HARD GIRLS

By Martina Cole and available from Headline

Dangerous Lady
The Ladykiller
Goodnight Lady
The Jump
The Runaway
Two Women
Broken
Faceless
Maura's Game
The Know
The Graft
The Take
Close
Faces
The Business
Hard Girls

MARTINA COLE

HARD GIRLS

headline

First published in Great Britain in 2009
by HEADLINE PUBLISHING GROUP

1

Cataloguing in Publication Data is available from the British Library

ISBN 978 0 7553 2868 0 (Hardback)
ISBN 978 0 7553 2869 7 (Trade paperback)

Typeset in Galliard by Avon DataSet Ltd,
Bidford-on-Avon, Warwickshire

Printed and bound in Great Britain by Clays Ltd, St Ives plc

Headline's policy is to use papers that are natural, renewable and
recyclable products and made from wood grown in sustainable forests.
The logging and manufacturing processes are expected to conform
to the environmental regulations of the country of origin.

HEADLINE PUBLISHING GROUP
An Hachette UK Company
338 Euston Road
London NW1 3BH

www.headline.co.uk
www.hachette.co.uk

For Gavin.
Always remembered.

For my lovely family.
And for all my lovely friends.

For Darley Anderson.
With all my love, and all my thanks.
It's been twenty years, and I have loved every minute of
them.

And for Barry and David.
You both mean the world to me.

Prologue

Danielle Crosby was very pretty, there was no doubt about that, but she wasn't exactly beautiful. This was mainly because of her constant frown. It was a habit that she had acquired as a child and now it was part of her make-up. She looked miserable, and she was miserable. It was just her nature.

Her mother always said she looked like the orphan of the storm and, as a kid, thanks to her mother's laziness, she certainly looked the part. Her nickname at school had been 'Scruff-bag', and even she had accepted the truth of it. Like most truths, it had hurt.

Fortunately, her attitude didn't interfere with her chosen occupation. Men, she found, were not too bothered about how she felt inside, they were more interested in how she looked on the outside. She had a body to die for, as her mother had often remarked to her during her short sojourns from the care system. She had learned at an early age how to fight off men, and distract other women. Along with the drinking and the drug-taking, she was pretty much immune to most things these days. She felt she had already lived a lifetime by most people's standards.

Now, at nineteen, she was a professional, and though she might not enjoy the actuality of her job, she loved the money, so it worked out quite well for her.

As she applied more deep-red lipstick, and touched up her Bobbi Brown blusher, she was more than satisfied with her appearance. Her hair was long and thick, a deep auburn with natural red highlights, and her wide-spaced blue eyes gave her an exotic appeal that the older men seemed to go for. Her skin wasn't that good, but a thick coating of expensive foundation soon put paid to that. She made the best of what God had given her, and she used it to further her career.

She rearranged her heavy breasts, showing them off to their full advantage which, in her case, meant spilling out of a tight top, and stepped back to appraise her handiwork.

She was pleased, though you would not have known that: as per usual she looked dissatisfied, completely unaffected by her own appearance. But she knew her own value, knew what she was worth down to the last penny, even if she did end up giving over most of her take to her boyfriend Jimmy. Though *she* was pleased with her appearance, she still looked like she had the weight of the world on her slim shoulders. In many ways, her demeanour actually worked in her favour because it allowed her to do her job without too much thought, and without any kind of real involvement, the main prerequisites for anyone who sold their assets to the highest bidder. Sex meant nothing to her, the men she engaged with were beneath her radar, she just wanted to earn her wedge, no more and no less. She fucked them, sucked them, and forgot about them.

Danielle heard the doorbell go and sighed, she knew she had to play the game as usual. Slipping on her impossibly high heels she walked awkwardly from the room and answered the front door, secure in the knowledge that her legs and her cleavage would more than compensate for her lack of joviality, personality or interest in the person she was about to meet. Sad bastards with a few quid and the determination to get laid. She hated them all.

Retired DCI Kate Burrows was smiling as she walked into Grantley Police Station. She loved coming back here, relished the feel of working again. It was supposed to be only two days a week, but she liked the fact she was keeping her hand in, that she was still making a small difference to the world. And in truth she usually worked much more.

'Hiya, Kate.' Annie Carr was genuinely pleased to see her. Despite the difference in their ages, as the only other female DCI she had forged a close friendship with Kate and often turned to her for advice. Though Kate was now only part-time, she still had a lot of sway where her colleagues were concerned, not least because she had up and taken notorious hardened criminal Patrick Kelly into her bed and, more surprisingly, kept the bugger there even though they had never married, but also because she had worked two of the most high-profile murder cases in living memory, as well as breaking the biggest ever paedophile ring in the South East. Kate had her creds and she knew it, she was also aware of the fact that she was kept on because she had a working knowledge of everyone and everything in her orbit. It was her nature, and it was why she had always been so good at her job. The grey that now salted her brown hair, and the wise look in her eyes were visual testament to her experience.

Kate came in twice a week in an advisory capacity. She

helped out in any way she was needed. This could be anything from giving her opinion on pending cases to clearing a pile of filing. She wasn't proud in that respect. There was so much paperwork involved with the job nowadays it was a wonder any of them had the time to get out and investigate actual crimes. It amazed and disturbed Kate that old-style policing was fast becoming obsolete.

Kate knew that, in many respects, she was considered a dinosaur as most police work was now done on a computer. Personally, she thought that was half the problem, but she was shrewd enough to keep her opinion to herself. After all, she just liked to keep her hand in.

'Hiya. I'm bloody freezing, shall I put the kettle on?'

Annie could never really understand how Kate was so normal. She was a legend in her own lunchtime, yet she never acted the big I am, and that was why she was so well loved. A few of the men in the station may have had a problem with her success, but they were not worth the proverbial wank, and she knew Kate didn't let them bother her. But Annie was aware that Kate missed the daily grind, and she also knew that only someone who felt the same way could really understand the attraction a dump like Grantley Police Station could hold. She felt it, and she knew that Kate understood that, it was why they got on so well.

'Sit down, Kate, I'll get the coffee. It's so quiet here I feel like a spare part.'

Kate grinned. 'Don't knock it, Annie. One thing I'll give Grantley, when it does finally kick off, it kicks off big time. I can vouch for that.'

They both laughed. Grantley had been without any real crime for so long no one in the force thought it would change at any time in the near future. It was a nice place to live, people came there because of that, and no one wanted it to change. It had the usual bit of vandalism of a weekend, and the usual domestics. A pub might go off occasionally after a football match, and burglary was not unheard of. But in the grand scheme of things, Grantley seemed these days to be immune to the greater sins of the world. In recent years it had fallen into a time warp of prosaic normality.

'Oh, that reminds me, Kate, it's the memorial service on Friday for Alec Salter. His wife Miriam will expect us all there.'

Kate nodded. She had expected to hear about that at some point. She sighed heavily. 'I really don't think I can face it. How is she? They were so close those two, a bit too close if you ask me. Is she coming back to work then? She'll find it hard without him. And they had all that church stuff together as well.'

Annie nodded and tossing back her short blond hair she said in a whisper, 'God forgive me, Kate, but she is so bloody boring. I know I sound like a bitch but she's such hard work.'

Kate knew how she felt, but she was also aware that it was the Miriams of the world who made their jobs easier.

'You're preaching to the converted but, in fairness, she is good at what she does. God knows why, but she really seems to be loved by the people she helps. Though in all honesty if I was a victim of a crime, she's the last person I would want hanging round.'

Annie loved that Kate would say that to her; everyone else spoke about Miriam in hushed tones. It was awful she had lost her husband, but there was no getting away from the fact she was bloody difficult to be around.

'I do feel bad about finding her so dull, but I can't seem to help myself.'

Kate grinned. 'Look, Annie, if someone's burgled your house, or mugged you, Victim Support is just what you need, but I know what you're saying, she's not exactly a live wire as such. She's lost her husband, and she's a part of the team, so I'm afraid we'll just have to be nice to her. God love her, she means well.'

Annie rolled her eyes in annoyance. 'Which is more than you can say for me, Kate! She drives me up the wall. The trouble is she's such a holy Joe, I feel like she is judging me all the time, don't you?'

'That's because she is, love. She has never really liked me because of Patrick. She is incapable of seeing the big picture.'

Annie grinned. 'Why do you think she gives me the evil eye then?'

Kate shook her head in mock despair. 'I think it's because you're a loner. You're only in your thirties but you're married to your job already. I understand that, I was like you, still am in some respects. That's why I keep on coming in here. Whereas she's like a lot of women. She defined herself and her life by her husband. He was everything to her, and she was everything to him. Women like us are beyond her comprehension, she thinks we are a pair of sad old bags. She wouldn't put it like that though, she's too nice. Now she's been widowed she's going to have to join the real world, and that will be hard for her.'

Annie nodded in agreement. 'She still gets on my tits.'

'Well, get over it. She is a civilian worker who somehow clears up the mess after a crime has been committed. She also takes the onus off us so we can get on with our job.'

They both laughed, conspirators together. They would never have said any of that to an outsider. Victim Support had become a big part of the job nowadays, whereas they both believed that it was more important to catch the villains responsible. So do-gooders like Miriam were worth the aggro because they left the police free to do their job.

Kate was aware that her presence was a boon to Annie and the other detectives, she was able to override the new practices and she didn't have to bow down to anyone. She was there to give her valued opinion and let them make use of her expertise. But it was laughable really, how much the times had changed. She hated that police work was now more about keeping the public happy, and less about actually catching criminals. She hated that the criminals they collared had more rights than they could deal with. She hated that they were treated with kid gloves. She saw how difficult it was for anyone in the service to do their job without worrying if they were going to be accused of all sorts. Criminals were being treated like fucking visiting royalty – the politically correct brigade had seen to that. Kate believed in being fair and working within the law. But that was all out the window now. Annie was like her, she just wanted to do her job. It was not easy any more. People watched too much TV, knew too much about the system, demanded far too much from the police, and they expected it far too quickly. The trust was gone. The papers and the news channels had seen to that. It was like working in a vacuum. Despite everything, Kate still loved it, still needed it. She was not young any more, she had fought long and hard to become a name, a Face, in her world. And she had had to work harder, and longer, than her male counterparts to earn her promotion.

She had always been proud of that, proud that she had been better than all the men around her, and yet it felt as if it had all been for nothing.

Annie and her ilk were put into the job *because* they were women, and consequently they had to prove themselves worthy of their promotions rather than having earned them first. It was all arse up, and let's see how we can look good to the world. Certain people were given key jobs, key promotions, for all the wrong reasons.

It was hard for Kate to admit it, but she actually felt that the old days, when women had to really graft to get forward, had been better for the women involved. At least then you knew you were there because you could do the job. Not because the powers that be had to fulfil a quota. Or they were frightened you would take them to a tribunal. It was hard then to even get someone to listen to your complaints, let alone do something about them. Kate loved the law, she felt the need to see people get justice, to see them get some kind of redress when they were wronged. Kate knew that it was when people were suddenly made victims, were stripped of their decency, left feeling vulnerable and frightened that they needed the law most. It was then that they needed to feel there was something bigger than them, something stronger than them.

Annie was like Kate in her heyday, and she loved her for that. She was a good policewoman. Annie also respected experience, and she was not only open to Kate's advice, she was also willing to absorb anything that Kate could tell her about her own experiences, she wanted to know everything and anything that could help her to achieve her goals. Kate valued her interest, needed it in many ways, she was so grateful that Annie wanted her and her expertise, it was an honour to be a part of Annie Carr's career. She knew that this woman would really make her mark. She would go far, but she would be lucky enough to achieve her success at a younger, more impressive age. She was not as naive as Kate had been. She was really on the ball. She was aware of just how corrupt and how dangerous the world was for a female in the police force. She also knew the pitfalls and the benefits available to anyone with the brains to sit it out.

Kate felt as if she continued to be in the loop, was still needed and, for someone like her, whose job had been such a big part of her life, had defined who she was, that was seriously important in itself. Annie Carr was her protégée, and Kate would personally make sure that she was given all the help she needed to reach the top of her game.

Patrick Kelly was tired out, and it was annoying him. He knew he wasn't in the first flush of youth but, all the same, he wasn't in his dotage. Things had been quiet recently. He still kept his hand in with his businesses but they were more or less legitimate these days. He'd pretty much handed the reins over to younger men since his friend Willy Gabney had died. The truth was he was bored. He knew he needed an outlet. Like Kate, he needed to be doing something. Something new. The trouble was, he didn't know what that something might be.

He poured himself a large Scotch, though he knew it was far too early and, as he sipped it, he looked around him. He had a beautiful home, but in reality, he didn't really see it any more. He didn't care about it now, didn't feel any pride or satisfaction in it. He just lived there and, as much as he loved being so settled, enjoyed his home being a refuge, he had not really looked at it for a long time. Now that he *was* looking he saw it as if for the first time. It was lovely, he knew it was something that most people would be proud of. Most people would see it as an achievement, as something they could regard as the pinnacle of their success. But Pat just saw it as a nice drum, and as his home with Kate. Nothing more. But she had put her mark on it, and he was glad about that much. She was a fucker for photos, they were everywhere, and though he pretended indifference, he loved them really. He saw his daughter in all her splendour, her short life was anywhere he cared to look. She was smiling, and she looked happy, she *was* happy. She *had* been very happy.

That was something he could now accept and enjoy, even though he missed her with every fibre of his being. Mandy had been his world, and her death had proved to him that no one was immune to heartache. It didn't matter how much money you had, or how much you were respected and revered. Shit could land on you from a great height at any time, especially when you least expected it. It had not been the first time life had seen fit to piss all over him, and he had a feeling it would not be the last. But he had found his Kate, and for that he would always be grateful.

Patrick could see himself in one of the photos, his arm around Kate, his smile genuine and his grief finally contained. She had made a home for them both, and he recognised he was a lucky man because of that. He knew he was looking a bit battered around the edges, his hair was greyer than he liked to believe, and his clothes were a bit too snug, but he also knew he was basically content, and that was because of Kate.

So many of his contemporaries were still out on the pull, having new families who were even younger than their grandchildren, but Patrick hadn't felt that urge. He knew they were chasing something they would never regain, no matter how many young birds they fucked. Kids were everything, but they had to be produced by the right woman. They had to be there because they were wanted. Not to prove a point.

It was sad to see old men chasing the strange, something they only did to show they were still worth a pull, to prove to themselves they were still in the game. All they seemed to prove was that they were silly old fuckers who ended up with another load of kids they would be lucky to see grow to adulthood. He didn't want any of that, he had been blessed with his daughter, and he would never, ever attempt to replace her. Mandy was gone, and he had accepted that fact, finally and irrevocably. It had been hard, but eventually it had also been a natural step. After all, he knew he couldn't grieve for ever. Life, such as it was, went on.

Pat saw himself as finally settled, and though Kate could make him seriously consider bashing her brains in at times, he couldn't ever harm her. Her brains were what kept them together. She was so bright, so fucking opinionated. She kept him on his toes, and that was more to him than all the little birds, and all the little babies, put together. He didn't want a new family, he didn't want to replace his girl. He wanted his Kate, even though she was still a straight-laced mare at times, and she was getting a bit long in the tooth. But that didn't mean he didn't want her, didn't love her.

He respected her too much, and that was the mainstay of

their relationship. They may never have found the time to actually tie the knot but Kate had been his lifesaver. Her opinion of him was all he really cared about if he was honest. Because he loved her, really cared for her. He still looked, and lately he had felt a great urge for the younger body, its fullness, softness, but it was not because he thought any less of Kate. It was because he was a man and he yearned sometimes for the feel of youth.

Patrick sometimes craved the faceless fuck, the use of a girl without the emotional ties. He had taken a flier now and again over the years, and it had made him feel young again. It made him feel virile, made him feel as if he still had it. That he still had the power to attract a good-looking girl. He had also admitted to himself that it was his money, his position in the world, that had been the real attraction. He knew this made him like the men he despised. But still he wanted the fuck, nothing more. He knew it was wrong, knew that he would be jeopardising all he had with Kate.

Not that it had stopped him from doing what he wanted, of course. He felt he needed it at times. He loved that he didn't have to do anything, talk, cajole, or care about it. He was once more feeling the urge, and yet again he was justifying his reasons for doing what he wanted. He wasn't proud of himself, but he wasn't that bothered about it either.

He picked up the phone on its third ring. 'Hello, Peter, long time no hear.' He was genuinely pleased to hear from his old mate. And Peter Bates was an old mate and a long-time business partner. 'What can I do you for?' Patrick's voice was loaded with friendliness, but as he listened to his friend talk his easy smile disappeared.

'You are fucking joking? Tell me you are having a laugh, Pete.'

Peter's voice sounded as gutted as he felt. 'I wish I fucking was, Pat. It's the truth and, as I have never been what might be termed a comedian, I resent you questioning my interpretation of the said events.'

Patrick sighed, and knowing that Peter Bates was renowned not just for his lack of humour, but also for his penchant for stating the obvious, he swallowed the retort that came immediately to his lips and instead said quietly, 'Well, it's your fucking problem, isn't it? I didn't know what you were doing behind my back, so you had better fucking sort it yourself. What the fuck do you expect *me* to do?'

Peter Bates was annoyed. Never one to hide his feelings, he got off the phone as soon as he could without causing offence and bellowed at his latest conquest, a twenty-five-year-old lap dancer who was not only younger than his daughter, but had also been her best friend. 'Turn the fucking telly down! It's like living in a fucking cinema! How many times do I have to repeat myself?'

Veronica Lamper looked at him with open disdain as she clicked off the TV. She was a lot of things, but she wasn't a fool. He was weighing out big time, and because of that she was prepared to overlook a tantrum or two. It still annoyed her, especially as she knew she was a keeper. She could have anyone she wanted. But he was a stepping stone. She would produce a child, and he would be fucked for the rest of his days. The government would see to that, but she knew he would see her all right because he was decent enough in his own way. He was also loaded, he would have to be. If he wasn't, she wouldn't fucking be there in the first place.

'All right, Pete, keep your hair on! What the fuck is wrong with you?'

But he didn't answer her, instead he stormed from the room and, shaking her head in annoyance, Veronica put the telly back on. She loved *Deal or No Deal*, and she settled back down to watch it in relative peace and quiet. Peter was one lairy ponce, and he was also old enough to be her father, but when the fancy took him, he was generous to a fault. It was much easier to overlook his shortcomings and concentrate on his good points.

He *was* caked up with money and that was enough for her. After all, she was hardly there because of his sparkling personality. He was a lousy shag and all; he was well past his prime and he was a bit too quick off the mark. But he was part of her game plan. A girl had to look out for herself and she was determined to do just that.

She settled back to watch her programme, she liked Noel Edmonds, he looked quite kind and he had all his own hair which as far as she concerned was a definite bonus. He was also possessed of a nice voice, she could listen to him for hours.

As she heard Peter slam the fridge door ranting and raving, she decided to get herself out of it. She had done her stint, and she felt she had earned herself a pension. It was time for the baby to be conceived. Her bonus, her wage packet.

The front door slammed and as Peter left the premises she felt herself relax. It was a hard old graft, but she knew how to play the game.

*

Terri Garston was sick, physically sick. She had never encountered anything remotely like this in her life. A tall girl, she had always been expected to look after herself, but she was really chicken-hearted. She cried at Disney films, and was still convinced that some day her prince would come. Though how she was supposed to meet him while on the bash, she wasn't sure. She was a nice girl who had fallen into her job like she had fallen into everything in her life, accidentally.

Danielle Crosby had introduced her to the life and Terri had been pleasantly surprised by how easily she had adapted to it. Lazy by nature, she had relished the short working hours and the large sums of money. It was a very seductive lifestyle and, as she embraced it wholeheartedly, she soon found herself with a large clientele along with an even larger cocaine habit.

She had not, however, expected to find her friend as dead as a doornail, and her employer doing his crust about it. Anyone would think *she* had murdered Danielle the way Peter Bates was carrying on.

'Will you clear the flat of any drugs that might be hanging round, *please*? Then you have to phone the Filth, so get your arse in gear. The last thing you want is to be done for possession. And if they ask, you know nothing about her or any of the customers, right?'

Terri nodded, but she was frightened now. Peter was clearing the flat of everything that could incriminate him or the girls and, as he searched, he made a conscious effort not to look at the dead girl on the floor. He knew he was probably removing evidence, but that was hard fucking luck, he had no intention of getting a tug for anybody, let alone a fucking brass.

They were a breed apart as far as he was concerned. He might have a struggle with a bird now and again, but he prided himself on never getting involved with the staff and, even though he knew he should feel responsible for the girl's demise, he wasn't going to let it intrude on his daily life. He just provided them with a roof under which to conduct their business, took his earn, and didn't think about them at all. He was annoyed that Patrick had blanked him. He might be a sleeping partner, but he wasn't in a fucking coma. Peter was grieved at Pat's reaction, that he wasn't going to help out. But he still didn't feel it was anything to do with him. She was dead, but it wasn't his fault. She knew the score, knew the pitfalls. At the end of the day, if he hadn't given her a base to work from, then someone else would have. And until now, it had guaranteed all the girls a level of security they would never have had on the street.

And after all, she was the one that had chosen to be a brass, he hadn't forced her, he had just provided her with the opportunity to spread her charms. Like all his girls, *she* had come to him, and he had provided her with a nice flat to work out of. He saw himself as quite a generous employer, as someone who helped his girls out.

He had been doing this for years without any kind of aggravation. Now he had a dead one, a very dead one, and he was not fucking impressed about it either.

He had nothing on his conscience, as he would tell himself over and over again. But the sight of her lying there dead, mutilated and naked would stay with him until the day he died. She had been done over good and proper; whoever had done it had really gone to town. Satisfied he had obliterated any kind of evidence that could incriminate him, he left hurriedly. She had been a nice girl and all, and the shame was overwhelming him even as he determined to save his own arse.

Terri was left alone, waiting nervously for the police, the horror of her situation finally taking hold. Seeing her friend's body, the blood everywhere, and the look of sheer terror on her face, it finally sank in that someone had actually murdered her. Someone had deliberately taken her young life.

Terri suddenly realised that it could quite easily have been her lying there. The men they dealt with all came through the adverts in the local paper, and at the end of the day, it wasn't as if they had ever known anything important about their clients. The men who frequented their establishment lied about their real names, as they themselves did. They had sex with them, were intimate with them, and yet she and Danni knew literally nothing about them. Some of them arranged their dates by text. Until now, the danger had never crossed her mind.

It was over five hours since she had found the body of her friend, and it didn't occur to her that for the police to find the culprit she should have been telling them the truth. Instead, she was still practising her story as they knocked on the front door.

'Are you all right, Pat? You're awfully quiet tonight.'

Patrick shrugged. 'Just tired, Kate, that's all.' He was watching her as she cooked for them both. She was a good cook, and he enjoyed her food. But tonight he was seeing her as if for the first time. She was still a looker as far as he was concerned, she was the only woman who had ever managed to keep his interest. She had aged, of course, but he never really noticed it, she was still his Kate. Now though, as she chopped vegetables and sautéed the veal, he marvelled at how much he loved her. The fear of losing her had made him aware of just how much he cared about her. He was still trying to get his head round Peter Bates's phone call. Still trying to work out what had happened.

Kate smiled at him, her eyes taking in everything around her. She saw more in a quick glance than most people did in a lifetime. She was one of the only women he had ever met who was happy to be quiet. He loved that she didn't feel the urge to fill up every silence with inane prattle. Pat opened a bottle of red wine and poured them both a glass. As Kate sipped hers, she winked at him mischievously and he felt the tug of her once more. He knew that she accepted him for what he was, as he had accepted her for what she was. Chalk and cheese, really; she was straighter than a weightlifter's grandmother and he was as bent as the proverbial corkscrew. Yet somehow it worked for them.

As they ate their evening meal, Patrick marvelled at how well they got along together. Even after all these years, she still had the knack of keeping him interested in her. Not that he hadn't been drawn to the occasional bit of strange but, as his old mum used to say, what you don't know can't hurt you. And so far, she had been proved right. His earlier thoughts of going on the hunt were at once obsolete. He had to keep Kate close now, couldn't give her any reason to doubt him. He was terrified that she would suss him out.

Old Peter Bates's call had rattled him and, though he hadn't known the full story, he'd only owned the property, he knew it was only a matter of time before Kate demanded that he explain himself. Be sure your sins will find you out. Well, his would anyway. But he couldn't tell her, he didn't know how to. She would find out soon enough. She was a shrewdie. Pat felt as if he had the Sword of Damocles hanging over his head. Once again, he knew something that she didn't, only this time, he feared that when she realised that, it would take more than a bunch of flowers to calm her down; in actual fact, the deeds to a diamond mine would be disregarded. She would be what was commonly known as pissed off, and that was putting it nicely.

Annie Carr was shocked by what she saw in front of her. That the girl had been murdered was evident, but it was the fact that she had clearly been brutally raped beforehand that was the real shocker. She had literally been ripped to pieces inside and the remains of what looked like a chair leg had been discovered by the girl's body. Whoever he was, he had acted with a tremendous rage. The poor girl must have died in agony.

The flat was nice, Annie had noticed that as soon as she entered it, all white walls and leather sofas. It was obviously a Tom's workplace, but that was neither here nor there at the moment. That just meant they would have to cast their net wider, after all Toms were called Toms because they slept with every Tom, Dick and Harry. Annie hoped they had some forensics to fall back on. What really pissed her off was that the girl was so young. She had died a horrific death, all for the lure of a few quid. It was such a pointless way to die, such an abrupt end for a young woman who should have had her whole life ahead of her. Annie hated that she had to tell someone that their child had been so violently slaughtered.

She could see that the girl had been tortured, she had burns all over her and what smelled like caustic soda had been poured down her throat, so this wasn't a random killing, a sexual deal that had gone wrong. This was a deliberate act of violence against a young woman who, it seemed, had not put up any kind of fight whatsoever. That in itself was a mystery, there were no signs of a struggle; her nails were still perfectly manicured, a deep-red, they didn't have a chip or a mark of any kind. Her face was contorted in agony, but that could have been the caustic soda, she had to have felt that coming, but there were no signs of her having been tied up. So the burns had to have been inflicted when she was unconscious, no one could have endured that much pain without fighting against it. She had them on her breasts, her genitals and her buttocks. And then her murderer had left her with her legs wide open, and with the object they had used to rape her by her side.

It was all wrong, none of it made any sense. Annie felt the jingle of alarm bells in her head. This was not the usual. In fact, it was so staged it seemed almost as if the person responsible wanted whoever found Danielle to be shocked over and over again. Shocked first by the dead body, then by the burning of the throat, the burns to the breasts and genitalia and finally the cuts that were deep and gaping. There was blood everywhere. She had been left to bleed out all over the floor. The sheer amount of blood told Annie she must have been alive when she had been cut. She had pumped out her life's blood as she died in agony.

Annie knelt by the body once more and looked at the cuts

closely. They were deep, they were open. She was stunned by the sheer brutality of the crime, someone had enjoyed themselves, had really put a lot of effort into this poor girl's death. The person responsible had known he would not be interrupted. Annie knew in her heart that this was not going to be a one-off, wasn't a random killing. This was planned and precise and, whoever he was, he was going to do this again. It was a textbook murder, in many respects.

Annie knew that she was out of her depth because this was the first time she had ever been confronted by something so heinous. She hoped it would be the last.

Annie stood up. 'Look, Terri, you being on the game is of no interest to us, we just want to know who killed Danielle, and we can only find that out if you tell us how you worked together. I swear I have no interest in your working life, I just want to find out who killed Danielle. So please will you stop pretending the pair of you lived the high life in a really posh block of flats, yet apparently neither of you have any kind of legal employment? Let's cut the crap and get to the fucking real-life bit, eh? Only I am getting the arse now, I've had enough of your bullshit.'

Terri knew that she should tell this woman the truth, but she was frightened. Peter Bates had warned her to keep stumm, and she knew he meant it. But Danielle had been murdered, and Terri knew she had to tell at least a bit about their daily lives.

'We would have the flat at different times. We didn't really have a system, we worked on bookings. We advertised in the local paper, men rang us up, and we . . . you know, we would entertain them. We always gave each other plenty of space. She had regulars like me, but we also had a lot of passing trade, you know. Men working in the area who might want a bit of company, men from nearby towns who look in the local papers for a bit of excitement. You know, as well as I do, that in our game you never know who's going to turn up, and as long as they have the money they are guaranteed a warm welcome. I mean, we ain't cheap, it's a onner a time, straight sex, no kissing and oral sex is extra. We ain't bloody stupid, we earned. But I can't think of anyone who would do that. Most of them are the usual fucking idiots who have to pay for a nice-looking girl. Let's face it, if they were on the ball, they wouldn't have to pay for it, would they?' She started to cry again and Annie instinctively put out her arms and, holding the girl gently, she let her cry.

She wished Kate would hurry up, she needed her expertise at this point, she had never before been involved in anything like this. This kind of murder would hit the papers and the place would be crawling with reporters by the morning. This kind of crime brought a spotlight down on the police involved that made their job even harder. She needed Kate's experience and her level-headed approach to life. She needed her to walk her through this because it was unlike anything Annie had seen before.

As Terri sobbed out her shock and her fear, Annie wondered what the coroner would find out from the girl's body. She knew it was imperative to get the autopsy out of the way as soon as possible. The door opened and a young PC said loudly, 'Mrs Crosby is here, ma'am.'

Annie saw that Kate was talking to the men outside. She was already taking charge, and Annie was grateful for that. It meant she had Kate's support from the off, and she needed that more than she cared to admit.

*

'Are you saying a punter murdered the girl in my property?'

Peter Bates liked Pat Kelly but sometimes he could quite happily smack him one. The fact that Pat Kelly was a foot taller and two stone heavier was the main reason he didn't bring that wish to fruition.

'Yes, Pat, but I wasn't to know that was going to happen, was I? The girls have been working out of there for yonks. How could anyone predict a fucking nut-bag turning up and outing one of them? I think it's a fucking diabolical liberty meself.'

'Oh you do, do you? How about the fact that I thought the flats were for renting purposes only and, forgive me for being somewhat obtuse, but why ain't I been paid the going rate for letting my drums be used as fucking brothels! Kate will have my nuts in a carrier bag for this, boy. She won't believe I knew nothing about it . . .'

Peter Bates was short and stocky and, when the fancy took him, extremely argumentative. He was known for his quick temper, and even quicker departures. Especially when he thought he might have overstayed his welcome. He could never resist a con, and now his partnership with Patrick Kelly had been dragged into the daylight his serious earnings were suddenly looking very precarious. He was a worried man, he had not let on about the flats' real use. He had not thought he would have to. It had been a doddle so far, an easy earn. Now though, it had well and truly fallen out of bed. In more ways than one.

Book One

Set me as a seal upon thine heart, as a seal upon thine arm:
For love is strong as death; jealousy is cruel as the grave.

Song of Solomon, 8:6

Chapter One

Janie Moore was tired out. She had been working for hours. She had a virus, and it had really knocked her for six. She had to keep going though. After all, once she finished, she had a few days off. She preferred it like this. She loved having a bit of time to herself, a bit of time with her kids. She liked the money, but she also liked the hours. It suited her to work all day, then she could have a couple of days off. She was new to the game and still had the wide-eyed naivety, the belief that it was only for the interim. That she would stop once she either found Mr Right, or she found another job that paid enough for her to keep her and her kids. Deep down she knew that was *never* going to happen. Some of the girls who used the flat were paying for themselves through college, or for some kind of education. They were determined to better themselves. Janie knew inside that she was never going to be like them. She was hoping for a man to take her life over, but she saw that, after this job, whoever it was would not only need to be passable in the looks department, but generous in the financial sense. Sex was not something she craved any more. In fact, it was something best left out of any marriage equation, she had had her fill of it in all its scummy, pretend glory.

But all in all, she thanked her lucky stars for the work because she had two kids under three, and the fathers had both gone on the trot early on in her pregnancies. They'd abandoned her and their offspring without a second thought. Janie had learned the hard way that money was important, and talk was bloody cheap. She'd learned that promises were something that only the rich could afford. She had been promised so much in her young life, and she had believed that the men making the promises would make good on them. Instead, she had been left with two babies, a mountain of debt and a drug problem. She'd been helped off that. She counted herself fortunate because she had not suffered physically after giving birth. She had hardly a stretch-mark on her, and she still looked good in her underwear. She knew how devastating a pregnancy could be on the body, had seen mates who had delivered a child and been left with a stomach that looked like a map of the London Underground. She had carried low and had not put on much weight. She had popped both her boys out quickly and cleanly, and she had loved them both with a passion from their first breaths. She'd nearly lost them over the drugs. She had ended up on the bash for them, to give them everything they needed. To ensure they had a better start in life than she had. She was saving, building a little nest egg, she wanted to take them on holidays, wanted to see them play in the sea, thrive under a foreign sun. They would have everything, and she would do anything to make sure that was the case. She dreamed of a man, a kind man, who would love her and her boys. Who would give her security and love.

Janie was already settled into the life, and she knew deep down that she didn't want a real relationship; the job she had chosen made sure of that. She would accept security over passion. She was too used to strange men climbing on top of her, using her for a given amount of time, and paying her for the privilege. She had her regulars, and she had her appointments. She also had her other life, with her sons, her mum, and her friends.

The only man she would want now was one who could offer her and her boys a good standard of living, and who would not make too many demands on her. A decent man with a few quid and a nice disposition. It wasn't really that much to ask.

Janie Moore repaired her lipstick and waited for her next appointment. She was tired and irritable, but what could she do? Work was work, and she needed the money.

Kate was sipping her tea. She stared out of the window at the cold winter's day. It was freezing. The frost was still glistening on the rooftops, and the wind was loud enough to be heard through the walls. The view from the police station was depressing – it was all cement buildings and car parks.

Every time she closed her eyes she saw the body of Danielle Crosby, saw the way she had been butchered. She could still see the terror etched in her young face. Even the coroner had been shocked by the severity of the attack, especially after death.

The coroner had been specific about the cause of death. It was the acid. The young woman had been drugged with Rohypnol and GHB then, when she had been unable to move, caustic soda had been poured down her throat, burning her, killing her. The bastard had set about his business, slicing, burning and raping her while she choked in agony, until, finally, Danielle Crosby was a bloody corpse. There was nothing left to remind anyone of the young woman she had been. All Kate saw was the devastation of her young body, the hate that had caused her death, and the reminder of how vicious human beings could be.

What a terrible way to die. How much fear had she endured before she had finally been released to death? It grieved Kate that she would have been happy to die just to escape her tormentor. It was tragic that a young woman had been cut down before she had even had a chance to really live.

Kate knew she was going to have to help Annie, that she would need her to take the brunt of the investigation because she was the seasoned detective and had experienced the bloody aftermath of a violent murderer. This wasn't a spur of the moment killing caused by rage, by anger. Kate knew this was a calculated and cruel death, and she also knew that this was simply the start. Whoever had done this would want to do it again, and soon. They would have been planning this for a long time; they had decided on their victim, and then they had arranged it so that they had not just the *time* to carry out their plan, but also the *privacy*. They had even taken the girl's mobile.

It was the staging of the body that bothered Kate, it was reminiscent of her first murder case all those years ago. George Markham, the Grantley Ripper. He had enjoyed the knowledge that whoever came across the bodies of his victims would never forget how each of them had been placed. That they'd never forget what they had seen, would never get the image from their minds. It was a form of humiliation against the dead person so, whoever the killer was, he had a grudge. It was this that told Kate that whoever had done this, they were going to do it again. He was already planning the next one, was already coming down from the initial high, needing the euphoria of feeling he had the power over life and death again. He needed to be noticed, and she knew the papers would make sure that he was granted that wish.

It was George Markham all over again.

Annie Carr was nervous, she knew that the press would be all over this murder, that it was gruesome enough to catch the attention of the dailies. She looked into her Chief Super's face. Lionel Dart was not a handsome man by any stretch of the imagination. He was tall, skinny to the point of emaciation, and he stooped when he walked, making him look as if he was on the defensive. That was not the case, however. He was, in fact, a very aggressive man, given to resenting slights, real and imagined, and he was known for his petty-mindedness and his ability to hold a grudge. He was not a man who could be trusted, he'd serve up his own children to further his career. And now he was terrified of the furore that this death would create; it would bring with it too many questions and the spotlight would fall on Grantley Police Station.

'Any idea how we are going to deal with this?'

Annie shrugged. 'In what way? Do you mean the media or the finding of the culprit? Only Kate thinks that whoever did this is not going to retire gracefully, it's not a one-off, and it's going to get worse.'

She felt bad about using Kate in this way, but she knew it was the only way she would get any kind of sense from her boss. He was frightened of Kate and her reputation. Unlike him, Kate was a real police officer. She hadn't wanted the career this man had craved, but she did have the experience and he couldn't argue with that. Kate just wanted the facts, and Annie understood that, it was all she was interested in too. But her limited experience had taught her that the truth was often unwelcome. Especially where this man and his cronies were concerned. He didn't respond, but then that was what she had expected.

'By the way, the place had been tampered with before we arrived. So it's going to be hard to get decent forensics.'

Her boss nodded, as if resigned to his fate.

Lucy Painter was as shocked as everyone else when she heard about the slaughter of Danielle. Though they didn't know each other very well, they worked in the same business. Sometimes they'd even worked out of the same flat. Like most of the girls in the know, she too was wondering if she had inadvertently entertained the nutter who had killed their colleague.

It had suddenly become crystal clear just how dangerous their job actually was. It was a risky occupation and, deep inside, they all knew and accepted that. But, like your house burning down or finding out you had HIV, it was always something that happened to somebody else. None of them really believed they were in danger, after all, they weren't on the pavement, were they? Because they worked out of nice flats and houses, and because they worked with other like-minded girls, they didn't see themselves as prostitutes, let alone being in any kind of peril. They earned a good wedge for a start and they didn't have to procure anyone; they had a good clientele thanks to the advertising. None of them had ever known life any different. They felt quite glamorous, that they were a cut above the usual brasses. It was a well-paid job, and it was a secret part of their lives. Danielle's death was tragic and shocking but, in all honesty, they were more concerned about being exposed as Toms. If their occupations were to become public knowledge, they would be destroyed. Like the men who frequented their establishments, the girls concerned primarily didn't want to be outed. They had no interest in the men's private lives, their wives, children or work, and they expected the same respect in return. They were a commodity, nothing more and nothing less. They provided a service, and that service was not something they dwelled on. They wanted them in, and out, with the minimum of aggro.

Personally, Lucy often felt a spark of sympathy for the men who used her. Most of them were more nervous than her, and she prided herself on being able to suss them out quickly and easily. She had never really had any trouble from them. Only once had she ever had to assert herself with a client, and that was because he had finished before he had even begun, and then had the nerve to expect a second go for free. He had been a short, bald-headed Turkish bloke with bad breath and a very expensive phone. It was strange what you noticed. She had sternly informed him that he had to pay again or she would call her husband. He had swallowed the bluff and left cursing her in his native tongue.

But, for the most part, the men who frequented her establishment were timid, overawed by her sheer height and statuesque build, and they tended to come back again and again. Recent events had made her realise she had become a bit too complacent and she was determined to make sure that never happened again.

As Lucy let herself into the flat she heard Janie singing in the kitchen. Taking off her coat, she walked through the hallway calling out, 'Pour me one and all, will you.'

Janie was already dressed in her street clothes, she looked like any other young girl now. Bereft of make-up and in baggy jeans and an oversized sweatshirt she was the archetypal young mum. Hair scraped back into a ponytail, and her feet encased in a pair of Nike Airs, she was still pretty enough to get a second glance from most men. She looked a thousand miles away from the girl she became while at work.

'What would you like? There's white wine or Bacardi Breezers in the fridge. I know you like a few before you start your shift.'

'White wine please. Did you have a nice couple of days off?'

Janie took a deep draught of her drink then she said quietly, 'Too right. I heard about Danielle.'

Lucy nodded. 'It's fucking mad, ain't it? Terri found her, and you know what she's like. Coked out of her fucking nut by all accounts. She reckons Bates cleared the place of anything that could cause aggravation. Wiped the whole place down because of prints, and poor Danni was lying there the whole time, dead as a doornail. She had been really done over and all, but no one can get the full bifta. Terri's frightened of getting involved; Bates told her to keep her nose out, and who can blame her? If her family finds out what she's doing, there'll be murders.'

'What did she tell the Old Bill?'

'That she came in and found the body. She pretended she was a newbie, though if they believe that, they'll believe anything; she's been on the game since she left school. The thing is though, what can she do? If she spills the beans she would be putting everyone in it, most of us do this on the quiet. It's not like the Filth would give us a swerve, is it? Do you think we're safe, Janie?'

Janie sighed heavily, her face as bewildered as her friend's. 'What's safe in this game? What with dogging and the internet, I'm amazed there's anyone who still requires our services, they can get a free fuck in any council car park providing they don't mind an audience. I know one thing though, we're safer here than on the streets, and whoever did Danielle will be loath to repeat it with all the furore it's caused. That flat is closed down, but all the others are still going. Old Batesy thinks it was the ex-boyfriend, she was seeing that druggie for years on and off. I can't see a stranger doing something like that, it's too personal. I heard she had a chair leg shoved up inside her. I mean, what the fuck would make someone do that to her? And if you remember, she had a few good hidings off that idiot over the years. He put her in hospital more than once.'

'Well, if it was him he's going to be collared sooner rather than later. Her mum will see to that, she hated him because he kept taking all Danielle's money.'

'Makes my blood run cold just thinking about it. What a way to die. I think we should consider working in pairs for a while, just in case it's not him.'

Lucy shrugged, her shoulders looking even more impressive than usual because of the sheer material of her

Matalan top. 'Well, let's wait and see. I am on till six and I have a full quota. I'm going to put a heavy ornament by the bed in case of emergencies. But I can't see anything happening tonight.'

Janie poured herself another wine and, taking a large swig, she said sadly, 'I never liked Danielle, she was a flash prat, but I wouldn't wish anything like that on my worst enemy.'

'Who the fuck would? But it will bring heat with it, you can depend on that.'

Jimmy Heart was worried. He had been arrested, but not charged, and he had been sitting in the interview room for over an hour and a half without anyone even looking in on him. He was terrified. He had last had a toot about an hour before his arrest, and he was just about to go and score when he had been rudely detained. Now he was starting to rock; he needed another hit, and he needed it soon. He was sweating and his heart was racing. He knew that there was something serious going down, but he wasn't sure about what his part was in all of it. He was shrewd enough to know that he was going to be accused of something, he was also shrewd enough to know that, whatever it was, he probably was involved in some way because he normally was. Unfortunately for him, he had no recollection of anything that might have brought him to the Filth's attention. He also knew that if he was being detained and ignored by the said Filth, it was a serious tug. But he had not done anything to his knowledge that warranted such a production.

Jimmy was genuinely bewildered, but he was also worried. The police were more than capable of fitting a person up when the fancy took them. He could name many people who had not only been accused, but put away for a crime they had no knowledge of nor, more importantly, the intelligence to prove their innocence of. It was a worry, but it was also a given. For all his fear, he knew he was nothing more than a junkie, a dealer. In the grand scheme of things he was a nobody. So his sensible head was asking him repeatedly why he was waiting for the big interrogation. He knew he did not warrant this kind of treatment. He talked a big game but, in reality, he had never actually experienced one. He was a ponce, no more, and no less.

It never occurred to Jimmy that he might be there because of his love life, his girlfriend. She was not even important enough to register on his radar, all she was to him was an earn. He supplied her drugs and relieved her of money on a regular basis. It was an arrangement that seemed to suit them both.

So, when he was finally confronted about his personal life, no one was more shocked than he was when he realised that Danielle had been erased. He played the part well; he looked shocked and horrified while thanking the powers that be because he had a cast iron alibi for the time of death.

Whoever had outed her had done it on the quiet. She had always favoured the evening shifts. She would. That was the real allure of her game, the hours. She worked the nights because it gave her the freedom to have the day to herself. She also liked the fact she was paid more on the night shifts. It was mental really, but men were happy to pay the extra for a late-night assignation.

So as Jimmy explained that while Danielle was being murdered, he had been scoring in a very public venue, her actual death didn't register with him at all.

*

Jennifer James looked over the books before her with a trained eye. A tall girl, she had the most unusual eyes, a deep blue with heavy black lashes. She had inherited the best of her parentage; her mother's English looks, and her Spanish father's colouring. She was striking. Well built, she had a presence about her. She also had a good head for figures, and she kept the accounts for Peter Bates. She worked her shifts like all the others, but her mathematical abilities were enough to get her a second earn.

The books were not for the tax man, they were for the sole use of the girls and Peter Bates. Most of the men concerned paid in cash and a small number by credit card – only a few of the girls accepted them. Jennifer made sure that Peter got his due from them all, and she collated the customers' details. She noted the purchase price and, where possible, a name and address. It was laughable the amount of men who were willing to part with that kind of information. The girls were booked over the phone, and they were encouraged to not develop any interest in their dates for the obvious reasons. Peter used the information for his own ends, and that was his business.

Jennifer's job was to make sure that Peter got his due. The girls were on a good earn, but they were also more than capable of trying to hide some of their customers. No one minded a bit of it as long as they didn't take the piss. They had to pay for the privilege of working the flats, as annoying as that might be, they had to do it. Peter Bates ran it like a taxi rank; they paid a percentage for the use of the premises.

As Jennifer looked back over the last few weeks of Danielle's appointments she tried to see if there was anything unusual, but she found nothing. She had wondered if the man who murdered Danielle was a regular. But when she looked over the list it seemed unlikely. They all seemed kosher. It was more likely that the night she died Danielle had to have taken the call herself at some point. There were often loners, as they were known, who rang on the off-chance after seeing the adverts in the local papers.

Sighing heavily, she wondered if she had enough time to get herself a quick meal before she had to take over her own shift for the night. Danielle's murder had thrown them off-kilter, and she knew that they would all have to be doubly careful in the future.

It grieved her that the girl's demise was being talked about in hushed tones, but by the same token, the girls concerned were not about to publicise their involvement in any way. Even though Danielle's death was horrendous, it still wasn't enough to make any of them step out of the shadows. Their whole lives were lived by a code of secrecy and they all had far too much to lose.

'Are you going back in then?'

Kate nodded. She had showered and changed after her meal, and she was dressed in what Pat had always laughingly referred to as her work clothes. White shirt, tailored trousers, and a well-cut, expensive black jacket, the only light relief was the jacket's purple silk lining. She looked good, though. If he was honest, her understated dress sense had always been a big part of her draw for him. But she was looking her age and they both knew it. He wasn't a spring chicken any more either, but as a man that was not really an issue. For women, however, it was different. Pat had the money and the reputation for women to see him as a viable option, young women as well as the older, more experienced women. His preference had always been for the more mature, sophisticated type of female. But as he looked at Kate's troubled countenance he had to admit that she was looking older these days, and this murder had really hit her hard.

She was already miles away from him, was already gearing herself up for the hunt. It had been her sheer determination that had attracted him all those years ago. Now he was seeing it again and it was frightening him. He knew she was going to find out things that she would not want to believe, and those things concerned him and his business ventures. He could cut Peter's nuts off and laugh while he was doing it, but he knew that would be a fruitless exercise.

'Why are you so sure this ain't a one-off, Kate?'

She shrugged, her eyes already had the haunted look of someone who knows they're about to experience a lengthy and protracted time of difficulty and heartbreak. She was preparing herself for it once more. Pat knew she worked on instinct, and her instincts were telling her that this was the start of something big, something horrendous and tragic. Pat knew that that something could possibly be the cause of them parting company. It was, after all, what Kate did, find out people's secrets. He had to try and sort it all out, and sort it out soon.

'I mean, it could have been a customer she tried to have over or something. You know, as well as I do, how these things can escalate.'

Kate shook her head dismissively. 'Not in a million years, Pat. Whoever did this was well prepared, it was a vicious and bloody act. It was planned, and executed, with precision.

Whoever killed Danielle Crosby has been thinking about it for a long time. I wish these girls would understand the danger they place themselves in every time they entertain some sad fuck. It's a waste, such a waste of a life.' She paused then and looked at him, concerned. 'Are you all right, Pat? You look awful.' She went to him and placed her arms around him. His blue eyes looked tired and he looked old suddenly, it was as if he had aged in a few hours. 'Is this bringing it all back, are you thinking about Mandy?'

Pat's daughter had been brutally murdered and it was the investigation into her murder that had originally brought them together. It pleased them both that something good had come out of George Markham's reign of terror. Pat didn't answer, just held her tightly and enjoyed the smell of her hair, the feel of her body. The familiarity of her was enough to break his heart. He knew she was too good for him on so many levels but, until now, until this moment, he had not really understood just how much he needed her in his life.

'Get yourself off, Kate, I'll be fine.'

'Are you sure, Pat?'

He smiled sadly. 'Go on, I'm fine. Like you say, this is a bit too close to home.'

Annie Carr was glad to have Kate back in the building. The place was a hive of activity, everyone was in, no leave, no days off, and no way of knowing how it would pan out. It was being treated as a one-off murder, but no one believed that. This was the gut instinct of every officer, an instinct that the good ones hone over years and trust to give them a heads-up when needed. It was telling them all that this was the start of something big. Annie knew that Kate's expertise would be invaluable, she also knew that she was going to be the cause of her friend being deeply troubled within the next few hours. She wished she knew how to lessen the blow. It was laughable really, but not so unexpected, if there hadn't been a murder it would have gone by without a mention.

Oblivious to the underlying tension in the room, Kate looked over the evidence reports and wondered at how no one could have heard anything. The block of flats was small. A low-rise with three storeys and a well-tended frontage, they were not cheap. Well built, they had an entry phone system, along with an expensive alarm system. They were not the type of flats that were easily accessible to the usual burglars or teenage thieves. They were in a nice, quiet road, and they backed on to the woods, from which you had access to the golf course. So someone had to have heard a commotion, had to have heard something.

Kate would talk to everyone who lived there herself. The neighbours would be over the initial shock of the slaying and might open up about the girls' work, the type of clientele that frequented the premises, if there was much foot traffic and, more importantly, how the men got access to the flats and if they parked in the car park or on the road.

They *had* to have seen something, someone. It was amazing what people didn't see, what people ignored, what they became immune to. They must have guessed what was going on there, and yet they were claiming ignorance. Kate had said as much to Annie Carr.

'Well, Kate, you know what people are like. Anyway, they were probably worried about complaining.'

'I suppose so. Annie, have we got the name of the person who owns the flat yet?'

Annie nodded, and passed her a pale buff folder saying pointedly, 'Peter Bates. But, Kate, I think you had better look at who he co-owns it with.'

Kate felt the breath leave her body as the implications of her friend's words sank in.

'I've kept a lid on it, Kate, but I don't know how long before someone else susses it out.'

'Is it Patrick by any chance?'

'I'm afraid so, mate.'

Kate could hear the sorrow in Annie's voice, and that just made the anger mounting inside her colder. She was numb with the shock of Patrick's duplicity. He knew she would find this out, and yet he didn't even attempt to give her a heads-up, allow her to at least have some dignity when the truth finally emerged. She had to be told by a subordinate, by someone who looked up to her and respected her.

It meant that they were living off immoral earnings, that even though he was loaded, he still had to have a dabble, as he would put it. What was running through her mind now was, what else was he up to? What else was Pat hiding from her?

Once this came out she would be implicated in it, and that was the last thing any of them needed. The crime scene had been messed with by either Bates or one of his minions, so that again put a different perspective on everything. Tampering with the evidence suggested to Kate that whoever visited the flat might not be just the usual weirdos, but could include rich, well-known weirdos. People with too much to lose and a lot to hide. It was an upmarket establishment, and that meant their job would be much harder.

Kate couldn't speak, she felt as if all the air had left her body, she could feel herself deflating with the hot flush of her humiliation. She closed her eyes, she was suddenly overwhelmed with tiredness.

'You OK, Kate?'

Kate shrugged and said flatly, 'Well, I've had better fucking days.'

Peter Bates was nervous, but then he always was. He knew that he was skating on thin ice. He had cleaned the flat up because he thought it was for the best. It was his first reaction, tidy away anything that could tie him to the offence. He was just protecting his interests.

He had assumed the girl had been on the receiving end of a nut-bag, it wasn't unheard of in their profession; after all, they were Toms. As well as the regulars, they took their own calls and arranged their own clients. The days of having a maid on the go were long gone, though a maid did offer them a level of security, he saw that now.

In the fifties and sixties, no Tom worth her salt was ever alone with a customer. Nowadays, there were a few who still employed someone to make the tea and change the beds, but they were a dying breed. Girls today didn't work out of their homes for a start, and they were a different sort to their forebears. When he cut into the game as a young lad, he had learned early on that a good pimp kept his girls chaperoned, not just for safety, but because they kept their eyes and ears open for any extra monies earned on the quiet. They also ran errands, kept the place clean and, more importantly, kept a beady eye out for anything of a suspicious nature.

The women and girls these days were more on the ball, they had lives outside of their work. They weren't as involved with the game now; it was basically just a job, a means to an end. While they were young and fresh-faced they had the chance to work out of a nice apartment, once the life took them over and they started to look a bit frayed around the edges, he outed them. It was only firm flesh that earned a wedge these days; men were inundated with young girls, and they were available at any time of the day or night. It was a competitive business now, albeit a lucrative one, but it was also a business that was being overtaken by the Eastern Europeans. They trafficked their flesh, and because of that they had most of the girls' earnings. Peter saw himself as far above those fucking thieves, his girls came to him for a job, they were complicit. He had never forced a bird on to the bash in his life. That was an outrageous situation for any man who ran an orderly business.

Peter might have done away with a maid, but he still had a head girl who kept an eye out. As far as he was concerned, he had taken all the precautions needed to keep his girls in the loop. But now the shock had worn off, and the enormity of what had happened had sunk in, he knew he had done a wrong one. But he had protected his business interests, protected his own arse. He had also attempted to protect Pat Kelly's arse, even if Pat hadn't been aware his arse needed protection. And he had the distinct impression Pat was not too impressed about it. And Patrick Kelly had never been a man to take aggravation without some kind of retaliation

Chapter Two

Patrick Kelly was fuming, and he knew he had no one to blame for his predicament but himself. That was why he was so angry. Even if Bates hadn't told him exactly what the flats were being used for, he had to admit he hadn't agonised over receiving the more than generous proceeds. It was bloody obvious really, particularly to someone like him. He could have got Danny Foster to check it out. If Kate found out she would de-bollock him without a second's thought. Yet he had turned a blind eye to what had been going on. He had to face the consequences of his actions and that was not something he had had to do very often in his lifetime. He was a well-respected Face, he had his creds, and he had his reputation. He also had a weakness for easy money and, once more, it had caused his downfall.

He was blaming Peter for his dilemma, but really it was all down to him. He knew what Bates was like, so he had to put his hand up and take the blame. Kate liked honesty; that was her biggest problem, she demanded it, and sometimes people were better off not being in the know. Not that he was going to point that fact out to her in the near future of course. He hoped she would look on this as an aberration of sorts, as a one-off. He would argue the fact that it was an investment, that was all. That he was just helping out a mate who needed a silent partner. He knew he was hoping for a miracle. Kate was not a fool and, worse than that, she was not a person who allowed herself to be treated like one. Patrick Kelly was up shit creek without the proverbial paddle and he knew it.

Annie watched as Kate smiled at the woman and accepted a cup of coffee with real appreciation, breathing in the aroma and hugging the mug with both hands. Each action told the woman she was in the company of a like-minded individual. 'You can't beat real coffee, instant is no substitute.'

Carmen Milke was thrilled with the compliment, most people didn't know the difference. At forty-seven she looked much older. Her husband had traded her in a few years previously for a younger model, and she had fought for a generous settlement, bought her little flat, and put a serious wad of cash in the bank. She was a victim of her husband's success; after the divorce he had kept his life, and most of their friends. She had found herself at the wrong side of forty, starting over. She had worked to keep him in university, she had worked to give him and their son a good home. She had done everything to see her husband get ahead, she had done the hard work, the graft, the dinner parties, the drinks and canapés. She had been beside him from the start. Along the way she had seen him change, seen the man she had loved become a selfish boor. Their success had changed him until she didn't recognise him. He had become a snob, something he had always accused her of being, and he became a bully, but she had still not seen it coming. He had walked out on her without a backward glance. Now he had his new life with his new wife. He had taken everything she knew, everything she had ever wanted; he had taken it all from her in a few minutes. Even her son preferred his father's lifestyle and now only visited her every few weeks.

Carmen was lonely. Lonely and suspicious, but she still loved her husband because he was all she had ever known. He had been her life. She was also worried that any man she *might* meet would be more interested in her money than her sparkling personality. After all, she was hardly a spring chicken, and she knew she was not the kind of woman men were attracted to. Sex had never been something she craved, she was born to be a wife and mother, not a femme fatale. Her husband could have kept the girl on the side, like all the others, and she would have done what she had always done. Ignored it. She had seen off more than her share over the years. She had learned to pretend she was clueless about his amours, even though she had occasionally felt the urge to stab the faithless bastard to death while he slept. Unlike him, she had been prepared to sit it out, that's what people were supposed to do. But he had decided to be different.

She was bitter, and she knew she was, but she was unable to overcome that. Now, as she sat with these two nice women and enjoyed the unexpected pleasure of some company, she opened up like a flower. 'I do prefer real coffee. It's one expense I couldn't forgo.'

Kate and Annie grinned in agreement. 'It's a rare treat for us, I can tell you. You have a great view here, you can see right over to the golf course.' Kate was looking out of the large picture window as she spoke. And it *was* a great view, all trees and well-tended grass. It also looked directly over the forecourt of the flats so Carmen would see all the coming and goings.

'I liked the view, it's why I purchased this property. I find it very calming, I watch the golfers sometimes.'

Carmen watched them because now and again she saw her husband, who she still wanted even after all that he had done. He played there frequently, and she hated herself for her weakness. He had taken everything from her, and yet she still held a blazing torch for him. She fantasised that he'd come back to her, cap in hand, sorry for not appreciating her and everything she had done for him. She knew it would never happen, he had been mentally gone from her for years, it was only when he had left physically that she had understood how shallow her life had been. Now she was saddened that a visit from the police was a highlight in an otherwise bloody boring day. As her son kept telling her, she needed to get out more.

'You also have a bird's-eye view of the road, so you must have wondered at the number of strange men coming and going constantly. I understand the flat was in operation twenty-four hours a day. I can't believe an intelligent woman like you didn't put two and two together. It must have been awful finding out you were living next to a knocking shop. Men coming in and out at all hours of the day and night.'

Carmen nodded, her sharp features seemed to be closing in on themselves; she was exactly as Kate had predicted, a small-minded woman who saw herself as above the general population.

'I don't know what I can tell you really, there *were* a lot of men in and out, and obviously I knew they weren't coming here for piano lessons. But what could I do? The people involved, those girls, they were common, low types. I was afraid to say anything to them so I just ignored it.'

Kate nodded in understanding. 'It must have been horrendous for you. How did the men get in, were they buzzed in by the girls?'

'Not always, sometimes the outside door was left open, that way the men didn't disturb us by ringing the wrong buzzers. That can be very annoying and, as you can imagine, very distressing.'

'Why is there no CCTV? You have such a great alarm system.'

The woman nodded and then shrugged theatrically. 'We did have it, but it was disabled a few years back. It was costing us a fortune every month, and that on top of the gardeners, you can imagine. And, in fairness, we were happy enough with the security offered in exchange. It made sense, after all, we're in flats. We have one entrance and one exit. Why pay out for something we don't really need?'

Kate smiled again. Annie watched her as she drew the woman out. Last night Carmen had been adamant that she knew nothing of the activities of the flat, and that she had never noticed anything untoward.

'Who offered you the security system?'

Carmen looked uncomfortable.

'I promise this will be off the record, Mrs Milke. But we really need to know what's happened here. I assure you no one will get into any trouble, what security you decide on is your business. I just need to know who was behind it, that's all.'

Carmen was worried about saying too much, but she felt that she should try and help if she could. After all, a young girl had lost her life, even if Carmen felt deep down that she had asked for it.

'A man called Bates. He said that what we were paying for the CCTV, he could get us all a much better deal, and also make us safer in the process. He wasn't a man who you felt would take no for an answer, if you understand me but, in fairness, he was as good as his word. We were given individual alarm systems that were on-site, as Mr Bates put it. Not something we had to rely on as a block. Even the windows are fitted with sensors, as are the doors. It really is a much better system.'

'Did you hear or see anything on the night of the murder?'

Carmen shook her head furiously. 'Not a word. I was asleep very early. I take sleeping pills because I find it hard to drop off these days.'

'Do you see Mr Bates around here often?'

'Occasionally, not regularly.'

'Have you noticed any strange men recently, maybe regular visitors to the dead girl's flat? Has there been any-thing at all of late that made you think something was odd, off-kilter? Raised voices, strange noises . . .'

Carmen snorted then, her face once more wearing its pinched look of disapproval. 'There were always strange noises, you can imagine . . . I can't hear anything from my bedroom, so I tend to spend a lot of time in there. In fact, now this has happened, I hope we'll be able to get some sort of normality. I mean, you will be closing it down, won't you?'

Kate heard the relief in Carmen's voice and wondered at

how people allowed themselves to be walked over like this. 'I think that's a given, but we have to prove the flat was being used for the purpose of prostitution, and without anyone giving us evidence of that, it could be argued that the girl who died had only been there that once. We need solid evidence of the flat's usage over a period of time.'

Carmen was quiet for a few moments. 'Talk to Mrs Brown on the ground floor, she knows more about it than anyone. She had words with the girls on more than one occasion. But you didn't hear that from me. She was frightened off by a man and, from what I gather, after his visit she did what we all did, she turned a blind eye.'

Veronica was tired out. After another hard day watching television and grooming herself to perfection, she was bored out of her mind, and fed up with the murder that seemed to be the only thing on everyone's mind. Even *Sky News* was milking it for all it was worth. Peter was like a bear with a sore arse, and she was fed up with the lot of it. So he owned the flat? Big news on the grapevine, he owned loads of properties. All he had to do was feign ignorance. As he walked into the kitchen she voiced her thoughts. 'Why are you so bothered, Pete? All you have to say is you rented the gaff out, and what the person did with it was their business, not yours.' As far as she was concerned, it was cut and dried.

Peter Bates looked at Veronica for long moments and saw the girl she had been, and the woman she had become. Never the sharpest knife in the drawer, she had been blessed with an innate cunning that had seen her sleep her way to a nice life. She was pampered, she was beautiful, and she was a fucking bonehead.

'Are you having a fucking laugh, you dozy bitch? Everything I have ever done, ever bought, or ever touched will come under scrutiny. If I farted in 1978 it will be found out and reported back to me: date and venue. A young girl has been horrifically killed, and I was the one who organised the cleaning of the flat and, in doing so, I erased any evidence that might have been there. More importantly, I have landed me mate right in it, and he ain't a person you can apologise to and guarantee a fucking friendly handshake and instant forgiveness. He's known to be a bit temperamental when the fancy takes him. I fucked up big time, and now all I can do is try and fucking extricate meself from a potentially lethal situation. So my advice to you is keep your fucking opinions to yourself, and try to restrain your natural ability to talk absolute shite. Am I making myself clear?'

Veronica didn't answer him. She knew that this was a turning point in their relationship. She would have to box clever for a while, he was capable of aiming her out the door without any worry. He had a lot on his plate, he was not a man who listened to reason and he was capable of taking out his aggravations on her. It was much better to retreat on this occasion, and wait until it had all died down. He was still looking at her with contempt and so she took his advice and restrained herself. Instead she went to him and looking into his eyes she said gently, 'I'm only trying to help, baby.'

Peter laughed then, a sarcastic and disbelieving laugh that told her she was on very shaky ground. 'Oh stop it, Veronica. You don't give a fuck about Danielle Crosby, you don't give a fuck about anyone but yourself. So save the amateur dramatics, and let me sort this out without your fucking big trap in me earhole.'

As Peter left the kitchen she heard the front doorbell go, and she stood quietly when she heard Patrick Kelly's right-hand man Danny Foster saying, 'Hello, Peter, I was worried you might be out, what with your new job as a fucking charlady taking up all your time.'

Danny Foster was a Face, a man to respect and someone who was seen as on the up. He was Patrick Kelly's sidekick, Patrick Kelly's mouthpiece. He was the son Patrick Kelly never had. If he was on the knocker then they really were in deep shit.

Diana Brown was in her late fifties. A small, heavily built woman, she was somewhat reluctant to let Kate and Annie inside her flat. As they followed her into the spacious kitchen Kate noted that the furnishings were very understated, and very expensive. That surprised her, the small neat woman she saw didn't strike her as having that kind of sophistication. Her clothes were well made, probably Marks & Spencer, but not that well put together. Her hair needed a decent cut and colour, and her nails were bitten to the quick, with traces of chipped pink nail varnish still apparent. She looked as if she had not slept for a while, and Kate assumed this was because of the girl's murder.

'I told your officers everything I knew last night.'

Kate and Annie smiled as they sat down at her breakfast bar. The kitchen was state-of-the-art, all black granite and stainless steel. It was not a kitchen you would associate with this woman in a million years.

'We know that, but often, after the shock has worn off, people remember things they forgot in the initial excitement. And also, Mrs Brown, things you don't think are important can turn out to be very important to us and our investigation.'

Diana sighed. 'It's awful to think of that girl up there dying, and no one knowing about it. But it was on the cards. I don't mean the murder by that, but there were so many men going in and out of there, something had to happen at some point.'

Annie got up and walked Diana gently over to a chair. She sat down heavily. Seeing a pack of Marlboro Lights on the worktop Annie took one out and put it into the woman's hand. Diana accepted it gratefully and picked up her lighter.

'I understand you had words with the girls on a few occasions over men coming and going twenty-four hours a day. That must have been difficult.'

Kate had chosen her words carefully, and she was rewarded by another deep sigh. 'I had a few words with that poor girl last week. It's so bloody inconvenient, cars pulling up at all hours, men up and down the bloody stairs, the music, the constant movement, you know. I wish I had never bought this place, and it's impossible to sell. I mean, you can imagine what it was like if anyone came here. Cars and more cars. I have to park on the road sometimes, I paid a fortune for my garage and, nine times out of ten, someone is parked right in front of it. I feel awful because I am glad that this has happened because it means we can all have our lives back.'

Kate understood how Diana was feeling. 'That's human nature, Mrs Brown. It can't have been easy living through all that. I understand you made a few complaints. Can I ask you, who did you deal with?'

The woman shrugged then, and looking directly into Kate's concerned face, she said finally, 'I was threatened. Not directly, of course, but I knew what was being said to me. I asked that man, Bates, if he could see how it looked to everyone. Told him how the place was ruining my home. I hated the whole bloody lot of them! Those girls would laugh at me, swear at me some of them. Bates said I was not someone he saw as significant, in fact, he assured me that I was not someone he would be seen dead talking to in a public place. Like I wasn't good enough. He did say he would ask the girls to keep it down, but if they were popular, what could he do? I even called the police a few months ago, there was a big row going on up there, the police arrived, went upstairs, and then left. I never heard another word. It went quiet after that though, and for a while life was bearable. But that man Bates is very intimidating, and I got the message. We *all* got the message.'

Kate felt sorry for this frightened woman. She knew Peter Bates was Patrick's friend, and that they had a few business dealings, but she had not dreamed that those dealings would be the cause of this woman's life being made a misery, and the reason a young woman was lying dead on a mortuary slab. Bates would have threatened her, Kate knew that; she knew him and what he was capable of. She also knew what Patrick was capable of.

'Can you remember anything else at all? Were there any strange men hanging round, did you see anything that was out of the ordinary?'

Diana shook her head. 'Strange men are the norm here. I got the most of it, as you can see, my flat is directly by the parking bays. The flat next door is rented by a businessman who is always off somewhere. He rarely stays there more than a few nights at a time. I had to put up with the cars in and out and the men looking in my window as they came up to the front door. I keep my blinds closed all the time now. The other residents work, they go out for the evening. They got a break from it all. I am stuck here with it all the time. I hated it, hated what they stood for. Hated that my life was invaded by their bloody whoring. My husband died and I got over it, I moved here to make a fresh start. I bought this place because it was quiet and it was pretty. I have lived here for two years and been at the mercy of those bloody girls almost from the start. I stopped taking notice of what went on after Mr Bates explained that I was not helping myself by complaining. The police ignored me, and I didn't know what else to do. Now we've had all this.'

Kate and Annie looked at each other, both aware that this woman had been badly let down. 'Can you remember the date you called the police out?'

Diana Brown smiled sadly. 'Sixteenth of April. It would have been my husband's sixtieth birthday.'

Kate was in her bedroom, she had showered and dressed. She caught her reflection in the antique mirror she had bought with Patrick years before and stifled the urge to smash it up. She didn't feel like this was her home any more. It was as if everything around her was alien, she felt so out of place. She had always accepted that Patrick was a wide boy, in all honesty, it had been a big part of his attraction. But she had believed him when he said he was on the straight. She should have known better. He had let her down before. But this time she had believed him.

All those years, and they had been good years. Happy years. She had moved in with him, enjoyed his affluent lifestyle. Had felt loved, cared for. Safe. He must have been laughing up his sleeve at her. Well, not any more.

Kate checked her bags, making sure she had packed everything she needed. Satisfied she had enough, she looked around the room once more then, picking up the cases, she walked out without a backward glance.

Patrick pulled on to the drive as she was putting the cases in the boot of her car. He got out of his Bentley and walked over to her. She sensed his approach and could feel the anger inside her bubbling as he said nonchalantly, 'Oh, for Christ's sake, Kate. I didn't know what the flat was being used for. I just invested in a property business, that's all.'

Kate slammed the boot of her Mercedes 220 saloon, a birthday present from Patrick two years ago and, turning to look at him, said quietly and deliberately, 'If it was with Bates, then you knew exactly what you were letting yourself in for. You always said you never trusted him, that you read the small print on every contract, and checked that there wasn't any really small print invisible to the naked eye. I laughed with you as you said it. Well, he will have been picked up by now, and charged with everything from tampering with a crime scene, tampering with evidence, attempting to hide a criminal act, living off immoral earnings, and anything else I can think of. Once he mentions you, I can't be responsible for what the police might decide to do. I can, however, distance myself from your fucking devious shenanigans and your obvious involvement in the violent death of a young woman.'

Patrick looked at her and when she saw that he was gritting his teeth, she knew she had hit a home run. She knew she had hurt him, and she was glad. She wanted him to hurt like she was hurting.

'I'm only on the paperwork, I am a sleeping partner, and I can prove that. So don't you go trying to stitch me up. I am sorry, I am fucking in bits over that young woman, but it wasn't anything to do with me personally.'

Kate pushed him out of her way. 'I don't believe you, Patrick. You could have told me the score when you heard the murder took place in your property and I would have been upset, but at least you would have spared me the indignity of finding out you were a born-again pimp from a colleague. I should have guessed you were involved, you were too quiet. You already knew about it, didn't you?'

Pat couldn't deny it and they were both aware of that.

'So this is it then?' he said. 'I get me collar felt for no more than investing in a legitimate business, and you walk out on our life as if it meant nothing. I have already had my brief explain the situation to your superiors and they are more than satisfied I had no knowledge of anything that went on in that flat. So calm down and stop being so bloody dramatic.'

He was always so cocksure, it had been what attracted her to him all those years ago. He had a way with him, a way of making you overlook his failings because his good points seemed to outweigh them. He was a fucking ducker and diver, a wide boy made good. If it had been anything else she could have swallowed it. But not this.

Now all Kate saw was that girl's broken body and his reluctance to admit his involvement. She loved him, really loved him. But she knew that his going behind her back, his trying to justify himself by using his brief to prove he was no more than an investor in a business, that he was a dupe, an innocent, was something she could not forgive. He could have come clean about everything, given her the chance to understand their situation. The outright audacity of the man was unbelievable, he thought she was overreacting. He'd let her down before with his tricks and secrecy. And she'd forgiven him then. How could he not understand that it would be impossible for her to swallow it again, and that his actions would impact on her? It would be all over the station by now. Everything that she had worked for over the years would be forgotten in a heartbeat, she would once again be nothing more than the villain's bird.

He wouldn't even think about that, it wouldn't occur to him that this was about more than him and his wants. He had not thought about her and how his actions might affect her and her life. He was a selfish man in many respects, but she had still loved him.

'You really don't see it, do you, Pat?'

He opened his arms wide, a look of bewilderment on his face. 'See what, Kate? What the fuck is there for me to see?'

Kate shook her head sadly and, forcing down the urge to cry, she said quietly, 'I can't stay under the roof of a man who has lied to me, who could keep something so important to himself, who would distance himself from any wrongdoing before he felt it was safe to tell his side of the story. You went in with your brief and extricated yourself from a sticky situation. Well, I don't believe you, or your brief. How can I believe a word you say after that? You must have been aware of what was going on, and don't fucking insult my intelligence by trying to spin me otherwise.'

'Oh, I see. So this is all about me trying to save you some embarrassment? I didn't tell you because I didn't know *how* to tell you, did I? Come on, Kate . . .' He was trying to talk her round now, he'd realised she really was leaving him. 'I panicked, I was bloody mortified . . . Surely you can see that . . .'

Kate shook her head slowly. 'I saw a girl who had been battered and tortured, and all you saw was how to save your own arse. I'm working on this case with Annie, we are going to find this nutter, and if that means you get a tug in the process then tough shit.'

Pat was weary now, he had no fight left in him. He saw the determination in her, felt the anger that he knew was justified in part, but he still felt was way over the top. She should have seen all this from his point of view, should have understood his dilemma. She should have been watching his back.

'Fair enough. You go. And, for the record, Kate, you ain't a real Filth any more, remember?'

With that he walked into the house and Kate got into her car. As she drove away she resisted the urge to look back. She knew he wouldn't be looking.

Lucy was already inside the flat when she heard the music and she smiled to herself. Janie loved Oasis, she listened to them constantly. The music told her that she wasn't entertaining a punter.

She walked through to the kitchen and put the kettle on, calling out for Janie as she went. She assumed Janie was in the shower, getting rid of her make-up and turning herself back into a regular person.

Lucy made the tea and noticed the answering machine was flashing. She pressed the Play button and listened to a litany of punters asking for a call back. That wasn't unusual.

What was unusual, however, was that these messages were all from the night before. They had started at eleven-fifteen, and each one asked why they had not been given access to the premises.

Lucy was nervous now. The Oasis music had somehow become the Spice Girls. She strained her ears in an effort to listen, was terrified that someone was in the flat, someone dangerous. She could hear her own heart beating inside her chest. She called out her friend's name once again.

She removed a knife from a drawer as quietly as she could and, holding it tightly against her chest, she walked out of the kitchen and towards the front room. She was sweating with fear. She knew something was wrong, knew that it didn't feel right. There was a really awful smell coming from somewhere and she couldn't place it, but she knew it wasn't good.

Pushing the door open she looked inside the room. It was perfect, not a thing out of place. She turned towards the bedroom and, breathing as quietly as she could, she stepped towards the door. It was shut tight.

The sound of the radio was loud in the hallway, and Lucy tried to convince herself that she was overreacting. But she still couldn't bring herself to open the door. She wondered if Janie had copped herself an all-nighter, they were rare these days, but not unheard of. Lots of men wanted to wake up with a girl beside them, it was only the price that stopped them getting their heart's desire.

Lucy saw her reflection in the hallway mirror; she looked ridiculous standing there with a knife in her hand and her face like a terrified child's. She wiped a hand over her face, her sensible head was telling her not to be stupid. Finally she plucked up the courage and pushed the bedroom door open, calling out gaily, 'You in there, Janie? You all right, mate?'

Kate was unpacking her bags. As she hung up her clothes and placed her shoes in the bottom of the old-fashioned wardrobe she tried not to think about the day's events. The room wasn't bad, she had just forgotten how small the house was in comparison to Patrick's.

This had been her home for a long time, and she had always resisted the urge to sell it. To get rid of it. Now she was glad about that. Glad she had chosen instead to rent it out. She had loved this house. As she sat on the bed she felt the pull of her old life overwhelm her. Her husband Dan had deceived her, lied to her, and eventually left her for another woman. He had also tried to win her back when he had realised his mistake. By then though, she'd had enough. She had met Patrick Kelly, and he had made her forget how lonely you could be when you were abandoned by the person you loved most.

It was strange really, how one person could have so much impact on your life. You didn't even know they existed for years, then one day you met them, and that was it. Your whole life would be changed overnight, you suddenly found you needed someone so much you couldn't imagine your life without them. Yet you had lived without them for years and years, you had gone to work, laughed, cried, gone on holiday, and all that time you had never even dreamed of them, heard of them, seen them, or even smelled them. Then, one day you crossed paths with them and your life, the life you had loved, had come to enjoy, wasn't good enough any more. Without that person you felt alone, unloved, unwanted.

Kate wondered how many people had missed out on that. How many people lay awake at night wishing for someone to come into their life and make it all seem worthwhile. When all along, what they really did for you was stop you from being your own person. Kate closed her eyes tightly, she could feel the tears of her disappointment flooding her eyes, the bitter tears that she knew would need to be shed at some point, but not now. It was too soon, it was still too raw. She was frightened that if she let them go, she wouldn't be able to stop.

Annie Carr knocked gently on the door before coming in with a large brandy and a mug of coffee on a small tray. 'I thought you might need this.'

Kate smiled at her. 'I'm sorry to land on you like this, it's not fair.'

Annie smiled at her sadly, her eyes taking in everything around her. 'It's your house, Kate. I never used this room, it always seemed a bit too personal, you know? I'm glad you came here, after all, this was your home for a long time.'

Kate poured the brandy into the coffee and sipped it gratefully. The trouble was, it didn't *feel* like her home any more, she had been away from it for far too long.

Chapter Three

Kate looked at the girl's remains, and remains was the only way to describe what was left of her. The acrid stench of acid was still hanging in the air. Janie Moore's face and genitalia had been slashed and burned like before. The counterpane underneath had melted. It was obvious the girl had not tried to escape.

'Have you looked at the toes, Annie?'

The girl's toes were relaxed, so at least they could assume she would not have felt anything. But she may have been conscious on some level of what was happening to her.

'How did he get in?'

Kate grinned wryly. 'This is a premises where letting in strange men is the norm. He must be targeting these girls for a reason. Think about it: Danielle Crosby was left like this girl, open-legged, body posed for the maximum shock, horror of whoever found her. Were these girls hand-picked for a reason, or were they just the ones available? Two girls in three days, that's a lot. It tells me that whoever this is, they have more than a working knowledge of this area. At least when it comes to the girls and where they're based.'

'You think he's a local then?'

Kate shrugged. 'Could be, but then again they might have lived here years back, could even have worked around here. Might even have relatives here. Until we find out something concrete it's all speculation.'

Annie looked around the room, it was a typical sex-worker's paradise. All peach colours, full-length mirrors and sex toys. It wasn't as seedy as some of the places she'd seen, but it wasn't exactly the Ritz either. She wondered at the men who frequented these establishments. What possessed them to come into these places? Nine out of ten of them were putting their whole lives on the line for a bit of strange. If their families knew what they were up to there would be murders. No woman in her right mind was going to accept that kind of behaviour, no matter how much she loved her partner. This was what they laughingly referred to in the station as a Jeremy Kyle situation; a man gets caught with a brass, they all know he's going to get far more of a punishment from his wife than Lily Law. This time though, there was no humour to be found in the circumstances. It was a tragic and violent loss of a young woman's life.

Kate looked around the flat with interest. She saw the usual paraphernalia indigenous to Toms, but she also saw that this was quite a homely place outside the bedrooms. The girls who worked here had brought in a touch of normality. She saw the usual mix of make-up and cleansers in the bathroom, the hall cupboard held an array of hooded sweats and warm jackets. There were boots and shoes that were not the usual Tom attire. She had even found a child's coat and hat in a carrier bag. Her first instinct was to wonder if the place was being used for paedophilia, but the garments still had the price tags on so she guessed they were just the property of one of the girls involved here. There was nothing else to make her think any different. Most of the girls were there to keep their kids clothed and fed anyway. Like lap dancers and hostesses, they were simply trying to keep their heads above water. In this climate it was the only way some women could exist. This place had obviously been used by the same girls over a long period of time. She guessed that they had got used to being here, felt safe, and had probably forgotten how dangerous the job really was. Perhaps they'd let their guard down, assumed that men were all friendly and easily controlled. The reality was so different. Most men were harmless enough, but there were plenty of nutters about as well. These were the men who saw working girls as beneath them and who felt it was perfectly acceptable to hurt them. These men felt a surge of energy by humiliating them, or causing them injury. It was these men that the girls often forgot about until they were standing in front of them with a knife and a smile. Only this one didn't use a weapon as such, he seemed almost to be trying to cleanse them. The use of acids and industrial cleaners on the girls was clearly important. It was as if he wanted to make them pure again.

Kate kept that opinion to herself because she knew that everything said or speculated upon could find its way into the press. It was a different world now, the old ways were long gone. Young policemen and women were as caught up in the celebrity culture as everyone else. Nothing was kept quiet any more, kept in-house, even if it meant that the person they were looking for was given an out. It was the era of the snide, the internal grass. Everything was fair game these days, even if it meant ruining an ongoing investigation.

Kate wondered how much of this crime scene would hit the papers by the weekend. How much of the girl's life would be plastered across the front pages. It was always the same now. Her family wouldn't be allowed the decency to grieve in peace, it would all be in the public domain and her whole life would be out there for anyone to read. And they would no doubt say she was asking for it because she was on the game.

She sighed in exasperation, wondering if her private life would be exposed along with these poor girls'. It wouldn't be the first time she had been the subject of the tabloid press's scrutiny. Only this time she didn't have Patrick's strength to see her through it. Twice she had been the lead investigator on very high-profile cases, and even though she helped solve them, put the perpetrators behind bars, each time she had also been publicly ridiculed because of her alliance with Patrick Kelly. Until now, she had held her head up and accepted it as part and parcel of her life, and the people she worked with had grudgingly admired her stance. She had fronted it out. Now, though, she knew that Pat's involvement in this investigation, however tenuous it might be, would be used against her. It was a different world to the one she was used to, and she also knew that if he was a part of this, then she had no option but to distance herself from him once and for all.

She saw the girl's Versace handbag on the worktop in the kitchen, it was a Jekyll and Hyde, a snide, a good imitation of the real thing. Opening it she saw the usual; a purse, a few bits of make-up and an Oyster card. In the purse was about fifty pounds in cash and a photograph of the girl with her two small children. She looked happy as she gazed into the camera, a huge smile on her face. The kids looked even happier, were well dressed and well cared for, which was not unusual for the children of brasses. Kate remembered reading somewhere once that, contrary to popular belief, the offspring of Toms were better dressed and cared for than the majority of the so-called regular population's children.

Janie Moore had been a lovely-looking girl with two beautiful children, and now her life was over. Snuffed out on a whim. Her kids were left motherless, and her life left without meaning. No one would remember her as a good mother or daughter, or as a friend, all they would remember was *how* she died, and what she was working as.

It was bloody tragic. Like Danielle, Janie Moore would be remembered as nothing more than a victim from this day forward. Everything else about her would count for nothing.

Patrick was going through all the paperwork concerning the properties he owned. He already knew that another poor girl had been offed on what was legally his premises and he was once more trying to convince himself that he was not in any way responsible.

He had already had what he would describe as a full and frank conversation with Peter about his stupidity in trying to clean the flat after Danielle's death. He'd now had to call in a favour to sort it out with the Filth. Kate would add that to his crimes. Peter Bates had been shown the error of his ways, thanks in part to Danny Boy and his persuasive personality. But it had been an eye-opener for him on a personal level.

Danny Foster was to all intents and purposes his manager, he was down on all the legal paperwork as the person who ran the businesses. After all, Pat was now retired. So any flak that might come in his direction would, in actual fact, be Danny's problem; that was what he was paid enormous sums of money for. But it still didn't make him feel any better. Danny was his fall guy.

Pat had always made sure that he was one step ahead of the game, that there was someone to act as a buffer between him and the law. It was what had kept him safe for all these years. He had been good for a long while because of his relationship with Kate, but once she had officially retired, he allowed his natural aptitude for a decent earn to surface once again.

It wasn't even about the money, though that wasn't to be sneezed at, it was more to do with the fact that he had felt alive once more. He felt the old excitement of the deal, had enjoyed being back in the world of skulduggery. Kate had made him happy, and he loved the bones of her. But he had missed the excitement of the life, missed the feeling of being a part of something. Danny Foster had done a good job as his number two, but it wasn't the same. He had felt old, and he had felt bored, and that was something he could not get used to. Now his involvement in all this had backfired on him, and he had felt compelled to put it right, and he had done just that.

This wheeling and dealing was making him feel alive once more. All he had was his businesses now, he had neither chick nor child, as his old mum used to say, he had nobody to call his own. Mandy was long gone, dead and buried. He had had no one except Kate, and she wasn't enough for him any more. She wanted him to be like her, settled and accepting, and he had tried. He had really tried to be what she wanted him to be. But now, as much as he loved her, he had to admit part of him was relieved at her going. He wouldn't have to pretend any more, he didn't have to convince himself that he liked the quiet life. She had chosen to walk away from the life they had made. She had been compromised, he understood that, but her anger and complete indifference to him and his life had only gone to prove that he had been right all along.

She had left him in a heartbeat and, in doing so, she had shown him just how much he had really meant to her.

He had smoothed over his ownership of the flats, and he had walked away from the problem without a stain on his character or hers. But it hurt the way she had reacted, and he was not about to forget that in a hurry. She had always been the same, it had always been about her and her bloody job. Now she was a consultant, working for a bloody pittance just so she could keep her hand in, as she put it. She still had to go into that poxy nick on a regular basis, it was all she really cared about.

Now she had another big case to keep her occupied, it would be the only thing she was really interested in. He respected her for that, knew she did make a difference to the world. He understood she was only doing what she felt needed to be done. But he also knew that *he* needed something in his life as well. Now Kate had walked out on him, he realised that he'd needed more than she had been willing to give him for a long time. He had felt disgruntled for the last few years, had felt the heaviness of his age and his loneliness weighing on him. He realised now that Kate, as much as he loved her, wasn't enough for him. Without her, he could do what he wanted, without fear or favour.

He was enjoying the prospect of having the freedom to do exactly what he wanted, having the freedom to go out and about at his leisure. She had kept her life right from the start, she had stayed on the force, and he had been happy for her to do that. Even though it had meant he had to change his life to fit in with hers. He had done that without a second's thought. Now though, all these years later, he was aware of how old he was getting, and how little time he might have left to enjoy the money he had accrued, and the thought of that was terrifying in itself.

But worse than that was the knowledge that it had taken Kate just minutes to decide that her job was more important than their life together. She should have been willing to stand by him, no matter what she thought he had done. She should have had his best interests at heart, as he had had hers. It had been a real learning curve because he had been so determined to make it all all right for her, and he had done just that. Yet she had walked away from him without a backward glance. As someone had pointed out to him many years ago, once a Filth, always a Filth. Never was a truer word spoken.

Tammy Taylor was still very attractive for her age. She was tiny like her daughter, but she had a way with her, a way of holding herself that made her seem childlike. She had the same eyes as Janie, and the build was the same. But whereas Janie had looked what she was, a capable and strong young mum of two, Tammy looked almost ethereal, as if a strong gust of wind would knock her over.

She was still in shock at her daughter's death, and her eyes were haunted, they were searching Kate's face for some kind of understanding, and Kate knew she had nothing to tell her that would make the news any easier to bear.

'Was Moore her married name?'

Tammy shook her head, making her long, thick hair ripple with the action. 'It's my maiden name. She was . . . I mean I wasn't married when I had her.'

Kate could see from the photographs all around the small front room that she was Janie's mother, no doubt about that. They were like twins born years apart, the two of them smiling into the camera together, Janie's lovely face radiant with youth and happiness.

Kate hoped that this woman wouldn't insist on seeing her daughter's remains, she knew if she did, it would be something she would regret for the rest of her days. Kate intended to find out if there was anyone else who could do the formal identification of the body.

'Do you know what time Janie normally started work?'

Tammy shook her head once more. 'I dunno. I mean, she never talked about it. She told me she was working for a nursing agency, you know. I can't believe she was . . .'

Kate let Tammy gather herself together once more. 'Would it be possible for us to have the keys to her house, we need to have a look around in case there's something that might help us . . .'

Tammy nodded. ''Course, do whatever you want to. What am I supposed to tell the kids? How am I going to tell them . . .'

'Is there anyone we can call? I think you need someone with you.'

Annie's voice was quiet, she was worried about how Tammy would cope with the shock of her daughter being murdered. Death was hard enough to accept at the best of times, but a murder was always harder because there was no reason behind it except hate.

'My sister, I better ring my sister. She'll know what to do.'

Kate nodded. 'Are you sure you didn't know anything at all about Janie's work?'

Tammy slumped heavily on to the leather sofa she had bought a few weeks previously with the money Janie had given her for her birthday. 'I guessed it had something to do with Lucy Painter and that Jennifer James, but I didn't think it was anything like this. I heard her on the blower to them a few times, but I didn't think anything of it . . . I heard Lucy was a bit of a girl, but I never thought my Janie would do that, she was a quiet type of girl. She lived for her kids.'

'Who's Jennifer James? Is that who Lucy worked for?' Annie asked.

'I think so, she's a hard-faced mare, and my Janie would talk to her a couple of times a week. She said she was just helping her get sorted with the agency. I knew deep down it was all a load of old fanny. She had too much money. But I didn't think she was doing anything like this, I thought it might be lap dancing or some such. She had a lovely figure on her. I never asked too much about it because I didn't really want to know. I wish I had put me foot down, had made her tell me what was going on . . . But she was a very determined girl, and she would do what she wanted no matter what I might have said.'

Tammy was crying again, and Kate motioned to Annie that it was time to go. A young policewoman would stay with her until her sister arrived to keep her company. It was the worst part of their job, seeing the families as they realised their nearest and dearest would never come home again. And Victim Support would follow up.

Outside, in the cool night air, Kate saw the ordinariness of

Tammy Taylor's life. A life that would never be the same ever again.

'I think we need to talk with Jennifer James and, once Lucy Painter calms down, I think we need to find out from her exactly how the flats work. The phone records should give us something, if nothing else at least we'll get a timeline of sorts. I can't understand why no one seems to have seen or heard anything. This man must be either invisible, or imbued with magical powers.'

Annie Carr opened the car door and settled herself behind the steering wheel. As Kate got into the passenger seat Annie said seriously, 'It's got to be someone who knew the girls' movements, they were both drugged and then attacked, that all took time.'

Kate nodded her agreement. 'But a punter can buy as much time with the girl as he wants, can't he, so that's a moot point really. If he requests three hours, then he gets three hours. That's why I want to see the phone records, the mobiles as well as the landlines. Someone booked that time, and we need to find out where they phoned from. The chances are it will be from a pay as you go, but we can only hope, can't we? Also, the fact the girls were almost unconscious before he felt confident enough to attack tells me he is not a typically aggressive person. He needed them to be pliant, unable to fight back in any way. I think he is a loner, not that strong physically, but not a weakling, if you see what I mean. He needs to be able to spend time with them, but he also needs them to be warm, almost active. The girls would have been groaning, making some kind of futile movements as he started in on them. The Rohypnol and GHB would have rendered them unable to function, unable to fight back, but they would have known he was up to no good. I think that he would have needed them to know that. I think he is a sadist who gets off on the thrill of the blood, who enjoys violating them with foreign objects such as the chair leg, then goes merrily on to the destruction of not just their faces, but also their genitalia. This man obviously has a serious hatred of women, but not just any women, he targets young, beautiful girls who sell their bodies to the highest bidder, so I think we can safely assume he will not be killing outside of that comfort zone. Also, the elaborate posing of the bodies to maximise the horror of whoever is unlucky enough to discover them makes me think he is getting as much from that as he is from the murder itself. He is just warming up, Annie. This man has taken two lives already, and we have literally nothing to say he was ever there.'

'Fucking hell, Kate. When you put it like that, I wonder how the hell we can hope to catch him.'

Kate grinned wryly. 'All we can hope for, Annie, is that he makes a mistake. So far we have found *nothing*. No prints, nothing that can even tell us he was in the room, let alone near the girls he murdered. He is not only cunning, he is also confident in what he is doing. He has planned it. I mean, think about it, even if we do track down any of the prints we might find, the girls' occupation is the perfect alibi as to why the prints were there in the first place. We can find the fingerprints, but we can't say *when* they were put there. They could have been there weeks, months, even years. But he is too shrewd, we won't find anything. It's the Grantley Ripper all over again. These people function in the world, they fit in somehow. We need to try and work out when and where he might strike, that is the only way we will be able to get some kind of head start on him. So we should start by finding out exactly how many properties and how many girls work for Bates.'

Annie lit a cigarette in the darkness and drew on it deeply. 'Patrick came in and saw the arsehole, so he is now officially off the wanted list. But you already know that, don't you?'

Kate didn't answer her.

Annie went on. 'But we can still question Bates and, as you said, that Jennifer James. We can easily find out what premises are being used, and we can also shut them down. But what we can't do anything about is the girls who work from their own homes.'

Kate sighed. 'We can only warn them, and hope they have the sense to listen to us. Now, as far as Bates is concerned, I'll go and talk to him myself. He will be a bit more forthcoming if I see him on the quiet. He will appreciate that and be more inclined to tell me what I want to know.'

Annie nodded and started the engine up. As she pulled away from the kerb she said sadly, 'I always wanted a big case, you know, wanted to make my name, and now I can't believe I was so fucking naive. Who in their right mind would want any of this on their plate?'

Kate laughed. 'You know the old saying, be careful what you ask for, you might just get it.'

Danny Foster was handsome, and he knew it. Not that he was vain as such, but he saw himself every day and knew that, on a scale of one to ten, he was at least an eight. Women of all ages loved him. He had the thick, dark hair and steely grey eyes of his Irish grandmother, and the height and strong build of his Scottish grandfather.

He was gorgeous and, unlike his parents, who had nothing remarkable about them, he had been blessed with a cheery disposition and an uncanny knack of sussing out a situation in nanoseconds. Coupled with his razor-sharp wit and his willingness to use extreme violence when the need arose, he had soon made a name for himself as someone of note. Patrick Kelly had seen the potential in him, and now they had a good working relationship. Danny liked and respected Patrick, he wanted to be like him when the time came. He wanted to be permanently solvent, well respected, and out on the lash as and when the fancy took him.

Danny had no yearning for a permanent woman in his life yet. He liked to play the field and, at thirty-five, the field was getting bigger by the day. His reputation guaranteed him the interest of the women in his world, and his looks were just a bonus for them. He could look like fucking Oddjob and there were certain women who would still profess undying love and devotion. But Danny was far too shrewd to let anyone interfere with his work or his very active sex life on a permanent basis.

As Danny Boy waited in Patrick's office he allowed himself to relax. He loved this house, it was everything he wanted for himself one day. When the time came for him to have a family, he wanted them to be brought up in this kind of splendour. Not that he felt the urge for any sprogs just yet, but he assumed he might feel the need one day. He knew that it was only natural to want to reproduce at some point, and he accepted that the urge to do so could be a strong one. When, and if, he did decide to have a family, he would pick the girl wisely.

Danny looked at the picture of Mandy that always caught

his eye. She had been a real stunner, all blond hair and baby-blue eyes. She was staring into the camera and laughing, head back slightly, and her perfect teeth looked almost fake in their whiteness. But he knew Mandy Kelly had been given everything in life, from love and care to good dentistry. He wondered how Pat could see her everywhere, knowing what had happened to her. It just proved that you couldn't ever be too complacent because life had a nasty habit of turning round and biting you on the bum.

Patrick walked into the room. He was still a big man, still powerful looking, and although his dark hair was more grey than black these days, he carried himself as he had always carried himself, as if he was someone of importance. Which, of course, in their world, he was.

'Here you are, Danny. Get that down you.'

Danny accepted the brandy gratefully. He knew it would be expensive, knew it would be smooth. He sipped it, and savoured the burn for a few seconds.

'Have you talked to Peter about the girls' safety?'

Danny nodded. 'Yeah. He reckons that we just need to keep them in pairs, it's only the girls on their own who are vulnerable. I agree with him, Pat. It's safety in numbers, so I got his assurance that the girls would be offered a cash incentive to work the shifts in pairs.'

Patrick nodded absently. 'What about the club?'

Danny shrugged gently, his huge shoulders reminding Patrick just how strong this young man was. 'What about it? Takings are up, the doormen are doing their job, and the skirt is fucking wall to wall.'

Pat laughed with him. 'You are fucking always on the horn, do you ever give it a night off?'

Danny grinned cheekily. 'I saw a great little earner yesterday. I was thinking of investing in it, so I would appreciate your advice, Patrick.'

'What is it?'

'Dicky Bolton is selling off his scrapyard, and he's offered it to me at a good price. I'd put someone in to run it like, but I reckon it could be a good investment.'

Pat nodded in agreement. 'That's a good earn. Dicky needs shot because he's gambled himself into a corner. He was always one for the fucking horses, even when we were young. His old man used to bail him out, but now he's dead Dicky's gone through all the cash and can't lay his hands on any readies. No, you take the yard on, it's a potential goldmine if it's run properly.'

Danny smiled happily. 'That's what I thought, Patrick, but I wanted to run it by you first.'

Patrick knew Danny Boy was asking his permission to take the scrapyard on, and he appreciated the lad's sense of decency. It was something that would go a long way in their world. Respect was everything to them, and so it should be. Without it, you had nothing.

'Offer him ten per cent less than his asking price, that's what he will be expecting anyway. Then see one of the Conroys, they know the scrap-metal game inside out.'

Danny was thrilled at the advice and it showed.

'By the way, Danny, exactly how much did the bookies take last week? Only old Lenny said you were late on the pick-ups?'

Danny smiled again, an easy smile. 'I have it out in the car, ready for you to look over, Pat. I was late because I had a lot of running about to do, remember?'

Patrick grinned back at him, but the job had been done. Danny Boy wouldn't be late with the figures again.

Jennifer James was fed up, and it showed. Peter Bates was like a fucking old woman about the girls and, as much as she understood his worry, she was sick of listening to him go on about it. He owned the premises, so he had to expect to get a tug at some point. He was lucky they weren't all over him. He had been given a swerve, and he still couldn't see how lucky he was. He was worrying over nothing. He had made a bad error of judgement, it had happened and it was over. Anyway, she always looked out for herself first and foremost. She knew where the proverbial bodies were buried, and she had the edge on the wealthy boys who were frightened of their carnal relationships becoming public knowledge.

'You'll have to talk to the girls' families at some point, Peter, they're going to want some compensation, and who can blame them? I told you to leave well alone, and you still insisted on doing a Kim and Aggie. Well, now we have to sort out the rest of the girls, and make sure we keep everything and everyone safe.' Jennifer sighed then. 'Well, as safe as anyone *can* be in this game. And we do need to listen to young Danny, he is doing the talking for Kelly so we need to at least look interested. We can only learn from our mistakes.'

Peter nodded, but he was not a happy man. 'Fucking animal, if I get me hands on the ponce that killed those girls I'll fucking gut him.'

Jennifer laughed wearily. 'Join the queue, but until he is caught, we need to get ourselves organised. We can safely assume that the bloke needs privacy so working in pairs seems the best option. It'll give us all a measure of security. What we don't want is any kind of heavies on the firm. The men who come to our girls will not want to feel intimidated, and a big hairy-arsed bouncer type will do just that.'

Peter nodded. 'How are the girls? Have any gone on the trot yet?'

'A few, but not as many as you'd think. What we need now is damage limitation, as the big banks would put it. We need to make sure the girls do not aggravate the neighbours, do not bring unwanted attention to themselves and, most of all, do not allow themselves to be drugged. Though with the majority of them, it would be hard to tell either way. Once this is all over, we can get back to normal.'

'Have you put the word out then, Jen?'

Jennifer nodded sagely. 'What do you think?'

Chapter Four

'I feel like we're running in circles, we have *nothing* to go on. Either this person is fucking invisible, or people are just not registering him.'

Kate and Annie had gone over everything again and again, and there was not one thing that stood out, not one thing that was even suspicious.

'George Markham was like that. A really nondescript little man. But for all that, he was a devious little fucker. The trouble with the working girls is they have so many people in and out of their lives on a daily basis. So we need to start collating details of the girls and the punters sooner rather than later. We will have to talk to them, all of them, and Jennifer James will help us with that, whether she likes it or not. She'll have their names, addresses and their fucking bra sizes, knowing her. We need to see if the girls themselves have any inkling as to who it might be. Anyone who freaked them out, scared them, or threatened them, has to be looked into.'

Annie didn't answer Kate for a while. 'Do you want me to talk to Patrick? Even though he has ironed out any personal involvement with the arsehole, he still needs to be talked to, we have to rule him out.'

Kate knew Annie was speaking sense, she just didn't want to dwell on Patrick's involvement. She had walked down this road before. 'You take him, Annie, I'll take Jennifer James. Bates is no good, as we've already found out. He can talk for hours and not say a word, have you noticed that? A born bullshitter. We need to get a list of all the girls in their employ, and also find out who else is running Toms for hire. As we said before, we need to try and find out who might be the most vulnerable. As it happens, why haven't we heard anything about prostitution in this locality from our own guys yet? I find that a bit suspect, don't you?'

'A lot of this is suspect, but there's such a fine line these days between the force and the people they are supposed to be after. Anyway, it's always the same with vice, no one wants to know. It's only the nice girls getting bumped off that makes the powers that be sit up and take notice. We both know that if these girls weren't being brutally butchered no one would give a toss. If they were being killed and dumped somewhere out of the way, who would really notice?'

Kate knew Annie spoke the truth, street girls were often reported missing, but their lives were so precarious anyway that the assumption was always that they had upped sticks and moved on to a new city. They lived transient lives and, accordingly, they were not regarded as top priority when they moved on. But these girls were being murdered in nice flats, and were in full possession of their families. They were not people whose disappearance would go unnoticed. Yet they were being slaughtered, and there had to be a reason for it. There had to be some kind of common denominator between them and, once they found out what that was, they might then be able to work out who was responsible. But at the moment, they were pissing in the wind.

'You look terrible, Kate.'

The words, spoken so honestly, made Kate smile. There was one thing you could never accuse Jennifer James of, and that was being indirect. She said it exactly how she saw it. Unless it was about her work, her actual involvement in the said work, or her whereabouts on certain occasions, that is. Jennifer was very close; she kept things she felt were unnecessary out of conversations. She was every Face's dream employee.

'I feel terrible, but then I am investigating two gruesome murders. It tends to make you feel a bit rough, Jen, as I'm sure you can imagine. After all, you knew the girls personally, so I reckon you must be taking this very hard too.'

Jennifer didn't react. Kate wasn't entirely surprised, Patrick had once remarked that Jennifer James was harder than a monk's jockstrap.

'What do you mean, *you're* investigating? I thought you were long gone from the Bill shop. Or was I misinformed?'

Kate sighed then. 'Are we going to fuck about all night, Jen? Only, like you, I'm a bit long in the tooth for the job I once held, but by the same token, my experience is invaluable. So why don't we have a drink and talk like grown-ups? If you can't find it in your heart to do that, then you can come to the station and talk to someone else, someone, I might add, who won't turn a blind eye to your involvement in not only the running of the brothels, but also your obvious involvement in the money that was earned. You're a money person, Jen, you always were. So cut the crap, I'm not in the mood.'

Jennifer shook her head in mock despair. She was still a looker, and Kate admired her for her stance. Like any woman in a world that was predominantly male, she had to be quicker, shrewder, and willing to hide her light under the nearest bushel until she knew she was safe to come out into the open.

'Patrick's like a dog without a tail, why don't you go and talk to him? You know he can't cope without you.'

Kate grinned. 'Well, he'd better learn. Now, tell me how the flats work, who the regulars are, and how you organise the girls and their earn. I want the truth this time; you and Bates have run rings round everyone else, I want the real deal. I can cause serious aggravation for you even though you are hand in glove with my boss. Everyone has a head that I can go over if need be, remember that.'

Jennifer walked across her kitchen. It was an expensive one, and Kate knew Jen was proud of it. It was, like the rest of her house, bought and paid for. It was modern, spotlessly clean, and it made Jennifer feel good every time she walked into it. Opening a cupboard she said quietly, 'Whisky do you?'

Kate smiled her assent. She took the glass offered her and waited for Jennifer to seat herself at the scrubbed pine table. Jennifer sat down in the chair beside Kate, not opposite, as might be expected. Lighting a cigarette, she pulled on it deeply before saying, 'Honestly, Kate, I don't think it's a regular. The girls talk, you know, and I ain't heard nothing that's alerted me to a nut-bag. It's hard these days. There are so many fucking opportunities now for the punters. Years ago, we would have been the only game in town, now we have to advertise on the internet as well as the local papers, and we are still up against it. It's a fucking hard graft, girl, and the people we employ know that. Some of them have a dabble off the books, and I accept a bit of that, and turn a blind eye. No one can be expected to hand over all their fucking dosh. I mean, it ain't like they are paying tax, is it? But anything on the off, I would have heard about, and I swear there ain't nothing been said.'

Kate sipped her whisky and let Jennifer's words sink in, they made a lot of sense. The girls always warned each other about any Looney Tunes they might encounter. Even if they hated each other, they wouldn't see any girl come up against a dangerous punter. It was an unwritten law; they had to look out for each other because they knew that no one else was going to do it for them.

'Some of the girls are paying their way through university, others are doing it to get a deposit for a flat or pay for their drugs. Most are trying to keep their kids and their heads above water. You know the score as well as I do.'

'Why were the girls working the night shift alone? I've not heard of that before. Safety in numbers has always been the mantra for working girls. What's changed?'

Jennifer shrugged and rolled her heavily made-up eyes. 'Do you know what, Kate, girls today are a different breed. They want to do their earn without the benefit of competition. They are happy to work alone, it's a different world now. They take the calls themselves, they email the punters and answer fucking texts. Some of them even have a code on Facebook, they're on there as cartoons. Avatars. I can't keep up with them, and I stopped trying to a long time ago. All I can do is warn them and, believe me, I do. But look at Danielle, she had three separate mobiles. One of them was a BlackBerry, Danni was online all the time, she did a lot of her business in *cyberspace*. A lot of the girls do now. You tell me, in all honesty, how the fuck can I police that?'

Kate could hear the feeling of futility in Jennifer's voice. She understood that she was way over her head where the girls were concerned. She had given up trying to keep up, and who could blame her? These girls were computer literate, were part of the cyber-generation. For them it was something to embrace, they were used to it and its convenience. But Kate and Jennifer, like many of their generation, were wary of it, didn't trust it, didn't understand how it was now an accepted part of life. They felt that it was something wonderful, but also something dangerous because it was something that was both easily accessed and easily abused.

'I read somewhere, Jen, that there are kids in China who have never physically interacted with another child: their only contact with other kids is through the internet. How scary is that?'

Jennifer refilled their glasses. 'Janie was online as well. I think they felt safer, as mad as that sounds. I think they also liked the anonymity of using the computer. It made it less personal for them. Does that make sense, Kate?'

Kate understood what Jen was saying, but she still didn't understand how the girls collated their earnings and paid their dues. And, if Jennifer James was watching over them, then that was exactly what they would be expected to do, and do it with the minimum of fuss. So there had to be some kind of legislation in place, Jennifer wasn't the type to let anything get past her.

'So how did you manage to crunch their earnings then? How did you know what they were averaging? You charge them for use of the premises, and you also take a hefty percentage of their overall wage. So how did you work that out, and how did you know how many punters they averaged, online or off?'

Jennifer was quiet for a few minutes, and Kate saw that she was battling with herself about how much to actually admit. Kate could understand that, after all, she was the enemy in every way. This time though, they were both after a common goal. So she said as much. 'I don't give a flying fuck how much goes through Bates's hands, or anyone else's hands, for that matter. I just want to know how you get to the end result.'

'I averaged it on hours. I couldn't find out anything for certain, so I done it all on averages. As I said, I also turned an occasional blind eye, it's par for the course in this game. No one can expect them to weigh up for everyone that comes through the door. But I tell you now, Kate, the girls pretty much police themselves. I just work out the average, it's all I can do given the circumstances. If the client rings in, then I can put them down as a definite. If they text the girls on one of the house mobiles, I can trace that, the same with the online registrations that come through our website. But if the girls themselves give the punters a private number, or a private email, then I am fucked. I can't prove anything and they know it.'

'How many flats are we actually looking at, just your girls?'

'Twenty in Grantley alone, that's without the ones spread all over the South East. With different owners. We can't keep up with the demand, not just from the punters, but from girls asking to be taken on.'

'I'm going to need all the information you have, you do realise that, don't you?'

Jennifer swallowed down her whisky. 'I have it ready for you, it's out in the hall. And I can email the computer files. All the girls' names and addresses, all the places we work them out of, everything. I hope you find the bastard, because whoever he is, he needs taking down a peg, sooner rather than later.'

'To be completely honest, we've got nothing, Jen. Not a fucking brass razoo. He comes and goes without anyone even noticing. But then that's par for the course in this game, isn't it? No one wants to advertise the fact that they have to pay for sexual favours. It doesn't matter how nice the girls might be, or how up-market the premises they work out of are. The men are still buying the girls' time, and that's not something they would want broadcast to the nation.'

Jennifer grinned then, and her whole countenance changed. She looked younger, brighter and Kate saw the girl she had once been. 'Now, all the regulars are in the file and so are the numbers we have for them, or their online bookings. I've also put in the details from the casuals. I warn you though, most of the men use public call boxes, or internet cafes. But saying that, a lot do use their own phones, even landlines or work numbers. In fairness, the majority are harmless, and won't think for a minute they are going to get a tug. But, as I said before, the girls all have their own little earners, and I can't help you with those. Our business is reliant on people's anonymity, not just the punters', but that of the girls involved as well. So you'd better understand how hard it's going to be to get the girls to open up to you.'

*

Lisa Blare was petite in every sense of the word. Just under five foot tall, she was well proportioned. Her hair was very long, past her waist, and she had a centre parting that framed her heart-shaped face to perfection. Her eyes were a very light blue, and she wore the minimum of make-up. She was twenty-two years old, but she knew she looked much younger. She dressed the part, from the schoolgirl skirt purchased from Marks & Spencer, to her long white socks courtesy of Asda. Coupled with a white shirt that barely covered her ample breasts, and a navy-blue tie, she knew she was every inch the jail bait her punters desired. She also knew better than to work in tandem, the other girls didn't like her because she was a bit too pretty and a bit too babyish. Against her, most of the other girls looked jaded. Lisa knew her worth, and she knew exactly how to extract it from her customers.

Against the odds, and despite growing up in care, Lisa was at university, and expected to earn herself a good degree in English literature in the near future. Meanwhile, she needed money, and she wanted a nest egg, a decent nest egg. She never wanted to be poor again. She knew as well as anybody how important money was, that without it you could do nothing. Without it, you had no independence.

She slipped out of her uniform and hung it up neatly in the small wardrobe. She rented this room for her work. It suited her purpose, and she knew the rest of the house was inhabited by like-minded individuals. She had branched out on her own so she could keep herself and her job as private as possible. She had decided she was better off alone, and she had been right. Now she kept most of the money she earned, and she chose her own hours.

She glanced at her watch, her last appointment was due any minute, and she checked her make-up and hair before slipping on a grey gymslip and black silk stockings. She forced her feet into impossibly high black stilettos and, lighting a cigarette, she put a jazz CD into the player by her bed. Then, after snorting a big, fat line of cocaine, she sat and waited patiently for her last call of the day.

Kate was stretched out in the bath, a glass of wine in one hand and a cigarette in the other. She was shattered, and she knew she needed to get some sleep.

Patrick had been leaving messages everywhere and she had not answered any of them. She needed time to herself. She needed to be able to concentrate on what she was doing.

She was still angry at him, angry that he didn't see what he had done as wrong. Pat was a law unto himself, and she had been attracted to that side of him but, as the years had gone on, she had come to resent him for his cavalier attitude to the world and the people in it. She knew he laughed at her because she was so straight, as he would put it. But it was how she lived her life, and he knew that as well as she knew that he couldn't be straight if his life depended on it.

But it was the use of the women that bothered her. The girls were dead, and they were dead because of people like him and Peter Bates. So why did she feel she was being unfair to him? Why did she miss him so much? Kate closed her eyes and tried to push him from her thoughts.

Annie came in and refilled her glass for her.

'Thanks, I needed this.'

Annie nodded. 'Join the club. I've left all the stuff Jennifer gave you with Margaret, she is a computer whiz-kid by all accounts. But to be honest, I don't think we'll get anything from it, do you?'

Kate shook her head in agreement. 'No. I think whoever this is, they are too fucking shrewd to leave a trail of any kind. The crime scene is almost sterile, and that takes a lot of planning, and a lot of guts. But that doesn't mean we can rule anything, or anyone, out. Speaking of which, how did your interview with Patrick go?'

'Exactly as you'd expect!' Annie laughed. 'He was more interested in asking me questions about you.'

Kate shrugged. 'So who are we looking for? Jennifer James reckons it isn't a regular but I'll put my money on it being someone we've had dealings with before. This person is in the system somewhere, even if not here in Grantley. He would have done other stuff before this, and that's what we need to be looking at. We need to see what we can dig up over the last ten years, men who've specifically targeted prostitutes. He's perfected his trade somewhere, we just need to find out where the fuck that was.'

'What do we need?'

'You need to request everything relating to attacks on working girls from all the different forces in the British Isles. But I think he knows this area, so I'll concentrate on anyone who was born here, lived here, or went to school here. He's chosen Grantley for a reason, he's killing here for a reason. Like I say, we just have to find out what the reason is.'

Annie sighed. 'Look, Kate, the arsehole wants to bring in another lead detective. He says it's to help me, but I think it's because he doesn't trust us to deliver quick enough. He's not even got the fucking guts to tell us to our face. He told me over the phone.'

Kate laughed then, a loud, cackling laugh. 'I expected him to do something like this. Don't worry, I still have a few friends I can rely on. Unlike him, I never made the mistake of tucking up my own colleagues.'

Kate gulped her wine down and held out the glass for another refill. 'I'll sleep like the dead tonight, Annie. Tomorrow I'll start pulling in favours. You'll be surprised at how many I am actually owed.'

Patrick looked around him with unusual interest. He was wondering how he had come to be so bloody domesticated, and trying to work out when this domestication had begun. He even used a coaster, despite there being no one around to remind him.

His mother had once run this place with almost military precision. After his wife had died, he had been bereft and he'd needed a woman around. He'd needed normality in a world where normality had been destroyed. His daughter had been all he had cared about then. She had been like a beacon, shining out to remind him that life still went on, that he had someone who needed him, someone he loved with a vengeance. Like most self-made people, Pat had gradually learned how to sort the wheat from the chaff, had got rid of the hangers-on and the spongers. He had learned early on that someone with his reputation was not always told the truth, even when it was requested. Only his old mate Willy Gabney had ever had the guts to disagree with him. He was dead this long time, and Pat still missed him.

Along had come Kate. He had admired her, her strength of character. She had awakened something in him and he had felt the pull of her almost from the start. That same strength of character now got on his nerves. She was too bloody good at times, she saw everything as black and white. Well, that didn't work for everyone, especially not the people in his world.

He had been terrified of her finding out about him owning the flats and the houses, but why had he cared so much? He had done nothing illegal, not in the eyes of the law anyway. He was a partner in a business, no more and no less. He wasn't about to be given any kind of tug, and he had ironed it out so she was safe from anything untoward. She wasn't even a real Filth any more, so why was she so fucking bothered anyway?

They would desperately need her on a case like this, she was very experienced and respected by everyone. Most of that lot in Grantley nick couldn't find their own arses with two Sherpas and a detailed map. She would be needed down that fucking dump if she had just got paroled after a bank job.

Now though, he was determined to show her that *he* didn't need her, or her bloody-mindedness. He was a businessman, and if his businesses were sometimes on the wrong side of the moral highway, then tough shit. He was still legal enough to guarantee he wasn't going to get any late-night door knocking. And if that was good enough for him, then it should have been good enough for her.

So why was he missing her?

He poured himself another Scotch and turned on the CD player. He liked the old records lately, Dionne Warwick, Dusty Springfield, they were soothing on the ears. They reminded him of better days, when life had possibilities, when he was still striving to make something of himself.

Then each day had been a new beginning in his quest to take over the world. Had he really woken up each morning with the urge to get up and out into the world, had he really felt that alive once? Had he always enjoyed the challenge that each new day had brought? All he had been feeling recently was discontentment, he felt as if he had wasted so much of his time, so much of his life, on nothing.

Pat had always looked down his nose at men with new wives and new kids, the kids often younger than their grandchildren. Perhaps he should have done that, he should have married again, had another family while he had had the time. No child could ever have replaced his Mandy, but he could have loved them, could still have nurtured and cared for them. He could have them around him now, and then enjoyed their children when they came along. Then he would have been a grandfather, would have had something, someone, to say he had lived on this earth when he was gone.

He should have been open to that kind of possibility. After all, there were plenty of women willing to produce for a decent lifestyle and a nice gaff. He would have looked after them, even loved them in a way but, most of all, he would have been given a new family by them, and for that he would have given them the world.

Until now, Kate had been enough for him. He felt her presence as an almost physical force; her being beside him had always calmed him, made him feel a level of happiness he had been grateful for. He had loved her deeply, and he had given her something he had never given a woman before; himself. But her leaving him like that, without any kind of hesitation, had made him re-evaluate their relationship. She had always loved and needed her work, and he had respected that, had even admired that about her. But now he felt different, felt that he needed a bit more than companionship and interesting conversation.

Alone in this hulking great house, it had occurred to Pat that he was, in reality, just waiting to die. Not a cheerful thought, but it was the truth, he was just biding his time. He was not a youngster any more, but he wasn't in his fucking dotage either. He looked at Danny Foster and saw himself as he had been. Now, when he looked in the mirror, he saw himself and what he had become. He was old, much older than he had ever thought he would be. And all he had to show for his long and eventful life was his money, his businesses, and nothing else. The knowledge frightened him, had woken something in him he had never even known was there. He was lonely.

It was as if Kate leaving him had opened his eyes to what was left of his life, of his future. He had more money than he would ever need, he had more friends than he had ever imagined, and yet he had nothing to show for his years of grafting, nothing of substance anyway. He needed to feel there was something left for him in his future, he needed to feel that his hard work and his graft would be appreciated, would be of use after he was gone. He wanted something to show that he had lived, wanted to feel that he would carry on living even after his death. He wanted a child.

Kate going had brought all these feelings to the fore, but Pat knew that they had been festering inside him for a good while. He had denied them, had felt they were somehow disloyal not only to Kate, but to Mandy, and even to his long-dead wife.

Kate's refusal to answer any of his calls, or even acknowledge him in any way, had shown him just what a tenuous
link they really had to each other. She could have stood by
him, she should have *known* he would never have allowed her
to be implicated in anything untoward. The girls' deaths
were not his fault and she knew that as well as he did. If they
had not been working for Bates, they would have been
working for someone else. He understood then that she had
used the circumstances available to her to do what she really
wanted. She had left him, and now he understood that, it
was probably for the best. But it didn't stop it hurting.

Jennifer James was drinking a large vodka and Coke and, as
she listened to Peter Bates droning on, she pretended an
interest that wasn't there. 'Danny Foster is trying to open up
the business by expanding the websites, he thinks he's Essex's
answer to Bill Gates. I can't see why you'd have a problem
with that. He's a sensible lad, and he can bring us in a lot of
dough. For crying out loud, Pete, what *is* your problem?'

Peter Bates liked Jennifer James. She had a shrewd
business head, the girls liked her, and everyone trusted her,
himself included. So he knew he had to be honest with her,
he knew she would suss him out if he tried to have her over.

'I don't like him.'

Jennifer laughed out loud, then began choking on her
drink. As she coughed and spluttered, and wiped the tears
from her eyes, she wondered at men and their rank stupidity.
'You don't *like* him? Are you telling me that's the reason you
are questioning his ability to bring us in more money? He
wants to streamline the business, bring it into another
fucking dimension, and you can only say "I don't like him"?

I don't like a lot of the people I work with, that includes you at times, but I don't let that interfere with my job. It's called being a grown-up, Pete, you should try it sometime.'

Jen's dismissive tone rankled, but her words were something he knew he couldn't argue with. Danny had not done anything to make Peter mistrust him. But he absolutely loathed him, he loathed him with an intensity that surprised him. It was irrational and it was groundless.

'Anyway, Patrick likes him and that's all that counts. Take my advice, Pete, leave well alone and find a way to work with him. We don't need any trouble.'

Peter nodded and smiled drunkenly. 'I know you're right, but he's so fucking smug. I want to rip his fucking face off, especially when he does that voice. He talks to me like I'm in me dotage.'

Jennifer grinned then, showing her expensively capped teeth. 'Well, you are to him, he's only in his thirties. He's still at the age where he wants to show his strength, prove himself. You were the same at his age, I bet.'

Peter smiled at the truth in Jen's words. Her mobile rang and he grinned as he heard the tune; it was Monty Python's 'Always Look on the Bright Side of Life'.

'Oh hello, Jill, how are you?'

Peter watched her as she listened attentively.

'Are you sure?'

Jen sounded worried now. 'Why are you ringing me, doesn't her mum know where she went?'

She listened again and Peter saw her nodding her head slowly. 'Do you know where she was working from?'

Peter filled her glass once more, and handed it to her as she put the phone down.

'What was all that about?'

Jennifer took the drink and swallowed it down quickly. 'A girl worked for us called Lisa Blare, a nice girl, but nervous. Very young looking, she had fantastic skin. Anyway, Jillian Barber had a call from her mum asking if she was with her, it seems she ain't arrived home. Jill said she hadn't seen her but thought she'd ring me in case I knew where she was. I'm sure I heard she was renting a room off old Maggie Dinage, she was a bit of a loner anyway. She didn't like working with the other girls. But with all that's been going on I think I'll give Maggie a ring just to be on the safe side. Lisa's mobile is turned off, so there's no other way of getting hold of her.'

Peter nodded. 'Is Maggie still going? I thought she was dead and buried.'

'No way, she's as sprightly as a ballerina, still likes a drink and still likes dirty jokes. Only these days she tends to stay close to home. She's got to be seventy at least.'

Peter sat down heavily and lit a cigarette. He remembered Lisa all right, she was a Brahma. She had a face like a madonna and the body of a porn queen. He hoped she was all right and they were worrying over nothing.

Chapter Five

'Jesus Christ, her whole face and chest are gone.'

Kate didn't answer, she was too busy looking around the small room. The smell of burned flesh was still hanging in the air making her feel slightly nauseous. The girl's few bits and pieces were still in place. Other than the monstrosity on the bed, the room was basically untouched.

It was eerie just looking at the girl's belongings. Her handbag was under the chair, her cigarettes and lighter were on the small bedside table, her few work clothes were hung neatly in the wardrobe. As before, there were no prints anywhere.

The girl's well-manicured hands were relaxed, and Kate felt grateful that she had not been aware of what was happening to her. To Kate it was outrageous that she was, once again, looking at the lifeless body of a young girl with her whole life ahead of her, and that she was pleased because the girl had not felt the pain as she was dying. It was so wrong. These girls were dead, and who knew what they might have become.

'It's personal, so personal, even more so than the others.

This was complete obliteration. Her whole face has been removed. What exactly did the coroner say?'

Annie opened her notebook and read back the words she had written down verbatim. 'Lisa Blare. No signs of rape, no signs of a beating, no sign of retaliation. The coroner believes she was already dead when he started burning her, but that will only be confirmed after her hair has been tested. Same acid used as before, same MO, and everything points to the same drugs having been used. In short, fuck all of any use.'

'And, once again, no one saw or heard anything?'

'Nothing, Kate. All the rooms here are used for the same purpose, people walking about at all hours wouldn't be anything unusual. In fact, most of the girls had already gone home by the time of death. When old Maggie let herself in, she was only expecting to find the girl asleep, apparently that happens on occasion after a hectic night. She's had to be carted off in an ambulance, she was really fucking freaked out about it. She lives on the ground floor, but she can't hear anything that goes on, she keeps the radio on twenty-four-seven. She's also a heavy drinker. I think she's a bit deaf and all, but then she is getting on.'

Kate was baffled once more. How could no one see or hear anything? 'What about the people who live in the road? Have they been questioned yet?'

'The boys are talking to them all now, but if anyone had anything to say, I'm sure we'd have heard about it by now.'

Annie sighed as she looked at the girl's remains. It was bloody disgraceful, to think he had walked in and out without a sound.

Kate looked at Annie with dark-ringed eyes. Even she was looking old, old and tired. 'He picks his time and his victims with care. These girls were all targeted for a specific reason, he has something against them personally.'

Kate examined the room again, looking at the girl's belongings, hoping against hope they would talk to her, tell her something. 'He knows when they are at their most vulnerable and he allows himself plenty of time to do his business. He has to have been a regular of some sort, or he had to be watching them for a good while, because he knew exactly when to strike. He knew when he would be safest. No one has heard a car or a motorbike, so I think he walks to his chosen destination. No one notices anyone strange in the area, or wonders what the hell is going on in a house in their street that is being used as a brothel. Is it me, Annie, or am I missing something here? Surely no one can walk in and out of several different locations without someone, somewhere noticing them.'

Annie shrugged, she was wondering the same thing. 'Maybe he's just been lucky up to now? Or maybe he looks like part of the surroundings? Either way, Kate, no one seems to have seen him.'

Kate nodded slowly, her eyes staring blankly at the girl's lifeless form. 'He knew them, he *had* to have known them. He was familiar with their movements. Which means *they* probably knew him and, if they did, then so must some of the other girls.'

Margaret Dole was very pretty, she had short, dark hair and large, doe-like eyes. Her looks were her downfall in some ways, because they made her look soft, made her seem vulnerable. She had a natural grace, even picking up a coffee cup was done with precision and an inborn gentility.

Margaret, though, was in possession of a brain capacity

that staggered the belief of those around her. She was a computer hound; she could hack, track or reroute anything that came her way. She also had a natural affinity for research that had brought her to the attention of her superiors, and she knew it was what would guarantee her getting fast-tracked to promotion. What she didn't have was a natural affinity with her colleagues, but it didn't bother her too much.

As she looked through all the information provided by Jennifer James, she knew there was nothing that would be of any use. The files were time-coded, and there was nothing she could see that might stand out as different or strange. Whoever had arranged to see the dead girls had done it by phone, probably text. As the phones were the only things taken, they were relying on the phone companies' records. So far there was nothing suspicious there either. She would bet it was a pay as you go so, other than the location of where the call was made, they were still none the wiser.

Margaret opened up another file and perused the data available. Frowning, she looked back over the previous five files. Now this was much more interesting, as far as she was concerned. Smiling to herself, she printed off the information that interested her and placed it in her locker. It was her curious nature that had made her want to be a policewoman and it was this same curious nature that was now telling her she had stumbled on to something else entirely. Something that might bring her promotion a step closer.

'Hello, love, have you got a minute?'

Kate smiled as she heard Desmond Clark's voice. He was not only Patrick's brief, but also a friend, and she had known him and his wife for many years.

'How are you, Des? It's lovely to hear from you.'

Desmond was quiet for a few moments. 'Look, Kate, this is hard for me, but I have been asked to tell you that Patrick has had all your belongings packed up and he wants to know when it will be a convenient time to have them delivered. He has also asked me to inform you that he has requested that I work out a fair settlement for you given the years you've been together. He hopes you will understand that he wishes you the best, and requests that you only contact him through my office.'

Kate was stunned. Not only at Desmond's words, but also by the way he so casually spoke them. The amiable man she had dined with, who she had spent holidays with, and who she had always regarded as a friend, was now talking to her as if she was no more than a stranger to him, someone to relay his client's wishes to and then forget about. He was treating her as a problem that needed sorting, and Pat liked his problems sorted as quickly and as painlessly as possible. It was a learning curve, and Kate was sensible enough to learn from it.

She felt the hot flush of humiliation as it washed over her, and she wondered at a man who could so easily wipe away the years of easy friendship and the memories of times gone by. Good times. Times that had been captured on camera and reminisced about on more than one occasion. Des had been a regular visitor, along with his wife and family. Kate assumed that his wife would also be giving her a wide berth now that she was no longer with Patrick.

She swallowed down her anger and shame with difficulty. Then, taking a deep breath, she said steadily, 'Tell Mr Kelly I will get in touch with *you* about the delivery of my belongings, as you so nicely put it, and you can also inform him that any settlement will need to be looked over by my own legal representatives. It's not that I don't trust *you*, Desmond, it's just that I have an intimate knowledge of how you usually conduct any business dealings that pertain to Mr Kelly.'

'That's not fair, Kate.'

Kate could hear the indignation in his voice and it pleased her. 'What's fair then, Des? You tell me. Only, from where I'm standing, it seems that the only fairness I see is being directed towards your client, but then, what's new?'

With that, Kate replaced the phone gently, pleased that she had not given into the temptation to slam it down with all the force she could muster. How dare Patrick try and remove her from his life like an errant mistress! How dare he get his brief to do his dirty work! She was finding it difficult to breathe, so great was her shock and disgust. That Pat could do that to her, and do it without a second's remorse.

She felt the hot tears of humiliation and tried to force them away, tried to keep her dignity if nothing else. But it was suddenly too much for her. She felt old, old and useless. Patrick had hit her where he knew it would hurt most. He had abandoned her without a second's thought, had reminded her that she wasn't a girl any more. She had invested so many years in him, and she knew she would never get that opportunity again.

Kate had always looked down on those women who put a man before everything in their life, who believed that if you didn't have a man, you had somehow failed. But it was important, she understood that now. It was about not being alone, it was about proving to yourself that you were still attractive, that you had the charm and the personality to be wanted by someone. She realised just how important it was to have someone in your bed waiting to put their arms around you and tell you how great you were. Having someone there to listen to you as you poured out your woes. Having someone to accompany you on holidays and make new memories with. Why had she never appreciated that before now?

She still had her job. She had her reputation and that had always been a big part of her life, of how she perceived herself. Kate was proud of what she had achieved, of how her work had penetrated so many lives. But now, one phone call had revealed her life for what it really was. She was on the wrong side of fifty and she'd been dumped. Pat had erased her from his life, and in a strange way she didn't blame him. She should have stayed and talked to him, should have known that he would make sure she was protected in any way he could. After all, she wasn't a real Filth any more, as he had so forcefully pointed out to her. She felt so betrayed, so unwanted, and yet she knew she had brought it on herself. What did she have left in life now that he was gone from her?

The future seemed bleak and frightening, she saw the years ahead as if she was already living them. She could see visits to her daughter Lizzy in New Zealand until she was unable to travel, she saw herself spending her time reading and wondering what might have been. But worse, she saw Patrick Kelly living the life he had lived until she met him. A life of money, skulduggery, and in the company of young women who would remind him that age was only a number.

She should have seen this coming, should have understood

that she was putting him second, should have remembered that he was happy for her to do that as long as she assured him it was only temporary, only until she had seen through whatever she was working on. She had walked away from him, not the other way around, and she had forced this situation because of her reaction to his involvement in the girls' working lives. He had to have known what the flats were being used for, so why didn't that matter to her any more? Why was she so willing to overlook that if it would bring him back to her? Why was she such a hypocrite where Patrick Kelly was concerned? It wasn't the first time either. She had overlooked much worse than this over the years. Love could do that to a body, it could make them do things they never believed possible.

Eventually, Kate laid her head on her arms and cried like she hadn't cried in years. She sobbed out her pain and her anguish, not just for herself, and her life, but also for the young women whose lives had been cut so tragically short, and who she knew made her own problems seem nothing in comparison. But even understanding that didn't make her feel any better. She wanted Pat, she always had, from the first time she laid eyes on him, and she knew that nothing was going to change that now. Unfortunately.

'But I can't see where you are coming from, Pat.'

Patrick swallowed down his annoyance. What was it with people that they always thought they knew better? Why did people he employed to run the businesses he had created, always think they had more of an edge than him?

'If we open up the casino and the restaurants we can double the take, surely?'

Patrick looked at Danny and forced a smile that told everyone in the room that he was aggravated. Very aggravated. 'Look, Danny, if we let any Tom, Dick or, in some cases, Danny, down those stairs, we will be just like any other casino or restaurant. We could be Southend, or fucking Canvey Island, use your fucking brains. What we lose out on with the roundabouts, we can more than make up on the swings. You see, a lot of our customers come to us because they ain't going to run into the bloke who does their garden, or the bloke who frequents their pubs, clubs or chippies. Or, for that matter, the people who work in said establishments. Whatever their business happens to be, we ensure that they only rub shoulders with other like-minded individuals and that, I might add, goes for *me* as well. We entertain a lot of people down there who wouldn't want the general public clocking their movements, if you get my drift. So, if you want to make suggestions in the future, my advice would be to try and think the fuckers through properly first.'

Patrick laughed and looked at Desmond in mock amazement as he continued. 'Can you imagine the boat-race of some of our more salubrious clientele as they shake hands with their own workforce, especially if said workforce were well oiled on free booze and in possession of a camera phone? I mean, far be it from me to piss on any lucrative fireworks, but I think the casino in question brings in more money through the contacts it attracts, than the actual gambling.'

Danny took the lambasting with good grace. He knew better than to disagree with Patrick in front of anyone. He also knew that, once they were alone, he could put his case across properly and succinctly and that he would get a fair hearing.

Patrick Kelly was a man of contradictions. Danny knew that his interest would now be piqued, and he would listen to the reasoning behind the proposal. He would then digest the information and give a fair response to it. But it was wearing sometimes, even though he knew Patrick could still teach him a good thing or two where business was concerned. Danny could feel himself chafing at the collar, but he also knew that was normal for anyone in his position.

Desmond, however, knew the real reason behind Patrick's angry tirade and he hoped he saw the error of his ways. Kate was the best thing to have ever happened to him, if he could only see that for himself.

'What about Bates and his involvement in the first incident?'

Desmond sighed. 'The other crime scenes are apparently all sterile anyway, cleaned and polished after the event, so we got a pass. It was lucky for us because if the mad cunt had left anything behind, Peter would have been responsible for messing with it first time around. Anyway, we've had a swerve so let's leave it at that. The other deaths are not being seen as anything to do with us or our involvement in the properties. Or any of our partners. In fact, as luck would have it, the girl who died last night was nothing to do with us at all, she was renting off old Maggie, so we can forget about it now. It's all academic. You're only on the paper-work, nothing can link you to the businesses personally.'

Patrick digested what had been said then, pouring himself a large brandy he said sarcastically, 'So, what a stroke of luck for us. The girl who died didn't die in vain. She inadvertently made sure we were all protected. I think we should find the culprit and shake his hand, maybe give him a night out in the casino, especially now we are letting anyone in.'

'I never meant it like that, Pat, and you know it. I was just doing what I always do, what I am paid to do, protect you and your business interests. In other words, I watch your fucking arse, and sometimes you know, I have to do and say things I don't particularly like, but I do it anyway, because that is my job. What I don't have to do though, is listen to this kind of shit. So, if you'll excuse me, I'll be on my way.' With that, Desmond got up and walked from the room.

Danny Foster was nonplussed for a few moments, he had never experienced anything like this before with Patrick or Desmond. They had always been perfectly in tune. He guessed there was an underlying problem here that he didn't know anything about. He also had the feeling that he didn't want to know what it was about either, if this was how it was affecting them both. Desmond and Patrick went back longer than the Ark of the Covenant; if they were arguing like this, then it was serious.

Patrick stared at the door for long moments then, turning towards Danny, he said quietly, 'Well, I think we can safely say I fucked him off, so how do you feel about me and you going out on the town?'

Danny grinned. 'After *that*, I think it's the only thing we can do.'

'Do me a favour, Danny Boy? Never let your head rule your heart, it only leads to heartbreak, suspicion and a general feeling of dissatisfaction. And that, my young friend, is on the *good* days.'

Danny had enough sense not to give Pat any kind of answer. He understood that this was one of those times when all that was required was a drinking partner and someone who would listen, agree and then promptly forget what had been talked about. He also knew that Patrick Kelly had been like a pressure cooker lately, and he was on the point of exploding. What Patrick needed was an outlet for his emotions, and Danny decided he would make sure that was exactly what he was supplied with. A warm-blooded outlet.

'You look fucking terrible, Kate. And coming from me, that's quite something, given that I spend my days looking at dead people.'

Kate couldn't help laughing, even though it was the last thing she had envisaged herself doing for a long time. Megan McFee was a tall, red-headed Scotswoman with a ready smile and a problem with food. Her eyes were a faded blue, but her high cheekbones and porcelain skin saved her from being plain. She had the skeletal figure of a supermodel, and the hands and feet of a ballerina, but it was her dress sense that really made her stand out. Like most people who secretly diet by forcing up anything they eat, she dressed in loose layers. It suited her somehow, she had good taste in clothes and they made her look almost normal.

'You don't look so good yourself. How's things?'

Megan looked around the mortuary and, opening her arms wide, she said, 'How do you think things are, Kate? I'm surrounded by the dead, the murdered, the unwanted and the relatives to match.'

'You love it, Megan, and you know it as well as I do. Did you find anything else?'

Megan looked at her friend and saw the damage the years could do, to women especially. Kate looked old, wrinkled and pale, she wasn't even trying to hide it. Bereft of make-up she looked every inch her age. Patrick Kelly must have had more going for him than she had thought if he had done this to her friend. Kate had always taken care of herself, and as someone for whom appearance was of paramount importance, Megan had admired that about her friend.

Kate said sarcastically, 'Calling Megan, come in Megan McFee.'

'There's no need to be like that, Kate. I'm just shocked at your appearance, that's all. You look like a bloody tramp or something. Sort yourself out, woman. You still have a life, which is more than I can say for this lot in here.'

Kate knew Megan meant well, but coming from some-one who had battled bulimia all her adult life it rankled. But she knew Megan was trying to help in her own strange way. She *did* look terrible, and she knew it was being remarked on. She also knew she didn't give a flying dinosaur about any of it.

'Seriously, Kate, you need to remember that you are being observed by everyone, including the press. Get a grip.'

Kate swallowed down the retort that came so easily to her lips. Instead she said calmly, 'Have you anything for me, Megs?'

Megan nodded. Suddenly she was all business and her whole demeanour seemed to change as she went to her desk and picked up some files. 'The girls were given a cocktail of drugs. It's taken a while to get the results back, you know what it's like. It was the usual, cocaine, amphetamines. And then there was something different. A paralytic was used on them as well as the GHB and Roofie. A drug normally prescribed only to chronic insomniacs, and even then only for a few days at a time because of its potency and side effects. These range from hallucinations to psychotic breaks. In large doses it's guaranteed to paralyse the patient so that, alongside the Rohypnol and GHB, would have laid these girls out in no time. They would have been unable to move, no matter what was being done to them. Danielle Crosby, the first girl, probably knew exactly what was happening to her and was unable to do anything about it. She would have put up a weak resistance, but some kind of resistance nonetheless. He must have learned from that as the others were given far larger doses. That rules out anyone in the medical profession. The girls would still have been aware of what was going on, for a short while at least.

'The drugs that were used are available on the internet, or on the street. The doses were huge, they would have killed them anyway, or in the case of the paralytic, would have left them in a coma. Whoever this man is, he is using trial and error on them, the doses were all different. No thought has been given to, say, the girl's weight, which, as with any drug, affects its potency. There was one anomaly though, that I found in all the girls. They had all drunk a mug of *tea* very close to the time they died. I think that's how they ingested the drugs, through the stomach lining.'

'Tea?'

Megan nodded, unfazed by Kate's obvious disbelief. 'Good old Lipton tea, to be exact. I made sure I found out the exact brand, I knew you would want to know. We aren't exactly *CSI Miami*, but we do get there in the end.'

Kate nodded. 'We didn't find any cups or mugs at any of the crime scenes that held tea.'

'I know that, there were a few used coffee cups, but they were harmless. Whoever gave these girls the tea took the time to take the drinking vessels with him when he left.'

'He really does seem to think of everything, doesn't he?'

Patrick was pleasantly drunk, and as he looked around the club he owned, he wondered why he didn't come here any more. It was nice. It had a great atmosphere and good music, but then it was Over Twenty-fives night. And, best of all, it had a really well-stocked bar. He was enjoying every minute of it. He had liked the out once upon a time, even when he was married he had liked to get out once or twice a week with his mates. Of course it had been necessary at first, it was how he had done a lot of his business. He enjoyed the company of his peers, and liked the camaraderie between them.

As he sipped his brandy and looked around him, he felt pride in what he had achieved. This was a nice club, it catered to nice people. The girls were a bit young, but that was par for the course these days. They were good looking, well presented, and up for a laugh. He saw the attraction for them; well-set-up men with money to spend and the time to spend it. After all, they were hardly doing the nine to five, were they?

Danny Foster was talking to a petite blonde with huge blue eyes and tits that were struggling to stay inside the tiny top she was wearing. Every time she laughed they were in danger of escaping once and for all. Pat smiled, he had always looked down his nose at the men who took advantage of the little birds, the young girls. Now though, he felt that he had been unfairly critical towards them. The girls were aware of what they were getting themselves into, and more than happy to get themselves into the situation in the first place. He spied a tall brunette with a slim frame and an expensive suit. She had a nice smile, and a very feminine way about her. He watched as she walked behind the bar and opened the tills, removed the notes with ease and placed them in a black suede money bag. He saw her observe what was going on around her while emptying the tills. She also made sure that the staff were aware that she was watching. He liked the way she was treated by everyone; they all seemed to defer to her, and when she called over a young barman and pointed to the empty glasses on the tables near him, Pat found himself looking around with her, and seeing the bar as she saw it. It was well run, he could see that. But it was also well cared for; the punters spent a lot of money, and she made sure they felt they were spending it in worthy surroundings. Pat knew the importance of making people feel they were being treated properly, it was what made a club or restaurant a success.

She saw him watching her and she smiled slightly, nodding her head in acknowledgement. She obviously knew who he was and he felt absurdly pleased. He smiled back, and winked mischievously. Her smile widened as she walked sedately from the bar towards the private doorway behind which were the offices.

Pat saw Danny raise his eyebrows at him in mock shock horror, and he heard himself laughing out loud. He was enjoying himself, really enjoying himself for the first time in what seemed years. Kate had made her bed, and she could lie in it on her Jack Jones. She had not allowed for him being fed up with always coming second best. And she had blanked him. Well, he was relatively young in comparison to some of the men here tonight, he was free, and he was single. He felt up for the chase once more, he wanted to feel desirable, feel young again. He needed to feel that his life was beginning, not coming nearer to its end. The woman made him want to throw caution to the wind. In short, he wanted to get laid, and that was exactly what he was determined to do.

Pat leaned towards Danny and said quietly, 'Who is she?'

Danny grinned saucily before saying, 'That, Patrick, is my sister. Eve.'

Book Two

For the wages of sin is death.

Romans, 6:23

Meine Ruh' ist hin,
Mein Herz ist schwer.

My peace is gone,
My heart is heavy.

Goethe, 1749–1832

Faust

Chapter Six

'Do you think we can assume this is all over, Kate?'

Kate shook her head. She hated it when she was asked questions no one could know the answer to. It was all speculation, no matter how they dressed it up.

'I don't think so. It's been over a month and I hope to Christ that I'm wrong, but I think this is just breathing space for him. He's waiting for it all to die down, waiting for the girls to feel safe again. Either that, or he's been nicked for something else, been run over by a bus, he might even be on his holidays.'

As she spoke, Kate wondered at how quickly the deaths had left the news. There was hardly a mention of them now. It was as if the murders had been relegated alongside the credit crunch and the Eurovision Song Contest. She hated that they had nothing to go on. All their enquiries, all the door-to-doors, all their hard work had yielded them precisely nothing. It was as if the man responsible didn't exist outside of the murders. He had left nothing tangible, had left nothing that could be used to identify him.

He had to have a knowledge of forensics, but that wasn't

unusual these days. Anyone who could read, use the internet, or afford a Sky package could learn about forensics in a few hours. Could be experts in a few days. From real-life dramas to handbooks on forensic science, it was all out there for anyone who wanted to know about it. It grieved her, she knew that any crime could be researched, looked into, and committed again, with all the flaws ironed out this time, and there was nothing she or anyone else could do about it. It was harder than ever to get a conviction because even juries expected the same kind of evidence they saw on their favourite television programmes.

It was all well and good seeing a profiler for the FBI solve a crime in under sixty minutes, or a forensics expert find a piece of glass that couldn't be detected by the naked eye, and subsequently tie someone to a murder, again in under an hour. That was the magic of television and novels. They were not meant to be real, they were there for entertainment, no more. And that kind of entertainment was not something she enjoyed these days. Not that she enjoyed anything that much these days.

Patrick Kelly was in her every waking thought. She missed him, missed everything about her old life. She wondered at how she could have been so stupid as to walk away from him without even attempting to iron out their differences. In her anger, she had only seen that he had not told her about his involvement in the flats. She should have understood that he had his fingers in so many pies he would be hard-pushed to tell her about all of them. But it went deeper than that, and she knew it. They had been steadily coming to an impasse, and it had taken them both by surprise when the inevitable had happened.

'Are you OK, Kate?'

She looked around her, saw the canteen with its dull grey walls and its metal chairs. She saw the newspapers scattered across the tables and the scratched floor tiles that she had been looking at for over twenty years. This place had been her refuge once; after her divorce from Dan, she had been wary of ever letting herself get close to anyone again. Her job had become her life, and she had thrown herself into a career in which she had become one of the leading figures of her profession. Once that had been enough for her, once that had made her feel as if she had really done something with her life. So why did it mean nothing to her now? Why was her involvement in this latest case making her feel as if she was in over her head, making her feel that she was somehow lacking?

Her confidence was at an all-time low. She was back where she started and, for the first time ever, her job just wasn't enough. She had given her life over to something that was without meaning to the majority of the populace. She had happily lived her life for what she saw as for the good, she had spent serious amounts of time chasing the bad guys and catching the good majority of them. So why did it seem pointless, why did it all feel so futile to her? She had finally come to realise that her hard work, when it came down to it, was worth nothing. She had put herself out, put herself on the line, had spent the best part of her life doing what she thought was right, and for what? She had caught two prolific murderers, and she was proud of that. But it had come at a cost, it always did for women. The young ones down the nick knew her by reputation and that she was only on board now because of her past victories. Kate understood that her creds were all she had left. And her creds were not enough to give the rest of her life meaning; she felt so alone, so very lonely. She wanted to find this murderer, wanted to see him pay for the young lives he had destroyed. But she also knew she needed something for herself as well. Before it was too late.

Geraldine O'Mahoney was new to the life, and she was more aware of that than anyone. At twenty-nine she was a bit old for a beginner, and she knew it. But her husband had gone on the trot with a young girl called Regina, who had once been the babysitter, and it had thrown her, had made her realise that life as she knew it was over. She had relied on him for everything, had not thought that would ever change. But she had been wrong, and how wrong.

He had walked away from his family without even a whisper. He'd gone from their lives like a ghost, not a word, not a hint, nothing. He had not even attempted to see her all right money-wise, and he had made it clear that he did not want to see his girls. They missed him, they still cried for him on occasion. He had always told them they were his life, had always made a big fuss of them. Then, suddenly, he had gone. Just left them all, and they were still reeling from it. She had waited patiently for him to return until her mother informed her of his new baby girl and his marriage to Regina, and she finally accepted that she was well and truly alone. Regina would go through the same thing one day, when the flush of youth left her, and the daily grind became too much for him. When the lure of another young girl possessed him.

Geraldine had been introduced to the life by her friend Alana; she had needed to pay the bills. Gas, electric, food, clothes and, on top of all that, she was trying to redecorate. Add to that the girls' dancing lessons and private tuition, and she was finding it hard. But she was determined to make a home for the girls and for herself and make sure they wanted for nothing. She saw this job as her only way to do this.

So as Geraldine opened the front door of her friend's house, she tried to calm the erratic beating of her heart. It was always the same, she felt overwhelmed by what she was expected to do, but at the same time she needed the money she earned.

'Hi, it's only me.'

Alana usually called out a response. But today the whole place was quiet.

Too quiet.

She made herself a coffee and leaned against the kitchen cabinets as she sipped it. It was too quiet, it felt wrong. She could smell bleach, it was overpowering.

'Are you in, Alana?'

Geraldine then knew there was something amiss, there was always noise of some description. Music playing, or the muffled sound of a blue film. Sometimes she even heard the strangled cries of the actual punter as he heaved away for his money's worth. Today though, there was nothing, and she was getting more and more nervous by the second. It was too bloody quiet, it felt wrong and smelled wrong.

She walked quietly to the bedroom door and tapping on it gently, she called out, 'Are you in there, Alana? It's me, Geraldine.'

There was nothing, not a sound, no movement, nothing. Opening the door a fraction, Geraldine peered inside and what she saw made her blood run cold. Closing the door, she walked back to the small kitchen and, after throwing up her recent meal into the kitchen sink, she wiped her sweating face with a dish towel. Then, almost as an afterthought, she went to the front door and locked it.

After she had called the police and an ambulance, she sat by the front door and hugged her knees to her chest until they arrived. Once they were inside, she allowed her feelings to get the better of her. Geraldine was still crying hysterically when the nice doctor gave her an injection that brought on perfect oblivion. She had never thought she would see anything so terrible, so heartbreaking in her lifetime. She knew that what she had glimpsed for those few seconds would stay with her for the rest of her life. She also realised that this new job of hers was well and truly over. She had thought she could cope, but she was wrong. Very wrong.

Patrick was nervous, and that was something he had not felt in years. Nothing had happened between Eve and him yet. But he was sure it would. And soon. Danny was her brother and as Patrick waited for him to arrive, he wondered at what he would make of the situation. As he heard his car pull up in the drive, Patrick walked through the entrance hall to the front door and opened it before Danny had even parked up. As Danny walked towards him, Patrick searched his face, but he was smiling as always.

'Bloody hell, Pat, you're a bit lively today.'

Danny followed Pat through to the office, and as they settled into their usual routine, which consisted of a large brandy and a few minutes of small talk, Danny said sadly, 'Have you heard, Pat? Another girl's been found.'

Patrick was in the process of pouring the drinks, and the

news threw him. He had not heard anything. 'One of our flats again?'

'Nah, nothing to do with us. I wondered if you might have heard anything from Kate?'

Patrick shrugged and handed Danny his drink.

'I haven't spoken to her for weeks, and she's got no reason to keep me in the loop.'

Danny watched Pat closely. He was still a handsome fucker, even Danny could see that much. He might be getting on now, but he still had the dark Irish patrician look that women seemed to go for. He still had that air of menace, that extra something that made him seem invincible. And a cool and calm exterior that belied the real man inside. Patrick Kelly was still a big player in their world, and he played the game close to his chest. It was what had kept him out of nick for so long and kept him in the forefront of everyone's minds.

'Do you think it's someone who works for us, Pat? Someone in the know about the girls?'

Patrick had wondered the same thing himself. Though the girls worked out of different places, for different people, they all worked to pretty much the same routines. Whoever this was, they knew the life well, and they knew how to get themselves inside the flats without alarming the Toms. Most of these girls could smell trouble at fifty paces. It was how they survived. So whoever this was, he knew how to allay their fears, knew how to respond to them without arousing suspicion.

Patrick shook his head in denial. 'I know where you're coming from, but I can't believe it's anyone in the game. It doesn't make sense, does it? Why would they shit on their own doorstep for a start? They would cast their net wider, away from anything that could be traced back to them.'

Danny Boy saw the logic of that but he was still unconvinced. 'But if it's a nutter, and this has to be a nutter, don't it? I mean, we ain't talking a fucking hundred per cent with it, are we? So this nutter might not have the nous to take it outside of his world.'

Patrick laughed. 'I lived with Kate a long time and she will tell you that whoever this is, he's a crafty fucker, and he probably makes Stephen Hawking look like a fucking dimlo. Not that anyone around him will suss that, of course. He will be a mild-mannered and quiet bloke, the last person anyone would think capable of such crimes.'

Danny grinned. 'Fuck me, Pat, you sound like Gil Grissom.'

They both laughed. Then Patrick said seriously, 'I had a daughter murdered, remember, and, believe me, Danny, the bloke who did that was a seriously sad fuck. George Markham. I see his face every night before I go to sleep, and every morning when I wake up. He was shrewd, he was clever, and he enjoyed every last second of his little hobby. My Mandy was young, beautiful, and all I had or cared about in the world. Whoever this bloke is, he has been working up to this for a long time, and he is madder than the maddest person who was ever mad, but he ain't fucking stupid. It seems that he ain't put a foot wrong yet, and that tells me he is taking all this very seriously.'

Danny didn't know what to say. It was the first time Patrick had ever talked about Mandy's murder, and he could see that it was still raw even after all these years. But then, how did you get over something like that?

'You're right, Pat. I think that's where we all go wrong;

we assume because they're mad, they must stand out somehow. We expect them to look what they are, a bloody nut-bag. When, in reality, it's their normality that shields them from us.'

'Well, whoever this is, he's clever enough to make sure no one suspects him, and that alone speaks volumes. I know from Kate that people usually come out of the woodwork at times like this, accusing neighbours, friends, even family. But that doesn't seem to have happened this time.'

Danny knew Pat was speaking sense. 'Have you spoken to Kate at all, Pat?'

'Nope. And to be honest, Danny, I don't want to. She made it quite clear how she felt, and I respect that. Now, let's get down to business, shall we?'

Danny knew when to leave well alone, so he deftly changed the subject. Patrick was miles away though, talking about Mandy always did that to him. It made him remember things that were best left forgotten.

'Look, Geraldine. We can see that you are overwhelmed with what's happened, but we really need to ask you a few questions, love.'

Geraldine was terrified, and Kate watched as Annie tried to keep her temper in check. She had to learn that wanting to know wasn't enough, you had to find things out gradually when these kinds of situations arose. Kate knew that Geraldine needed gentle prompting, she needed to feel she was not to blame in any way.

'Do you have any idea who her last punter was?'

Geraldine shook her head in denial. Kate knew the symptoms well, she was still in shock. She was also frightened in case whoever was responsible knew her, knew who she was. That they would come after her.

'If you do know who he was, if he was a regular, or someone you'd seen before, you can rest assured that we will not ask you to stand up in a court of law and accuse him. All we want is a name or a description. That's it.'

Geraldine looked away from them and stared out of the hospital window. Her nerves were shot and her body rigid with fear.

'I didn't see anyone, I swear. If I did, I would say, I would tell you. Alana was expecting me, she worked the late night, and I was supposed to take over from her. I got in early and thought she was still at it.'

Kate grasped her hand, and said quietly, 'You must have seen something, somebody as you went into the building.'

Geraldine shook her head once more. Kate could see she really wanted to help them now, knew she was racking her brains trying to find something she could tell them so they would leave her alone.

'Well, it was so early, no one was about. I think there was a lady who passed me as I walked to the flat. I park the car a few streets away to make sure no one can put me near the place, so I can't be certain which road it was on. Other than that, the streets were deserted. It was still dark. Please let me go home to my kids. If I knew anything at all I swear I would tell you . . . My mum and my friends think I work nights in a nursing home . . . I can't tell them the truth, can I? No one will find out, will they? You won't tell anyone?' Geraldine was on the verge of hysterics once more. The fear of people finding out about her, coupled with the death of her friend, was really taking its toll.

'Who was the woman you saw? Could she have seen anything? Did she go into any of the nearby houses?'

Geraldine shook her head in abject terror. 'I wasn't taking any notice, I didn't think it would be important. I mean, who really bothers to look at people?'

The girl was absolutely petrified, and Kate thought she probably didn't have anything to say worth hearing now. She was a bloody useless idiot, a fucking no-brain, as Patrick would say. She wouldn't notice if a madman brandishing a machete asked her the time. But she was all that stood between her and the murderer.

Alana Richards had been drugged, mutilated, burned, and left naked and open for whoever was unlucky enough to find her. This time, however, the cause of death was manual strangulation. As before, the whole place had been wiped over, and there was nothing untoward to be found. The girl's phone had been taken away, but nothing else was missing. He had once again chosen his victim and his time frame so well that no one had seen anything, or heard anything. He was too clever by half.

Jennifer James opened the front door and seeing the uniform she said aggressively, 'And what can I do for you?'

Margaret Dole smiled and said quietly, 'Can we talk inside?'

Jennifer grinned. 'Have you got a warrant, darling, only this is my home, and I don't have to let you in if I don't want to.'

'I haven't got a warrant, and I don't need one. This is private business and I don't want to talk about it out here.'

'And what kind of business would that be?'

Jennifer was intrigued now. This girl looked interesting; she had the look of a bent Filth about her and she was still in uniform. Best time to get them, while they still thought they knew it all.

'I looked over the evidence you gave to Kate Burrows, and I found some interesting anomalies that I would like to discuss with you.'

Jennifer opened her front door wide and, waving her arm in a grand gesture of welcome, she allowed Margaret into her home. Then, shutting the front door, she said quietly, 'One word out of place and I'll aim you out that door so fast you'll burn a hole in the carpet.'

Margaret accepted the threat with good grace and followed Jennifer into the kitchen. She knew she had something that would get her what she wanted.

Kate went over everything once more and, once again, she could find nothing that was useful.

'Are there no CCTV cameras anywhere along that road?'

Annie shook her head. 'It's hardly bloody footballers' wives territory, is it?'

Kate kept her temper, she knew that Annie was as frustrated as she was about the lack of anything even remotely resembling a clue. They were both on short fuses these days.

'I am aware of that, but people in less salubrious areas often need the comfort of CCTV more. I just wondered if anyone had come up on the database, that's all. It's not a bad little road, it's quiet, the houses are set well back to afford privacy, and often it's the privacy that makes burglars think the house might be a viable option.'

Annie wiped a hand across her face. She knew she was

being unfair, but she was tired and she was hungry. She was also feeling that she and Kate were living in each other's pockets. She had rented the house from Kate two years previously, and been glad of it. Now though, Kate was back for good, and she had gone from being an apologetic friend in need to the actual owner of the house and Annie didn't like having become the lodger.

Kate sat back at the kitchen table and opened the files once again. 'We're missing something, we have to be. There's nothing we can find that ties the girls together in any way, in fact, two were complete strangers to the others. We know that he takes their phones with him, but from the phone logs we can get nothing except that he rings them all from differing locations, providing it's him ringing, that is. Of course most of the girls take calls on pay as you go, and so do the men. Who can blame them? So we have nothing to learn from that. But I believe he is *choosing* these girls, they are not random. He makes sure he has enough time to do his business with them, he *has* to plan for that, he can't take the chance of someone interrupting him. He needs time to clear up after himself, and take away anything that might incriminate him. We are missing something.'

Annie knew Kate was right, but she also knew that, as much as she wanted her expertise and help, she wanted to come home sometimes and just forget about work for a few hours. She also realised that she was using work as an excuse because she didn't like Kate taking over her home; it was her home now, and Kate should understand that.

'Look, Kate, it's been a long day, and I need a bath. I also need a few hours' sleep so, if you don't mind, I'd rather not go through it all again.'

Kate sat at the table, staring at the paperwork in front of her, aware that she had stepped over some imaginary line. She could hear the bath running upstairs, and she knew that Annie was feeling the pressure as much as she was, more so in fact, because while Kate was there in her capacity as a long-serving officer, was there because of her expertise, Annie was the one who still had to prove herself. Kate knew, better than anyone, how hard that could be.

She looked around her, saw the kitchen she had once been so proud of, remembered her mum waiting for her to come home with a good meal on the table and a ready ear if she needed it. She had also brought up her grandchild and cleaned and scrubbed the house. She had been the reason Kate could follow her star, and she had.

Now her mother was dead and Lizzy and her family lived in New Zealand, they were reduced to cards and phone calls and the rare visit. She had not felt the gulf between them until now, had not realised that her daughter had slipped from her life so completely. She had assured herself that she had been a good mother, she had let her child go, encouraged her to escape from Grantley and follow her dream of a better life. Now she felt that she had just let her go because it made her life with Patrick easier.

Kate suddenly understood her mother's insistence that life was to be lived, to be enjoyed. Because of her mother's goodness she had been allowed to make a career for herself, she had been allowed to do something with her life. But her mother had also warned her that sometimes people were more important, and she should remember that.

She sat at the table with her head in her hands. She knew she still looked good for her age, she kept her hair short, and she was the same size she had always been. But it didn't change the fact that she was older, a lot older, and she was lost. Patrick had been everything to her, and she had walked away from him. Getting up slowly, she went to the fridge and, opening it, she took out a bottle of white wine and poured herself a glass. The fridge was full of food that was alien to her, Annie's food. Processed and unhealthy.

She glanced around the kitchen and saw Annie's pots and pans and Annie's personal belongings, her mail, her handbag, and the cosmetics that she left on the window sill. It dawned on Kate that she was a stranger in her own house.

She sipped the wine that had been purchased by Annie, and, sitting back down at the table, she lit one of Annie's cigarettes. Inhaling the smoke deep into her lungs, she wondered what the future held for her. Then, taking a deep breath, she once more looked over the paperwork she had brought home, as if it would miraculously make some kind of sense to her.

Chapter Seven

'Come on, Des, you know I can't get involved in all that old fanny. I'm the number two. I can't start criticising Patrick's mates. What do you think I am? On a death wish?'

Danny was annoyed, he had no intention of pushing his nose in where it wasn't wanted. He also had no interest in doing Desmond's dirty work. He was a brief, dirty work was what he got paid for. He heard Desmond sigh heavily, and Danny knew he was trying to keep his temper in check. Desmond wasn't used to people refusing him anything. He worked for the Faces, and that gave him his credibility.

'I just want you to ask around, Danny, that's all. I can't, because it would look odd if I started asking questions, wouldn't it? But listen to me and listen good, we need to get the SP *before* Patrick starts snooping for himself and, believe me, if he susses anything before us, and starts creating, the first thing he will want to know is why *you* didn't notice anything peculiar. Why you weren't watching his interests.'

Danny saw the logic of that. He also knew that Patrick only dealt with people he trusted, so how was he supposed to go and investigate people Patrick thought were beyond reproach?

'But I don't have anything to do with the girls as such, I just collect. How can we be sure there's a scam going on?'

'We can't, but I don't like the way the monies have dropped off. It isn't because of the nutter. After all, the punters know it isn't them so they aren't that bothered. Bates keeps saying the business has dropped off lately, but I know for a fact that it hasn't. Look at the website; we are getting more interest than ever. We've never had so many hits. How can we be losing out?'

'OK, Des, I'll look into it, but Peter won't like it.'

Desmond laughed. 'Well, you'd better make sure he doesn't find out then.'

Desmond put the phone down and sat back in his very comfortable and expensive leather chair. He looked around his office; all art deco and leather furniture, it looked class, and it was class. Right from the antique law books to the stripped pine flooring. He was proud of this establishment, and he knew it was because of Pat Kelly and his cronies. He knew he was a very lucky man, he had a good life, and that life was dependent on people like Pat Kelly.

He prided himself that he could smell a dead rat before it was stinking, and all his instincts were telling him that something was not right. Now it was up to Danny, and he hoped against hope that the boy would use his loaf and not attract too much attention as he sniffed around.

Peter Bates was not a man to suffer insults lightly, and he would take any questioning of his integrity as a personal affront. He was, to all intents and purposes, one lairy fucker when the fancy took him, especially when he was in the wrong.

Eve was dressed to impress, and she knew exactly who she wanted to impress. As she applied her lipstick, she looked herself over with a critical eye. She knew she looked good. She made a point of looking good, it was part and parcel of her job. She had to be seen to be in control, and that meant looking in control.

It was strange really, she ran the club with a fist of iron, and she employed very young, very good-looking girls because they brought in the majority of the customers. She was also surrounded by very young, very good-looking girls because they were a large part of the clientele, they were out on the pull and looking for Mr Right or, in most cases, Mr Right Now. Even so, she knew a lot of the male customers gave her more than a second glance. Yet she was always suited and booted, as befitted the manageress of a busy nightclub. She didn't show her body off, just a hint of cleavage, and the benefit of very high heels. It seemed to attract a better class of man, they liked the fact she wasn't on permanent display.

Patrick Kelly was one of those men and she knew he was as aware of her as she was of him. Which was strange because she had never really been attracted to the type of men who frequented the club before. She saw herself as a bit too shrewd for that, saw herself as above that kind of male. In her thirties, she felt she was far too experienced for the kind of men she met during her work. Most of them were married, a lot of them were on their second or even third wife, or live-in mistress, depending. Most of them still had their eye on the main chance though. Privately, she thought of them as incorrigible. Still on the search for a bit of strange, for the latest conquest.

Eve only dated men who had proper jobs and proper lives. But she had to admit to herself that they had never kept her interest for long. Plus, they had been few and far between the last few years, she worked the wrong hours for any kind of proper social life. But that didn't bother her too much. She liked her independence, and she liked her own company. She didn't usually feel the need to be part of a couple – she liked the sexual freedom that her lifestyle afforded her. She had no illusions of marriage or babies, all she wanted was good sex, and a good time. Eve prided herself on not wanting a perm-anent relationship, especially not with a local villain who could, and would, move on to another pretty face sooner rather than later.

Now though, she found herself looking out for Patrick Kelly. She knew it was silly, it was like a schoolgirl crush, but she couldn't help herself. He was old enough to be her father, but she didn't care about that, there was something about his eyes, his demeanour, that made her want to be near him. Touch him. That her brother Danny worked for him didn't help, she wasn't sure he would be too pleased if he knew how she felt. He thought the world of Patrick, and he respected him, but she had a feeling he wouldn't exactly be thrilled at the prospect of her lying down for him.

As she thought of having sex with Patrick Kelly she felt an excitement she had not felt for a long time. She thought about sex with Patrick a lot, and the more she thought about it, the more she wanted it to happen. He attracted her, and she knew she would not rest until she had him beside her in her bed.

He was coming in tonight to look over the books, something they both knew was a sham, a pointless exercise, an excuse, as it was a job normally split between three different parties. The tax man, the accountant, and the managers. Still, she knew it was make or break time, and she was ready for whatever might come her way. She wanted to smell him, feel him, fuck him. He interested her in more ways than one. He made her think about something other than work. He made her think about herself, about how she felt sexually. He reminded Eve that she was still alive and it had been a long time since she had felt like that.

Her hair looked good, her make-up was perfect, and she had worn her sexiest underwear, just in case. She had been plucked, waxed and moisturised within an inch of her life, and it felt good to be a part of the world again. Even for just a short while. It had given her the rare urge to be part of a couple, even though experience had taught her that it wouldn't last, it never did. But she always enjoyed the chase.

She went back into her office and poured herself a neat vodka on the rocks because she needed Dutch courage. She threw it back in one swift movement then, stretching like a cat, she waited for Patrick Kelly to arrive.

Kate was walking quickly, the cold was settling around her, and she could see her own breath. It was damp and raining again, the start of the real cold weather. She walked the streets looking at the houses near the scene of Alana's murder, trying to work out if any of them had vantage points from where the occupants could have seen someone arriving, either from their windows, doors, drives, or even the pavement.

Kate still couldn't believe that no one had seen anything, she knew from experience that often people saw something important, but at the time it looked innocent, uninteresting. She also knew that people didn't really take any notice of their surroundings any more. Years ago, people looked out for their neighbours, they noticed a strange car or a noise late at night. Not any more. People ignored things now, they didn't want to get involved. They were frightened of comebacks, retribution. So Kate walked the streets to try and find some kind of common denominator, something that could help her make her case. She found herself doing this a lot, and each time she didn't see anything that could be of any help, yet she still did it, still tried to understand the logic of the crimes. There was a logic somewhere, she just had to find it. So she watched, she saw the girls arrive, and she saw the men arrive. And she waited to see if anything untoward might occur. The men were always furtive, but not unduly worried. She guessed from the websites that many were from out of the area, and she understood the sense of that. She also knew that some of the men were locals, others were willing to travel long distances for their entertainment. It was soul-destroying in some ways, these were men whose wives and daughters would never even suspect that they were capable of such blatant skulduggery. She knew that sex caused people to do things, reckless things, that they often found left them surrounded by guilt and shame. She also knew that these same people would nevertheless repeat those acts time and time again. It was the fact they were doing something so heinous that got them going in the first place. But for all that, the majority were harmless, they were looking for a quick buzz, a sexual high they felt they couldn't ask for and, in most cases, wouldn't want from their wives or long-term partners. It was sad really, that in this day and age men could find anything they wanted at the click of a button, things that were once only available to them in their fantasies.

So, she would walk the streets or sit in her car and observe, hoping deep inside that the man she wanted would turn up. But instead, she saw them come and go without incident. She was always surprised at first by how low-key things were. How nondescript the flats were, perfect for that secret liaison. She could almost understand why the men seemed to feel relatively relaxed going there. It was like they were visiting a friend, the flats were in nice buildings, but not too nice, the streets were quiet and the neighbours were all workers. Most of them were out during the day, and too tired at night to be watching what was going on around them.

But for all that, it didn't change the fact that one of these girls was eventually going to entertain the wrong person. Kate desperately wanted to prevent that from happening, but she knew she couldn't, there were too many girls and too many punters out there. It would be impossible to police the whole area.

She started to walk back to her car and as she felt the rain on her face, and the cold seeping into her bones, she saw Patrick's car coming towards her. It threw her, it was the first time she had encountered him in weeks. She stepped into the shadow of a garden and waited till he had passed her by, she didn't want him to notice her.

As he drove past the streetlight she caught a glimpse of him. He looked good, but then he always did. He was wearing his heavy overcoat, and she knew that meant he was going out somewhere nice for the evening. She knew him so well. But where was he going? And, more importantly, why wasn't she going with him? Why had this happened to them? She opened her car and sat behind the steering wheel. She was suddenly freezing, and she sat for long moments, wondering how her life had come to this.

Patrick was nervous, he felt like a schoolboy on his first big date. He was suited and booted, but then he had always been a man who liked to dress well. He believed that a man was judged on how well turned out he was. But as he stood in the bar he felt overdone, the younger men around him were dressed casually, all open-necked shirts, collar-length hair and Italian loafers.

He saw Danny arrive and cursed him under his breath. It was his sister he was hoping to see tonight, not him. He felt almost ashamed about his feelings for her. As if he was doing something wrong, something out of order. But he knew that was stupid, he was in a world where men of his age sought youth, where younger women were part and parcel of their credo. Look at me, I can still get it up. Look at me, she could be me daughter, but she ain't. It was like an unspoken rule among them all: I can still pull the birds.

Kate had been different, she had been someone to respect, someone he had felt was on a par with him. Now though, he felt she was no more than a fucking albatross that had been hanging round his neck for far too long. She had voided him in a moment, so she could get fucked. He had a life to live, and he was determined to live it with or without her.

Danny waved at him happily, and he nodded an acknowledgement. Then Peter Bates came over to him and said loudly, 'Here, Patrick, have you heard about Kevin Daly? His wife died this morning. Only thirty-nine, she had food poisoning of all things. Three kids under ten, what the fuck is all that about?'

Patrick was shocked. Kevin was a good bloke and his wife had been a nice girl. Quiet and well dressed, she had sat out a hefty prison sentence for Daly, had waited patiently for him to come home.

'That's terrible, how is he?'

Peter was busy getting the barmaid's attention for a refill. 'How do you think? He's in a right fucking two and eight. Do you want a refill?'

Patrick nodded.

'Just shows you though, Pat. Enjoy your life while you've got it, you never know when it's going to be over. Three little kids. Girls and all, they need their mums, girls.'

Patrick nodded. 'I know that, Pete. Girls do need the female touch.'

Peter turned to face him then and Patrick could see the sorrow on his face as he said, 'I'm sorry, Patrick, you know better than anyone what it's like to lose your wife, and your daughter. My fucking big trap, I say things without thinking them through . . .'

Patrick smiled sadly. 'You're right though, Pete, you *should* enjoy your life. Take it from me, you don't know when it's all going to be snatched from under your nose. Let's face it, I found that out a long time ago.'

He picked up his drink and looked towards the door that led to the office. Peter grinned then, a mischievous glint in his eye. 'Go on, my son, get in there, she's fucking right up for it. I've noticed you two circling each other like a pair of bare-knuckle boxers. She's a nice girl and you ain't getting any younger, boy.'

Patrick looked into Peter's face and he saw the age that had crept up on them all. They had known each other for well over thirty years. He had been best man at Peter's first wedding; seventeen years old and on remand for robbery with violence, he had married his longtime girlfriend of three years to get himself a reduced sentence. But Peter had loved her, and the sad thing was, he still loved her. But he had fucked her over once too often. Women weren't like men, they couldn't turn a blind eye unless it suited them. Women knew the score from the off, and their mates gave them the strength to put up with it, until they decided different. Then they moved heaven and earth to see the man concerned pay through every orifice he possessed. Men though, if they had a bird who put it about, they either nutted her on the quiet or, in extreme cases, they swallowed their knobs rather than confront the truth. If they still wanted her back after she had seen fit to stretch herself out for a stranger, then that was their prerogative. It even made sense in some ways. Pat understood how a deep love could overcome the humiliation and the shame that a woman out on the cock could bring to a man. Personally, he would rather die than be made a fool of by anyone, let alone a female. Females, to his mind, should be above reproach, and intelligent enough to know that without him having to point it out to them.

Winking saucily at Peter Bates, he made his way through to the office. As Pete said, life was too fucking short. He felt the excitement deep in the pit of his stomach, it had been years since he felt like this. He was almost breathless at the thought of her waiting for him.

As he slipped through the doorway, he wondered what had kept him from approaching her for so long. After all, as he knew better than anyone, you really did only live once.

Annie Carr was tired, and it showed. She looked at herself dispassionately in the toilet mirror and felt once more that she had long passed her sell-by date. She looked dishevelled, unkempt. Her skin was grey from lack of sleep and bad nutrition. Her hair needed a wash and a decent cut, her shoes were scuffed and worn for comfort and familiarity. At her age, she was in her prime if she believed the magazines she read in the canteen. She was also aware that she was letting life pass her by at an alarming rate. Turning from the mirror, she hurried away from her own reflection.

As she walked into her office, she smiled sheepishly at Kate. Kate was very quiet, and Annie knew it was because of how she had been acting towards her, she knew she had been out of order. She'd taken out her frustrations on her friend, even going as far as to question Kate coming back to her own home. It was outrageous, because she knew that Kate would have welcomed her wholeheartedly if their positions had been reversed. 'I don't know what's wrong with me, Kate. I'm sorry.'

Kate looked at her friend, saw the stoop of her shoulders, the scruffiness of her attire, the sadness that enveloped her, and knew she was no different to her really. She had also taken out her frustrations on the person closest to her. And she'd also walked back into her house and taken it over without a thought for Annie, who had lived there for a long time and paid her for that privilege. But it went deeper than that, and they both knew it. She opened her own arms wide, and the two women hugged each other tightly.

'I am so sorry, Kate . . .'

'Listen, Annie, this is all part and parcel of being on a big case. You live, breathe and eat the fucker, and anyone who stands in your way gets the flak. If you want to stay in this game you have to accept that no one else matters in the pursuit of a resolution. I've fallen out with everyone in my time, and so will you. But take my advice, Annie, don't make the job your whole life. Leave something over for someone else. Don't leave it until it's too late, you'll regret it.'

Kate was genuinely sorry for Annie, because she knew that if she wasn't careful she would end up not only alone, but achingly lonely. Annie reminded her so much of herself all those years ago. Still young enough to believe that there was time for a real life, but she would keep putting it off like Kate had. Then, one day, when you looked around, it was all gone, and the worst thing was, you never saw it happening until it was all too late.

Annie smiled sadly. 'I think it's already too late for me, Kate. I stopped dating while I still had the looks. It didn't seem to matter so much then, I just wanted a career. I wanted to be successful, wanted my life to make a difference somehow. But this has shown me how fucking futile it all is. We have all these dead girls, and nothing to go on. We have the papers and the public on our backs, wanting answers sooner rather than later. We have a man who has enough time to not only knock these girls out, but to torture them. After he makes them a cup of tea, of course. He then cleans up after himself, and wipes the whole place down. There is nothing for us to use, Kate, he has *always* pre-empted us. He has always made sure he is at least one step ahead. You're right, I shouldn't make my job my life, because I can't even say with any certainty that I have any kind of life outside of work. All I ever wanted was this.' She opened her arms wide, taking in the room and everything it encompassed.

'This was all I needed. Now what I think about is the fact that I can't work out how this man can bypass us on such a regular basis. It's like we are outside looking in. This man knows more about crime scenes than I do. He leaves the girls dead and no trace at the scene. Nobody sees him, or hears him. We are chasing a ghost, Kate, a fucking ghost.'

Kate knew that Annie was doing what everyone in their job did at some point, she was blaming herself for not stopping him. She was blaming herself because he had got the better of them.

'He's not a ghost, he's a living, breathing person. We just need to get a break that's all.'

Annie looked at her as if she had never seen her before. 'A break? Kate, he's fucking laughing up his sleeve at us. We have *nothing*, do you get that? *Nothing*. He must think we are all complete idiots.'

Kate hated the disillusionment in Annie's voice, hated that she was already giving up, that she felt they wouldn't be capable of finding this man.

'Oh, Annie, you *stupid* girl, you *stupid, stupid* girl. Do you think we just wake up one day and *know* everything? This all takes time and experience, love. No one in the world can really understand why some people choose to do really terrible things to other people. Innocent people, people that end up dead. We have to try and find out who killed them, and why. That is our job, it's what we do. Now there will always be someone who writes about it all, *after* the event. Psychiatrists who will try and explain away why this ponce felt the urge to kill these young girls. But listen to me, Annie, it's *crap*. No one *really* knows why they do it. No one on God's green earth can pinpoint what made that fucker decide to get up one day and go on a killing spree. It's all conjecture, all shite.

'Our job is to try and make some sense of it, try and bring him to task. We have to trawl through the statements, and the evidence we have gathered, and somehow we are expected to make some kind of sense out of it. You can't just assume you will work it out. You can only work with what you've got. So try and remember that all that is expected of you is that you do the best you can. It's all any of us can *ever* do, Annie. Our best, and sometimes we have to admit that our best just isn't good enough. So, do me a favour, will you? Fucking grow up.

'This bloke has been planning this for a very long time, and he has the edge because of that. We have to try and understand his logic. Even though it makes no sense to us, it makes sense to *him*, and that is what you have to remember. He has a reason for what he does, and he has the added benefit of planning and forethought. We come in *after* the main event, love. We basically clean up after him. We are the ones who see them dead and bloody. We are the ones who tell the families. We are the ones who try and make it right for the people left behind. But don't you dare think that you will always find the answers, because you won't, Annie. You can only work with what you've got, and if that isn't enough, then you have to accept it.'

Annie held her hand across her mouth, as if to stop herself

from being sick. Kate felt the pain she was in. It was hard the first time, not that it ever really got any easier. But murder was part and parcel of their job. Most murders had a weird logic to them. A reasoning of sorts. It was the serial murders that made you lose faith, not just in yourself, but in everyone around you. They made you realise that there really were people out there capable of such hate, such extreme violence, and that they lived amongst us. These people were capable of feigning a normality that hid their crimes from the people around them. These people were out there, and they would *always* be out there, no matter how hard you tried to bring them to justice.

Annie had to understand that their job was like any other. You just do the best that you can, even though the difference was that, in their job, if you fucked up, there was often a high price to pay. Annie believed that she would *always* catch the bad guy; well, the reality was that all they could ever really do was try their hardest. It wasn't a guaranteed result. That was the difficult part. Sometimes you also had to watch people walk, even though you knew they were as guilty as hell. You had to learn to let it go.

'Are you all right now, Annie?'

Annie laughed then, a hard little laugh with no humour in it. 'How can we ever be all right, Kate? It's so fucking pointless.'

'Now you're finally getting it, Annie. Everything is pointless in the end. No one really gives a toss about *anything* five years after the event. There're new murders, new cases, and our job is about the here and now. But what you have to remember is, when everyone else has forgotten about it, when no one cares any more, you *will*. You'll remember the kids left behind, the mothers whose hearts are broken, and you will still be determined to find out who was responsible for all that heartache years later, even though no one else is interested any more, even though it seems an impossible task. It's what makes us get up in the mornings, and it's also why we wake up one day and find that, somewhere along the line, we've lost everyone we cared for. And even then, knowing all that, we still can't walk away. Look at me, I am still here, still in this shit-hole, and still more interested in my job than my personal life. Don't make the mistakes I did. I can't let this life go. I retired, but I still can't function without this place somewhere in my life. It *consumes* me, and do you know why that is? It's because it stops me from having to join the real world.'

'Oh, Kate, you don't mean that.'

'But that's the trouble, Annie. I mean every word of it. I'm trying to help you. I watch you, and I see myself. Don't allow yourself to give up on the people who care about you. At the end of the day, it's really not worth it. I should have put my family first, but I never did. Patrick always stepped aside, allowed me to do what I wanted, and I took him for granted. I always put my feelings first, put my needs before his, before everyone's. I always believed that he would be there for me, if and when I needed him. I walked away from him for my job, just because he was implicated in all this crap. And he wouldn't have me back in his life now if I lay down and sang "Swanee" for him. So don't tell me I don't mean it, Annie. This is all I have left now, and I am trying to make sure that this never happens to you. One day you will wake up and find you are getting old, love, and you didn't notice it happening. It creeps up on you, and you ignore it, pretend it's not important. But it is, Annie. We can't control what's happening, we can only control the course our lives will take.'

'Why don't you go and see Patrick? Try to make amends? It's not too late, but you have to be the one to make the first move, even I can see that.'

'That's the point I'm trying to make, Annie. I can't do that. I can't let this go. I walked away from him without a backward glance because my work, such as it is, still means more to me than anything. That's what I am trying to tell you. If you're not careful, one day you will find that the job really is all you have left.'

Annie knew Kate was right, she saw she was trying to help her. But she still knew that, like Kate, she wouldn't rest in her bed until she had found out who was responsible for those girls' deaths. Like Kate, she understood it was already too late for her to change.

Chapter Eight

Patrick was impressed with Eve's flat. It was large and well proportioned, with high ceilings and original wood floors. She had done a fantastic job of bringing the place together. He knew from experience that it would have cost her a small fortune to have the floors sanded, relaid where necessary, and brought back to their former glory. He also liked the subdued colour scheme and the carefully chosen pieces of furniture. None of the brand-new, DFS, pay-for-it-three-years-later rubbish. Each piece was a work of art in itself. Eve had a good eye for detail, and she obviously liked the comfort that handmade furniture guaranteed. The place looked warm, inviting, and it made Patrick relax. He liked that she was intelligent enough to live in such an environment. It had been a long time since he had visited a woman like this, seriously, with an eye to seeing her again.

Eve seemed as nervous as he was, and he appreciated that she was not accustomed to having men in her home. She had a femininity about her that he found endearing; his first wife had been a lady. That was important to him, he had always had a preference for women who had not been round the turf more times than Shergar. He liked those types now and again, most men did if they were honest, but for the most part they were not really of any interest long-term. Pat was old-fashioned in that respect. He had never wanted an easy lay, not on a permanent basis anyway.

Eve was pouring them both a drink and he saw that the brandy was good, the glasses crystal. Once more, he approved of her choice. He looked at her again and was thrilled by the outline of her clothes. She had a good body: supple, lean and heavy breasted. Pat knew that she was as aware of him as he was of her. There was a tension in the air between them, and it was good, he was enjoying the chase.

Eve smiled at him, and he looked at her face as if for the first time. She was older than he had first thought, and that pleased him. He liked grown women, for the most part always had. Not that he hadn't taken a flier now and again with young girls, but he didn't see that as anything important. Eve was ripe for the picking, and they both knew that. It was why he was here, they had been leading up to this from the first time he had laid eyes on her. So why had he waited so long to make a move? Guilt had played a big part, but he was not going to allow himself to let that spoil his enjoyment. Kate was in the past, she had made her feelings quite clear. He pushed her from his mind, she was all he needed now, putting a damper on everything.

He watched Eve as she put on some music. Amy Winehouse filled the room, her dark, smoky voice, full of heartbreak and cigarettes, seemed to encompass everything he was feeling. Sipping his brandy, he put his glass on the mantelpiece. Then, suddenly full of bravado, he went to Eve and pulled her into his arms.

She settled into his body easily, and he enjoyed the smell of her, she wore a subtle perfume, and he could still catch the scent of the soap she used. He pushed his face into her hair. Rubbing his hands across her back, feeling her shape, he brought her face up to his and she kissed him, a deep, brandy-tasting kiss that made them both realise that the kiss would not be enough.

Eve pulled off her clothes and he watched her quietly, knew that there was no going back now. As she stood before him, naked and proud, he wondered what the fuck had taken him so long.

Peter Bates was drunk. Not too drunk, but drunk enough to have a punch-up if the fancy took him. His girlfriend was getting on his nerves, and he had given her a swerve earlier on in the evening.

Now he was settled in a small drinking club in Stepney with a few old cronies and an assortment of attractive and not too fussy young women. Not that they interested him at the moment, he'd had enough of young women for the time being. But they were not causing any trouble, and were easy enough on the eye, so he was happy enough to let them join the company.

Danny Foster was sitting opposite him, and he had a bad feeling off him. He couldn't put his finger on it, but he sensed a general feeling of unease around him. Danny was a good kid in many respects, a handsome little fucker, of that there was no doubt, but Peter felt he was also a bit of a snide. Patrick had taken him under his wing and that was all well and good, Peter had no problem with that. There was just something about Danny that he didn't like, he had never really quite taken to him. He felt the coldness in the boy, as if he was looking down on everyone. Felt that he was watching, questioning, biding his time.

Now Peter was watching him surreptitiously, saw the way he blended in with the company. How he had an answer for everything, a joke for every occasion, and the capacity to drink large amounts of alcohol without getting too drunk. But then that was youth for you, he had been like that once. As he watched Danny exchange banter with the girls, while at the same time talk business with the men at the table, Peter decided that there was some kind of skulduggery afoot. He didn't know what kind, but he was still convinced that there was something seriously amiss. His instincts were usually spot on, and they were warning him to keep a wary eye out. This little cunt was out for the big purse, and it wasn't going to be his. Not that his purse was that big these days, but it was the principle of the thing.

At the table, George Parnell was also watching the proceedings with a weather eye, he knew when Bates was working himself up for a row. He had known him for years, and he also could see that young Danny Boy was as aware of the situation as he was, and he admired him for that. It took a lot of bottle to sit there and take that kind of attitude without retaliating. He didn't think any less of him for not saying anything, it just proved Danny was level-headed. If he had jumped in, all guns blazing, that would have shown a weakness, that he was stupid, too hotheaded to be taken seriously as a player. It was the quiet lads, the ones who had the nerve to wait their turn, that always ended up in positions of real authority. The lairy little fuckers brought too much attention with them, especially the Filth, and that was the last thing anyone wanted.

As Danny leaned forward to listen to the girls' conversation, George saw Peter also move forward in his seat. That would herald the start of the badgering. Peter would start a war of words, then he would take sudden offence, and a fight would ensue. It was Peter's stock in trade and, in his day, he had had some blinding rows, bless him, but that was then and this was now.

George saw that the other men at the table were unaware of the petty drama that was about to unfold before them.

'What did you say, Danny?' Peter's voice was heavy with belligerence and fake umbrage.

Danny leaned back in his chair, and looked Peter in the face. 'About what, Peter? I was talking to the girls.' He was laughing as he spoke, the ultimate insult to someone of Peter Bates's mentality. 'You got a problem with that, Peter? Only I thought we were all grown-ups here.'

It was a warning, a friendly enough statement of fact, and it should have calmed the situation down. The men around were quiet now, wondering where this was going to lead.

Peter picked up his drink, a large vodka and tonic and, taking a deep swallow, he said nastily, 'Talking of girls, where's your sister tonight?'

George Parnell sighed heavily, and gave the eye to the other two men at their table. In seconds, the atmosphere had become charged, threatening, and everyone was waiting to see what was going to happen. The girls instinctively moved backwards, none of them wanting to be in the line of fire.

Danny smiled easily. 'I think she's out with Patrick, at least that's what I heard. Unless you know different, Pete.' It was said without any anger or spite. But the challenge was there nonetheless.

'I know he's been sniffing round her. But then who can blame him, I wouldn't kick her out of bed.' Peter was laughing at his own wit. 'But you should have a talk with her, stop her making a fool of herself. He won't stay away from Kate for long, she's a Filth, but she's got class. Something Patrick has always aspired to. His wife was the same. A real lady. No notches on the bedpost, know what I mean, Danny?'

Danny didn't seem to register what was being said to him, and George Parnell was impressed. Personally, he would have taken Peter out by now; family, especially the female members, was not something anyone would be expected to overlook in the grand scheme of things. His father had once glassed a bloke for chatting his mother up while she worked in a bookies. The problem being, of course, that his mother, God bless her, had never been averse to a bit of flirting, but that still didn't make it right.

'Eve can look after herself, Peter, she's all grown up. Unlike some of the girls you knock around with, she's old enough to drink.'

Peter Bates snorted in contempt. 'She's well over the age of consent, mate. She won't see thirty again. Funny that, you can see you're related, can't you? She looks like you in drag.'

George had had enough; this was uncalled for, and without foundation. Peter was out of order and he said as much. 'Give it a rest, Peter, that's enough. I don't think Patrick will appreciate you discussing him and his private life in a pub, do you? Eve's a nice girl, and she hasn't done anything to warrant you talking about her like that. Danny is in our company, and he's been a fucking diamond where you're concerned, so either shut the fuck up, or let me get you a sherbet dab.'

Peter was aware that he had crossed the line, he knew he had no right whatsoever to say anything about Eve; she was a good girl, a hard worker, and he had chanced his arm a few times himself. And he also knew that Patrick would not be impressed if he found out he had cast aspersions on her character. But it still galled him that Danny Boy was not rising to the bait. He rounded on George Parnell.

'Who are you then, George, his fucking minder? Is young Danny here sucking your cock on the side, is that why you're sticking up for him?'

Danny was out of his seat before George could react, he physically dragged Peter from his chair, and had him up against the wall in seconds. He was livid, but he still didn't look angry. Externally, he looked perfectly calm, it was only that Peter could see the hate in his eyes, and feel the trembling of his hands that told him he had finally gone too far.

Leaning forward, Danny whispered angrily, 'You cunt, I'll fucking see my day with you. I'll fucking demolish you and laugh while I do it. You're old, and you're past it, but you just can't fucking lie down and die, can you? Well, you got what you wanted, Pete. You got yourself an enemy, and I am a fucking good enemy to have, mate. You just wait and see.'

Peter pushed him away, and Danny let him do that. He knew he had more than kept up his end, knew he had been pushed into a reaction. No one had heard his threat, but Danny guessed they had half expected something like it. He also knew that George Parnell was rooting for him, and that had been a bit of a shocker in itself. He had expected him to take Peter's side, and he wouldn't have thought any less of him for that, after all, they had been friends since they were little kids.

But the fact George had shown his allegiance so openly had proved something to Danny; Patrick had obviously let it be known that Danny was his boy. Danny had worked his arse off for Patrick, but he had also understood that, in the world they inhabited, it often took a while to be properly accepted. Now he saw that he was. George Parnell had a puritanical streak, everyone knew that. Peter had asked for a front-up, and he had got it. George's coming out on Danny's side had thrown him a side bar, and Bates wasn't sure how to react to that. He had assumed George and the others would automatically take his side.

Peter was watching him warily, and George Parnell gestured for Danny to come back to the table so they could resume their evening. Danny walked back over to Peter and, smiling easily, he held out his hand. 'Let's shake on it, Pete? Too much drink and too little sleep, eh?'

Danny grasped Peter's hand in both of his. 'You'd better fucking get that temper of yours under control, mate, it's like your book-keeping, all over the fucking place. I want to see the books for meself, I've heard so much about them.'

Danny laughed again, acting as if it was all a big misunderstanding, but no one sitting at the table was fooled by him. George Parnell looked at Peter and shook his head in dismay. Peter would now have to bear the consequences of his actions. And not before fucking time.

George bought Danny Foster another drink and, at the same time, he arranged a cab for Peter Bates. Then he personally put him into it. It was the final insult, and they all knew it.

*

Patrick lay in bed and listened to Eve as she murmured softly in her sleep. She was beautiful and yet she was completely unaware of how lovely she actually was. Though she was not body shy – she was definitely not averse to getting her kit off and joining in the fun and games.

Pat had enjoyed her, enjoyed the feel of her, the taste of her. He was still reeling from the whole experience. She had loved it, had thrown herself into it without any inhibitions at all. It had been a revelation to him, he had not expected her to be so forthright. Not that he was complaining. But she had been the instigator and the principal participant, and that bothered him as much as it had excited him.

Pat had never before been the passive partner and he couldn't help wondering if it was his age. He had kept up with her all right, but he knew that if he was expected to do that on a daily basis it would fucking wear him out in no time. He'd need forty-eight hours' kip to get over this little lot.

He loved seeing her body in the lamplight, the smoothness of her skin and the tightness of her belly. As he looked at her, it made him aware of how much older than her he actually was. He was in pretty good shape for his age, but he wasn't in his prime. Yet he knew Eve had not cared about that. He had felt the need in her, and loved that she had wanted him so much.

Pat had felt like a boy again, had felt that exquisite rush a new body could produce through nothing more than its utter strangeness, its difference from what he had been used to. He had loved feeling someone different in his hands, loved that she was so willing, and so amenable. She had not tried to talk afterwards either, and that in itself was a bonus where women were concerned. She had not felt the need to discuss love or relationships, she had just been there beside him. Sated and tired, until eventually she had curled into him and drifted off to sleep. It was the easiness of her that Pat wanted to pursue, the uncomplicated way she had with her. She just felt right to him, and that was what he wanted at this moment in time.

He had missed Kate more than he wanted to admit. If she had only answered his calls, responded to even one of his messages or texts, he would have believed that they still had a chance. But she had not even tried to contact him, all he knew was that she had refused his offer of a settlement, a very generous offer at that. She had declined it through her legal representative. It was harsh that they could part like this after all these years.

Well, it had given him the chance for a new life, had enabled him to get out there and find someone different.

Pat pulled the quilt up off the floor and covered them both with it. Then, turning off the lamp, he allowed himself to finally sleep. He had not felt this good in years, and he decided that he liked the feeling. It was about time he did something reckless, thought about himself, because Kate had only ever thought about herself, and he had been quite happy about that at the time. But, in hindsight, Kate had never really stopped being a Filth. Even after she had retired, and they'd attended the party, listened to the speeches, and accepted the fucking carriage clock, she had gone back there, to that dump, as soon as she could. Part-time, and with a smile on her face, she had walked back to her old life and not even thought to ask if he minded.

He pulled Eve into his arms, savouring the feel of her as she instinctively moved her body so it perfectly fitted into his. Kate had made her bed, and she could now lie in it alone. He was happy enough to lie in *this* bed, and re-live his youth for a while. He just hoped it was going to be nice and easy, he liked Eve, liked what she stood for. She had a good way about her, and he needed someone, needed to feel he was still in the game, that he wasn't past it. He hoped Eve felt the same because he had a feeling she might be good for him.

Peter Bates was not that surprised to see Danny Foster on his doorstep, he was only surprised that the boy had come round to his house first thing.

He had left the bar in disgrace, got into the cab ordered for him, and he had assumed that Danny had stayed and partied the night away. So to see him standing there on his doorstep, all bright-eyed and bushy-tailed had, once again, put his back up. He had the grace to feel ashamed at his behaviour today. Last night he had been drunk and coked up, and unable to contain the resentment he felt towards this young man and his place in the world even though he knew that Danny had worked hard for it, knew that Patrick had never suffered fools gladly. The fact that Patrick had put his faith in Danny Foster should have been more than enough for Peter to accept the boy on face value.

But it didn't work like that, he had just taken a dislike to him overnight, and he couldn't hide it. He knew it was irrational, knew he had no reason for his antagonism, but it was there all the same.

'Come in.'

Danny followed Peter into his house, it was a nice place

and Peter knew it. Not that he really liked it there. It was somewhere to crash, somewhere he could do his business in relative peace and quiet. Somewhere his bird could watch television and give him fucking earache.

In the kitchen, Danny observed Peter as he poured coffee from a stainless-steel American percolator; he was surprised to be offered one, and he accepted it with good grace.

'So, what's this visit in aid of?'

Danny grinned, he couldn't help it, he had to admire this bloke's fucking front. Even when he was on the losing side, he still couldn't resist playing the hard man.

'I have been asked, on the quiet, to question the books you have put in regarding the girls. It seems that the amounts expected aren't anywhere near those that have been paid in before. Now, I can see you are about to start explaining yourself in your usual forthright and aggressive manner, but I have to point out that I am looking for any excuse to fucking lamp you one. Do you get my drift, Peter? So calm down and answer the questions to the best of your limited fucking ability.'

Peter was already incensed – that Danny was speaking to him like that, in his own drum and base, was unbelievable. 'You come here like fucking Dilly Daydream, accusing me of being on the con, and expect me to fucking keep me trap shut? I don't have to answer to you, boy, I don't have to answer to anyone.'

Danny laughed out loud. A derisory, insulting laugh. 'You answer to the same man I do, Patrick Kelly, and, incidentally, he hasn't yet been informed about any of this, but then I'm sure you've sussed that much out for yourself. Only, I think we can safely assume that if I had mentioned this to him, you would now be talking to me through the services of a fucking medium. So cut the crap, and let's get this sorted, shall we? Where's the money gone?'

Peter sighed heavily, his whole body seeming to collapse inwards with the exertion. 'I don't know what you're talking about. I collect and I pay out, that's it, mate. I can only think that it's Des who's tipped you the wink. Well, you tell him from me that he's been fucking creaming off the top for long enough and, unlike him, I don't feel the need to question every penny that goes through the flats. The girls have to have a bit of leeway every now and then, that's what keeps them sweet. But if Des thinks there's a con afoot, then he had better make sure he can prove it. Since the murders, the girls have been a bit skittish, so I've turned a blind eye now and again, it's called good business sense. I have also made sure that Patrick was kept out of it all.'

Danny didn't answer him for long moments, waiting for Peter to fill the silence, it never failed in situations like this. Guilty people couldn't shut up, they kept trying to talk themselves out of any trouble they might find themselves in.

'You tell Patrick from me that this is out of order. If he wanted to give me a tug, he should have done it himself. I ain't a mug, a fucking errand boy.'

'No, you're absolutely right, Peter, but as I've already pointed out, Pat doesn't know about this yet. Now, what you are, Peter, is a gambler. And you owe serious poke to some very serious people. So I think that is why you've been on the snatch. You have a bird with expensive tastes, an ex-wife who costs you a small fortune, and a coke habit that makes Pete Doherty look like a fucking choir boy, so taking all that into consideration, I think we can safely say you're well and truly fucked, mate.'

Peter knew when he was beaten, he also knew that this boy was here to offer him some kind of deal, otherwise he would already be history. Danny had a reputation as a hard little fuck, he was all sweetness and light until you crossed him, then he was a violent bastard. Now his sister was Patrick's new amour it seemed his position was even more solid. Danny had earned his place in Patrick's affections and had proved himself worthy on more than one occasion. So Peter knew he was being unfair.

Peter wondered if that was his problem. All around him were new young bloods, all of them coming up in the world. They were making their mark, looking towards a bright new future and he was still dependent on Patrick Kelly's earn all these years later.

He was hocked up to the hilt, he owed money left, right and centre, and he had found himself at sixty-five years old without any real poke to his name, and without the wherewithal to start afresh. He remembered when he was a young man, he had worked hard, and he had flourished, he had made his mark on the world he inhabited. But he had never seen the need to rainy day it. Like all money easy earned, it was easy spent. Years ago, there had always been more money just waiting to be blagged.

Now he found himself working for a *wage*. It was fucking outrageous what he had allowed to happen to himself. He was ashamed, he had nothing left to fall back on and, worst of all, he was now at the mercy of this little prat.

'So what do you want from me then? Why haven't you gone running to Patrick?'

Danny looked at the waste of a man in front of him, and wondered how someone like Peter had allowed it to happen. Danny had admired him, he knew he had lived the stories and had the experience that young men like him had grown up on. He had heard Bates talked about with awe, he had been a real fucking earner in his day. Now he was nothing, he was just an old man trying to talk himself out of trouble. It was only his reputation from years gone by that had stopped Danny from dragging this out in public. He had been willing to try and help Peter, but he could forget that now, one more insult and he was done for.

'Is Jennifer in on this? She's going to be my next stop, Peter.'

Peter sighed, he knew it was over for him. ''Course she is, but it was all my idea, she didn't want to do it. She's only doing what I told her to.'

Danny liked that Peter was trying to protect Jennifer, that was what he would have done. What he expected from him.

'You are a gentleman, trying to save a lady's reputation. But come off it, Peter, do I look like I just came off the banana boat? You couldn't have worked this out on your lonesome, you ain't got the fucking nous. Now Jennifer, she's got more mouth than cows have udders, and she has a mathematical way about her. At least, that's what Pat tells me. So I think we need to ask ourselves what we are going to do next. Now that I have sussed you out, so to speak, you and me have got what some people would refer to as a connection. In plain English, that means, if you don't fucking sort yourself out, my boot will be making a connection with your arsehole, and that is putting it nicely. Now, Patrick is none the wiser. As you so astutely remarked, Desmond is behind this little contretemps, but you see, I've been thinking about all this, and I have a feeling that Desmond wants you out of the picture for reasons best known to himself. So, I think me and you need to have a little chat, because I think you know more about his little scams than he realises. Am I right, or am I fucking right?'

Danny was grinning now, his arms were opened wide, his whole demeanour friendly and approachable. Peter Bates looked at him as if for the first time, and he decided that Danny Foster was worthy of his reputation. He was hard, but so were all the people in their world. Danny Foster, however, had that something extra, he was a fucking shrewdie. He had the sense to think in the long-term and play the long game.

Desmond would have expected Danny to come round firing on all barrels, he would have assumed that he'd take him out, but instead Danny had thought it all through, and he had come up trumps, so to speak. Now that Desmond had shown his hand, Peter didn't feel he had any reason to keep him out of it. In fact, he had a good reason to put the fucker right in it. And that is just what Peter intended to do.

'You want Des out of the way, don't you?'

Danny nodded simply. 'I'm willing to gloss over your involvement, but I want that cunt finished once and for all. He is a liberty-taker, and I intend to see him broken and borassic.'

Peter Bates laughed then. 'You're a holder of grudges, not a bad trait in our game. But all the same, be careful, he gathers information on people and then he uses it. How do you think I got roped in?'

'Well, Peter, let's just say that I think he will be hoisted with his own fucking petard. Now, start talking.'

Peter pulled out a chair, offered Danny a seat then, opening a bottle of Scotch, he cleared his throat and started from the beginning.

Eve woke up to no one. She stretched in the bed and then sat up. Patrick was gone. She was slightly disappointed, but not overly. She had expected it in a way. Patrick was probably like most older men, he would be an early riser by nature, and unwilling just yet to want the whole breakfast scenario. That didn't bother her, she liked to read the paper and drink her coffee in peace.

She lay back in the bed, and let her mind go over the night before. She had enjoyed it, had enjoyed him. He was quite tame sexually and she was quite voracious. She knew that a lot of older guys thought they were sexual gymnasts when actually they were quite tame. She was the product of her generation; sex was to be enjoyed by all, not something to be endured. Pat had risen to the occasion, she couldn't complain about that, but she also knew he had been hard-pushed to keep it going.

But, all that aside, he had excited her. He was dangerous, and she also liked that. The danger was half the attraction, she liked that he had treated her with respect. She was pleased by the fact that she shocked him, that her sexual appetite and her willingness to be a very active partner had been something new for him. It was clearly something that he had not experienced before with a woman he really cared about. Most men of his generation had a strange belief about women; there was the good girl they married, and the bad girl they fucked.

Eve knew that, for the first time, Patrick had seen the

sense in having both those traits in one woman. She hoped he had anyway, because she was determined to repeat the experience as soon as possible. He intrigued her, he was urbane, witty and also dangerous. At one point he had been completely and utterly hers, and though she didn't want a husband, and she didn't want a *partner*, as people referred to their lovers these days, she just wanted the excitement. No more and no less.

Going down to the kitchen she saw that he had made himself a cup of tea before he left, the mug he had used was in the sink, and for a split second she felt a rush of affection for him. She pictured him sneaking around, trying to keep quiet so he didn't wake her. He was a nice man, and nice men were dangerous in a different way because, if you weren't careful, they made you start to care about them. And that was when the trouble really started.

Chapter Nine

Margaret Dole was waiting for Annie as she walked to her car, she was all smiles and Annie was pleased to see her. She respected her well enough, and thought she would make a good plain-clothes one day if she could maybe learn to control her strong personality.

'Hey, Annie, has anyone spoken to you yet about me being on the team?'

Annie frowned in consternation. 'You're already part of the team, aren't you? I thought you were working on the computers, the website and that.'

'I am. Whoever this is, he isn't contacting the girls through the website. He uses a phone and, as we already know, it can't be traced to anyone in particular. It's a clean mobile and, until he puts some more money on it, we haven't a hope in hell of catching him. He doesn't use it for anything other than contacting the girls in question. He never uses it from the same location, and never for more than a few minutes at a time. He's got that well sussed. No, what I was interested in was whether anyone had maybe recommended me to work with you and Kate Burrows so I could get a bit more experience, you know.'

Annie shook her head and smiled. 'I can ask for you, love, you'd be a real asset. So much of our work is done on computers these days. I think I spend more time filling out bloody forms than I do actually out on the pavement. It's ludicrous but, as Kate always points out, it's to cover our own arses, as well as make sure no one can say we didn't follow all the correct procedures.'

Annie saw the frown on the younger girl's face and knew exactly how she was feeling. It was hard when you wanted to work on a particular case, especially one like this where it was high-profile and guaranteed to give you a leg up. Everyone wanted in, and who could blame them, it was invaluable experience and it gave the younger ones the chance to be a part of a large investigation.

But Annie wasn't sure Margaret Dole would fit in, she had a very forceful way about her that often put other people's backs up. She could come across as a know-all, which she was and, when she lectured you on her knowledge of computers, and anything pertaining to them, she made you want to drop into a self-induced coma. It wasn't just the way she spoke to you so directly, it was that she could make the most interesting of subjects sound boring and repetitive.

Annie didn't really like her, and she also knew that she drove Kate to distraction after a few minutes. People like Margaret didn't even see that they were getting on people's nerves, they were too busy being the big I am. Even this, waiting by her car to talk to her, made Annie feel that there was something not quite right about her. Why was she being so furtive? Why not just ask like anyone else would, in the comfort and warmth of the station house?

'So you'll ask for me then? Put in a good word.' It was a statement more than a question, and Annie nodded her answer.

As she drove away, Annie felt uneasy about it all. Margaret Dole had acted like she had some kind of inside knowledge and Annie wondered exactly what that knowledge might be.

Jennifer wasn't surprised to find Peter Bates on her doorstep with a sob story and an apologetic air about him. He was terrified, and he had every reason to be. She knew this had been on the cards for a long time and they had agreed that, when this time came, they would face Patrick together, and let him in on the big secret. She just wasn't expecting it to be today.

With all that was going on with the girls and the flats, the police crawling all over the place, and the fact that Des was all for keeping it quiet, she had expected a few more months before the balloon went up, as it were. By then she would have siphoned off enough to make the consequences bearable, after all, she was not as involved as the others. She had made sure of that. Plus Patrick would more than likely give her a natural swerve as a female, he would understand that she had had no real option but to go along with it all.

It was the deaths of the girls that had caused the skulduggery to come out into the open, and it had frightened them all in one way or another. And, on a scale of one to ten, they had come off far better than the poor girls who had paid for their so-called sins with their lives. But it seemed that Desmond was not just on the grab, he had also tried to palm off his thieving on Peter Bates. Young Danny Boy had seen through him from the off though. Now all she had to do was do some digging, ask the right questions and make sure that she kept herself out of the firing line, and protected her end. Something she had been doing for years. So, with a smile and a cheery demeanour, she explained to Peter Bates that she had the problems well in hand, that forewarned was forearmed, and she was already making sure they were both kept out of the eventual showdown.

Peter was thrilled. He had always had a grudging respect for old Jennifer James, and today he was very tempted to give himself a pat on his proverbial back but, until this was sorted out once and for all, he would leave that until he could guarantee the outcome. He knew he was not quite out of the woods yet. But Jennifer had come up trumps, and for that he would be eternally grateful.

'Come on, Eve, you must like him.'

Eve shrugged nonchalantly. 'So what if I do? He's a nice man, and he's interesting.'

Danny was unsure, for the first time ever, about how to treat his sister. Never before had he felt uneasy about her love life. It had always been her business and he had made sure it had not been anything to with him. But her involvement with his boss made him uneasy. He didn't want her to get hurt. After all, no matter how tall and strong she was, she was still, and always would be, his little sister.

'I just want to know you are OK, that's all. It's a brotherly thing, indulge me.'

Eve laughed and Danny saw the humour that was an intrinsic part of her personality and yet seen quite rarely. It always showed her to be far prettier than anyone realised. There was something about her demeanour that hid her true character, she had always had a way with her. She acted like she was better than everyone else, but in reality she was quite shy of new people. Once she got to know them she was a different girl but, until then, she could come across as bolshy.

Danny had seen it all their lives with people, even their mother had not taken too well to her only daughter. In fact, she had always had a big problem with her. Lily Foster always had to be the star of her own life story, her little daughter's beauty and intelligence had not been something she found easy to come to terms with. Although she had liked it when Eve had been at an age where she could still be controlled, it was when her daughter had stopped being a child that the real problems had begun.

At thirteen, Eve could have passed for twenty. Physically well developed, she had looked like a watered-down version of her mother. By fifteen, her mother looked like a watered-down version of her. Eve had blossomed, opened out like an exotic flower, and she had an easy sexuality that had been as frightening as it had been natural to her. Danny had always known, deep down, that his mother had not been like other mothers. She had used her children as nothing more than appendages to her and what she wanted to stand for. The beautiful mum had not been able to cope with the beautiful young daughter when said beautiful young daughter had started to outshine her. Both he and Eve had been in and out of care, and in and out of foster homes, but one thing had stayed constant: they really cared about each other. Both of them had only ever had a real relationship with the other, people came in and out of their lives, but they had only ever really had time for each other.

It was strange that neither Eve nor Danny had ever had

any long-term relationships. Neither of them had ever lived with another person, the closest either of them got was when they spent Christmas together at their mother's, providing she was not incarcerated, of course. She seemed to be either in a mental institution or rehab, depending on how her life was going at that particular time. Men being the bugbear, naturally. Danny wondered at times how he and Eve had turned out so normal. Neither of them had substance abuse or alcohol problems, though he knew that they had had problems letting other people get too close to them. But, on the whole, he thought they had got off pretty lightly.

'Do you think he's the one?'

Danny was laughing as he said it but deep inside he felt Eve could do a lot worse than Patrick Kelly. Age difference aside, Danny felt that Patrick had the money and the influence that a girl like Eve needed in her life. He also had the added benefit of being someone Danny knew and liked, so the usual asking around and digging into the man's background wasn't necessary. Plus, Eve looked happy and that pleased him, they needed to take their happiness where they could.

Danny's only worry was Kate really, she had been a big part of Pat's life for a long time and, even though it looked like it was all over, that was no guarantee that it was. Long-time relationships had the benefit of memories and comfort, they were about more than excitement and sexual chemistry, even if they had once started out just like that. So Danny would keep a wary eye out and, if needed, he would step in to pick up the pieces. But it was early days, and he was just pleased to see his sister looking so happy.

Eve smiled, but she didn't answer him. Instead, she changed the subject. It was too early to say where the relationship was going and, for the moment, she was happy just to see what developed. Danny working with Patrick could be a problem, so the less he was told about it the better. Though she knew her brother well enough to know that if he wanted to find out anything, then he would. She changed tack quickly. 'I hear you've been seen with that little blonde bird twice this week, does that mean there's an engagement on the cards?'

Danny grinned easily. 'That just means I let her stay over, she's a bit too fucking aware for my tastes. Put it this way, sis, she knows all the moves.'

Eve laughed. 'She seems nice enough.'

'She is, sis, but, like you, I don't want anything more than a casual relationship at the moment. And, when I do, I certainly won't go looking in any of the places I tend to frequent!'

Eve didn't answer him, and they were both happy to change the subject as soon as possible.

Kate was tired, but she felt better than she had for a while. As she knocked at Tammy Taylor's front door she was ready once again to re-ask all the questions she had asked before. It was her way, she often went back, again and again, asking the questions in a multitude of differing ways, it was amazing what people didn't realise they knew until you asked them the appropriate question.

Her old mentor, a crusty old DI who she had loathed, had taught her that many years ago. He had been a seriously sexist, misogynistic and clever man. She hadn't liked him when they worked together, but she had come to respect him in a strange way. They had become close after his retirement, his enforced retirement because, like her, he had understood too late that he had no life outside of his work.

As Tammy showed Kate into her neat and tidy house, she was reminded of him, and the part he had played in her life. She had not only learned her skill from him, she had also developed his habit of long working hours and the same determination to find out the truth of any situation. A double-edged sword in any walk of life.

'Any news?' It was asked tentatively, Tammy's eyes wondering if she really wanted to hear what was going to be said to her. Kate hated that she was not only the bringer of bad tidings, but also the harbinger of even worse news. It was part of the job, but it still didn't make her feel any better.

Kate tried to give people the closure they needed after a violent death invaded their life. It was a job that she loved, a job that had to be done. Sadly, it was also a job that only certain people seemed capable of doing, not only well, but for any length of time. It was a depressing fact that, most of the time, her presence was not only unwanted, but was also seen as a necessary evil. Something to be endured while, at the same time, she was the only link people still had with the person they had lost.

'Nothing concrete, I just wondered if I could run a few things past you again? I know it's hard, Tammy, but it can often help us to get to the crux of a situation.'

The woman had aged overnight, but that was par for the course where murder was concerned, especially a murder like this: a deliberate, calculated act of hatred. People tended to understand murders that were the result of anger or other extreme emotion, a death that was caused by jealousy or drink. Even a death caused by a person's involvement in drugs or crime at least had some kind of reasoning behind it.

Killings like this were always harder because they were without any obvious motive at this stage of an investigation, and motive was something everyone could somehow get to grips with. It might be hard, it might be shocking, but at least with most murders there was a logic of sorts to hang on to, to look back on. People needed to feel that the person who had died had died for a reason, *any* reason. Somehow it made their life easier if they could lay the blame somewhere, even if some of that blame had to be placed on the victim.

'Anything, Kate, if it helps. Can I get you a coffee? I'm on the vodka if you fancy one.'

Kate smiled gently. 'Just coffee please. Look great if I was done for drinking and driving, wouldn't it?'

Tammy smiled back wanly. As she prepared the drinks in her kitchen, Kate looked around the small front room. Janie was everywhere, and the smiling face was like a beacon of happiness and hope. It was obscene to think that those girls' lives had been wiped out like they meant nothing to anyone.

'Here you are. Cheers.'

Kate clinked her cup against Tammy's glass, and moved straight on to small talk. She knew it was easier to warm people up first, get them relaxed before she asked any really difficult questions.

'How are you coping, Tammy, if that doesn't sound too stupid a question?'

Tammy shrugged. 'As well as can be expected, I suppose. The kids miss her. I still expect to hear her voice at the end of the phone, or see her come into the house as usual. If we could bury her it would be half the battle.'

Kate could understand how difficult it was when you couldn't even make funeral arrangements for the one you loved. 'I think you should hear something soon.'

Tammy nodded, but she looked haunted and upset by Kate's words. Once more, Kate knew she couldn't tell Tammy what she wanted to hear, needed to hear.

'It doesn't make it any easier though. Still, whatever needs to be done.'

'Are you getting all the help you need, Tammy? Is there anything I can help with, anything at all?'

Tammy gulped at her drink. 'Funnily enough, Victim Support have been great. Miriam has been a real diamond. Do you know her?'

Kate nodded. 'Ah, she lost her husband recently, very suddenly. She's experienced at her job, and very understanding. I'm glad you've got her to help, she really does care about people.'

Tammy frowned. 'She lost her husband? She never said a word. Bless her, she must be in bits.'

Kate was quick to say conspiratorially, 'Don't let on I told you, she probably thinks you have enough on your plate. She'll tell you in her own time. She is a good person, Tammy. She really cares, you know. She's also very private and she wouldn't let her personal grief interfere with her work.'

Tammy nodded. 'My old mum used to say, everyone's troubles are their own. It's like everything I believed, or I used to believe, was wrong. I thought we were safe, that we'd all live long and prosper, as they used to say on *Star Trek*. My baby loved that programme, she loved all sci-fi things. She believed in ghosts as well, the paranormal, she loved all that rubbish. She relished it, believed in life after death. Shame really that she didn't believe in life before death, only, no matter how I try and dress it up, she never really had one, did she? A young girl like that, her whole life ahead of her, and she's gone. Snuffed out, *gone*. I don't know what I am supposed to do about that. I don't know how I am supposed to get on with my life. I still expect her to walk through the door. I mean, I ain't stupid, I know that *ain't* going to happen, but I still *want* it to happen. I just want my baby back. I want everything back like it was before.'

Kate could hear the heartache in Tammy's voice, knew that she didn't have any answers for her that would make any real sense. Murder was a strange thing, it left a resonance that never really went away. She knew that first hand. Every so often, Patrick would get up out of bed, and she had sensed he was reliving his daughter's death, knew that the anniversary was due. She understood that Patrick was caught between the good memories of Mandy, and imagining the terror and fear she had experienced before her death.

Life was a bastard in many respects, it threw you curves you couldn't ever understand, didn't want to understand.

'I know this sounds lame, Tammy, but this is all part of the grieving process. Anger, bewilderment, raging at the gods. It's natural to feel like this.'

Tammy sighed heavily. 'That's the good thing with Miriam, she sits there and lets me get it off my chest. She reckons people need to be able to talk about the person who's passed on, about their bad points as well as their good points. She says it makes them real again, and it's true. I can talk about Janie to Miriam and she doesn't say a word, she just listens and listens until I've had enough. Then we have a cuppa, she dries my tears, and I feel I can cope again for a while.'

Kate laughed, and Tammy understood why she found her words so amusing.

'I mean, she's a bit of a God-lover but, at the moment, Kate, God is all I've got left really. How fucking sad is that?'

'That's not sad, Tammy, that's real life, love. I'm just glad you feel you have someone you can talk to. Miriam is not everyone's cup of tea, but she cares about what she does, and she is very good at it. Miriam knows what people want after such a tragic experience is someone they can unload on, can rail at. She knows the benefit of allowing someone to get it off their chest.'

'She does that. I tell you, Kate, I fucking do my crust and she doesn't bat an eyelid. She's good with the kids as well, she's got them in a nice nursery, everything. I've promised I'll have a proper service for my girl when the time comes, and Miriam is helping me plan it. She reckons that, once Janie's planted, I'll start the proper grieving process. I got to say this, I think she's right. I need to bury my baby. Once that's over, I will be able to move on. At the moment, I feel I'm in limbo, you know? I hate to think of her in a fridge in the morgue. Alone, cold, with no one able to visit her. Once she's in the ground, Miriam says I will feel better because I can visit her. I'll know where she is, and can bring the kids. As mental as that sounds, I think she's right.'

'She's spot on, mate. Now do you mind if I ask you a few questions about your girl's working hours and her usual habits? I know I seem to be asking the same things over and over again, but I am a person who can't let something go and in my job, that's a bonus. I need you to go over everything again, and don't leave out anything. Give me every tiniest detail.'

'Miriam thinks the world of you, Kate. She said you are the best of the best. It's strange for me, though. All my life, the Bill were people to avoid and now, suddenly, I *need* you in my life. I know you are doing your best for me. Miriam made me see just how hard you work to make things right, she said it's people like you who make the world a safer place to live. She says you were blessed with the gift of policing, and through you and the other police, my daughter's murderer will be found, and once that happens, I will find peace. Janie was a good kid. However she lived her life, she was a good kid, and I want to keep that memory of her close to my heart.'

Kate smiled tightly. Tammy's words had made her feel bad, she had never really liked Miriam, and she knew that Tammy would have crossed the road to avoid her if this hadn't happened. It was odd really, something like this brought together the strangest of bedfellows. She should know, it had once brought her Patrick Kelly, and though she was missing him desperately, she knew that her problems were nothing in comparison. It was strange, but sometimes it took someone else to make you understand just how easy your life actually was.

Kate decided then that she would pop in and see Miriam at the earliest opportunity. Not just because she felt guilty, but also because Miriam might have learned something from the victims' families that could, in some way, help her with her enquiries. People often said things that had real importance to them, only they didn't know that. As far as they were concerned, they were just reminiscing, remembering. It was only when their thoughts were taken into careful consideration, when a timeline of sorts had been established, and when someone like Kate saw a connection, a link, that the innocent words took on a more sinister, and useful, meaning.

Kate wanted to find something, anything that could tie these girls' deaths together. Up till now, there had been nothing of value, nothing that even put the girls together at any given time. They had not socialised outside work, had not even drunk in the same pubs. The victims were relative strangers to each other. The only common denominator was they had been murdered by the same man. He had to have known them as a customer, and perhaps that meant that a lot of girls knew him, not just the girls who had died. The problem was, none of the girls who worked out of the victims' premises could think of anyone who they thought might be dangerous enough to harm anyone.

He had used paralytics, he was not physically strong, not powerful. But then that could just be personality-wise, he could be twenty stone of sheer muscle with a domineering mother and a quiet personality that belied the fact that he was a murdering bastard. There was nothing, nothing at all to go on, nothing she could even grab hold of and try and make sense of. So all Kate could do was ask questions over and over again until she found out something, anything that made her think twice. Failing that, she had to wait and hope that he might make a mistake and leave a clue with the body of the next girl he murdered. It was Hobson's choice, and it made her feel terrible. He was a clever fucker, but even clever fuckers made mistakes. But, until then, all she could do was keep asking the same questions and hope against hope that she got some interesting answers.

But as Kate listened to Tammy, she knew that now there was nothing she could ask that would make her re-live her daughter's life in candid black and white. Thanks to good old Miriam, Tammy would always see her daughter through rose-tinted spectacles. And why not? After all, anything had to be better than the truth.

Kate held her cup out for a refill, and Tammy went into the kitchen with some hope for the future. Kate could not deny the woman that.

Patrick was nervous again, he was not sure about having Eve round to his house. He knew it was silly, he was a grown man and he wanted to see her again, but it still felt a bit too much like his home with Kate. Of course, that was natural. It *was* his home with Kate. Just because she wasn't there now, didn't make that fact any different. He had toyed with the idea of removing her photos, but had decided against it. After all, why should he?

Instead, he decided to take the photos out of the lounge area, and put them out in the other rooms. Eve was unlikely to go walkabout at any point and, if she did, he still couldn't justify to himself removing every trace of Kate from the house. It was early days, and he wasn't ready to remove Kate's image, any more than he had ever been ready to remove his wife or his daughter's images. As Kate always said, there was plenty of room for everyone if you loved them. Kate had never felt jealous of his wife, in fact, she had always ensured that Renée had a presence in the house, because as she always said, she had been the mother of his child, and so she deserved to be remembered. But Pat wasn't sure if Eve would be as generous. After all, he didn't know anything about her except that he liked her, fancied her, and that she had somehow invited herself round for the evening. He wanted to see her again, but it was a bit too soon to have her in the family home. Though family home was stronging it a bit these days, considering he was living here all on his Jack Jones.

Pat looked around him. The place was tidy, too tidy, really. Kate usually left her coat on the back of a chair, her bag in the hall, her shoes at the bottom of the stairs. She was one untidy mare. But now she was gone, and he was suddenly embarking on a relationship with a girl who would be younger than his daughter, had she lived. And he was finding himself enmeshed in a whole new set of rules and regulations.

Eve was a beautiful, sensual girl with a killer body and a cracking smile. A girl who he was frightened of, in many respects, because she had made him want her, and he had not really wanted anyone but Kate for a long time. Eve made him feel like a young man again and he felt the want of the younger woman.

Kate had once explained to him, in graphic detail, why she didn't wear a dark lipstick any more. She pointed out the tiny wrinkles around her lips and explained how a dark lipstick bled into them. But if she had not brought the subject up, he would not have noticed the wrinkles, he wouldn't have seen the ravages of time. He had always looked at her and just seen *his* Kate, the Kate he had fallen in love with, not the Kate she had become, the older, wrinkled Kate. Kate had felt the need to tell him every fucking step of her descent into old age. But Pat had not wanted to hear any of it, he liked his illusions and didn't want to admit that, if Kate was getting old, then where the fuck did that leave him?

Suddenly Pat made a decision. He rang Eve and arranged to see her at her flat once more. As he put the phone down to her, he was overwhelmed with relief; it was far too soon.

Chapter Ten

'I still feel bad, Kate, but you can understand my feelings, can't you?'

Kate didn't really, and she was fed up with pretending that she did. She and Annie had been good friends, but both of them knew that they were spending far too much time together. Kate took a deep breath and steadied her growing anger before saying quietly, 'Can we just let it go, Annie? I know you feel I have invaded your space, and I have. But you know that, in reality, it's actually *my* space. I mean, I own the bloody house. But I will leave, if you really feel it's necessary, because this is starting to get on my wick.'

Annie felt bad about her resentment, and it was just that, real, raw, resentment, but she couldn't help it. After all, she had rented this house fair and square. Now Kate was back, and she was suddenly the lodger. She felt like a stranger in what was, in effect, her own bloody home. But this went deeper than that, and they were both aware of it. Annie knew that Kate needed her, but she needed Kate even more. Especially with all that was going on. The resentment had really surprised her. In fact, she had not expected the depth

191

of feelings she had experienced since this all started.

Annie felt ashamed of herself, even though she knew her feelings were perfectly natural. After all, she had done the psychology courses, she knew that her bad feelings were caused by the fact that the person she was determined to learn from now seemed to be taking over everything. How unfair was that? Hating the person you wanted to help you get on in life. How selfish was she? But she already knew the answer to that, she was jealous of Kate, and it killed her because she also loved her as a friend. But Kate made her feel so inadequate at times. Annie was thrilled at being given the experience of working on such a high-profile case with someone like Kate, but she also knew that she came second to Kate in every way. People talked to Kate before they spoke to her, and *she* was supposedly the lead detective. Kate was supposed to be there as a consultant, two days a week. In truth she had never stuck to that though. She was the person in charge of everything and, even though Annie knew that was because she had the experience, the reputation, and the good grace to help out, it still rankled. It made Annie feel she was on the sidelines, that she was once again the ingénue, the youngster. And why did she feel that needing Kate's help was like admitting defeat?

Annie was out of her depth, and that frightened her. The way the girls had died frightened her. The fact that there would, more than likely, be more deaths terrified her. Unlike Kate, Annie had not learned enough to set her feelings aside, to concentrate only on what was relevant. Unlike Kate, she felt overwhelmed and nervous about the seriousness of everything that was going on around her. Unlike Kate, she wasn't sure she could cope with this pressure which was like nothing she had ever experienced before in her life.

'Please, Annie, let this go, will you? We should be pulling together, not moving apart. I get that you're pissed off with me, I get that you want a fight. But I don't want that. I really don't want to fall out with you again.'

Annie knew how pissed off Kate was, she could hear the annoyance in her voice, see the impatience in her face.

'I am willing to go to a hotel, do anything if it will get us back on an even keel. But it doesn't change the fact that this is *my* house, or the fact that I don't want to be here any more than you want me to be here. And do you know what really hurts? I've lost everything that really mattered to me, and I've done nothing but try to help you in any way that I can. I have prioritised, and made you as much of a priority as the girls who have died. But I can't cope with any more of this crap. We seem to have fallen out again and I don't understand why. I thought we had got over all this. I know the situation is not ideal but, if you want, I can give you notice to quit and we can go from there. The contract allows me to give you twenty-eight days' notice, don't make me do something we'll both regret.'

Annie looked into Kate's face and she could see the sorrow. She could also see that Kate was just about at the end of her tether. She was missing Patrick, regretting that she had forced the issue and that it had ended their relationship. She also knew that Kate would need to see this case through to the bitter end, and she also saw that she herself was turning into Kate. It was this knowledge that bothered her so much. She could see herself in ten years time, how lonely she would be. But Annie knew that there was nothing she could do to stop that happening. Even though she was aware that her chosen career was going to be the cause of her being alone for the best part of her life, she couldn't change anything. She wasn't annoyed with Kate, she was annoyed with herself. Annie looked at Kate and saw the person she would eventually turn into; a lonely woman, well past her sell-by date, whose only interest was in the lives of other people. People who had been murdered, raped, or robbed. These people would become her only reason for living.

Annie had no man, no real social life, she didn't even own her own home because she was more interested in getting on in her career, and if that meant she would have to move on, go to another station, she didn't want the added aggravation of having to sell up.

'I'm sorry, Kate. I don't know what's wrong with me. I can't explain why I've been acting like I have, I can't put it into words. I feel like this is all too much, the girls, the way they died. The pressure, the constant pressure, and the feeling of inadequacy because we can't seem to put anything together, that we can't link anything up to make any kind of connection, no matter how many people we interview. I hate that everyone defers to you, even though I am doing that as well. It's like all this has shown me just how fucking useless I am really. I *know* that I am out of my depth, but I don't know what I am supposed to do about it. I feel like an amateur, like everything I have learned over the years means nothing in the face of all this. I can't sleep, all I can see when I close my eyes is their bodies. I see their families and wonder at their pain and their terror. All I do is try and work out over and over again what kind of person does this, how they can hurt another person and not care about it. I lie there, hour after hour and, in the end, all I seem to be capable of is absolutely nothing. And I don't know what I am supposed to do, what I am supposed to feel.'

Annie was nearly in tears, and Kate saw the bewilderment in her face, heard the fear in her voice. She knew that Annie was experiencing the exact same emotions as every other detective who was involved in serial murders. Serial murders were always senseless, always distressing, and always left the people involved, from the families concerned right through to the lowliest of PCs, in a state of complete and utter shock. These deaths made no sense to anyone except the person responsible, and that person was generally living in a parallel universe. They lived by their own secret code and were capable of great deception, they had to be to carry out their plans. They were clever, they were devious, and they were the reason Annie Carr would never sleep through the night again.

The silence was heavy between them. Kate understood that Annie secretly felt guilty because she had wanted a case like this, she had yearned for a case that would enable her to make her mark in her world. Now she had it, and it wasn't anything like she had expected it to be. Kate had been there, and done that. She also knew that like her, Annie would find out that even if they caught the person responsible, it ultimately wouldn't make her feel better. All it would do was give her a temporary feeling of relief.

Shaking her head sadly, Kate said, 'Come here, you bloody fool. We need to be together on this, not arguing or having a pissing contest. Leave that to the men, all we can do, love, is stick together and hope for the best, because no matter what anyone says, or whatever you might have read, we will not find this fucker till they make a mistake. So embrace your anger and your feelings of failure, because it will always be like this. I should know, I've done this before and, even when you find the bastard, it doesn't make you feel much better.'

Annie was hugging her now, and Kate felt sorry for her because it never really got any better. All Annie could ever really look forward to was some kind of ending to this case. And even that was never going to be a happy one.

Patrick knew there was some kind of trouble afoot, he just didn't know what that trouble might be. He could feel it closing in on him, knew that somehow his world was going to be rocked. Des was on his way over, and he had sounded nervous on the phone. There was something fishy going on, and Patrick was honest enough to admit to himself that, at this moment in time, he really didn't want to have to deal with more aggravation.

Eve was becoming a part of his life. He liked her, she was a good girl. He also liked that she was extremely fuckable, that she was interesting, and that he felt good around her. Eve made him feel young again, that he was still a part of it all. She saw him as being someone of value, and he needed that these days. After Kate and her defection, Pat craved someone to boost his ego again.

Kate's departure had hit Pat harder than he had thought possible. He missed her and when he saw her picture in the paper or watched her on the news, it hurt all over again. Pat was still reeling from the fact that he was now alone. Even with Eve, he was alone. It was as if suddenly he saw his life through a magnifying glass, and it showed him just how little he actually had. If you stripped away his money, he was left with basically nothing of any value any more.

Pat felt that he was just drifting through life, and he didn't know what he was supposed to do to make it better. He had lived a good life: he'd travelled, eaten in good restaurants and dressed well. He had cars and property. He basically had the means to do anything he wanted. So why did it mean nothing to him? Why did he feel it was all a waste of time? Pat felt that he had to make something happen soon, make something of his life again. He looked around him and saw himself as he really was, and he didn't like it. He didn't like what he had become. An old man with no one. He had lost all his zest for living, felt the silence of his home like a cloak around him, mocking him. He needed young Eve, he wanted her youth to make him feel alive again. He prayed that some of her natural enthusiasm might rub off on him, that she might give him back the will to live. She could make him want life again, want and enjoy it. Give him a second chance before it was too late.

Sandy Compton was beautiful. Small-boned, she had a delicate, heart-shaped face that was reminiscent of a Victorian doll. She had natural blond hair and baby-blue eyes that were framed by thick, dark lashes and her Cupid's bow mouth made her look as if she was smiling, even when she wasn't. She was given to wearing very feminine clothes, lacy, old-fashioned attire that suited her look. She pulled it off, and somehow she managed to look both sexy and innocent. Of course, her picture on the website showed her at her best, Sandy was a very photogenic girl. Her eyes were the first thing men noticed, they were very enigmatic eyes. Women also looked at her, she was so unique. Sandy had very good manners. Unlike a lot of the girls, she came from a very good background and was well educated and well spoken. She also had the benefit of being twenty-seven, but looking nineteen in the right light.

Sandy actually liked the job. She had worked the life to pay her way through uni, a lot of girls did. It was good money with good working hours and Sandy found she had a knack for it. She enjoyed it. It was fun, and she liked the excitement of it. She now had more money than she needed, and a comfortable lifestyle. Her parents thought she was running her own interior design business, and they never asked her anything too taxing about her work, were never too intrusive. If her mother was ever sober enough, Sandy would give her a fancy little story about a lottery winner's house, or a magazine spread that she knew pleased her, but didn't really provoke her interest. She'd even hidden the time she spent in prison behind a story of a gap year. That was the great thing about her job, she loved the anonymity of it. She also loved that she was breaking the law, yet wasn't breaking the law. She was breaking a moral law, but she didn't care.

The girls who had died recently were something she thought about a lot but, on a personal level, she felt very safe. The men she attracted tended to be old-fashioned gentlemen who treated her with the utmost respect, liked the saucy side of her, and the fact that she enjoyed her work. Unlike most of the girls, Sandy didn't need any chemicals to do her job, not even alcohol. She always attracted the kinder, more refined men who liked a drink before, and casual chatter. Sandy made them feel like they were on a date, were in charge. She knew the majority respected that because they didn't feel like that at home. Men came to her to escape the family, the wife, the responsibility, they came to her to relax in nice surroundings with someone who agreed with everything they said, laughed at their jokes, had some eager sex with them and waved them off with a smile and a cheery little wave. But as she poured herself a small sherry and relaxed back into her chair, Sandy said a little prayer for her friends and colleagues. After all, they were all girls together, and that was why they looked out for each other.

Sandy was more or less finished for the night, and she yawned delicately. Then, repairing her hair and make-up, she waited patiently for a Mr David Spalding, a mature gentleman with rather nice hands and a very generous nature. It was the generous nature that appealed to her; he had already bought her three necklaces, a diamond pendant, and a very expensive watch.

Oh, she liked Mr Spalding. He was a nice respectable man with two grown daughters and a wife who spent most of her time tending to her elderly mother. He spent most of his time as far away from his wife and her elderly mother as possible. He was as worried about Sandy's safety as she was, and she assured him that he was her only customer. She told them all that, it made them feel better and gave her the edge. But she could see that, at some point, she would need to get herself a nice, rich husband with a good job and a kind nature. She would produce a child, and play a new game, motherhood. Everything she did, she did to the utmost. She allowed herself another three years before she snared herself a live one, and when she did, he would be wealthy, of a certain age, and he would allow her free rein to do what she wanted. Her mobile beeped and Sandy smiled greedily to herself. Another day, another dollar.

*

Kate answered her front door, expecting it to be Annie who she assumed had forgotten her keys. She was not expecting Jennifer James.

'Hello! What can I do for you at this time of night?' Kate could hear the surprise in her own voice and it annoyed her. Jennifer followed her into the warmth of the house, and Kate wondered what she could possibly want that would bring her to her home. Kate wasn't sure she was happy about it, given the circumstances of their association. But for a few wonderful seconds, she had thought that maybe Patrick had sent her round. Deep down she knew that she was fooling herself – that didn't stop her wanting it to be true though.

As they walked into the kitchen Kate was suddenly aware of how shabby the place looked, it was old-fashioned and in need of a lick of paint. She was embarrassed because she didn't want Jennifer seeing her living like this. But then she thought, how utterly vacuous that she would let something like that bother her.

Opening the fridge, Kate took out a bottle of white wine and pouring two glasses said archly, 'So, what's all this in aid of? Have you something of interest for me?'

Jennifer sat at the breakfast bar and lighting a cigarette and accepting the wine she said sadly, 'I wish I did have something for you, Kate, but this isn't to do with the girls, this is personal.'

Kate felt her heart miss a beat at the words and, once more, her hopes were raised. Perhaps Patrick had sent Jennifer round as an emissary, a go-between. Though why he would ask Jennifer to broker a meeting between them, she didn't know. If she was honest, she didn't care either. She missed Pat like she had never missed anyone before in her life.

'Then why are you here?'

Kate sat opposite Jennifer, and waited for her to start speaking. Her heart was racing with the sheer want inside her; to know Pat wanted to see her was like hearing she had finally been given her life back. The life she missed with every fibre of her being.

'I don't know how to start, Kate. You're the only person who can help me out. I have been involved in a scam with Peter, a scam that directly involves Patrick. Des has been on the skim, and now he is trying to lay the blame at our door. Now young Danny has got wind of it all, via Des, and he's causing all sorts of fucking aggro. I suppose I've come here to ask your advice on how best to deal with it. Personally, I think Danny is a good kid, but he also looks out for his own ends. It would suit him to get Des off the firm, and Peter as well. He wants to be the fucking dog's gonads.'

Kate held her hand up then. 'You can't tell me anything dodgy, Jennifer, remember that. Especially if it concerns Patrick.'

Jennifer smiled then. 'Oh, Patrick ain't done nothing wrong, it's me and Peter who was skimming the girls. What worries me is that Desmond, the two-faced fucker, has not only been skimming Patrick, it turns out he is also responsible for the girls getting access to cocaine. Now, Kate, you know that it's a drug of choice for millions of people, but you also know, as well as I do, that in my game it often comes with the territory. Desmond saw the gap in the market and he decided to fill it. So, along with all his other fucking cons, he is earning off that as well. I've been asking around and it looks to me like this is all being done in Patrick's name. After all, he has the rep needed to ensure good gear and quiet distribution. However, I don't think Danny has sussed this out, I only found out because I heard a bit of chat off one or two of the girls and put two and two together. Now, my dilemma, if you like, is this: who do you think I should talk to about it? Should I go to Patrick, or should I talk to Danny Boy?'

Kate was shocked at Jennifer's revelations. One thing she did know, Patrick would not want his name anywhere near a drug deal. Not just because the prison sentences were fucking astronomical, but because he was well past the need for that kind of money. She felt fear grip her heart now, knowing that Pat was being dragged unaware into something like this. Her instinct to warn him, to protect him, was overwhelming.

'I'm scared, Kate. This is serious shit, and all I signed on for was the skimming. Greed is a really destructive emotion, and I admit I am greedy. What I ain't, though, is fucking stupid. I'm worried that if we ain't careful, then Des is going to sell us all down the river, and that includes Patrick.'

Kate could hear the genuine fear in Jennifer's voice and knew that she had to be very worried if she was asking *her* advice.

'I never saw Des as being violent. He's always been a money man, a legal eagle, Pat always called him.'

'If he's as involved as I think he is, then he's dealing with some seriously heavy people, and he's only had access to them because of Pat. All Des has to say is that Patrick wants to tuck them up, or hint that he is not happy and thinks he's being shortchanged to see them come back at him with all guns blazing. Only Patrick won't be aware of any of that, will he? He'll be in the fucking dark about it all and, as much as I don't want to get involved, he's always done right by me, and I certainly don't want to be in the middle of a gang war.'

'What do you mean, a gang war? How would this turn into a gang war?'

Jennifer sighed heavily before saying quietly, 'The people supplying the coke are the O'Learys. Now, you and I know they are not people who would bother with pennies and halfpennies. I could be wrong, Kate, but I think Des isn't just supplying the girls, he's opened it up to the general public. He's supplying it all in Patrick's name, with Patrick's money, and it's the money trail that the Filth follow, isn't it? Des has carte blanche with Patrick's money, doesn't he? And now we have Danny Boy in the mix. Des ain't going to wait around for him to open his fucking gob, is he?'

Kate was in complete and utter shock. If Jennifer was telling the truth, and there was no reason why she wouldn't, then this was a very serious matter for all of them. Especially Patrick. Kate knew Desmond well enough to know that he would make sure he was nowhere to be found in any investigation. In fact, that was why Patrick thought so highly of him, he always said Des could write a contract or broker a deal and, by the time the tax man finally worked it out, they would all be in their graves.

But the tax man and the O'Learys were two completely different entities. For a start, the tax man wasn't liable to have you shot for having them over. The O'Learys, on the other hand, would feel honour-bound to see that that happened. Not just for the retribution they would insist upon, but also as a warning to anyone else who might harbour such disloyal thoughts. Kate knew that whilst Terry was the charmer, the front man, Michael O'Leary, would shoot his own family if he thought they'd had him over for a five-pound note. He was a man who did not see the relevance of any kind of communication after what he perceived as a direct affront to him personally. Whether that was by an insult, a slight, or the removal of a serious wad of his money, it was all the same as far as he was concerned. Whenever Michael O'Leary was miffed, he reacted in the same way. Michael would retaliate with a violence that was not only disproportionate, but also guaranteed to ensure that anyone who heard about it would be very loath to bring such a punishment down on themselves. It was this knowledge that would make Des frightened enough to serve up not only Patrick, but anyone else he thought might add to his own downfall. No wonder Des had been so quick to get her out of the house, her curious nature must have worried him. For all his sorry-sounding excuses, he must have been over the moon at her leaving Patrick like she had.

'Jesus Christ, Jennifer, are you sure about all this?'

'Why the fuck do you think I came here? I think that they've got a personal agenda, and I also think that they are off their fucking heads. Patrick is bad enough if you cross him, but the O'Learys are in a different league. I'll be honest, I want to help Patrick, but I am also frightened for meself now. And, let's face it, Peter won't swallow what's been going on, not with his name being bandied about.

'I'm scared, Kate. Des, Peter, Danny and Patrick are all going to collide and I don't know who I should be talking to. Des is the bad seed, I've known that for a while, and I hold me hand up to it. But all this latest shit is frightening the fucking life out of me.

'The trouble is, Kate, Patrick believes his reputation is enough to stop this kind of fucking problem. What he doesn't realise is that it's a *different* world now. He has been out of it for too long. He has his creds, but he doesn't understand how much has changed since he retired. Fucking youngsters who, in the past, would have to work for years to get themselves a decent stake and a foot in the door can now do it overnight. All they need is the money for a flight to Colombia and a few decent contacts when they arrive. A jewellery heist these days is collateral for a drug deal or an arms deal. Twenty-year-old Russians come over here with a bad attitude and enough guns for sale to equip a small army. I've been approached many times by traffickers asking me if I want girls and, believe me, I ain't proud of my job, but I never forced anyone into it yet, and I ain't going to start now. It's a new world now, and a fucking scary one, Kate. Take that chief of yours, he's in all this up to his fucking eyebrows. He makes sure we are left alone. He also makes sure that the O'Learys get some warning if there's a chance they might be in line for a tug. Even the Serious Crime Squad are part and parcel of it all. They give the O'Learys a fucking swerve, and who can blame them? I mean, would you put your family in danger for a collar, especially when it's easier to take the poke on offer and give them the chance of a better life? Money, that's what makes this country go round, money. And plenty of it. I have girls who work for me with degrees, girls who, twenty years ago, wouldn't dream of doing this kind of job. I have girls in the clubs who are from well-to-do families and pole dance because they seem to believe that it gives them some kind of fucking sexual freedom. Silly fucking bitches they are, but that's what I'm trying to say to you. We are dinosaurs, Kate, fucking dinosaurs. Anyone over thirty now is over the hill apparently. I feel that I'm out of my depth, not just with the way the games have changed, but also with the people I'm inadvertently mixed up with. So tell me, what am I supposed to do?'

Kate didn't answer her for a while. Instead, she lit one of Jennifer's cigarettes and puffed on it gently. She rarely smoked these days, it was only like now, when she was really stressed, that she felt the need for one. She welcomed the light-headedness and the nausea, she needed something to make the numbness inside her go away. Then the feeling, the magnificent feeling as the nicotine hit her brain washed over her, she needed that now. And, as always, the cigarette delivered it in just a few seconds.

Kate was unprepared for what she had been told and she needed time to digest it all, to think about it. She needed to understand who played what part, and why. This wasn't a question she could answer without real thought. Patrick meant far too much to her.

Kate looked at Jennifer's impossibly smooth face. She looked good, but in this harsh light she also looked what she was, a frightened woman of a certain age. For all her Botox and her maintenance, as she liked to describe it, this had aged her overnight. Fear did that to a body, no matter who they were.

'What about young Danny, Jen? Patrick trusts him, do you think he's wrong to do that? Tell me what you think about him, *really* think about him.'

Jennifer shrugged her shoulders inside her expensive shirt. 'Well, it's all academic now, especially since Patrick is seeing his sister. She's not a fool, Kate, she is already running one of the major clubs, and overseeing the casinos. It seems to me that they make a good pair.'

Kate had met Eve once, and she had thought her a handsome girl, if a bit hard looking. She was younger than her, much younger. She felt the enormity of Pat's betrayal as if he had sliced her open with a knife. He had already moved on, already sidelined her for a younger model. She should have guessed that he would not stay alone for long, he had the male ability to attract younger females. It was to do with not just money, but also reputation and the knowledge that he was capable of taking care of his conquest in every way. Kate knew, better than anyone, that there were certain young women who looked for the meal ticket, and looked to the older men to provide it for them.

She felt physically sick, felt her stomach rebelling against the wine and the nicotine. 'What do you mean they make a good pair, Patrick and Eve?'

'No, stupid. Danny and his sister. Those two are closer than a packet of fucking Rizla.'

Jennifer could see the devastation on Kate's face, could feel the mortification she was feeling at her words. She realised, too late, that she should have given her the news of Patrick's betrayal gently. Instead, she had thrown it at her, shoved it into her face without a thought for how it might make her feel.

'Look, Kate. I am sorry to be the bearer of bad news, but you were the only person I felt I could talk to, could trust. I don't know what to do for the best. Patrick needs a heads-up, and you are the only person I can think of who he would listen to.'

Kate nodded gently, attempting to hold on to the last shred of her dignity. She was frightened she would break down and not just cry, but rage at the God who always seemed to make sure that women were destroyed as soon as they started to age. It was as if nature played a joke on them; for years they had the advantage: make-up, hairdressers, good clothes; all those things staved off age for a while. But men, they aged without any kind of help whatsoever, and they got *better* with age. They had the ultimate advantage and if they were well heeled and well known, they could pick and choose.

Jennifer put out a well-manicured hand and placed it over Kate's. She squeezed it gently before saying, 'Where do you keep the brandy, girl? I think we both need something a bit stronger than wine, don't you?'

'The bastard, Jen, the two-faced bastard.'

Jennifer laughed snidely. 'No, he's just being a bloke. He's having what they call a mid-life crisis, only he's having it a bit later than most blokes. They say you walked out on him, and for a man like Patrick that's got to be hard.'

Kate didn't respond. Instead, she went and retrieved a bottle of brandy from her dining room, all the time wondering if Patrick was with the girl now, if Eve was currently lying beside him in the bed she had shared with him for so many years. Her instincts told her he was, and the knowledge was like a physical blow.

Chapter Eleven

'Are you all right, Kate? You look awful.'

'Oh do I? Well, thanks, Annie, for pointing that out to me. I really appreciate it.'

Annie knew when she wasn't wanted and took the opportunity to go upstairs for a shower. Kate looked troubled. She had a feeling it was to do with Patrick and she knew that if Kate wanted to discuss it, which she very much doubted, she would do so in her own time.

In the kitchen, Kate closed her eyes tightly, she felt sick with a hangover that was making her head pound, and her hands shake. She had carried on drinking after Jennifer left, and she had finished the remainder of the brandy alone. Without it, she knew she wouldn't sleep.

She kept seeing Patrick with Eve, kept imagining them together sexually. She knew that she couldn't compete with Eve in any way. Not in any way that mattered, he was looking for something new, something different. That much was evident. If Patrick had already replaced her it was clear to Kate that she was old news, and it was not something she felt ready to deal with just yet. It was still too soon, too raw for her to take on board. God knew, he had every right to be annoyed with her, but she had never thought for a second that he would have replaced her in his life so quickly. Especially with a woman so beautiful, someone who had the added advantage of being related to his surrogate son, which was exactly what Danny Foster was to him. She understood that now, he was the son he had never had, would never have had with her anyway. He might get better luck with Eve though, might get himself a whole new family when he should be having grandchildren. Pat wouldn't use Danny's sister for sex, he would have too much respect for Danny to do anything like that.

It was bad enough that he was being tucked up by Desmond, and she knew she would have to get to the bottom of that, if for no other reason than her own natural inquisitiveness. Kate was also interested in what else he was involved in. This was big, and she had a feeling that Patrick wasn't as savvy as he made out. He had softened over the years and that had made him vulnerable, not that he would believe that, he still thought he was the big Kahuna. Funny how men never thought they were out of the loop, not until it was too late anyway.

On top of all that, she now knew the O'Learys were on the case, so she understood the seriousness of Pat's predicament. They were like the Brady Bunch with machetes, not that Patrick would see that. He loved them and so he should, he had been mates with them for years. Or at least he had been. Desmond ought to be shitting it by now. He was about to get fucking scalped, and that was putting it mildly.

Patrick might have mellowed over the years, but he was

not a man who would allow anyone to get the better of him. Especially not someone he had placed his trust in. Kate knew Pat better than anyone, much better than the young girl he had taken up with.

Oh God, the thought of them together was torture to her. Kate felt sick with the thought of it, even though she knew that there was nothing she could do about it. Pat had replaced her with a younger model, it wasn't exactly something new where men were concerned, she just had not thought he was capable of doing that to her. The urge to go around to his house and have it out with him was strong, she felt almost murderous with hurt and betrayal. She wanted to smash his face in, really hurt him. She wanted to ask him if he had let that girl into the bed they had shared for so many years. She wanted to demand if he knew how much he had hurt her, how he had destroyed her with his actions. But she couldn't bring herself to do something like that. She had her pride and, at this moment in time, that was about all she had going for her. There was no way she would compromise that. It was literally all she had left.

As she poured herself another coffee the phone rang, and Kate answered it with trepidation. She felt as if she was living in a nightmare, and it grieved her that it was a nightmare of her own making.

Flora O'Brien was a very pretty girl. She was very aggressive, but her fine features and angelic demeanour belied her true nature. Everyone liked her, although no one really knew her. She was a transient from Newcastle on Tyne and she came from a family where her mother was a lunatic who had systematically fallen for men who impregnated her and consequently left her quick smart, and her brothers were both off the scale where mental ability was concerned. Flora had left as soon as she was able. Both her brothers were like their mother, small-minded, mentally incapable, and without the sense to get away from their mother's overbearing and lying nature. Flora had learned to look after herself, and she made a point of doing just that.

So when she opened the door of the flat she worked out of three days a week, she was not expecting the sight that was awaiting her. Seeing poor Sandy like that was a real blow, she had liked the girl, admired her. She had no real care for her as such though; like the other members of her family, it would always be about just her and her life, and what she wanted.

So, instead of phoning for the police there and then, or at least phoning someone involved in the flat's ownership, and who thereby had given her a place to work from, she cleared the place of anything connected to her then walked out and locked the door behind her. It was not until hours later that Flora had felt the need to let on that her friend and colleague was lying there, all alone. She finally phoned the news in to Jennifer James from a pay phone at the Watford Gap. She had told Jennifer the news and put the phone down before she could be questioned. After having a coffee and a quick wee, she was already making her way to pastures new.

Flora felt no kinship, no affiliation with young Sandy. Why would she? After all, as her mother had taught them all at a very young age, no one mattered unless they could be used in some way.

She had a new name and a new date of birth by the time she arrived in Liverpool, and she had forgotten the scene of her friend's death before she hit the M1. She was already looking forward to the future, and had no intention of revisiting the past. She was sorry for Sandy, but at the same time she was not about to let her misfortune rub off on her.

'You're telling me that this was an anonymous call?'

Annie nodded. 'Well, not that anonymous. Jennifer said it was definitely the girl who should have worked the next shift. I've run her though the computers and she's got more aliases than a bank-robber's driver. The sad fact is that if she had phoned an ambulance, the girl might have survived. According to the coroner, Sandy would still have been alive when the girl was due in to work. She left her to die basically. The perp would not have been gone long, and the girl could have saved her. Though looking at the body, who would want to be left looking like that?'

Kate nodded. The girl's eyes had been burned away, but her throat had been left untouched. It seemed this girl had been treated differently to the others. She had been tortured, but not to the extent of the previous victims. Her hair had been cut off, her breasts slashed but, other than her eyes, she had not been burned as severely as the other girls. There was no mutilation of the genitals. She had been slowly blinded. The only explanation was that the killer had been disturbed. If Sandy Compton had been given emergency treatment, she would have survived. She might have been able to give them something, anything that could have helped them find out who was responsible for all this destruction, all this hate.

'Fuck that cow, I don't care what it takes, I want her found and I want her charged. She could have saved this girl's life. And Sandy might have seen the bastard responsible. Fuck her, fuck her to hell and let's see how she feels when we lock her up. Jennifer knows who she is, let's put her on the fucking national news as a person of interest.'

Annie nodded in agreement. She also wanted to find the person who had walked away from this girl when she had needed her most. She had still been alive, God love her. If only that bitch had phoned an ambulance, they could have saved her, and they would have had someone who had come through something fucking horrendous, but they would have still been alive, still breathing. They might even have been given a clue of some kind. Instead, she had left this girl to die alone and in fucking agony.

Kate had always liked the fact that the working girls stood together, they might fight and argue, but the bottom line was always the same. They stood by each other and they protected one another because *they* would want someone to protect them if the need arose. Sandy Compton had been alive, but unable to move at all. She would have been aware of what was happening to her, and aware that her friend had left her to die alone. It was *that* which was bothering Kate so much. Even if she had thought the girl was already dead, it made no difference to Kate. She should have wanted that girl to have some kind of help.

Flora O'Brien, or whatever her name was, would be on her shit-list for as long as it took to track the bastard down. Though she had a feeling that if Jennifer got to her first, there wouldn't be much left for her to put away. Jennifer was as angry as she was and also assailed by guilt.

Mariska Compton was staring at Kate and Annie as if they had just both grown new heads before her very eyes. She was visibly shaking, the denial of their words was not something she believed with all her heart, but it was also because she felt they were tainting her daughter's memory. Her beautiful daughter who she had known, deep inside, was not as successful in her interior design business as she had liked everyone to believe. Mariska's real fear was the neighbours finding out, her friends knowing that her daughter had been murdered by a serial killer. Not just any serial killer, but one who targeted whores. She was already wondering how her husband would react to the news, she was already relishing his humiliation.

'This is outrageous. It's a mistake, my daughter would never do something so heinous. It's a case of mistaken identity.'

Kate's heart went out to this woman, she understood how hard it must be to hear something like that about your child.

'Please, Mrs Compton, we wouldn't be here if we weren't a hundred per cent sure that this was your daughter.'

Mariska looked at the two women. She would normally have just started on her daily drinking. She should have been nice and numb by now, but she had needed to drive to the bank, and her biggest fear was to be pulled over for drunk driving. So every Friday she made a conscious effort to stay off the drink until she had done her chores. But if ever she needed an alcoholic drink, today was that day. She knew that this would never be something they could live down.

How could Sandy have done this to her? How could that girl have left this mess for her to clear up? She had never interfered in her daughter's life, she had never wanted to. The girl had no real meaning to her as such. She had tolerated her all her life, just as she had tolerated Sandy's father. She remembered all the times she had bragged about her daughter's career, and now it seemed her career had been just like everything else about her, a bloody lie.

'Could you leave, please? If that *is* my daughter, I would ask you to make sure that it's known that we had turned our back on her. Disowned her. I had a feeling she was lying to us, and you have proved my point. Now, if you don't mind . . .' She waved her arm in a gesture of dismissal.

'Your daughter has been murdered. You do understand that, Mrs Compton?'

'I said, would you please leave? Don't make me throw you out because I am quite capable of doing just that.'

Kate was nonplussed at the woman's vehemence, she realised there and then that Mariska Compton was not so much bothered by her daughter's murder, but more interested in how it might affect *her*. What kind of mother would feel like that? She had guessed the woman had a drink problem from the moment they had entered the house. All the signs were there, and Kate knew how to read them. The empty vodka bottle beside the bin. The nervousness of a woman who has not yet had a few drinks that morning to take off the edge. The shaking of the hands as she lit her cigarettes, but the real decider had been the smell of her breath. Drunks could never really disguise the smell of their own destruction. It was an odour so toxic it could be noticed from three feet away. It was an acrid, disgusting aroma that all the toothpaste and mints in the world were eventually unable to mask.

Kate knew it well, as did Annie. It was something you became familiar with from early on in your career in the police force. Drinkers came from all sections of society, it wasn't just the poor, the underclass who turned to alcohol to relieve their problems. It was something that cut a swathe through all sections of society. It was legal, and that was its allure. No one took a second look at someone buying alcohol, it was socially acceptable. Everyone liked a drink and no one would look askance at anyone purchasing it in a supermarket or off-licence. Yet it was the cause of more deaths, and more criminal offences, than drugs.

Looking at this woman, smelling her addiction and seeing her looking down on her own child made Kate want to slap her face. She hated that drink was the reason this woman had no interest in her child. The pubs were now open all day, the supermarkets sold drink so cheaply it was available to school children in their lunch hour. They bought drinks that were flavoured by oranges, cranberries and melons. They were brightly coloured bottles of alcohol that were like drinking lemonade. Oh, Kate hated drugs, but she hated excessive use of alcohol more. There were so many young men doing life because of strong lager and a brief argument resulting in a violent fight. Young men who, without the drink, would have walked away from the argument in the first place. But who bothered to take the makers of the alcohol to task? No one. The government came up with more and more taxes so that publicans were unable to give their customers a reasonably priced pint. Pubs that had once been the centre of a community were now outpriced by the Chancellor. And for what? Just so the supermarkets could corner the cheap booze market. Could make sure that people drank at home instead of being with friends, with people who would have looked out for them.

Now, looking at this sad excuse for a woman, for a

mother, Kate knew that, as drunk as this bitch might be in her daily life, she would never be drunk enough to accept her daughter's lifestyle. Even though she was now dead as a fucking doornail.

She got up to leave with Annie in tow; they were both shocked by the woman's complete disregard for her daughter's death. At the front door, Kate turned to the woman and said sadly, 'Do you know something, Mrs Compton? Whatever your daughter might have been, she had one thing going for her. She wasn't *you*. Like all drunks, nothing really means anything to you, all you think about is yourself. I have a feeling that was probably what sent her on the game in the first place. I bet she lived her life around your drinking, knew you had no interest in her at all unless it suited you, unless it was something you could brag about to people who meant fuck-all. I bet she helped you into bed, cleaned up after you, pretended that everything was normal to her friends, and lived the lie you have forced on her. Now she is dead, so you go and have another drink, I'm sure you need one now even more than usual.'

Kate could still hear the woman cursing them as they walked down the well-kept drive, but she didn't care. She saw all sorts in her job, but the hypocrites were always the ones that made her see red. The worst thing of all was that Mariska Compton had not even asked about her daughter's demise, if she had been in pain. She had not even cared enough to wonder, or even think to ask in passing, exactly how her daughter had wound up dead. That told Kate this was a woman who was so well versed in the drink that she had forgotten how to care for anyone else but herself.

As they drove away from the large, prosperous house,

Kate was tempted to see that Mrs Compton was followed and watched until she was done for drink driving, dangerous driving or driving without due care and attention. *Anything* that could make her life a misery. It was the least she could do for the girl who had died so slowly, so horribly, and who had died without anyone to really mourn her passing. It was that, more than anything that got to Kate. Whatever that poor girl was, whatever she had become, she was still that woman's own flesh and blood. She deserved so much better from the woman who had given birth to her. She had at least warranted a few tears.

It never ceased to amaze Kate how people treated other people, how selfish and greedy so many turned out to be. Well, God paid back debts without money, and she knew that was true. God always saw a way to make people understand their mistakes, and she relied on that knowledge to keep her sane. Her old mum had said that scum floated to the surface, but that it eventually sunk without trace. Kate had always laughed at her mum's Irish wisdom, her old Irish sayings. Now though, years later, she felt that there was an element of truth in them. She hoped that she was right, because after today she wanted Sandy Compton's mother to one day realise just what she had turned her back on.

'You OK, Kate?'

She laughed loudly then. She realised that she needed a laugh, needed to express her anger, her disappointment at the human condition. She needed to vent her own feelings of abandonment, feelings that were even worse now she knew the poor girl who had died alone and unwanted had felt as unimportant as she, in turn, now felt.

'Of course I'm not, Annie. Are you? As much of a bitch as

that woman was, we're still no nearer to finding out anything about the girl's last few hours, are we? We know she was terrified but unable to even move a muscle. She was aware of what was happening to her, and she could see her killer, until her eyes were dissolved inside her head of course. Then, as if that wasn't bad enough, her mate left her dying without a second *fucking* thought. So *no*, Annie, I'm *not* OK. If that's all right with you, of course? I mean, unless you think I'm taking over again, you know, pushing you out. I would hate for you to think that I'm only here to take all the glory. Perhaps you think I'm not really interested in finding the actual murderer, that I'm only interested in making a name for myself. A name that I have already earned, darling. A name that has kept *you* on board for a long time. Long before all this.'

Annie was not just shocked at the way Kate had gone at her, but more by the words she had used to knock her down. She made Annie feel useless, as if she had no real talent for what they were doing. She heard the contempt in Kate's words, in the timbre of her voice. She heard the scorn and the disrespect that was aimed at her, and she pulled the car over into a lay-by.

Kate was still fuming. She could feel the anger coming off her in invisible waves and knew that one wrong move and she would, once again, demolish this woman with a few more well-chosen words.

'How dare you speak to me like that? How *dare* you. I have never given you anything but the utmost respect. I expected you to treat me in the same way.'

Kate shook her head sadly and, sighing loudly, she said honestly, 'Oh will you fuck off, Annie. You expected me to give you the benefit of my experience, and I have done that, darling. Without me, you haven't got a fucking case. The arsehole has given me carte blanche, and do you know why? Because he doesn't want anyone else sniffing round, and I have the creds to stop them forcing the issue. You think you can do without me? Well, I'm here to tell you that you can't, love. And I'm not in the mood any more to mollycoddle you. You live in *my* house, very cheaply I might add, and you're aspiring to do my job. A job that I did very well, very, *very* successfully. *You* asked me to help you out, give you the benefit of my expertise and believe me, darling, I have more experience than that fucking lot at Grantley put together. *You* included. And I was willing to do that for you, but you've turned on me a couple of times now and, as Patrick would have said, you are giving me the ache. Because without me, you are basically nothing. Do you get that? *Nothing.* I have tried my hardest to help you along. I know better than anyone how difficult it is to be a woman and a Filth. But if you don't fucking change your attitude, I will personally bury you, my darling, professionally and personally, and don't think I won't. I have had enough, Annie. You need to sort out who your friends are, and my advice is, sort that out sooner rather than later. I have swallowed your petty grievances, and your fucking imbecilic jealousy. But that's it for me now, and I'm not in any way inclined to let this murder inquiry become muddied because of your fucking ego. So get off my back, and work with me on this, or leave me be. If the arsehole has to choose between us, darling, we both know who he will pick.'

Annie was dumbstruck at Kate's attack, and it *was* an attack, they both knew that. Kate laughed then, really laughed. 'Have I upset you, Annie? Well, that's too fucking bad. I'm not in the mood for your histrionics any more. We both know that you are the second fiddle, so get over it and stop trying to become the top dog because, believe me when I say this to you, you have a long way to go before you could even come close to me and what I have achieved. If I was a man, you wouldn't have dared challenge me and you know it. And, while we're being honest, if you don't like living with me, get somewhere else, go and find yourself a flat. But remember, you won't learn half as much from books or talk. I am willing to make you into the policewoman you want to be and that is something that I've never offered to anyone else. Only you, because I really believed you had it in you. Don't you go and prove me wrong now. Don't make me regret all the time we've spent together, just because you think you finally have a big case because, without me, you have more chance of getting a kiss off Brad Pitt.'

Annie couldn't believe that Kate was capable of talking to her like that. It was as if she didn't know her, was as if she was listening to a stranger.

Kate could see the confusion in Annie's face, saw the hurt and the disbelief and knew that she had struck a chord with the selfish little mare. She had wanted her help, but she didn't want to admit that it was Kate who would most likely be the one to break this case. Annie Carr had wanted the glory all for herself. Well, she had to learn something that they all had to learn at some point. It was all about team effort, even if one of the team had the most experience. If Annie used her loaf, one day that person could be her. Until that day came, she would have to do what they all did; look, learn and try to understand. It wasn't fucking rocket science.

'Oh dear, have I hurt your feelings? Well, the truth hurts, doesn't it? And I am not, in any way, prepared to pussyfoot around you any more. I have done my best to try and help you out, from letting you rent my house to giving you all my case files and answering your questions to the best of my ability, no matter how inane they might have been, and all so that you could make a career for yourself. Well, that's all by the by now. I am going to *find* this fucker and, when I do, I will see to it that he gets so much time Prince Harry will be on his third wife before he can even dream of a parole hearing.'

Annie Carr was unable to speak, she had never seen Kate like this before. The worse thing of all was that she knew she had asked for everything that had been said to her. Kate was over the edge, they all were, and she guessed, rightly, that now was not the time to say anything. Instead she started up the car and drove them both back to the station house. She was very aware that she needed to rethink her role in Kate's life, and find a way to make things right between them.

Danny was on a mission. He was on his way to Patrick's to inform him of all the skulduggery that was going on around him. He now knew that it was Des who was the alpha male involved. Peter was just after a few quid, like all gamblers he needed the poke. Jennifer was the one who had made sure it was not a piss-take. He had a lot of respect for her, she was a real diamond in that she was loyal to everyone, and yet she also had the brain capacity to see what was going on and cover her own arse. He decided he would give her a real leg up in the future. Loyalty *and* brains were rare, he knew that better than most people.

But that aside, he was still nervous of telling Pat Kelly the whole nine yards. Patrick was a funny fucker, he could just as easily decide that Danny's information was tantamount to grassing. Patrick was in a funny mood most days, this latest murder would not help his frame of mind either.

So Danny was nervous, but that was healthy. Once you started being too sure of yourself it normally indicated that you were losing the edge. In their world you never trusted anyone, no matter who they were, or how many fucking creds they might have accumulated over the years. They were all born villains, and that fact alone said that they were always willing to listen to another earner, even if that meant treading on someone else's toes. It was the way of the world.

Any big business was the same. The people who put you in a position of power were often the same people you toppled so you could then harness that same power for your own ends. Bankers paid their mentors off with big pensions and even bigger investments. But in the world of villainy that kind of offer wasn't always an option. Most of the people involved were not liable to accept a hefty wedge and then see fit to swallow their knobs and retire gracefully. They were more inclined to want to *shoot* the person they saw as the instigator of their downfall, and therefore it was often a tricky and dangerous situation for all concerned. Especially for the fucker who had been the cause of the aggro in the first place. They were mostly ostracised by all and sundry, and that in itself was not something to be encouraged. It was more often than not something that caused their career to be cut short. Along with their lives, of course.

So Danny knew he was walking into a fucking nightmare, but he was also not a bullshitter, and Patrick was aware of that much at least. Patrick was shrewd, he kept his own counsel and made up his own mind. Danny also had the added knowledge to impart that Pat had been ripped off, royally ripped off, and for longer than any of them would care to point out. Danny wasn't looking forward to bringing fucking aggro to Pat's door, but he had to. He knew he had to.

As Danny pulled up in the driveway, Patrick was already walking towards him. As Danny parked his car, he took a deep breath. Then, opening the car door, he looked up into Patrick's eyes and saw anger there, along with the disappointment.

'You, Danny, had better come in here and tell me everything. Only I think me and you need what my ex-brief used to call a full and frank discussion.'

Chapter Twelve

'So, you thought I wouldn't find out the score, that I was too fucking stupid to suss any of it out for meself?'

Danny was frightened. He had never seen Patrick so angry. He had heard about his colossal temper, knew it was something that only emerged if he was seriously pissed off. Now he was seeing it first-hand and he could understand how Patrick had stayed at the top of his game for so long. He knew that this man in front of him, this angry man, was capable of walking out of his house and hunting down any-one who he thought *might* have been involved in this trouble. He was so incensed he was incapable of listening to reason or excuses.

Danny was clear that all his prior dealings with Patrick Kelly, and his sister's place in both their lives, meant nothing to Pat now. Patrick Kelly too was on a mission, and he would not rest until he had seen it through to the end.

'Did you know the full extent of Desmond's fucking skulduggery?'

Danny didn't respond, he knew he wasn't really expected to. Patrick wanted to vent his anger first and if he answered him now, all he would do was annoy Pat even more. That was the last thing he had any intention of doing.

'Did you know that he used Kate, *my* Kate, Kate Burrows, a *Filth*, and the woman I shared my life with, did you know that he used her name to launder the money he skanked off me? The money he made off *my* name and *my* reputation. Did you know that, clever bollocks? I sussed out Peter from the off, he ain't the sharpest knife in the drawer, know what I mean? But he's an old mate, and that means a lot to me. I also knew that Jennifer would watch *my* arse, she is more trusty than a fucking cricketer's cockbox. You see my point, Danny Boy, it was *Desmond* I never saw coming. And he used the O'Learys. I didn't expect it from Desmond. But apparently *you* did. Apparently *you* saw fit to keep your fucking trap shut about the things that were most important. So, given all that, I can only assume that you are either a *cunt* of Olympian standards, or you stood to gain from my fucking downfall. This is something I feel very strongly about, as I am sure you realise.

'I can also inform you that Desmond went missing today, but then I have a feeling you might know about that. You come here, telling me all your gossip, but you keep the real gossip to yourself. So now I have to start digging on me own. And I am the digger of diggers. I can find out anything I want. Like you and your sister's stints in care, your mother's fucking nut-bag lunacy. But I let that go, I thought you were worth the effort. I thought you were worth my time. What I never allowed for was that you would throw my good nature back in my boat-race. I am stressed, really stressed, about all this. I think that *you* owe me an explana-tion, and it had better be a good one. I have never suffered fools gladly. In fact, fools have never entertained me. I hate fools, I hate idiots and, back in the day, I had a habit of making them disappear. Permanently. But then I am sure you already have a working knowledge of my past endeavours.

'Well, my advice to you is, think about what I am saying, and find my fucking missing money, and find it quick. I pay you exorbitant amounts of poke to do my dirty work, and this is not just dirty, it's fucking disgusting. I also have a long memory and I never forget a slight. I never forget someone who mugs me off and, do you know something, Danny? They never forget me either.'

Danny took it all, and he took it calmly. Danny knew he had to prove himself to Patrick, not just with his loyalty, but also his ability to take what was coming without fear or favour. Patrick had to know that he was not someone who would hold a grudge, was not someone who would see his own personal ego as more important than the person he was being employed by. Danny Boy saw that this was a watershed, not just for him, but for Patrick too. After all, Patrick had taken him under his wing. He'd trusted him. And now he needed to prove that the trust placed in him was not misplaced, he had to prove that he *was* loyal, *was* dependable, and that he was more than capable of taking a bollocking. A bollocking that he knew he deserved, because he had tried to sort this out without going to Patrick and telling him everything that he'd found out. He had been a fool, had believed he could sort it out himself.

He had dropped the proverbial, he had wanted to come to this man with all the answers but, unfortunately, the answers had not been as forthcoming as he'd expected. In fact, he had not realised that Desmond had covered his own arse in many respects. Or how far he'd gone. He now understood that he was still a novice where Patrick and his ilk were concerned. The knowledge hurt Danny, but it was also a learning curve. He recognised that experience far out-weighed front, and it also outweighed pride.

'I am sorry, Pat, I wanted to nip this all in the bud and come to you when it was sorted. I wanted to prove to you that I was capable of sorting out any little discrepancies, that I didn't have to come to you for every problem that cropped up. I wanted to show you that I was keeping an eye out. I wanted to prove to you that I was on the ball, had your interests at heart.'

'Little discrepancies? Are you having a fucking tin bath at my expense? Little discrepancies are when a onner or a monkey goes amiss in the betting offices. Little discrepancies are when a till is out in one of the clubs, it is *not* classed as a *little discrepancy* when *my* fucking money is being used to bankroll drug deals and my name is being used to garner said drug deals. Especially when, after all that, I ain't even getting a fucking drink from it all. I see that as more of a major fuck-up. Not on my part, you understand. More on the part of the fucking imbecile who thought it might be a good idea at the time. I don't want your apologies, Danny Boy, I want you to sort it out. I pay you to front my operations, and I pay you fucking well. So now, I want you to sort this, and sort it soon.

'The O'Learys have the right arse with Desmond, so I can only assume they have had a word with him. I suspect that Scott of the Antarctic has a better chance of turning up in the near future than our Desmond. So you had better make sure that Kate is without stain, as they put in the Bible. Kate never asked to be a part of this, and I will not let her be crucified because of her job. As much as I hate the Filth, and I do hate them, make no mistake about that, Kate is not one of the ones we avoid. She is the one we really want to be there if one of our family get murdered. Know what I mean, Danny? She is one of the good guys. She is also someone who is not deserving of losing her reputation over a piece of shit like Desmond. Incidentally, Desmond has left his wife power of attorney, and she knows where the money is, the stuck-up, two-faced whore, and I am relying on you to make sure that she returns it to its rightful owner. That would be me, by the way.'

Danny had always known that Patrick Kelly had been a force to be reckoned with back in the day, but he now realised that Patrick might have retired from the game, but he had not lost the power to roar. Patrick Kelly was as powerful as he had ever been.

Danny understood then the authority he commanded. Patrick had always concealed his strengths though, had understood that it was far more sensible to keep your power hidden away.

All the time Danny had believed, deep down, that Patrick was finished, was over the hill, he had actually been at the height of his power. Patrick Kelly had something that most people never really attained. He had respect. Desmond had used Patrick's name to broker his deals, and the O'Learys had taken that on face value. Now they knew the score, they had taken out Desmond, not Patrick. Patrick was still powerful enough to ensure that his demise would bring unwelcome aggravation on the people responsible. Someone had tried to take him out years ago, but he had survived, and gone back after them with a rightful vengeance that made sure no one would attempt anything like that again without the help of at least a tactical nuclear weapon.

231

Patrick saw the truth dawning on Danny's face, and it grieved him, even though he knew it was inevitable. He had always hidden his light under the nearest bushel, it was what had kept him out of trouble from day one.

'Oh what tangled webs we weave, when first we practise to deceive. My old mum used to say that to me, and I never understood it for years. She was a shrewd old bird, and she could have more fights than John Wayne. I take after her, Danny, I feel it is only fair to warn you about that. I want *you* to sort this, and sort it sooner rather than later. As for the O'Learys, I could swallow them *whole*, you remember that, boy, because I can assure you that they do. They will do anything to make it right with me. The man ain't been born who can frighten me. And I can be one frightening bastard when the fancy takes me. Kate calmed me down, but even she knows that, push me too far, and I'll hunt you down like a fucking rabid dog, and I'll smile while I do it.'

Danny understood that he had made a fatal mistake. Patrick Kelly was back in the driving seat and, the worst thing of all was, he was relishing every fucking moment. He was loving every second of it. Without Kate to hold him in check, he was like a kid in a candy store. Overexcited, pumped up on sugar, and determined to do whatever he wanted. Patrick was enjoying himself, and that was what could well be the cause of not only his downfall, but also that of everyone else involved. These were dangerous times, and Danny knew he had better prove himself, once and for all.

Kate smiled at Miriam Salter. She didn't need her and her determined personality at this exact moment in time, but she knew she had to humour her.

'Have you got a few minutes, Kate?'

''Course I have, what can I do for you?'

Miriam shrugged, her heavy shoulders seemed to rise up like a hunchback's. She was even bigger than she was before. Kate hated that she thought things like that, but the Miriams of the world irritated her.

'I think Sandy Compton's mother is an alcoholic, and I desperately need your advice. She won't even acknowledge her daughter's death and worse still, neither she nor the husband want to arrange a funeral for her. Do you think I should try to get some public money to pay for it?'

Kate didn't know what to say. 'Look, Miriam, the body will not be released for a good while yet, as well you know. Why not wait until it's relevant? By then the parents might have come around.'

Miriam nodded, barely moving her head. She had a knack of making her feelings known with a subtlety that was extremely annoying. 'Maybe you're right. I have always trusted your instincts, Kate. You are rarely wrong. I should wait, I should have the patience to step back and wait until the Comptons are prepared to bury their child. But it's hard, Kate, you know. Hard to help people who are so angry and hurt that they can't see how destructive their feelings actually are.'

Kate felt the guilt rise up inside her. People like Miriam were hard work and she hated that she resented her so much. Miriam did so much for the families of the dead. She was the one who sat with them, listened to them, and eventually helped them come to terms with their loss. She visited people who had been raped, burgled and mugged. She ensured that Kate and her colleagues were not burdened with their emotions when they needed to be clear-headed to solve the crimes.

'Tell you what, Miriam, I'll talk to the brass, see if they can get someone in from outside, a professional grief counsellor . . .'

Miriam puffed herself up to almost frightening proportions. She straightened up like a demented, podgy runner bean, and her grey eyes became little slits of anger and distress. Kate immediately regretted her words, understood that she had inadvertently insulted this woman and all the work she had done for the families of the deceased.

'I can't believe you just said that, Kate. If you think I'm not experienced enough, then all you had to do was say. I am willing to step back and let the *professionals* take over. In fact, as I have recently been widowed myself, I can see why you might think I don't have the necessary qualifications for dealing with people who have lost their nearest and dearest . . .'

Miriam's voice was rising with every word, and Kate was aghast at her faux pas, but she had not meant it as it had come out. She was only trying to offer some kind of help. Miriam had a couple of older women who assisted her for a few hours here and there, both were do-gooders like Miriam but, unlike Miriam, they did not see their role as pivotal, as important, if not more important, than anyone else's. It occurred to Kate that this was what really needled her about Miriam. Like her husband before her, God rest his soul, she thought she was doing the most important job of all. Taking care of those left behind was a mantra that both Miriam and her husband had lived by. On top of all their church work, and their other charitable labours, they had seen themselves as the modern-day equivalent of Mother Teresa and St Francis of Assisi combined.

'Calm down, Miriam, for God's sake.'

People were staring at them, young PCs were smirking at the sight of Kate Burrows and Minging Miriam in what seemed to be a full-blown argument.

'Calm down? You're telling me to calm down? How dare you! I'm not averse to speaking my mind, and I do not take kindly to someone like *you* speaking to me as if I mean nothing.'

Kate was shocked at Miriam's vehemence. 'What do you mean, someone like me?' There was a challenge in Kate's words now for anyone to hear. The onlookers were thrilled at the continuing saga.

Miriam shook her head in a slow gesture of disgust. 'You, swanning around with that man, like Burton and Taylor, thinking you are better than everyone else when you are living with a criminal. You, a policewoman. Someone who should know better . . .'

All Kate could think of was, Burton and Taylor? Was that an insult? She wasn't sure, all she knew was that she felt a terrible urge to start laughing. Rip-roaring, loud laughter. The woman was off her bloody head. So she said as much. 'I think you came back to work too early, Miriam, you are obviously still not in your right mind. Grief can do that to a body. Listen to yourself, woman. Screeching and hollering in the hallways, making a spectacle of yourself. I apologise if I offended you, but I didn't mean to. I was just trying to offer you some help, offering to try and take some of the burden from you. That was all, there was no hidden insult, or underlying offence. But do not talk to me like that, do you hear me? No one talks to me like that and gets away with it.'

Miriam was suddenly calm, her whole body seemed to

deflate in an instant. 'My husband and I have done more for the people of Grantley than anyone else, and I say that as a fact. I am proud of what we do. He might have gone, but I am determined to keep his memory alive. I do not need any help, or anything at all, from the likes of you.'

With that, she walked away, a certain rough dignity in her rounded shoulders, and a surprising spring to her step given her immense size. Kate stood and watched her retreat. She saw Annie make a comical face of mock horror while saying loudly, 'What the fuck was all that about?'

Kate shrugged. 'I'm fucked if I know.'

And they both started laughing at the total incongruity of it, their earlier fight forgotten.

Mariska Compton was in bits. Her daughter's death had finally hit her. It was the way her girl had died that was hurting her, it was the way her daughter had been tortured, abused. It didn't help that she also felt some responsibility because she had never been interested in the girl. Not on any real level anyway.

'How are you?'

'Fine.'

That had been the sum total of their conversations for many years. As long as Sandy was clean, tidy, and in employment, and as long as she was as far away from her as possible, Mariska had not really given her a second's thought.

Now, as Mariska looked at her daughter's possessions, looked around the girl's flat, she wondered what she was supposed to do. What did one do in these situations? She certainly had no intention of looking through all this stuff, did she? She wasn't sure.

She glanced around the room, it was a lovely room. Sandy *could* have been a designer if she had really wanted to. She had made the most of the space, the light. She had a flair for the dramatic; she dressed dramatically, like Theda Bara or a very young Joan Collins. Very Hollywood, very feminine, and yet Sandy had been very strong inside herself. It was one of the few things she had ever admired about her daughter. She saw a photograph on the mantelpiece, it was of the two of them, mother and daughter. It was a very pretty picture, they both looked happy and connected. No one seeing it would guess at the true nature of their relationship and, for some reason, this made Mariska feel tearful.

She was suddenly aware that there was no chance to change their situation, they were lost to one another. The daughter she had never really had any time for had finally become important to her, only it was too late for either of them to do anything about it. She knew the next step was to go and see her daughter's working environment. As much as it repulsed her, she knew that she needed to see it. It was the only way she would ever be able to put this whole sorry mess behind her.

As Miriam had told her over and over again, without the men, these girls would be out of work. It was simply supply and demand. They had men working in the background, men who made sure these girls were sucked in before they knew what had happened to them. They kept them there with fear, intimidation and violence. She made it all sound so much easier, made her feel that it wasn't her fault, or even her daughter's fault. Miriam had made her realise that she had nothing to reproach herself for.

She was so glad she had listened to the woman, it had

helped to get it all off her chest to someone she knew she would never see again once this was over. Miriam was kind and helpful, but not exactly someone one would choose as a friend in normal circumstances. But there was nothing normal about any of this and, as the old saying went, any port in a storm. That sentiment seemed very apt at this moment in time.

Sitting on her daughter's chaise longue, Mariska Compton finally cried. Not for herself this time, but for her daughter and the tragic loss of such a young life. If she had only given her a bit more of her time, none of this might have happened.

Kate and Annie were back on track and they were both glad. Kate was throwing herself into work; knowing about Patrick and that girl had all but destroyed her, but she was a realist. She knew that it was going to hurt, and hurt for a long time. Her best defence was to be as busy as possible and, with all that was going on, she could easily achieve that much.

Also, seeing the devastation of the girls put her own problems into a much-needed perspective. She knew through Jennifer that Patrick had sorted his troubles in his own inimitable way and she was genuinely glad about that. But the pain was still there, aching inside her whenever she allowed herself to think too much about it.

Kate looked at Annie and smiled wanly. 'Did you get the other girls' names together?'

Annie nodded. Kate noticed she looked as harassed as she herself did and that, she felt, was a good sign. She never trusted police who could leave the job behind when they went home. It was a job that needed twenty-four-seven interest, and twenty-four-seven time and effort.

'Quite a few more. Jennifer has been very forthcoming.'

'Where are they? Are they coming here or do we visit them?'

'Both. Most of them are happy to see us here, a few insist on seeing us on neutral ground.'

Kate nodded. 'We'll take some ourselves and give the others to a good WPC. That new young one, what's her name? Amanda?'

Annie smiled. 'Yeah. Mandy Tooley. She's good with the working girls. I'll get her on to it. I thought we could do the others either alphabetically or by location. You decide.'

Kate shrugged. 'You decide, it's your call.'

Annie was inordinately pleased that Kate was deferring to her. She knew it was petty, but somehow it made her feel as though she really was the one who was actually orchestrating everything. She knew it wasn't true, and so did Kate, but it had gone a long way to getting them back on an even keel.

'In that case, I thought we could go alphabetically, cross them off our list and move on.'

Kate nodded. Personally she would have mapped out the addresses and therefore prevented them both from crossing town over and over again. But she didn't say that. Instead she smiled happily and picked up her handbag.

Janette Carter was tall, very tall, with a boyish body and thick, silky hair. She was wearing coloured contacts so her eyes were a very bright green, her teeth were white, and just perfect enough to give her a lovely smile. Kate liked her on sight; she had a warmth that was endearing.

'How often did you work out of the flats?'

Janette raised her heavily made-up eyes to the ceiling, she

seemed to be genuinely trying to answer the question honestly. 'I worked out of them all at one time or another, not that I can be that specific about dates. Now, young Sandy, God bless her, she kept a notebook and she wrote everything in it. Names, dates, amounts. She was quite a clever girl in that respect, very well educated, you know.'

Kate nodded, startled by this bit of information. They had found nothing in the room Sandy worked out of, nor in her flat. It had to have been taken. Her credit cards, money, all her personal jewellery were still *in situ*. But this notebook, if it existed, had not been catalogued.

'What kind of notebook?'

Annie's mind was clearly going along the same lines as Kate's.

'A little black one.' Janette laughed. 'A little black book. One of them Moleskine ones they sell in Paperchase. I remember because she gave me one too once. I admired hers and the next time I saw her she had bought one for me. I was really touched because they ain't cheap, the bit of paper inside said it was used by Ernest Hemingway.'

She laughed good-naturedly once more. 'Not that he had used that one, if you see what I mean. Really nice paper. I know that sounds silly, but it was something I would never have thought to purchase for myself. It was a reporter's notebook, had a lovely elastic band that kept it shut and stopped the pages from curling up. There's even a little envelope in the back for notes and things. It's the only notebook I would use now, very luxurious and handy.'

'And she always had it with her?'

Kate's voice was low and inquisitive. Janette turned to face her and said honestly, 'We all used to take the piss, but she said that one day it would make her her fortune. I assumed she was writing client names and car numbers in there, that kind of thing. The dates they visited her too, she had quite a regular clientele. She was known to be a bit over the road, if you see what I mean. Not that I want to say anything bad about her, but she was known to do things other girls wouldn't.'

Kate nodded again, this time as a conspirator. 'Did you ever see this notebook? I mean anything she had written down in there?'

Janette's eyes once more perused the ceiling in earnest. 'No. Nothing important anyway. Just numbers and amounts.'

'Do you all get to see the same men at times?'

'Oh yeah. Most of them don't care who they get, but if they request one of us personally, we tend to up the charge like. It's a perk of the trade. I would have a drink with Sandy now and again at the casino. The girl who used to run it was great with us, she never minded us working the tables for a few extra quid. She was Danny Foster's sister, so she had her creds like. The punters weren't averse either. But Eve Foster would know more, I think she had some kind of working relationship with Sandy. She was a fucker for making herself busy. Chasing the dollar, if you get my drift.'

Kate felt her heart stop in her chest. If Danny was being brought into this, then so would Patrick, and that meant, at some point, so would she. Pat might have swerved the owning of the properties, after all, that was a legal business transaction and he could easily argue the case of the sleeping partner. But if any of the other girls frequented the casino then he would have a problem explaining that away as a coincidence. It gave them something called association. He was now associated both with the houses and the females who worked from his premises.

But Kate knew, better than anyone, how a coincidence could get you hung, drawn and quartered by the British judicial system. People had been put away for a lot less, and for very serious amounts of time. Plus, where the fuck would all this leave her? She might be retired, but she still had a reputation to uphold, and without Pat in her life she had nothing but her part-time work. Without that, she knew she would never survive.

Annie was thinking along the same lines, only she was ashamed at the tiny jolt of pleasure she had garnered from this girl's thoughtless honesty. Annie had the grace to admit her failings and push them to the back of her very overcrowded mind. She was still harbouring a jealousy that was not only immature, childish even but, worse than that, she was also aware that without Kate and her experience they would never find this fucker in a million years.

Janette sensed the tension in the room and wondered if she had said something wrong. 'Look, Danny and his sister have nothing to do with all this, I was just trying to explain a point.'

It suddenly occurred to Janette that she might just have inadvertently put herself in grave danger, the Fosters were not a team to cross. Especially Eve. She could be a hard cow where the girls were concerned and Janette didn't fancy having her on her back because she had been loose-lipped.

Chapter Thirteen

Margaret Dole was waiting for Kate outside, in the car park. It was just getting dark, and a chill had settled in the air. It was one of those nights when the weather was finally letting up, and the rain was easing off for a while. Kate hoped it would keep up, she hated the bitter cold, especially when she had to work all hours. It could become depressing.

Kate inwardly sighed when she saw her, but forced a smile and said gaily, 'All right, Margaret, what can I do for you?'

Margaret gave a small grin showing slightly yellowing teeth. Like a lot of the force, she chain-smoked, it was part of the job and the no-smoking law would never change that. It had just turned the police station grounds into one large fucking ash-tray.

'It's more what I can do for you, actually.'

Kate was intrigued. 'So? Tell me.'

She settled herself against her car and waited patiently. Instinct told her this was going to be something interesting. Margaret was a lot of things, but she wasn't a fool, not by anyone's standards.

'Let's go somewhere and grab a coffee, shall we? Only,

what I want to talk to you about is best said away from prying eyes.'

Kate was even more intrigued by Margaret's words and her tone. Smiling archly, she answered her quietly, 'This sounds more like we need a drink, a real one. Any preferences?'

Patrick was not a happy camper. He missed Kate. That was the crux of his problem. He was out and about like a geriatric clubber, and it was starting to wear a bit thin. In fact, it was getting on his fucking nerves; the same faces, the same smells, the same old war stories he had heard a hundred times before. His liver was on the verge of packing its cases and going on holiday for a well-earned rest, and he had a rash on his old boy that was driving him to distraction. The doctor had told him he was suffering from a fungal infection and given him some cream. He was relieved that he had not caught something suspicious, and felt badly that he had assumed Eve had given him a round of applause, the clap. Pat had known in his heart that Eve had not been the culprit, but it was only now that he knew it was because of his new-found penchant for tight Speedo-type underwear that he was finally calm enough to see things rationally. But it was embarrasing in an old man like him.

Mainly though, as a realist, he had to tell himself the truth, no matter how painful. He wanted Kate back. He wanted the body that he had grown to know so well, the conversation that he enjoyed, her argumentativeness when challenged. He now appreciated that her need for a job had actually given him plenty of time to play golf and listen to his music. Pat missed the meals Kate cooked too, the glass of wine together at the end of the day, he missed the companionship. For all his annoyance that they didn't travel more, do more together, at this particular moment in time, he would accept her back on any terms.

So what the fuck was he going to do about Eve? Who, in fairness, also had her charms. He didn't want to hurt her, and he knew the situation with Danny could get a bit fraught, what with her being his sister and all, not that he really gave a monumental fuck about that. But he respected the boy, even more so now he had seen fit to sort out the O'Learys.

Pat was itching again, and he went into one of the downstairs bathrooms to apply more cream. The incongruousness of the situation hit him: he was well past retirement age, he had a rash on his dangler, and he was dreading the arrival of his young lady friend. It was time he took serious stock and sorted this whole fucking sorry mess out. What he needed, he decided, was to get his Kate back and get his old life back. He missed it, missed the normality, the knowledge that, even though he was getting older, it didn't matter so much when they were together. At the end of the day, Kate wasn't a spring chicken herself. His brush with a second youth was over, he had never particularly liked the first one. Now he had made his mind up, he felt easier. All he had to do was get a plan and put it into action. He opened the whisky and poured himself a drink.

First on the agenda, though, was getting shot of Eve. Something he felt was going to be easier said than done.

Chief Superintendent Lionel Dart was almost beside himself with glee. He had, at last, found something on Kate Burrows, or Patrick Kelly's tart, whatever you wanted to call her.

That he had to kowtow to Patrick was neither here nor there, he expected that, it went with the job. No self-respecting Chief Super would be anywhere in this world without the helping hand of the local bully boys. It was how the world worked. It was about scratching backs, making a decent wage, and ensuring the proper villains went to prison.

While Patrick had been trumping Kate, Lionel had been forced to stay his hand in the interests of keeping him happy. Something that most people seemed to realise was important very early on in their acquaintance with Pat.

But Kate, now *she* was another story. Lionel was honest enough to admit that it was her attitude to him that really rankled. Considering she was *living* with the man, how she could disapprove of his relationship with Patrick was beyond his comprehension. So what if he allowed himself a few perks? It wasn't entirely unheard of, he liked the finer things in life. He also liked the association, for the more obvious reasons. It held a certain cachet, while allowing him certain freedoms he might not otherwise have been party to.

Lionel was a petty man by nature. He was also a disappointed man, he knew he had sold out too early in his career and that was why he was finishing his days in a shithole like Grantley. He had thrown in his all and, like many before him, he had found out too late that personal fulfilment was the real deal. His life was all but wasted, and there was nothing he could do to change anything now. He had made his fucking bed, and the last thing he wanted to do was lie in it, especially with the woman he had married all those years ago. She made statements that would have raised the blood pressure of a deaf mute.

But now he was looking forward to putting Kate Burrows firmly in her place and although it was childish and petty, he didn't care. This, he felt, had been a long time coming.

Jemimah Dawes had always been a reckless individual, but the death of her friends had made her understand just how dangerous the life she was living actually was. Thanks to Miriam, she was seeing that there was a different path, a different way of life, that might not be so lucrative, but was definitely safer. Unencumbered with children, and without any real close family, she felt she had a good chance of making a fresh start.

In fact, thanks to Miriam and her contribution from her church fund, she was getting herself ready to make the change. Seven hundred quid wasn't exactly a fortune in these troubled times but, together with the money she had saved, it would help her afford a new start in any place she felt attracted to. Spain was one option. She could do bar work, or even, she smiled to herself, go back to her usual occupation, only this time without the added burden of a fucking twenty-four-carat nut-case on the horizon.

She had been the victim of a right strange cove herself, and a part of her wondered if he was the man responsible for the other girls' deaths. She knew he had been around for a long while, and that more than a few of the girls refused to deal with him. Unfortunately, there were always the girls who were willing to take the risk. It was because they felt that they deserved what they got, not that they would admit that, of course, but she had worked that one out a long time ago. Most of the girls in the game felt they were worthless, it happened to them gradually, over time.

She really wanted to change, she did. She just didn't see how she was supposed to survive on a tenth of her weekly earn. She liked clothes, having a nice place to live, and she liked the safety net that money gave her. She liked her current address, it had a proper intercom and it was quite smart. She had never made the mistake of entertaining at home, her neighbours all thought she worked as a croupier.

But Jemimah was genuinely nervous these days, and a new start was just what she needed. She had also upset a few of her so-called friends by omitting to tell them of calls they had received, then taking the client herself. So she knew she was living on borrowed time as far as the other girls were concerned, and she felt it would soon be necessary to vacate the town of Grantley and spread her charms in a different location entirely.

She had one last punter, a regular, the first and only one she would ever entertain in her own home, then Miriam was coming around to give her a speech and, hopefully, the dough she had promised. She would look at flights later on. There was no hurry.

Eve was getting ready for her date with Patrick. She was pleased with her choice of dress, it was a fitted black silk number that clung where it touched, yet didn't reveal anything you wouldn't want your nan to see. She knew it was sex on legs, and the black, strappy high heels gave it a definite thumbs up.

Patrick was a man she liked enormously, that he was older than her didn't bother her too much. He talked well, though he was a bit dated in his opinions at times, but then that was to be expected. He was also a man who could do wonders for her and her career. She wasn't averse to the fact that an association with Patrick Kelly was opening all sorts of doors for her.

Pat was a clever and thoughtful man and she knew that he realised that she genuinely cared for him and liked his company. She was also aware that she was a bit of a feather in his cap. There were not many men out there who would turn her down. She should know, she had turned down enough in her time. He also liked that she understood him and his businesses. Reading between the lines, Eve felt that Kate had been kept in the dark about a lot of his interests.

She applied another layer of red lip gloss; this dress needed the vamp look: red lips and eyes heavy with mascara. Luckily, it was a look that suited her. She had swept her hair up in a neat chignon and placed diamond studs in her prettily shaped ears.

As she surveyed herself in the full-length mirror she had to admit, without the least bit of bravado, that she was a very, very good-looking woman. She had always known that she would go far, and she had, further than even she had imagined. Though her brother was a big part of that, and she loved him for it.

But as she pondered her future as Patrick Kelly's amour, she felt the blood quicken in her veins. If she played her cards right, and she was an expert card player, she was looking at a whole new life. A lucrative, easy life that could afford her a position that would guarantee her a lifetime of respect. She knew that, by most people's standards, she was being crass. Thinking ahead, though, had always been one of Eve's strongest points and, coming from her background, it had also been something that had kept her from falling by the wayside, and gotten her to where she was today. She understood only too well how hard life could be if you didn't plan ahead, just look at all those poor fuckers who had never thought of their old age.

Well, she thought about it every day of her life. As Danny had once remarked, I don't mind getting old, I just don't want to be old *and* poor. Well, she didn't want to be poor, period. She had been there and done that. She always smiled at successful people pontificating on their humble origins. Funny, she always thought, how a few quid made poverty seem so fucking honourable and life-affirming. The truth was, poverty was shite, and anyone who disagreed with her needed serious psychiatric treatment.

Eve walked to the door. She had no underwear on beneath the dress, and the feel of the silk against her body as she walked was sensuous, she could hear the faint rustle that told her, and anyone that cared to know, that she was wearing in the region of three grand. Three grand was cheap at half the price, because she knew that this dress made her look like a million dollars. She was confident the effort wouldn't be wasted on Patrick, he liked the fact she had class.

She had to pop into the club, sort out a few things, and then get over to Patrick's house. Being a very progressive woman, she never took a swimming costume with her, preferring to swim naked knowing he was watching her, knowing he couldn't help but watch her. She had affected men like that all her life, and she loved the power it gave her over lesser women, lesser females. If you've got it, don't flaunt it until the right man comes along, then flaunt it for all it's worth. That was a sentiment Eve felt should be on a T-shirt.

Peter Bates looked sheepish, and Patrick felt the urge to laugh at him as he quietly came into the house. He looked like someone who wasn't sure whether or not to take off their shoes.

'Well, well, well. What brings you here? Good news, I hope?'

Peter grinned then. 'Fuck me, Pat, thought you was going Filth. All we need is a hello, hello, hello, and you could be Sherlock Holmes's little brother.'

Patrick laughed, despite himself. Peter was funny, there was *no* doubt about that. 'Sherlock Holmes wasn't a Filth, you fucking ingrate, he was a coke-headed fucking *amateur* detective. A bit like old Lionel from the Billery down the road. He likes a snort and he's a fucking amateur. Now, let's cut to the chase, have you got my fucking money?'

Patrick watched as his old mate sighed. He knew Peter of old and he knew he was now thinking on his feet, wondering how best to deliver the news. Pat loved Peter, but he wouldn't trust him further than he could throw him. He never had, which is why he knew far more about this skulduggery than was good for either of them.

'From what I can gather, Desmond should be surfacing somewhere along the Thames any day now. He was left to be found, if you get my drift. Knowing that ponce, he got stuck under a rock, which is something he should have thought about while he could still breathe. However, I digress. His old woman is not what you could call being cooperative, as such. In fact, I would go so far as to say that she is one stroppy cunt. Well, she is now a very frightened stroppy cunt. I hear young Danny went round there earlier today and she was left, how can I put it, wondering how best to extricate herself from the serious situation she has found herself in. Needless to say, her husband's disappearance hasn't bothered her as much as he might have liked. In fact, I think she sees that as a bonus of sorts. Knowing what we do now, we can, of course, appreciate her sentiments. Though, on the plus side, his bird is devastated by all accounts. So at least there is someone mourning his abrupt departure. I reckon his old woman will be playing by the rules tomorrow latest.'

'So what's the bad news?'

Peter grinned then, having expected Patrick to ask that very question.

'She wants more money than we are willing to give and she has booked herself on a flight to Israel tomorrow, and thinks we don't know about it. Fair enough. We all try it on, as you well know. However, I will point out to her that if she doesn't toe the line, she will be lying on the Mount of Olives with a stone ten times the size of Joseph of Arimathea's resting on her skinny corpse. As I said, we should get our poke by lunchtime tomorrow. She is a hard bird, and I quite liked that she tried it on, it shows spirit. What annoyed me was that she was mug enough to think that we would let her swan off with a serious wedge of stolen money. I mean, didn't she learn anything from her husband over the years? His demise should have alerted her to the danger involved in trying to scam off your mates. If she had not waited around for the insurance, the silly whore would have been home and dry.'

Patrick started to laugh, really laugh. Only Peter could stand there and take pity on someone for not getting the rip-off right.

Peter smiled then and said seriously, 'He's a good kid that Danny. I have to take me hat off to him, he has placated everyone involved, recouped the money, and no one has fallen out too much. If he wasn't such a handsome cunt I might actually start to like him. His sister ain't bad either, but then I'm sure I'm preaching to the converted here, ain't I?'

Patrick knew that a lot of Peter's talk was *because* he was seeing Eve. His association with her gave added weight to Danny Boy's position and he understood that. He would have thought exactly the same in Peter's position. It was another reason why he had to stop this liaison now, before it all went too far. Eve was a lovely girl, and he thought the world of her, but the tea break was over and he wanted to get back to normal as soon as possible. He only hoped that Kate was feeling the same as he was.

One thing Pat knew for sure, though. He had averted a great disaster. As much as he liked Desmond, and he *had* liked him, if he had got his hands on the ponce before the O'Learys, he wasn't sure he would have been so lenient. Some people just seemed to push it all too far, some people just never seemed to know when to call it a fucking day. The bottom line here, though, was that he had taken his eye off the ball. Well, that was not something he was going to be doing again in the future.

He had trusted Des with his life and, like Kate had always said, trust was great between couples, but in business it never hurt to take a gander at the books now and again on the QT.

She was a shrewdie was his Kate and, as much as she had annoyed him and, make no mistake, she had fucking nearly had him demented with fury, he knew in his heart that she was the only person he had ever really been able to trust one hundred per cent. Considering she was a Filth, that in itself was no mean feat. Anger was a strange thing, once it had burned itself out, all that was left, more often than not, was the truth. And the truth of all this was, he felt like a drowning man without her stabilising influence, without her level-headed approach to life. He knew he could tell her *anything* and she would stand by him, just so long as he took the time to *tell* her, just so long as she didn't find out before he had. Now that kind of trust was impossible to buy, and even harder to find in the world. Especially his world.

Pat poured two large brandies and passed one to Peter Bates, who knew then and there that he was almost forgiven. But only almost, it would take a while to get back the usual camaraderie. Peter was confident though that if he kept his head down and his arse up he would be completely forgiven. He learned his lessons well. He only hoped that he'd remember.

Annie and Kate were finally at home, and both were aware that they had to talk properly about what had occurred earlier in the day.

'I'm having a glass of wine, do you want one?'

Kate smiled gently. 'I think I need one, don't you?'

Annie's earlier flash of euphoria was long gone and she felt the flush of shame once more as she remembered it. She also knew that it was only human nature, that the best of people were capable of bad feelings. Today, she accepted, had not been her finest hour, but she consoled herself with the fact that at least she had been big enough to understand that.

'I think that Patrick will have some kind of explanation. Pat is not a fool, by anyone's standards. As for that girl, she wasn't exactly a fucking candidate for *Mastermind*, so don't start putting two and two together and making twelve.'

Kate gulped at her wine, grateful for Annie's attempt to make her feel better.

'You and I know that what she said is an association, and if Pat has an association between the flats and the girls, that's something that's worth exploring. As a policewoman *you* should be looking along those lines, even if I'm not.'

It was a challenge and they both knew it.

Annie shrugged. She saw that Kate was trying to be fair to her, was trying to tell her that she would understand if she decided to pursue those revelations further. Kate was trying to make it easier for her and she would always be grateful, she knew how hard this had to be for Kate. She also knew that, whatever happened, Kate could always be relied on to do the right thing, not necessarily the right thing for her personally, but the right thing nonetheless.

Annie refilled their wine glasses and lit a cigarette before replying. 'Look, mate, I think that what we heard today has no bearing on this case whatsoever, Patrick Kelly has something most men in his position don't have, and that's you. I know you well enough, Kate, to see that if you thought Pat knew anything worth knowing about this case we would be round his drum right now with a warrant and a serious amount of back-up. So my instincts, which you are always telling me to listen to, are telling me to forget what was said and get on with the job in hand. If anything else should arise then, of course, we'll have no choice but to investigate him. Until then, I am quite happy to let sleeping dogs lie.'

Kate was overcome with gratitude. She was angry with Pat, no doubt about that, but she had no desire to see him humiliated because of a young girl's careless talk. If anything, she would personally vouch for his behaviour in this respect. Kate knew that Pat would have nothing to do with the day-to-day running of the girls. That had Peter Bates stamped all over it.

'Don't feel you have to do anything for me, Annie. I wouldn't hold it against you in any way, shape or form. Remember that.'

Annie smiled then. A real smile, a genuine smile.

'To be honest, Kate, I think we need to put the past back where it belongs – in the past. We have enough to deal with without muddying the water with leads that will take us nowhere.'

'I'll drink to that.'

As they toasted each other the telephone rang. Annie went to answer it, something Kate was still having trouble getting used to. Although this was technically her house she had to remind herself that, to all intents and purposes, it was Annie's home now.

Kate could feel the tension as it seeped from her body, her relief was almost tangible. For all Patrick's faults, she didn't want to be the harbinger of his downfall. As much as she sometimes felt the urge to fell him to the ground with one almighty blow, she still cared enough to want him safe from harm. Especially harm that could easily be avoided if the people involved remembered that he was a Face all right, but not a scum-bag. He might sail close to the wind, but he had always made a point of being at least three people away from any actual proof of involvement. He was a lot of things, but not an idiot.

It still rankled though, the knowledge that he had replaced her so quickly. She wondered now if he had been secretly pleased she had walked out so fast. In the dark of night when sleep evaded her and the loneliness enveloped her, she wondered if she had just played right into his two-timing, double-crossing hands.

Kate knew she was at an age when her looks, while still apparent, were no longer enough to keep a partner by her side, but she had always thought, had always believed, that she and Pat were better than that. Apparently she had been wrong. No matter how much it hurt to know that you were no longer wanted by the person you loved above all else it didn't stop you caring about that person anyway. Deep feelings were never going to be banished overnight. Especially when those feelings were all you had known for so many years, you were frightened when you counted them up. He had been everything to her, and she had believed they were destined to spend the rest of their lives together.

Annie came back into the kitchen then, her face showing utter disbelief and her whole body alive with enthusiasm.

'You're not going to believe this, Kate. I'm not sure I believe it myself.'

Kate could hear the utter incredulity in Annie's voice and she felt the adrenaline rush through her at Annie's sudden fervour.

'What, Annie? Believe what?'

'Get your coat on and come with me! I think this could

be just the break we are looking for. You won't believe this, I can guarantee it!'

As they both rushed from the house, Kate thanked God for giving her something to take her mind off her own troubles, even though she knew it might be a high price to pay for peace of mind.

Chapter Fourteen

'This is Jemimah Dawes, I think you should listen to what she has to say.'

Miriam's voice wasn't loud, but she was being what Kate would call forthright. It was as if she was proving her worth to them all, and Kate knew she had good reason to feel as she did. None of the people at the station, police or civilian, had much time for her at all, and her husband had not fared any better. Like all holy Joes, they put people's backs up. They judged everyone by their own standards, as did most people in the world admittedly, except other people's standards were not so high. Miriam and her husband had set themselves up from day one. Praying and talking about faith were all well and good, but when it was a constant mantra to anyone who would listen, it became wearing. It wasn't that people didn't believe, it was just that they felt they should worship, or not worship, privately. Alec Salter had not been as bad as his wife, but he had been hard work nonetheless. A very ugly man, with a problem with hirsuteness, he was a real holy roller and he had been brought up in a children's home and had met Miriam there. No wonder he'd become a social worker and had run a halfway house before getting the job at Victim Support. They were a well-matched couple and, except for their determination to do good, they would have fitted in. Their holier-than-thou attitude succeeded in alienating everyone around them. Especially given that in a police station people see the worst of humanity on a daily basis.

Kate smiled at Miriam in a show of what she hoped was solidarity, with a hint of apology and more than a smidgeon of humble pie. Whatever it took to keep them all on an even keel.

Then Kate focused her attention on the girl as she smiled tentatively at them all. She looked what she was, and Kate saw Annie get out a notebook as they settled down on the well-upholstered sofa. In the background, Kate heard Miriam in the kitchen making them all tea.

It was late, but the girl looked chipper. Her make-up was perfect, her clothes were well pressed.

As Miriam walked back into the room, she said with authority, 'Young Jemimah is giving up the life and starting afresh. I have got her a grant to help her set herself up, keep her afloat until she finds gainful employment. I ascertained that she wants to make a fresh start in Spain, and I think that's best for her. Away from all she knows, Jemimah will hopefully find it in her heart to turn over a new leaf. I have given her a few numbers out there should she need further help. Now, young Jemimah was good friends with a couple of the girls who died. I have been counselling her about her grief and about the life she is currently leading, and she opened up to me about the darker side of her job. She told me about a man who attacked her one night and she felt lucky to come out of it unscathed. It turns out this same man also frightened a number of the other girls as well. I told her then that she needed to talk to you.'

Kate looked into Miriam's eyes, she was really trying to help them. As much as it galled her, Kate knew she had to do some serious grovelling in the near future and she was prepared for just that. She knew immediately that Annie Carr was feeling exactly the same. It was a sobering experience.

Miriam poured them tea, and even handed round a plate of digestives, and it felt almost surreal. Settling her huge bulk on a chair by the window, Miriam said gently, 'Go on, child, tell them what you told me.'

Jemimah cleared her throat. She was nervous of the police, but that was natural. She was also worried that if she said too much she would be expected to give evidence or something. She wasn't prepared to put her face or her name in the frame unless she had to.

'Look, before I say a word, I think you should know that I have no interest in becoming part of your investigation. I mean, not publicly anyway. I just want to help if I can.'

Annie smiled reassuringly. 'That's your prerogative, Jemimah, just tell us what you know.'

Jemimah took a deep breath. She *would* tell them the truth. After all, she'd be gone in a few days and if it helped, then that was all to the good. Plus, the bastard had hurt her, and she wanted to see him pay for it. If she had reported him herself she would have been laughed out of the Bill shop, no matter what these two might think to the contrary. Girls like her were still classed as Untouchables, especially where the male Filth were concerned.

'It was a Saturday night and I was working out of a flat in Merton Street. It's a nice location, quiet like, you know?'

Kate and Annie both nodded their agreement.

'Well, I had a call earlier on, at about six-thirty, from this bloke who called himself James. He arranged to come and see me at nine-thirty. Well, when he arrived, he was well on the drink. Not falling over, like, I don't mean he was pissed as such. But he was mean, if you can understand that. Some of the men are aggressive. Not all of them, in fact, the majority are nice as pie, but every now and then you'll get one that we refer to as a harmer. It's strange, but they are all alike. Not in looks but in their behaviour. They swagger in like the fucking dog's gonads and they always want a bit more than you are offering to give. They think they're entitled to do what they want because they're paying you. Well, he was like that. He smells, reeks of beer and cigarette smoke, and he is also unkempt in his personal appearance. He wears a suit and that, but it's seen better days. He also has a strange look about him, his features are off-synch. He looks like he's had a stroke or something. But it's not immediately noticeable, it takes a while before you realise what looks wrong.'

Jemimah picked up her tea and sipped it slowly. 'Well, he was all hyped up. Loud and crude. And I knew he was going to be trouble. We offer a drink to the men, you know, if they're nervous. He insisted on me getting him a vodka shot, and he also insisted that I get naked, sooner rather than later. I told him I wanted me money up front and he refused. Just refused down and out. He told me he would pay me if, and when, I had performed my duties to his satisfaction. Those were his exact words.'

She sipped at her tea again and, suddenly, talking about it to people who were actually interested, who cared, upset her and, for the first time in years, she cried. It occurred to her now, with the police and Miriam sitting there, that she really could have been killed. She could have been tortured and murdered. It was a sobering thought. Until now, she had not fully appreciated the danger she had actually been in. Her answer had been to run away, but then that was her answer to everything. It always had been. First from home, then from the care system, and she had done all right for herself up until now. But she had no intention of hanging around too long for these people to question her further; who knew, if he found out, he might come back and look for her.

'Miriam said that telling you would help other girls, and I agree with her. I think this man needs to be stopped. He has a vicious streak, he really enjoys the fear he creates. I was left with a badly bruised face and a cigarette burn to my arm.' Jemimah held her arm out to show them.

'How long ago was this?'

Jemimah thought seriously for a few moments. 'A few weeks ago. He got the number from the paper. We have adverts in there, you know, masseuses et cetera. But he's local, I know that much.'

'How do you know that?' Annie's voice was low, and she leaned forward in her chair to listen even more attentively.

'He used a cab service to get here, but he left on foot. Now, Merton Street is not somewhere you could find on your own, it's on the outskirts. But he left his wallet on the table and it was open. He had a Grantley Library card. He also had a Blockbuster membership card.'

Kate and Annie both knew that Jemimah had trounced his wallet. They also knew that it was likely being caught in the act had caused the trouble in the first place. It wouldn't be the first time a girl had found herself on the receiving end of a punter's anger over a near robbery.

'Did you get a last name?'

Jemimah shook her head. 'It was foreign, I can't remember it. I couldn't even pronounce it.'

Kate smiled ruefully. 'And you say some of the other girls were also victims?'

Jemimah nodded. 'A couple. I've just found out. None of us had mentioned it before. Stupid really, now I think about it. We don't do it often enough, talk about who is safe and who ain't. And even then, of course, you only talk to the girls you know. If he's done it to other girls, girls we don't know, strangers, then we wouldn't know about it.'

Kate nodded. 'Can you give me a description of him? Hair colour, style, that kind of thing?'

Jemimah nodded solemnly now. 'I'll never forget him, put it like that.'

Kate smiled at Lionel Dart, but she could feel the animosity coming off of him in waves.

'Bit early for you, Lionel, if you don't mind me saying.'

He hated that Kate Burrows called him Lionel, hated that she felt she was better than him even though he knew she had good reason for feeling that way. Well, he could finally mark her card and get her out of this station, once and for all. He smiled then, and she saw the tiny, pointed teeth of a predator. He *was* a predator, in every way. She was almost looking forward to this.

Kate sat down opposite Lionel without being invited, another thing she knew he didn't like. He was a bully and, like all bullies, he was basically a weak individual. She loathed him, and she knew that the feeling was mutual.

'So, what can I do for you, Lionel? I assume it's about the name and description Annie and I provided last night. We obviously want to keep this in-house, don't want the press getting wind of it. By the way, I think we should move the press even further away from the station house. Not only do they make it difficult for access, I also think that people are now nervous about coming here to be questioned and subsequently being caught by journalists or the TV cameras. What do you think?'

Lionel shrugged nonchalantly. 'I think, Kate, that you should consider taking yourself off this case, even though you are a consultant. After all, you are retired. And in any case, I'm going to bring in a new lead detective.' Lionel smiled, trying to look like a benevolent uncle.

Kate sat there, stony-faced.

'Not that we don't appreciate your expertise, or the valuable assistance you have always given this station and its regular policemen and women, Annie Carr in particular. But as it has now come to light that Patrick Kelly has too many connections with the women involved, I feel it's not really appropriate for you to be part of this investigation. As I'm sure you understand, the press could really make something of this, and it would dilute any lines of inquiry. Dare I say it, it could even shed doubt on to any arrest that might be procured.'

Kate smiled. It was a nasty, *I know something you don't* smile. 'God, Lionel, you do talk fucking shit at times.'

She lit a cigarette, ignoring the no-smoking policy and his outraged expression. She was pleased to see the fear now on his face. She pulled a plain buff envelope from her bag and she knew he could see his name, written in large black letters.

'You can't talk to me like that.'

Kate laughed then, a harsh, smoky laugh.

'Oh yes I can. Now you listen to me, you fucking moron. I know everything there is to know about you. I'm not with Pat any more, which makes you think you have the upper hand. But suppose I was to get a bit snidey, eh? I know about you too. I know where all the bodies are buried.'

Kate let her words sink in before saying, 'I also know that you were acquainted with at least two of the dead girls, thanks to Peter Bates. I understand that you got them free, gratis. How lucky are you? So as far as associations are concerned, I think we could reliably look in your direction, don't you? There has never been any reason to question *my* honesty or *my* integrity. Or have I got this all wrong? Only I wouldn't want to pass this lot on to your boss, a personal friend of mine, and Patrick's, come to that, as I am sure you know, if you think it's all lies.'

Lionel could feel the blood draining from his body, then he felt the heat envelop him at what she had just revealed. But Lionel Dart had always been a man who looked after number one, that had always been his priority over the years, and it was not about to change now. He hated this woman, but his ire would have to wait.

'Oh, and I can prove it, Lionel, I wouldn't be here if I couldn't. Now, you listen to me, boy, and you listen good. I was given this information by someone looking into the internet accounts. It seems to me, judging by the emails I have in this envelope, that you were discussed in graphic detail on more than one occasion. So, if I were you, I would think long and hard before you dare to give me any fucking ultimatums. I also think that you should make a point of keeping Patrick's name out of anything because, unlike me, he can be a vindictive bastard. I am holding your career, your pension, and a prison sentence in my hands, and I won't hesitate to use any of it. Neither will the young woman who uncovered it all. So do me a favour, *shut the fuck up*, and let us get on with the job in hand.'

Kate threw the envelope on the desk. 'Keep that for your own personal records, I have plenty of copies.'

Lionel stared at the envelope as if it had been hand-delivered to him by an alien.

'You're a ponce, as Patrick always said you were. A fucking parasite who thinks he's immune to everything around him. Well, you're not. You're a bully, a coward and, on top of that, you're a fucking joke, especially in this station house. Also, the body of your mate Desmond surfaced late last night, so, if you even attempt to get Pat involved with that, I will personally blow you out of the fucking water. All lines of inquiry will ultimately lead back to you, especially if I have anything to do with it. So, remember that, and remember that you have pushed me too far this time.'

Kate stood up then and, as she got to the door, she turned back and faced him. 'Now, move the press further away, they stopped photographing *you* ages ago, and make sure that Margaret Dole is assigned officially to this case with me and Annie. Unlike you, she has the makings of a good police officer.'

As Kate walked out the door she saw Annie waiting for her. They laughed loudly, aware that the arsehole, as Lionel Dart was unaffectionately called, could hear everything.

*

Patrick opened his eyes, it was past ten. He could hear the shower running, and he sighed in annoyance. By the time Eve had arrived, he had been half pissed, and he had also been almost incapable of any physical activity. She had cooked him an omelette and chatted to him until he passed out.

He could vaguely remember dragging himself up the stairs to bed and he had, in all honesty, not even realised she had been beside him. He secretly wondered if his behaviour might have put her off ever seeing him again. He soon realised how wrong he was.

She walked into the bedroom provocatively draped in a towel, she really was a good-looking girl. 'You look better today.' She was half smiling as she spoke.

'Well, I don't fucking feel it. Why don't you get yourself off home?'

Pat saw the hurt look on her face and felt bad at his words. But the last thing he needed with a marathon hangover was this young woman standing at the end of his bed looking like something from *Spanking Weekly*. She made him feel old, and she made him feel vulnerable. He didn't want to get up in front of her, didn't want her to see him in the harsh morning light.

'Look, love. I ain't at me best this time of the morning, and if you plus one that with a massive hangover, I think you might just understand how I'm not feeling the friendliest bloke on the planet at this moment in time.'

Eve smiled, and he was impressed at how easily she had recovered herself. She looked serene again, her usual enigmatic self. 'You look all right to me, Patrick. In fact, you look good enough to eat.'

It was not meant how it had come out, and Eve regretted

her words immediately. For the first time ever, she had lost her reserve, her cool. She genuinely liked this man, and not just because of what he could do for her. She respected him, cared for him, and it was the first time in her life where a man had made her feel she wanted something more than just a sexual liaison. She understood, though, that Patrick Kelly was not a man who would be wanting the same thing as her any time in the near future. She wondered how this had happened to her. She never let her guard down, what on earth had caused her to do it with this man?

'Look, Patrick . . .'

Pat held up his hand in a gesture of quietness. 'Nothing to say, darling. Now, if you don't mind, I want to get up.'

He watched sadly as her tight little ass wiggled its way back into the bathroom. He gave her serious Brownie points for her lack of anger, a lesser woman would have smashed him one by now, and he would not have blamed her. This girl had offered him herself, and he had knocked her back, just as well, all things considered. As he pulled on his dressing gown he felt dizzy, and he finally accepted that, once and for all, his days on the Rémy Martin were well and truly over.

He staggered downstairs and caught a glimpse of himself in the large Venetian mirror in his entrance hall. He looked old, old and debauched, in fact. He was not proud of himself, he saw himself for a fool, and an old fool at that. He knew that Kate would have swallowed eventually, all he had needed to do was tell her. What had really upset her was that he had not let her in on the big secret.

The phone rang and he picked it up angrily. 'What?'

'It's me, Pat.'

Hearing Kate's voice threw him for a few seconds. 'Hello, Kate.'

Kate could hear the uncertainty in his voice, and knew she was the last person he expected to be hearing from. The knowledge saddened her.

'It's just a quick call, Patrick. Desmond surfaced late last night. I've already smoothed it over with Lionel, no one will be asking you too much about it. It's over with. Finished and done.'

Pat knew how hard this call would be for Kate, and he knew how hard it would have been for her to go against the grain and help him out in a sticky situation like this one. The O'Learys would be eternally grateful as well, they would assume it was forgotten because of him. Naturally, he was willing to let them think just that. As always, Patrick was first and foremost a businessman.

'Thanks, Kate.'

Kate heard the affection in Pat's voice, and it was all too much for her. After not speaking to him for so long, hearing him now was getting to her. 'What are friends for?'

As he went to answer, Eve bounded down the stairs calling gaily, 'You got that coffee on yet?'

If Patrick had possessed a shotgun at that moment in time, he knew he would have aimed it at Eve and blown her away without a second's thought. Just to shut her up.

As Pat looked at the receiver in his hand, as he realised that Kate had rung off, he turned to Eve and said, 'Did no one ever teach you fucking manners? I was on the phone. I was talking to someone important.'

Eve was shocked, but also unsure what exactly she had done to warrant Pat's fury.

Patrick saw the stricken look on her lovely face and immediately felt ashamed of his outburst. He knew he was being rude, boorish, all the things he despised in lesser men. He put the phone down and, smiling sadly, he said with brutal honesty, 'Look, love, it's been great and all that, but I can't do this any more. You are *too* young, *too* energetic and far too fucking good-looking for the likes of me. And, if it's all right with you, I prefer to drink my coffee alone in the mornings.'

Eve was aware that she was being royally outed and the way he had done it annoyed her. Patrick's arrogance was legendary and she saw now why he was a legend in his own lunchtime.

'Look, Pat. You're a nice bloke, but a bit too long in the tooth for me, if truth be told. It was a bit of fun, and now it's over. I'm sure I'll recover from the devastating shock in a few hours. If you don't mind, you can shove your coffee right up your arse.'

As Eve clattered across the marble entrance hall Pat felt the urge to cry. Kate had done all that for him, and he knew just how hard it would have been for her to face Dart and his supercilious smile. And now she believed she had already been replaced in his affections. He knew he had to see her, and see her soon. She would probably blow him off like a nuclear missile, but at least he could try and explain the situation. He only hoped he could find the words to make her listen to him.

Jemimah was packing her bags, aware that she had done her bit for society, and also aware that she was actually considering giving up the life.

She'd listened to Miriam, who she knew was talking sense and was only trying to help her understand that, if she wasn't careful, one day this could be the cause of her own demise. Like Miriam said, she was a lovely-looking girl who *deserved* a home and a family. No one had ever said anything like that to her before, she'd always believed she wasn't good enough to want things like that. That she didn't deserve anything even remotely good, honest or clean.

Miriam told her about other girls she had helped with her husband, how they had been so proud of them and loved them like their own children. She'd explained that they had kept in contact with them to help them through the transition from working girls to working members of society. She explained that they loved that they were now all settled, some even in relationships as mothers and wives. Miriam reminded Jemimah that the girls in the life aged prematurely, and found it hard to fit in with the rest of society. She told her stories of girls dying of AIDS or being beaten once too often. She talked about how so many women often turned to drink and drugs to blot out the grind that had become their daily lives. From wanting to scam Miriam, Jemimah now felt she wanted to make her proud. When she got to Spain, she *was* going to turn over a new leaf.

She had given the police a detailed description of James, and she hoped they caught him. Whatever anyone else thought of the brasses and their way of life, they were still people and deserved to be treated with respect. Jemimah was humming when she packed her bag, she was going to have one last scam. The rent was due on this place in ten days' time, she was already a month behind, so she would knock them. That, she decided, was going to be her last crime.

Except that it wasn't a crime, was it? Not really. After all, whoever owned this gaff was rolling in it, and she needed as much money as she could get to start her new, legal and hopefully happy life on the Costa del Sol.

God bless Miriam. She was a strange old bat, but she had a heart of gold. And she had even managed to do something that no one else had ever managed to do before, talk some kind of sense into her thick head.

Kate was out of sorts, and Annie knew better than to question her about it, she would talk about it if, and when, she felt the urge.

Margaret Dole, in contrast, was like a dog with six lamp posts but as much as she irritated Annie, she had to admit that the girl was *trying* her hardest not to get on anyone's nerves. As they drove to Grantley Library, they were all tense. It seemed that the suspect James Delacroix spent a good deal of his day there. In fact, he spent all day, every day there. He was working on a book, according to the Chief Librarian and, from the tone of her voice, he was not someone she was enamoured of. She had described him as a rather colourful character, library-speak for headcase, by the sounds of it. She had promised to ring them if he left the building before they arrived. So far they had heard nothing from her, so he must still be there, doing whatever it was he did there, all day every day.

The library was a beautiful old building, it looked very much like an American courthouse, all columns and statues. The steps leading up were steep and Kate was gasping as she reached the top. 'If there's any chasing to be done, I think it had better be done by you two!'

273

They laughed, but they were all nervous. This man could be dangerous and they were about to confront him in what was, in effect, his comfort zone. Kate quickly scanned the road and surrounding buildings. The police presence was heavy, but very low-key. Inside were plenty of plain-clothes and she hoped that they had walked out as many civilians as possible.

As they entered the foyer, the Chief Librarian, a tall woman in her mid-thirties, beckoned them to follow her. Inside they walked to a large reading room on the second floor, and there she signalled towards James Delacroix. He was slumped in a chair, his feet on a desk, reading a copy of Edgar Allan Poe's 'The Raven'. He looked demented, even while relaxed, engrossed in the poem. Even his hair looked mad, shooting out in all directions where he obviously kept running his fingers through it. He needed a shave, and his heavy body was encased in a dirty suit that had the green shiny patches of wear and tear and rumpled look that said he slept in it. His shoes, Kate noticed, were as threadbare as the rest of him, the sole of one flopping down.

Kate and Margaret stood back as Annie approached him.
'James Delacroix?'

He turned then. He looked Annie up and down with interest, his eyes seemed to take in everything that was going on. He noticed Kate and Margaret and the uniformed officers at the doorway, and the librarian, who was watching it all with undisguised interest.

Then he placed his book on the desk, unfolded his body out of the chair and, bowing politely, said, 'Good afternoon, ladies. I have been expecting you. Are we going out to tea?'

Then all hell broke loose.

Book Three

Chains do not hold a marriage together. It is threads, hundreds of tiny threads which sew people together through the years. That's what makes a marriage last – more than passion or even sex!

Simone Signoret, 1921–85

Chapter Fifteen

'How come he's not on our radar?'

Margaret was amazed that James Delacroix was not in the system anywhere. He had gone berserk in the library and it had taken four uniforms to restrain him. He had then literally been dragged from the building, shouting to anyone who cared to listen about the police working for government agencies and trying to stop him from writing the truth. All he had against him were two minor offences, many years previously, for being drunk and disorderly as a teenager.

He was under the local psychiatric facility's care for schizophrenia. According to his doctor, he could go for weeks without any delusions. But when he had them he believed he was invincible and that there were dark forces at work trying to stop him from achieving his true potential. The government were extraterrestrials, and Steven Spielberg was working with them to take over the world. The doctor also explained that James's aggression would almost certainly be directed at the female gender, men seemed to intimidate him. His only living relative was a sister who wanted nothing to do with him and, as he seemed to find her presence as abhorrent as she found his, they didn't meet up unless by accident.

James Delacroix was very ill, anyone could see that, and Kate felt sorry for him having to live a life that was so blighted as to be no kind of life at all. Paranoia, what a dreadful affliction.

As Kate observed him pacing the interview room, counting the steps and then, after every eighth step, spinning around as if he was at a disco-dancing competition, her heart sank. This man wasn't organised enough to kill anybody. He would be hard pressed to sort out a bus journey. She wasn't ruling him out altogether, but her experience told her that whoever killed those girls had a very analytical mind.

They had planned the deaths down to the last detail and this man wasn't capable of that. He simply wasn't capable of something so well executed. James Delacroix wouldn't think of wiping the surfaces down and taking the evidence away with him. He might be faking it with this act, but Kate had the feeling that he wasn't. All her instincts told her that he was not the man they were searching for.

She stepped inside the room with Annie, and they sat opposite his chair, their actions relaxed and easy just as the doctor had recommended.

'Come and take a seat, James. We'd like to have a few words with you.'

James looked at them then, as if seeing them for the first time. 'I don't like you. You are both mean. Mean to James.'

They had been warned James often referred to himself in the third person, especially if he felt threatened. If he did commit the murders, there was no way he would ever get near a courtroom.

'Come and drink your tea, it's getting cold.'

'Don't like tea. Not your tea.'

Kate's voice was low, friendly. 'Would you prefer something else? Water, coffee, a Coke?'

As James watched them warily, Annie saw he was digging his nails into his palms, the blood visible on his hands. He was extremely agitated and seemed confused.

As they observed him, the door opened, and Miriam bustled in, her huge bulk almost taking over the room. She was followed by a small man in a cheap suit and carrying a vinyl briefcase.

'This is Mr Victor Blaine and he is here to represent Mr Delacroix.'

Miriam was very respectful, and Kate saw the compassion in her eyes for James. As she turned to leave he suddenly launched himself at her, almost rugby-tackling her to the ground. As big as she was, Miriam went down like a sack of spuds, taking the unfortunate Mr Blaine with her. Her head gave a loud crack as it hit the cement floor.

Pandemonium ensued.

Patrick and Danny were sitting in frosty silence in Patrick's office at home. They both wondered how they could start the conversation they knew needed to be had. After all, they needed to talk about this problem sooner rather than later.

'Look, Danny, I think we should get this out in the open. I treated Eve badly. I am ashamed of meself.'

'So you fucking should be.'

Patrick admired Danny for his anger, for the fact that he had not tried to pretend that nothing untoward had happened. That would be a coward's way out. Danny Foster was a lot of things, but a coward was not one of them.

'I made a mistake. I was trying to get over Kate and Eve . . . well, you know the effect Eve can have on men. To be honest, she reminded me of Kate. Strong, open, forthright. Then it all just got out of hand. I apologise, Danny, from the bottom of my heart. I never set out to hurt her.'

Danny saw the genuine sorrow in Patrick's eyes. In a way, he had guessed the truth. He had warned his sister not to get too involved. In fact, he had been surprised at her reaction to Patrick Kelly. He knew that, like him, she wanted to further her career, and Patrick Kelly would have been ideal in that respect. But he now knew that Eve had fallen for the man, hook, line and the proverbial sinker.

Danny sighed. 'You hurt her, Patrick, she deserved better.'

Patrick shrugged and held his arms out in a gesture of forgiveness. 'I know that better than you do. But she caught me off guard, and you know me by now. I don't mince my words when I'm cornered. If she had left last night none of this would have happened.'

Danny nodded slightly and Patrick breathed a mental sigh of relief. 'So, can we put this behind us?'

Danny nodded. There wasn't anything else he could do. He had the apology he craved and he knew that if he pushed it, their partnership was over. They shook hands and were both extremely glad that the episode was behind them. They were adult enough to draw a line under it now.

'So, you heard about Desmond then?'

Danny nodded and smiled at the glee in Patrick's voice. 'God pays back debts without fucking money. The O'Learys are over the moon.'

Patrick grinned. 'I bet they fucking are. Us Micks, for all

the jokes about us, are shrewder than the average person. My old mum always said that the Mick mentality, when used to its fullest extent, is the equivalent of a locomotive. It steams along and runs over anything in its path.'

Danny laughed, but he couldn't stop himself from thinking, *I'll tell my sister that.*

'Now then, Danny Boy. Down to business. When do I get my money back?'

Colin Charter was a heavily built man in his forties. He had a bald head, merry blue eyes, and the arms of a bodybuilder. Kate liked him at once.

'James has lived at Buxton House for about nine years. When the illness allows him to be, he is *very* intelligent. It's a shame really, without the disorder he could have made something of his life. If you look at him properly, full on, you can see where he was operated on. At nineteen, he took to his own face with a cut-throat razor.'

Colin waited for Kate to compose herself after that little bombshell but shrugged when he noticed that, unlike most people, she didn't wince.

'Go on.'

Colin sighed. 'I checked the list of dates the murders occurred on. James was here on all but one of them. He plays Monopoly for hours with another resident, Andrew Spark. They are obsessed with it, and argue all through the game.'

'Do you know where he was the other night?'

Colin nodded. 'Because he had refused his medication, something he does occasionally, he was in hospital, so that when he had his break with reality we were ready for him.

We can't make him take his medication if he chooses not to, we'd need to get him sectioned first.'

'Did you know he used prostitutes?'

Colin shrugged. 'He's over eighteen and we understand that he is a fully functioning male in that department. We can't stop him from doing anything unless it's dangerous.'

Kate understood that the doctor's hands were tied in many respects. 'It turned out to be very dangerous for the young women involved.'

He shrugged. 'We can't watch him twenty-four-seven, and he isn't currently sectioned.'

'Has he ever attacked anyone here before? Only today, he went on the rampage twice in three hours.'

Colin shook his huge head and said sadly, 'He is a paranoid schizophrenic. If you surround him at any point then I think we can safely say that he would attack. We know better than to do anything like that though. He was frightened, the voices were telling him God knows what. Like anyone who felt threatened, he attempted to defend himself. It's not rocket science. He won't wash because he believes there are drugs in the water that will sink into his skin and dissolve him from the inside out and he cut his face off because he thought he was someone else, he believed a stranger was taking over his body. Not just any stranger, an extraterrestrial stranger at that. So, no, he's never attacked any of us. But we are always prepared and we know how to deal with people with his condition.'

'Prepared, like the boy scouts?'

'More like the CIA and the FBI combined. But listen, Miss Burrows. James is not your guy. We'll review his care plan in the light of what you've told us though.'

'Thank you for your time.'

Colin nodded. 'You're welcome. I know this sounds strange, but he can be good company when he's on his best behaviour.'

Kate didn't answer him, she just didn't know what to say.

Annie and Margaret Dole sat in the canteen drinking coffee.

'She's a bit concussed, but she'll be all right, bless her.'

'Poor Miriam. I bet it was funny in a sick kind of way though!'

Annie grinned. 'It was. I mean she took that poor little solicitor down with her. She's a big girl.'

They laughed again at the image.

'He really looked good for it.'

Annie nodded. 'Kate didn't think so though. She said at the outset that he was too disorganised, too manic, and she was right.'

Margaret smiled slightly. 'She's *always* right from what I've heard.'

Annie knew she could take the comment in one of two ways. She could either agree with Margaret in a nice way, commenting on Kate's experience and years in the job. Or she could decide to be a bitch and remark on Kate being a know-all and hard to work with. Neither of which were true. It amazed Annie that she even had to think about which way she was going to go and proved that her jealousy was far deeper ingrained than she had realised. After everything they'd been through together, of late, and she *still* felt jealous?

'Look, Margaret. Take a tip from me. Kate was the one who got you on this gig because, to be totally honest, I didn't want you. You're a marler, and you need to develop a bit of loyalty. You can learn more from Kate Burrows in a few hours than you could from anyone else in the police force if you shadowed them for the rest of your career. So save the innuendo for someone else.'

Margaret's wide blue eyes were stretched to their utmost. She knew she had just made a really bad move, and she was desperate to cover it up.

'I was only joking around, Annie. I mean, come *on*.'

Annie stood up then and, smoothing down her trousers, she said nastily, 'If that's your idea of a joke, Margaret, I'd rethink me whole comedy standpoint if I was you.'

As Annie left the canteen, she knew that her reaction had been so vehement because she felt just like Margaret, and it galled her.

Jealousy was such a destructive emotion. Kate said that to her about eighteen months ago, when they attended a homicide to find three young children crying hysterically and their young mother stabbed to death by their own father. The father had believed that she was having an affair, a rumour that turned out to be totally false. Jealousy had destroyed five lives, and been the cause of one life being ended brutally and viciously. It had been Annie's first run-in with the aftermath of a jealousy-fuelled murder and she knew that it would not be her last.

The image of those poor children still haunted her. As did the images of those poor young working girls, tortured and dying in agony, not even able to make a sound.

Jealousy had nearly stopped Annie from doing her job to the best of her ability and getting justice for those girls. She knew they were *all* very lucky to have someone of Kate's stature on the case, as it were. So she determined to learn everything she could and maybe one day, some young up-and-coming murder detective would feel the same way about her. The thought made Annie smile.

But it still didn't make her feel any better. Whoever was out there, preying on these girls, was still at large. It was like he was invisible. Why did no one see him come or go? He had to have been seen by somebody at some point, surely? But, as Kate said, some people blended in so well they were like wallpaper, no one noticed them after a while. Well, this bloke had to make a mistake soon and, when he did, they would be waiting for him. As Kate said, sometimes you had to play the long game. Without any forensics or sightings they could only wait and hope. But knowing all that didn't make it any easier.

Kate saw Patrick's name flash up on her mobile phone screen and cut him off. She felt thoroughly satisfied by doing so.

As she steered the car into the hospital car park, she wondered what poor old Miriam had inadvertently done to be targeted by James Delacroix. She could only assume it was her sheer bulk. In the tiny room she must have looked even bigger than normal and with her wacky hair and open-toed sandals she could look very intimidating.

As she parked and walked up to the ward she made a point of not smiling, Kate wanted to look contrite and concerned for the woman's physical welfare. After all, Miriam had taken a major blow to her head. As Kate walked on to the ward she saw Miriam immediately, she was hard to miss, after all.

She approached Miriam's bed with a bunch of flowers and a box of chocolates purchased from a nearby petrol station.

'Is that you, Alec? Where have you been, dear? I've been waiting for hours.'

Kate felt a deep sorrow suddenly overwhelm her. This woman had lost the only person in the world who seemed to care for her. It occurred to her just how lonely Miriam must be. Neither she nor Alec had been what you would call popular. But for all that, they seemed happy enough with each other, it appeared that they didn't need anyone else.

'It's Kate, Miriam. Kate Burrows.'

Miriam's eyes cleared and she was once more lucid.

'Oh, Kate. How kind of you to come.'

She saw the flowers and chocolates Kate had laid on the bed, and her eyes filled up with tears.

'Are these for me? How kind of you to think of me in here when you have so much else to do.'

Miriam was visibly shaking with emotion and, instinctively, Kate put out her hand to grasp Miriam's. The gesture was interrupted by Miriam slowly and painfully pushing herself up in the bed. Sitting upright, the huge lump on the left-hand side of her head was clearly visible.

'You took quite a blow there.'

Miriam nodded. 'It hurts like hell. But I'll be out before the morning. Just a precaution, they said.'

'Well it's better to be safe . . .'

'. . . than sorry.' Miriam finished the sentence with her and they both laughed.

Kate was amazed at the difference in Miriam's demeanour. That crack on the head must have done her good. She was ashamed by her thoughts, but felt them just the same. Miriam was easier, light-hearted even. Kate wondered if it was because she had had a bit of attention, because someone had bothered to see if she was all right.

'Well, it's an old saying, but a true one.'

Kate smiled her agreement.

'How's that poor man?'

Kate filled her in on James Delacroix and his condition. Miriam tutted and shook her head sadly. 'They do a great job there, you know. People don't like having those kind of people on the streets, and I can understand that to an extent. But, at the end of the day, Kate, we all have to live somewhere, even those poor unfortunates.'

'I suppose so, Miriam. Not everyone is as generous-hearted as you though.'

Miriam sighed gently.

'Have you anyone to look out for you, when you get home?'

Miriam shook her head but replied gaily, 'Oh, I'll be fine, it'll take more than a knock on the head to stop me from doing my good works.'

Kate felt her heart sink, she had a feeling that the holy Joe part of Miriam was about to burst back on to the scene. Miriam seemed to read her mind. 'Why do people find religious belief so distasteful? Religion is the founding block for all the great civilisations of the world. I devote my life to the Bible because that is exactly what it tells you to do. If you live by it, you will be rewarded. Not here, not on earth, but in the afterlife. I just want to help people, Kate. That's all. People who have been written off by society for one reason or another.'

'And you *do* help people, Miriam. You are a good person.'

Miriam looked almost tearful again. 'I try to be, Kate.

Especially now my Alec has gone. It's been hard without him.'

'I'm sure it's been terrible for you, Miriam.'

'I still listen out for his key in the front door, I still expect him to walk in as if nothing bad had happened and he was still alive. He won't, I know that. It doesn't stop me from wanting it to happen though, does it?'

Kate sighed. She was humbled in the face of such abject sorrow and determined to be nicer in the future. It took all sorts and she, better than anybody, knew the truth of that old nugget.

'Well, ring me when you can leave, and I'll pick you up, OK?'

Miriam started to object but Kate waved her protestations away. 'I mean it. I'll leave my mobile number with the nurse on duty. She can ring me.'

'That's very kind of you, Kate. I appreciate it.'

'You're welcome, Miriam.'

As she made her escape, Kate felt the shame wash over her once more. Life was strange.

'I'm thinking of selling the lot. Do you want an in?'

Peter Bates was nonplussed for about ten seconds at Patrick's words.

'Are you having a laugh?'

Patrick shook his head, but he was laughing nonetheless. 'I am on a mission to get my Kate back. And this is the first step.'

Peter grinned lasciviously. 'I heard about your bunch of roses being kicked all over the club by Eve. She must have the right fucking hump with you.'

Patrick grinned in mock shame, pulling the corners of his mouth down and making him look like a naughty schoolboy.

'She has every right to have the right fucking hump with me. I treated the girl badly. But, joking aside, Pete, I miss Kate. We'd been together a long time, you know. I miss her being around, even though she can drive me up the wall.'

Peter knew just what he meant. 'I miss my old woman, but don't tell anyone. The kids fucking give me swerve, and that hurts, but then I hurt their mother, didn't I? It's true what they say, Patrick. Hindsight is a wonderful thing.'

'Don't I know it? I went past my Mandy's hairdressers the other day. Well, what would have been her salon anyway, had she lived. And it brought it home to me how fleeting happiness can be. One minute everything is wonderful and, within a few minutes, your life becomes an emotional fucking car wreck.'

Peter was chastened by his words. 'You've had more grief than most, Pat, no doubt about it.'

Patrick shrugged. 'Life is never fair, it doesn't matter who you are, how much money you've got. There's always some piece of shit determined to snatch it all away. I might have been a bit dodgy, but I always played fair by the people in my life.'

'Which is more than I can say, Pat. I tucked up all the people who cared about me, really cared about me. I chased the strange, and look where it got me.'

'I'll talk to the O'Learys, make sure that if you take up my offer they'll see you all right.'

'Are you really getting rid of it all?'

'Yes, and this time it's for good. Truth be told, Danny will run the legitimate businesses for me, and I'll retire properly this time. I just thought you might want the more lucrative parts, the businesses that could be open to interpretation, if you get my gist.'

Peter was touched at Pat's offer, and wondered how he could get the money together. He was an inveterate gambler and that often caused problems with his cash flow.

Patrick smiled, reading Peter's thoughts. 'You can pay me back over three years. I made a contract for you and, provided you keep to the scheduled payments, you're safe.' He passed a folder across the table to his old friend. 'I think the world of you, Peter, but if you attempt to tuck me up I will come after you like an Archangel, all batting of wings and serious vengeance. Your gambling is your affair, but you make sure that it doesn't interfere with my few bob. Only, I know what a slippery cunt you can be when the fancy takes you, you'd sell your own mother and buy a new one when the time was right. Now, that's only all well and good when it doesn't interfere with me or mine.'

Peter laughed then. He knew he was getting a serious warning off Patrick Kelly though and he also knew that it was only their lifelong friendship that had kept him alive on more than one occasion.

'I give you my word, Patrick. I needed something like this, a good earn, my *own* earn. That ponce I saddled meself with goes through money like a hot knife through butter. My ex still expects her wedge, and the kids want a lot, but who can blame them, eh? I treated them badly. But I swear you can trust me on this one, Patrick. You know me, mate, I can gather the money, I just can't keep me hands on it for any length of time.'

Patrick grinned again only this time there was not a hint

of his usual friendliness. 'As I said before, there's a contract. Keep to the payments, to the dates therein, and me and you will be tighter than a nun's crutch. But I tell you now, if you even fucking attempt to have me over, there will be consequences.'

Peter laughed out loud as the enormity of Patrick's generosity finally sank in. This was the break he had been looking for, it was the answer to all his prayers. He would be able to access the earnings in full, not just a cut. Not that his cut wasn't generous, but it still fell well short of everyone else's.

'No probs. I'll make sure you get paid out. Believe me, that will be my main priority.'

Patrick knew he had given this man the winning lottery ticket, but he also knew that Peter Bates was cunt enough to lose the fucker if he wasn't careful.

'And so it should be, but remember this much. I know you better than anyone else in the world. If you abuse my trust and friendship again I will personally see to it that neither you, nor your fucking outrageous taste in clothes, are ever seen again.'

'Sounds good to me, Pat.'

They shook on it then Patrick said happily, 'I never thought I would ever utter these words again, but do you fancy a glass of Rémy Martin?'

Peter laughed then, feeling the tension leave the room. 'Is the Pope a fucking Catholic?'

Laughing together, they toasted their new partnership. Patrick felt that Peter had learned a few valuable lessons over the years, the main one being never bite the hand that feeds you because, nine times out of ten, it would be in possession of a gun that defied ballistics.

Chapter Sixteen

Kate was tired out although she tried to stay awake in case the hospital called. She regretted her offer of a lift to poor Miriam, but she was determined to make good on it. She *did* feel sorry for the woman but, at the same time, she didn't feel the urge to be in her company unless it was deemed really necessary.

She knew that she was being unfair – Miriam was one of life's misfits and, as such, should be entitled to some kind of compassion. The trouble was, Kate only felt that compassion for short periods of time. It might be unjust, but that was how she felt about it all.

Annie had already turned in. After the emotions of the day – the excitement and then the disappointment they all felt – it seemed they all needed some well-deserved space from all that was going on.

It didn't help that Lionel had issued a press statement saying that they had apprehended the murderer. He was a fool of the first water, a fucking moron, but then he always had been, so why she was feeling surprised at this latest balls-up, she wasn't sure.

She had precisely ten missed calls from Patrick. Well, he could whistle 'Dixie' for all she cared now. When she had spoken to him before she could hear a hangover in his voice and she mentally shrugged. It looked like he needed a drink before he could trump Eve. Well she was welcome to him. He was a two-faced ponce, and that was something she would tell him to his face if she ever saw him again. The hurt was easing though. With all that was going on, it certainly put her own problems into perspective.

Kate opened her eyes and realised that she was on the verge of dropping off. She shook herself awake, then picked up the phone, called the hospital, and asked for Miriam's ward. She assumed as it was evening that Miriam was still there. She put the phone down five minutes later. Miriam had discharged herself and gone home earlier. She sank back on to the sofa and cursed her under her breath. However, she did hope she was OK, and considered calling her, but it was late and she knew Miriam would be an early-to-bed kind of girl. She would call her first thing, that was all she could do for now.

Pouring herself a large glass of wine, Kate meandered upstairs and settled herself into bed. But, as usual, she had trouble relaxing, and knew that she wouldn't sleep. Not properly, anyway. She seemed to spend her nights napping and waking at regular intervals. She missed Patrick's snoring, his weight on the other side of the bed but, most of all, she missed the warmth of knowing there was someone beside you.

In the restless early hours of the morning, her mind was filled with pictures of Pat and Eve together. Not just sexually, those images hurt enough, but them sitting and talking, eating together in the big kitchen she had helped to plan, taking a shower together. It was the mundane, everyday things that really hurt her, because she missed them so much. She missed *him* so much. Pat had taken the chance to get rid of her, he had even had her belongings packed up and sent to her former home. He had wanted shot of her, and she had never even *suspected* a thing. Some kind of detective she turned out to be.

Still, it was easier to think about Patrick's treachery than to keep seeing those dead girls in her head. But she did see them, every minute of the day. What was the connection between them all? Who was the person responsible? Did they choose the girls at random, or did they stalk them first? If it was random, they had next to no chance of finding him until he made a mistake and she didn't see that happening at any time in the near future. If he was stalking them, it stood to reason that someone, somewhere had to have noticed him, even if it was only for a split second. She determined to do yet another round of all the people connected to the murders. It was strange, but sometimes what you asked provided answers to questions that you had not even thought about asking. It sounded crazy, but it had worked for her before, and she was prepared to do it again. Life could be really shit at times. Kate gulped at the wine and resigned herself to another restless night.

Margaret Dole was going through the computer evidence once more. She had names and dates, which all pertained to the girls who had died. She kept staring at the screen, trying to find some kind of common denominator. That was how she had sussed out Lionel Dart, the filthy animal, but she couldn't see anything this time. There was nothing that could tie the girls together.

Margaret felt that she was missing something, and the feeling was so strong that she wondered if she was making it up. She was determined to prove herself, not only to Annie but to Kate too. She wanted to prove that she could be a vital member of the team. That was very important to her, especially after she had mugged herself off with Annie. She should have realised that loyalty was all they had, when everything was said and done. She should have realised that this wasn't a girlie night out, a meeting of friends, that these were her work colleagues, people she had to see on a daily basis for a long time. It was much better if they all got along and kept the back-biting to a minimum.

Margaret was still staring at the screen and her vision was beginning to blur, so she closed her eyes for a few moments to rest them. When she opened them she once more began scrolling through the different girls' appointments. She was convinced that if she looked hard enough she would find some kind of link.

Later, she poured herself another black coffee. She liked the station late at night, she worked better in the quiet. As she strolled back to her desk, she decided to pull all the dead girls' police files again.

Whoever this was didn't necessarily need to have known them as brasses, he might have known them all from school, a workplace, he might even have seen them in a shopping centre. Margaret knew, in her heart of hearts, that whoever this man was, he had picked on these specific girls for a reason though. She didn't know why she thought that, she just knew it was how she felt inside. As Kate said, work with your instinct, and all her instincts were telling her she was right.

Margaret rubbed her eyes and, after finishing the coffee, she started collating the details of the girls' lives together as best she could.

It was nine-fifteen in the morning and Kate was amazed Miriam was back at work already. The lump on her head had gone down significantly, but Kate was aware that close up, Miriam still had the dead eyes of a head-trauma victim.

'Are you sure you're well enough to be back here, Miriam?'

Miriam nodded her head quickly. 'I thought it best to get back to normal. As I always tell my clients, the best thing to do after a crisis is to get back to their routine as soon as possible. That way they won't have allowed the person responsible for their trauma to win. The sooner they start living their lives again, the better.'

Kate smiled. She certainly couldn't argue with that. 'By the way, did young Jemimah get off all right?'

Miriam nodded happily, her ruddy face almost beaming. 'She left me a text message last night, bless her. I hope she finds peace wherever she lands up. God is good you know, Kate. These days He just has a hard job getting the word out there!'

Kate smiled once more, unsure how to answer the woman.

'I'd like to take this opportunity, Kate, to thank you for your concern, it meant a great deal to me, much more than you could imagine.'

Kate was embarrassed at the woman's openness. 'Well,

Miriam, you're a part of this team, and we respect what you do. You are invaluable, really. Thanks to you, we can get on with our jobs without having to hold the hands of the relatives. It's very important what you do, and I think we don't appreciate you enough at times.'

Miriam swelled with pride at Kate's words.

'Well, it's always nice to be appreciated, and it's wonderful to know I have a good friend in you. I thought maybe we could have a spot of lunch next week, you know, catch up.'

Kate heard the words but did not really believe she had said them. She floundered, unable to think what to say to her.

'Or a coffee, a quick coffee? I understand how busy you are. It's just so we can get to know each other better. I think you were right, Kate, I need to get out more. Make another life for myself.'

Kate nodded her assent as her heart sank. Miriam grabbed her hand in hers and said girlishly, 'Poor James, I hope he's OK.'

'He'll be fine and, though it didn't work out, we can't tell you how grateful we are for your help. It was wonderful the way you got Jemimah to open up to us.'

Miriam was almost preening with the praise and Kate thought to herself how little it took to make people feel good about themselves.

'Well, Alec and I, we counselled a lot of the young street women over the years. The secret is gaining their trust. Like anyone, once you have that, the rest is easy. These girls are often brought up not to trust anyone, not to get too close. I think me and my Alec made them aware that they were worth something to someone. We were aware of how they felt, always having been classed as odd-bods ourselves, and we both understood how hard it is when people look down on you for no real reason.'

Kate felt awful once more at her words, because she knew they were true. 'Well, Miriam, I think what you did was wonderful. You tried to help us and we appreciate that more than you can imagine.'

Miriam shrugged then, and finally let go of her hand. 'I'd better be off, and I'll look forward to that coffee.'

Kate watched her as she walked away. That, she decided, was surreal. It was as if, overnight, she had just gained a new best friend, only it wasn't a cuddly little puppy, but a full-grown Rottweiler. She wondered at a loneliness so great that a tiny hand of kindness could make so much difference. She'd have to go for coffee with Miriam, after all, that's what the canteen was for.

Still, as Kate walked back to her office she felt immense dread wash over her. She had a terrible feeling that she was stuck with Miriam for life now. It wasn't a pleasant thought. She knew it was awful to dislike someone for no reason, but the truth was, she *did* dislike her, and she didn't really know why.

As she entered her office she saw Annie and Margaret deep in conversation, behind them were the white boards with all the relevant information regarding the dead girls. The pictures of them smiling, alive and happy, next to the photos of their corpses was as incongruous as it was tragic. At least Miriam had tried to help them, she had to give her that much.

Patrick was contemplating his removal of the businesses that Kate had had such a problem with. He knew he needed to get her back, and he wasn't quite sure how to go about it, but reckoned this would be a good start.

She refused to even talk to him, so the phone was out. He wouldn't show himself up by arriving at the station house, she was capable of fucking him off in broad daylight, and he couldn't go to her house because Annie Carr was lodging there. So he had to think carefully about how to proceed.

The phone on his desk rang and he picked it up.

'Oh my God! Why the fuck are you telling me?'

He slammed down the phone and felt the panic rising within him. Kate would have his balls for this latest fiasco. Picking up the phone again he dialled the number for Grantley Police Station. It was the only thing he could think of to do.

Kate and Annie arrived at Number Twelve Rossiter Crescent at eleven twenty-five. Kate saw the neighbours outside their houses, all rubber-necking and wondering what was up. The forensic team were already cordoning off the premises and setting up a perimeter. She knew it would be only minutes before the press and camera crews arrived.

Back at the station, Lionel Dart had done as she asked and moved them too far away for there to be any point in their hanging around. Only the newspaper journos with their telephoto lenses had remained, and even they looked decidedly dejected by the lack of photo opportunities.

As Kate walked inside the house she heard the first squeal of tyres that denoted the arrival of the press hounds.

Inside the house Kate was amazed at how luxurious it was. It was a big, detached place, and it looked like something from a magazine with all its over-stuffed furniture and fine art prints. She guessed that this was the higher end of the brothel market. The kitchen was state-of-the-art, and the only items in the huge, American-style fridge were champagne and vodka. She sighed heavily, the smell of caustic soda was making her eyes water.

She looked into the enormous, double-sized butler sinks and saw that one of them contained a skimpy La Perla bra and knickers set. They were hardly recognisable as they had been drenched in bleach and caustic soda, but the label was still just about readable, and she wondered at how much these girls were earning if they wore something that expensive to work.

Annie came down from upstairs and Kate turned to face her.

'Same MO. Paralysed, tortured and burned and then left on display. Only, this time he's changed his routine – she was suffocated with a plastic bag. He placed it over her head and, my guess is, he watched her suffocate. The torture this time was mainly on her genitalia though, for some reason, he cut off all her hair. Lovely hair too, long, naturally blond, thick and with a slight curl. If he hadn't scattered it around the room I might have been tempted to make meself a wig from it.'

Kate smiled. Annie was at last learning to distance herself from the dead girl with lame jokes. It seemed terrible to outsiders, but black humour helped put things in perspective for the people whose job it was to come and catalogue the lives of the deceased.

'It's a big place, I wonder why she was here alone?'

Annie held her arms out in a gesture of complete bewilderment. 'I think she lived here. And maybe yesterday was the cleaner's day off, which is why she wasn't found till today.'

Kate turned and walked from the kitchen. 'Come up and walk me through the crime scene, give me your first impressions.'

Annie followed.

Margaret Dole was proving herself a valuable asset, and both Annie and Kate were pleased with her. She was adding the dead girl's information to that of the other victims, trying to establish a common connection.

'Her name is, was, Valerie Kent and she also went under the name of Candy Cane. I would guess that explains the spanking equipment we found at the house. She lived there, on campus so to speak, and she was the sole occupant of the house when it was not in use. The last men she entertained paid by credit card, and they have viable alibis, nothing unusual there. Same as before. She was in and out of the care system, like most of the others, and she has a mother and two younger sisters who live in Liverpool. The mother remarried and left Valerie here in Grantley when she was eighteen. Mrs Dowse, as she now calls herself, is willing to claim the body. Other than that, we don't know jack-shit. No forensics, no nothing, basically.'

'You found anything yet? Anything to tie any of them together?' Annie asked.

Margaret shook her head. 'Not a thing, but I have a few ideas of my own I'd like to work on.'

Kate nodded. She was pleased that Margaret was willing to try other angles. Sometimes that was the only way to get a different perspective on a case.

'Good, you do that, and me and Kate will go back over the witness statements. Not that there's much to go on.'

Kate stood up. 'I'm going to talk to the neighbours again, see what they have to say a few hours after the initial shock has worn off. Do you want to come with me, Annie?'

Annie got up quickly, too quickly, Margaret thought. She was a bit like one of Pavlov's dogs, desperate to please her lord and master. She was sensible enough to keep that thought to herself, however. She had already rocked the boat once, she wasn't about to do anything that stupid again.

'I'll carry on with this, there has to be something, anything that these girls had in common.'

Kate nodded. 'Go for it, girl. After all, at the moment, we have fuck all to go on.'

'Do you think I should go back through medical records et cetera. I mean, I think we should look at any angle, no matter how off the wall.'

'I think that sounds feasible. Maybe they were treated by the same doctor, who the fuck knows?'

Annie was interested by the idea. 'Aren't medical records private though?'

Margaret grinned. 'Not to me, I can hack into anything.'

Kate smiled then. 'Really? Well, look at the case notes for the girls in care as well. Anything you can find, no matter how insignificant it may appear to be. But I don't need to know how you do it.'

'Will do. It might take me a while though, I warn you.'

Annie and Kate left the room, and Margaret turned back to her computer screen. She was excited now that she had the green light and, in her best Clint Eastwood voice, she said loudly, 'Are you feeling lucky?'

*

Danny was impressed, but he kept the feeling to himself. Patrick had given them the perfect out, and he liked that he had done it without any fuss or aggravation.

'Peter won't get the necessary poke, so I think you should go in with him. That way, you get a decent-sized stake for yourself, and a guaranteed earner for years to come. The properties themselves are worth a small fortune alone. Now, I think me being out of it all will enable you to take over in your own inimitable style. I've talked to the O'Learys, and they are quite happy to let Peter in the game, so long as there is someone there to watch their interests. They believe, like me, that you are more than capable of doing that, so what do you say?'

Danny was overwhelmed, and he let that show. 'Fucking hell, Patrick, this is fantastic.'

Patrick grinned. 'You might not think that a few months down the line when it hits you that you're watching over your own poke, not mine. But Peter Bates needs someone to temper his addiction to the gee-gees. He's a fucker for them, and once he gets in a card game, he couldn't leave if his life depended on it. When he ain't on the gamble, he's a diamond but, like all addictions, it's an illness. As long as you remember that, and don't let your guard down, for even five minutes, you'll be fine.'

'I don't know what to say, I'm fucking dumbstruck.'

'Say yes, and remember I have given him a contract to sort out the payments, I've got a copy for you. Keep your eye on it, and make sure he pays up. I'm not about to let a friendship get in the way of business.'

Pat said that in a joking manner, but Danny was clear that he was being deadly serious.

'Am I still working for you afterwards? Or is this like a severance thing?'

Patrick liked the way the boy thought, it was worthy of himself. That was what he appreciated about him.

'Do you think you could do both? I mean, do both the jobs well? Anyone can do two things at once, especially women, it's the childbirth thing I reckon, but really it's whether you think you can do both jobs properly.'

'I know I can, Pat.'

'Good lad, I had a feeling you'd say that. I want you to groom a number two, someone to take on the smaller businesses. That will leave you plenty of time to devote to the main issues. The main issue, of course, being the paying back of my money. Have you anyone in mind?'

Danny thought for a few seconds before saying, 'Would you object if I said Eve?'

Patrick was quiet, then asked, 'Why her?'

Danny shrugged nonchalantly. 'She's shrewd, she's good with people, she knows the game inside out and, most importantly of all, I trust her.'

Patrick grinned. 'Then you've answered your own question. I ain't got a problem with it. As long as she ain't coming here when we discuss anything, then that's fine by me. I know she's got her creds and she's got your trust. That means a lot to me, as I am sure you understand.' Pat smiled, a gentle smile that made him look almost benevolent. 'How is she, by the way?'

Danny laughed then, a real laugh. 'She was fucking fuming, Pat, but she's a realist, like us. As she said to me, no point flogging a dead horse. She was hurt, but she'll survive. The thing with Eve is that she's like me. We don't really open up to people that often. When we do, and it goes wrong, we feel exposed all over again. She's all right. A bit battered around the edges, but she'll be fine.'

Patrick didn't know what to say. 'She needs someone her own age, and so do you. Settle down, Danny. It can be a pain in the arse, it can be fucking irritating but, at the end of a long day, it's worth it all to know that there's someone waiting for you.'

'Like Kate, you mean?'

Patrick sighed heavily. 'She's the most awkward ponce in the world when the fancy takes her, but in all honesty I miss her. I tried not to, but it didn't work out. I filled my head with dreams of another family, kids even. But it's too late for that. I'd be dead before they started big school. I can't live without Kate. She's under my skin. Women can do that to you, you know. They burrow deep inside you and, before you know it, you're unable to function properly without them. Find yourself a decent bird, Danny, not one of the ones that hang around the clubs. They're all after the main chance. Find yourself a decent woman, and you'll not go far wrong, boy.'

Danny didn't know what to say, it was rare for Patrick to be so open, so honest. 'Do you regret not having any more kids, any family?'

Patrick thought long and hard before answering. 'Truth be told, I do. Without kids to work for, it all seems pointless at times. But, by the same token, you have to play the hand you are dealt and realise that just because you want something, doesn't mean it will change anything. Hindsight is a wonderful thing, remember that. I look in the mirror and I'm shocked at how old I am, but it happens so fast. One day you have years ahead of you, and then suddenly you realise that time has passed you by and you didn't even notice it. I would advise you to start taking stock now, because you really are only on this planet for a short time.'

Danny never thought he would ever feel sorry for a man like Patrick Kelly, but at this moment in time he genuinely did. He had buried a wife and a daughter, and he had lived through some horrendous events, even getting shot. Yet, for all that, he wasn't sorry for himself, wasn't constantly pissing and moaning at the hand life had dealt him. He got on with it, and Danny determined that he would do the same. Life, as they all knew, really was too short.

Chapter Seventeen

Once again, they had hit a dead end. They had interviewed everyone and followed every lead. No one had seen anything, no one knew anything. But the houses down at Rossiter Crescent were high end, they all had quite large driveways and the houses were not easily seen from the road. Peter Bates and Jennifer James were both being as helpful as possible, but it was obvious that they didn't know anything important. All they knew were names and dates and they had furnished the police with them quite happily.

Annie agreed with Kate that, if these murders were random, then whoever he was had the luck of the fucking Irish on his side because no one seemed to have noticed anything out of the ordinary.

Kate sighed heavily and rubbed her tired eyes. She looked a mess but she couldn't concentrate on anything. All she thought about were the dead girls.

If Patrick encroached on her thoughts, she pushed him away. Pat was an added problem she couldn't deal with just yet. She knew she still *loved* him, but she didn't *like* him very much right now and that was the issue.

She pushed him from her mind and concentrated once more on the pictures of poor Valerie Kent, or Candy Cane depending on how you knew her. The girl's face with the plastic bag over her head was horrifying. The bag had stuck to her skin and you could see the girl's perfect features, her high cheekbones. Valerie had been a beauty all right. That was why she would have been working the high end, of course. The real beauties were always marked out for the big money.

But judging by the girl's reading material she was also a brain-box. A lethal combination for a girl in her business. Kate had found books by everyone from Flaubert to Ibsen. She also liked the old classics, such as Aesop's Fables and Alexandre Dumas. It was odd to think of her doing what she did, with all those thoughts going around in her head. She could have really made something of herself, why the easy option? But people were odd, Kate knew that better than anybody.

And if she was on a night off, how did the man get inside the house? There was no sign of forced entry, no sign of a struggle. He had to be someone she trusted.

They had already sounded out Peter Bates, Jennifer James, and Danny Foster, along with all the other men who worked in the business. They each had airtight alibis, if not for all the murders, then at least for most of them. And this wasn't the work of a killing duo, a team kill, it had the hallmarks of a single man. A clever, calculating lone male who was sitting somewhere, right this minute, thinking about his next victim. If only she could read minds, how much easier her job would be.

Kate's mobile rang and Patrick's name flashed up. She cut

the call, but she was secretly pleased that he was still trying to contact her. She wondered what had happened with Eve, she hoped the girl had sacked him. That would not do much for his gigantic fucking ego. It would do him the world of good, in fact. He had far too high an opinion of himself. He always had done. The thought satisfied her for a few moments and then she went back to the proverbial drawing board and concentrated on the girls' faces, hoping against hope that something, anything, would start to make sense to her.

Peter Bates was not happy and he was as usual being very vocal about it.

'So he's actually going to end up with more than me, is that it?'

Patrick nodded, his smile still fixed in place. 'It's what the O'Learys want and, unfortunately for you, it's also what I want.'

Peter was shaking his head in despair. 'This is fucking outrageous, Patrick. A little fucking scummer like him having precedence over *me*? That's unheard of.'

Patrick was getting annoyed now, and Peter should have taken heed of that fact. 'Oh stop it, you fucking drama queen. If you weren't so enamoured of the fucking horses you might not be in this position. No one trusts you any more, Peter, you should have guessed that much by now. The flats and houses have been put under a difficult spotlight, and those poor girls should have been looked after. You knew CCTV was the best option but you vetoed it, and now we are all under the fucking microscope, because of you. So just swallow and keep a low profile for a while.

Danny is a good kid, and you get on with him well enough. Well enough to work with him anyway, though at this moment I can't imagine you spending Christmas together, but who cares? As long as you can sustain a working relationship, I can't see the problem.'

Peter Bates was disgusted at the turn of events and unwisely he let his ire show. 'I think you've tucked me up, Patrick. I think you and the O'Learys have rowed me out. I might have a flutter, but so do a lot of people . . .'

Patrick laughed, a loud, irritated laugh, then he bellowed, 'A *flutter*, a fucking *flutter*? You owe more money than Northern Rock, Peter. I'm trying to do you a favour here. I am trying to keep you on an even keel. You've got creditors coming out of your arse. You are up the proverbial creek, and I am trying to hand you a paddle. You're finished. Your reputation has been sunk lower than the *Mary Rose* for a long time. People keep you around because I still vouch for you. But listen to me, and listen good. When I start getting phone calls about your debts, there's a problem, Peter. Even you must understand that much. You're up to your fucking neck in it. I can't do any more than this. I am offering you a positive earn here. I want shot, and you and Danny need a good wage. You for the obvious reasons, and Danny because he is getting to that age. He needs to spread his wings a bit, and I trust him, which is more than I can say about you. If you throw this back in my boat I will disown you, and the next call I get saying you owe money, I'll give them the green light to personally sort it out with you. Once and for all.'

Peter slumped down in his chair. He could see that Patrick was only trying to help, but the humiliation was too much.

'I like the buzz, Pat, I like the fact that the horses might bring me untold rewards.'

Patrick waved a hand in front of his face to shut his friend up. 'No matter what you win, you always gamble it away. But that's your business, do what you want. I couldn't give a flying fuck. But the O'Learys won't be as amenable as me, so remember that and stop fucking trying to justify your bad behaviour. It's me you're talking to, I know you better than anyone.'

Peter was chastened. He was still very angry, only now he was angry at himself.

'I can't help it, Patrick, I love the thrill.'

Patrick sighed heavily. 'You're a fucking imbecile, Peter, a fucking earhole. But for all that, you're me mate and, for that reason alone, I want to see you sort yourself out.'

Peter was broken, and Patrick knew that as well as Peter did.

'Look, Pete, I need to get rid, and I am going to do that with you or without you. I want shot of the lot of it. I want to get my Kate back.'

Peter nodded, resigned now to his fate. 'She'll be back, Patrick, you and her were made for each other.'

'That's what I thought and all, and look where my double dealing got me. You were the first person I approached about all this, I gave you first refusal, then I made sure you had people around you who could guarantee you didn't fuck up. I can't do any more than that, Peter.'

Peter sighed heavily. 'I know that, Pat. I understand more than people think.'

'So we're back on track?'

Peter smiled faintly, the colour gradually returning to his face. ''Course we are. We're mates, aren't we?'

*

Jennifer was annoyed, really fucking angry. The last thing she needed today was to have to chase up the rent from some bloody lazy little mare too idle to bother paying her dues.

As she opened the front door of the block of flats, she shook out her umbrella. It was pissing down again, and she was drenched just coming from the warmth of her car to the front steps of the flats. She stepped into the foyer, leaving her umbrella in the lead-lighted porch.

This was a lovely property, and Jennifer had toyed with the idea of moving in herself. It was quiet and very pretty around this part of Grantley. It also had a low crime rate, there were never any teenagers hanging around, and burglary was almost unheard of.

She was annoyed that Jemimah had not even bothered to answer her calls. Well, she'd have to face her now, and she was going to tell her straight that she wanted her out. She had done her a right favour and all, letting her have this place. She was a right little piss-taker. She owed too much money now, and she was not going to pay it back unless she absolutely had to. That was the trouble with debt, people balked at paying what was due, they'd rather keep the money and spend it on something else.

Jemimah had been a good little earner, and she had initially paid her rent on time and without any moaning, a definite result in their world where trying to rip people off had become second nature. Then this was the upshot. Well, Jennifer wouldn't give her the chance to explain herself. She had given her all the chances she was going to get.

As she walked up to the first floor, Jennifer marvelled at the cleanliness and the quiet. She liked that about Cosett Court, it was built for privacy and comfort. She hammered on the front door, taking her frustration out on the ornamental knocker. When no one answered her, she called through the letterbox. She suspected Jemimah was inside, trying to avoid her. Well, she had better think again because Jennifer wasn't going anywhere without the rent and that was a fact of life. This girl needed a lesson, and she was going to get one, even if it meant she had to give her a well-deserved slap.

So, using the spare keys, she opened the front door and stepped into the hallway. It was clean and tidy, and she said a private prayer of thanks for that much anyway. At least the place wasn't trashed, it wouldn't be the first time that had happened. She called out Jemimah's name once more. Nothing, it was as quiet as the grave.

Jennifer's eyes were stinging and, for a few seconds, she wondered why that could be. There was an acrid smell, and it was making her cough. When she opened the bedroom door, she saw the cause of her discomfort. It was her hysterical screaming that brought the neighbours running, and the police not long after them.

'Unlike the others she's been dead a few days. This girl was already bloated and putrefying when she was found, that's because of the central heating. It was on, but timed, so this young girl was heated and then cooled down. I would say it's the same MO as the others.'

Kate nodded at the coroner and as she looked down on the destroyed face of young Jemimah Dawes, she wondered why she was not sunning herself in Spain. According to Miriam, she had already gone. According to Miriam, she had had a text message from her.

She looked around the apartment. The bags were all packed, so Jemimah was obviously going somewhere. This was Jemimah's home. She lived here, she didn't entertain here, there were none of the tell-tale signs. No answerphone, no laptop, no mobiles. Most of the girls had a work mobile and a private mobile and they logged on to their sites or shopped for things they hadn't earned the money for yet. This was odd.

The place was wiped clean, but she'd expected that much. Jemimah's body was now the second in three days, and Kate wondered if whoever was responsible had not expected her to be found so quickly.

She looked around her once more, there was nothing. Not even a cup on the draining board. It was pristine clean, and it was wrong. Jemimah had let her killer in, that much was obvious, even to the untrained eye. She had been packed and ready to go, her jacket was hanging by the front door. She was wearing street shoes, still high, but more like the kind an office worker would wear.

'I wonder if it could be a fake cabbie. I know we've already looked at the cab drivers in the area, but it would make sense. He could have a police radio, intercept the calls for a certain taxi rank, then turn up before the actual cab does?'

Kate was intrigued by this girl's death. It was the same as the others, but somehow very different.

'Get Margaret to look through the cab companies' computers, see if any of their drivers turned up somewhere and the fare had already been picked up.'

Annie nodded. It made sense. The girl had opened the door, as this particular door had a very expensive lock system, they knew it could not have been picked. Plus, on the inside of the door were two deadbolts. People who had that kind of security were rarely fool enough to let a stranger inside their home. Working girls were no fools, they knew the dangers of their job better than anyone.

James Delacroix came into her mind, but she dismissed him straightaway. But maybe there was another regular, one that the girls weren't afraid of. But then, they had interviewed so many of the girls' contemporaries, and none had ever said anything that rang any warning bells. All said the same thing, a few nutters, but that's why they worked the flats and the houses. They were safer there. This man had the girls' trust, and only certain people gained the trust of the brasses. Working girls were hard in many respects, immune to the usual daily banter and emotions. If they weren't that way inclined, then they couldn't do the job.

Kate looked around again. Maybe it was a policeman; after all, they were guaranteed admittance anywhere. But she had asked all the witnesses, on the quiet, if they had seen a uniform at any time and all had answered no. Lionel Dart sprang to mind. She half dismissed the notion, even as she knew she would have to actually question him about his association. He should know, better than anyone, that no one was above the law. She was quite looking forward to it, see how he felt to be on the hook for once.

'Jennifer, calm down. You did the right thing, you called me, and you called Peter. Kate will sort it out. Now, drink that brandy, you're in shock.'

Jennifer was white-faced and shaking, she looked every year of her age and then some. Patrick had never seen her look so terrified by anything before. And Jennifer was not easily frightened, she was as hard as nails. She had come up the hard way as well. Her mother had been a drunk, and her father had been an even bigger drunkard, if that was possible. She had dragged herself up and, to her way of thinking, she had made something of her life.

Pat knew the murders were gruesome, but ordinarily he would have had first-hand knowledge from Kate, and so he had not really understood just how macabre they actually were. It was his fault, he had not read about them because he didn't want to be upset by them. Not just because they were too awful to contemplate, or he didn't care. He cared deeply because he owned some of the properties where the girls were murdered. Though he knew that was just a coincidence, he still felt a level of responsibility. But his main reason for not wanting to know too much was because Kate was at the centre of it all. She would be pivotal in the investigation, and he knew she had every right to feel angry with him.

Jennifer held her hand over her mouth and bolted for the bathroom. He could hear her retching loudly, and poured her a glass of iced water. He had never seen Jennifer so rattled and, for the umpteenth time, he wondered how Kate did her job on a daily basis.

Margaret Dole was still trying to access files and information. It was a slow process because hacking into government databases was getting harder and harder. They were difficult to access, but not impossible. She was working on a computer that was still waiting for the latest in technological advances, and consequently it was a hard slog. She looked around her desk and picked up her coffee cup, only to find it empty.

She walked through the building to the canteen and, as she poured herself a large black coffee into a Styrofoam cup, she saw Miriam Salter sitting alone. She wondered, like a lot of the officers, whether she ever went home these days. She was still wearing the outlandish clothes she had been wearing two days previously and she was staring into space. She had taken a nasty blow to the head and Margaret wondered if this might be what ailed her.

As Margaret passed her table she asked gently, 'How are you, Miriam?'

Miriam broke out of her reverie and said happily, 'Why thank you for asking. I'm fine. Just thinking. Poor Jemimah, it's unbelievable that she's gone, poor child.'

Margaret sat down opposite her. 'I hear you were quite close to her.' She sounded sympathetic and concerned, and was amazed to find that she was.

'She was a lost cause. I really thought she had turned over a new leaf, she seemed desperate to get out of the life. I suspect she must have taken on one last punter for a bit more cash to take to Spain, and look what happened.'

It sounded feasible, it was something a girl like Jemimah would do, and Margaret nodded her agreement. 'Well, she picked the wrong one this time.'

Miriam shrugged, her heavy shoulders almost making contact with her ears. 'The trouble is, they think that what they look like is everything, that they are doing no harm to anyone, least of all themselves. They never stop to think of the families they help destroy, or the danger they might be in. It's all about them, and making money. They look all sweetness and light, but they aren't, Margaret. They're hard. Hard girls, and they think about no one but themselves. But I know that if they would just listen to their hearts they would see the error of their ways. Then they would see that they're living their lives in a vacuum, that they're not allowing themselves to reach their full potential. But it seems I have been wasting my time.'

There was a deep sadness in Miriam's voice that made Margaret feel, for the first time ever, a genuine liking for this strange woman. 'You tried, Miriam, which is more than most people do. You help lots of people, the victims of burglary, victims of rape and other violent crimes. You do a lot of good. It's like us lot, we can't solve every case. We wish we could, but there're always those that get away from you.'

Miriam nodded, and her wiry hair looked almost alive. 'Alec and I were kindred spirits and we really believed we had a vocation. But since I lost him, I wonder what I'm doing at times. It's so very hard. He always knew the best thing to do, always had the right words for whatever situation we found ourselves in. I miss him so much.'

'I'm sure you do, Miriam, but your faith is strong, isn't it?'

Miriam sighed, softer this time. 'Yes. My faith is still strong. But you see, Alec and I, we were a pair of misfits. I know that people stare at me, but I was born looking like this. I suffered my whole life because I wasn't like the other girls. Alec and me, we teamed up as kids and we looked out for each other. We both felt the power of religion, and of helping people less fortunate than ourselves. Since he's been gone, I don't know anything any more. I feel shaken, unable to deal with everyday life.'

'Well, I think you are coping marvellously, everyone does. My mum was the same after she lost my dad, she felt nothing was worth the bother any more. She didn't care whether she ate or washed. It's a natural part of the grieving process. This will pass, I promise you. It's only natural to feel out of sorts after losing someone so close to you.'

Miriam nodded, and wiped her eyes with a napkin. 'You should consider going into counselling, my dear. You'd make a wonderful, caring ear for someone who needed to talk about their feelings.'

Margaret smiled then, and grabbing Miriam's pudgy hand, she squeezed it gently. 'You'll be back to yourself in no time. Just remember, you've suffered a great shock, and you need time to let yourself adjust to that.'

Miriam nodded, and watched Margaret as she picked up her coffee and walked from the room. She really tried to be good, be kind, but it seemed that it had taken the death of her Alec to make the people in this station house even give her the time of day. Life was strange, but then people were strange. She knew that far better than anybody.

Patrick was watching *Sky News*. Jennifer was asleep in one of the spare rooms and he wanted to catch up on the latest developments. Especially since it was poor Jennifer who had found the girl. He knew it was selfish, but he was pleased she had come to him. That meant Kate would have to come here to talk to her. Jennifer had already been routinely questioned, but she'd been in no fit state to talk about anything of importance. So he was hoping that Kate would come to the house to question her further.

Pat felt almost excited at the thought of seeing her. At

their age, it was difficult. When you were young you were quite happy to make a prat of yourself. He would have turned up at her house and refused to leave until she agreed to speak to him, but those days were long gone, thank fuck, and he had a bit too much pride for those kinds of shenanigans. Not that he wouldn't use them, as a last resort of course, if he thought they would do any good.

He also knew that flowers would not be appreciated by Kate, she was not that kind of woman. She would see them for what they were, a beautiful bribe, nothing more. What he needed was a face to face, to explain everything to her in glorious technicolour. Right from his initial attempt to hide his ownership of the properties, to his insanity at trying to replace her with a younger model.

He saw the latter was going to be the hardest, and he understood that. He knew how he would feel if the boot was on the other foot. Unlike Kate though, he would have fronted his rival for her affections and taken the bastard's head off.

It suddenly occurred to him that Kate might be out on the razz herself, but he dismissed the idea almost immediately, she always put work first. But the thought frightened him, and he felt a sickness well up inside him at the thought that he might have lost her for good. She was proud, and she would know that his dalliance would be common knowledge amongst their friends and acquaintances.

Pat heard the crunch of gravel on the driveway and sighed with a mixture of fear and excitement. Kate knew the combination for the gates so he would sit here until he heard the doorbell, he didn't want to look too eager. He was shaking with nerves, and it made him feel like a schoolboy again. He felt the pull of the only woman who had ever made him feel whole. He didn't count his wife now, she was dead this longtime, and although his love was still there, it wasn't all-consuming any more. It was a good memory, but he didn't miss her now. Not like he did Kate. She was a physical need that festered inside him, and he couldn't seem to function properly without her beside him. And God Himself knew, he had tried. It was like eating or drinking, Kate was something that he needed to stay alive.

He stood up abruptly, she was taking her time coming to the door. As he walked out of his office, he saw a paving slab crash through the morning-room window. Picking up a baseball bat from his hall, he ran out of the front door. There he expected to find a crowd of men gathered by someone who obviously had a grudge against him.

Instead, he saw Eve standing there, dressed up to the nines, and wiping her hands free of dirt. Pat was shocked to the core. Eve had come across as a guarded person, a very serene, in control kind of personality. He realised that he had been wrong about her, very wrong indeed. She was a bit of a headcase, and he needed to get her calmed down and off his premises as soon as possible.

But unfortunately, Pat's anger and his fear of Kate arriving in the middle of it all set him off. 'What the fuck do you think you're doing?'

Eve laughed. 'What does it look like?'

She did not seem to be at all intimidated by him and that galled him somehow. It made him feel less of a man.

'Does your brother know you're here? Only I don't think he'll be too chuffed when he finds out about this, do you?'

'Fuck him, and fuck you, Pat.'

Pat was startled by her vehemence. 'Well, that's charming, I must say. I thought you were better than this. I thought you had a bit of self-respect, girl.'

She walked over to him and poked a long and very well-manicured finger in his face. 'I did, and I have. But you treated me like shit and no one, *no one* does that to me and gets away with it.'

He was ashamed then, she was so hurt, so upset. He had honestly never thought she cared about him so much. She was clearly devastated and, while his manly ego was loving it, after all, there was nothing like a young girl on your case to boost you up, make you feel good again, his sensible head was telling him he had treated her very badly. He had been a fool if he thought she was just going to walk away without a fight.

'Look, Eve, I'm sorry, love. I truly am sorry. I didn't expect this to happen, I didn't expect you to take it so seriously . . .'

'Blow it out of your old and sagging arse, Pat. Because I'm done here.'

With that, Eve walked back to her BMW convertible and screeched off the drive. He watched her drive away, relief at her departure overwhelming him. He was losing his touch, he would never have had her down as a fucking gooner. She had also shown him just how much dating had changed over the years. Come back, Kate, all is forgiven.

As he walked back into the house, Jennifer was standing there quietly, waiting for him in the entrance hall. She looked better after her sleep and she said to him sadly, 'Jesus, Patrick, you should have known better at your age.'

He pulled her into his arms and hugged her close. 'Don't

you think I might have already sussed that out for meself?'

She laughed, a laugh she didn't think she had in her, but it soon turned to tears, and she sobbed into his chest as he held her tightly.

Chapter Eighteen

Annie was impressed by Patrick's house, even the broken window didn't detract from its beauty. She had just seen a young woman in a BMW tearing off the drive, she assumed that was the lovely Eve. She also guessed from the look on Patrick's face that she had been the cause of the broken window.

But that aside, the house was breathtakingly beautiful, and the grounds were amazing with lawns like parkland and huge electric gates. She tried to imagine what it must be like for Kate, relegated back to her old home. Not that it wasn't a nice house but, in comparison with this place, it was almost a slum. She knew now why Kate never asked anyone from the station back here; it wasn't just because it was so luxurious, it was also because she knew the other person would feel out of their depth. That was Kate all over. She always thought about others before herself. But Annie knew Kate well enough to understand that this house and its trappings wouldn't make any difference to her feelings for Pat Kelly.

Annie had never in her life seen such a look of disappointment as she had glimpsed on Kelly's face when he realised that Kate wasn't with her. She felt sorry for him, he looked lost. As he waved her inside, he said gruffly, 'Where's Kate?'

Annie half smiled an apology as she said, 'Still at the station. She's hard at it.'

Patrick snorted in annoyance and embarrassment, he knew she had clocked Eve on her way in. 'Yeah, I bet she is. Jennifer's inside. Go easy on her, she's had a fright.' Pat pointed to a doorway to the left of the front door.

As she entered the large room, Annie noticed that Jennifer James was looking agitated and very nervous. She suddenly felt desperately sorry for her. Finding Jemimah's body would have been a terrible shock. She let her talk.

'It's strange, you know. The other girls, because I didn't see them, I didn't know what had happened to them first-hand. It didn't really register what they had gone through before they died. But seeing her like that . . . I had gone round there because she was late with the rent. The man who usually collects for me, Tom Prior, was umming and ahhing and I assumed she was paying him off in kind, if you get my drift. She wouldn't be the first one to do something like that. If I'd depended on him to go and see her, it would have been at least another few weeks before I got the money.'

The thought of the girl lying there like that for weeks on her own set Jennifer off again. She stood up and started to retch. She couldn't help herself, every time she thought of that damaged and tortured body, she wanted to vomit. It was as if the image had been burned into her mind and she knew she wouldn't ever again have a decent night's sleep because of it. She felt guilty, she was the one who had given the girls the opportunity to do the work they did. She saw the houses and the flats used by the girls as being somewhere safe, somewhere they could work in relative peace, without the eyes of the world on them. She'd felt she was helping them by giving them somewhere to work and to earn.

How wrong she had been and now, as she realised the consequences, she wanted just one thing. She wanted out, out of it all, and she wanted out sooner rather than later.

Suddenly Jennifer had had enough and she turned to Annie and said loudly, 'I *didn't* see anyone, I've already told you that. If I had, I would have said. For fuck's sake, I *want* to help you more than anything, can't you get that through your thick head?'

Annie sighed. 'Can I ask you something, Jennifer?'

Jennifer nodded, her voice filled with angry determination. ''Course you can. I want to help you, how many fucking times . . .'

'Have any of the girls ever said to you, however fleetingly, that they were spooked by a customer? Now, think hard, and think carefully. It doesn't matter how long ago they might have said it, just try and think about it for a while before you answer.'

Jennifer did as she was asked. She racked her brains for the merest hint that any of the girls had been frightened, then she shook her head in sadness. 'No, nothing. To be totally honest with you, the girls would be more likely to talk among themselves. And they would have told you anything they know because they want this man found, not just because he is killing their mates, but also because, until he is caught, none of them are safe.'

Annie knew she was telling her the truth.

Jennifer sipped at her glass of brandy once more and,

settling herself in the chair again, she said seriously, 'There's something you need to understand.'

She cleared her throat gently and took an alarmingly large gulp of brandy before continuing, 'A lot of these girls don't see pain like me or you would. Some of them were brought up in homes, in the care system, *whatever*. Their idea of pain is our idea of a living nightmare. They are used to being used and abused so, in some respects, this job gives them a bit of power. I know that sounds crazy, but it's true. For most of them it's the first time in their lives they have earned enough to live well, to live like the people they read about in magazines. They can dress nicely, they can eat what they like, and, for the first time, they answer to no one else. That's pretty heady stuff for a girl who has been pushed from pillar to post all her life. They've usually grown up lying, cheating and doing whatever they can to survive. They are a breed apart, love. Remember that, and you'll be all right.'

Terrence O'Leary was huge. He was a bodybuilder and he had a mass of curly red hair and an engaging, very expensive, smile. Kate had always liked him, even knowing what she did.

As she was shown into his office, she felt the full force of his personality. He walked around the desk and gave her a bear hug. He smelled clean, of Lifebuoy soap and mouthwash. 'Sit down, can I get you anything? A drink of some kind? Coffee, tea, water, a drop of the hard?'

Kate grinned. Terrence was impossible not to like. He was a naturally affable man, and his Cork accent gave people the impression he was a big softy, which he was, to family and close friends. But he was not a man to fall foul of. People who did tended to disappear, never to be seen again.

His answer to their whereabouts when questioned by police or his contemporaries was always the same. 'Sure how the feck would I know anything about your man? He's probably on his holidays.'

'I'll have a small Scotch if you've got one.'

Terrence was pleased. That meant he could have one as well. Ever the gentleman, he wouldn't drink in front of a lady unless she was drinking as well. It was those same good manners around the fairer sex that had got him into trouble with his wife on more than one occasion.

He poured one for them both. 'You're looking good, Kate. Are you back with Patrick yet? I heard you two fell out. I saw him the other night, he looks like shite, and I told him as well. He's missing you, girl, I know that much.'

Terry O'Leary could talk like that and not offend you. He always seemed so sincere and genuine that you didn't mind, it was one of the things Kate liked about him. She grinned. 'He can take a flying fuck as far as I am concerned. Now, Terry, I still work for the police, as you know. Purely in an advisory capacity.'

He nodded. 'So, what is this then, Katie? An *official* visit?' Terry's voice sounded incredulous, and Kate could understand that, he paid out a hefty wedge to make sure that official visits didn't happen to him very often.

Kate laughed, but Terrence's eyes had become harder, and she saw the real man sitting opposite her. 'Sort of. You own the house that Valerie Kent was working in. At least, you are *one* of the owners. I thought it best if I came and had a chat, unofficial, like? See what I mean?'

Terry visibly relaxed then refilled their glasses before saying warily, 'I might have an interest in the property, but I never went there myself. I've never stepped a foot over the threshold. All that having the bejesus knocked out of you isn't my cup of tea.'

He was smiling now and Kate knew that he appreciated that she had come here personally, that she hadn't sent a uniform or, worse still, a DC. Terrence O'Leary hated the police with an all-consuming passion, seeing them as trying to stop a man like himself from earning a living. Which, of course, is exactly what they *were* trying to do. It paid them to pay them, as Pat always said. It galled her, but she knew it was true. As Patrick said, it was all economics. The black economy was a valid part of the daily lives of most English people. If things were sold at the right price, without the humongous mark-up, people wouldn't get into debt and, ergo, the country could only prosper.

Pat believed that it was like the war, when people lived off the spivs. After all, the whole ethos of a consumer society was to *consume*. If people weren't *able* to consume because it was too expensive, you couldn't sell the product. If you can't sell the product, you have no market. Why outprice the man on the street? It was ludicrous to expect people to get into debt with credit cards or loans, why not sell them their goods at a reasonable price?

'Who ran the place? I promise this will be in the strictest confidence. All I want is someone who might be able to give me a heads-up on this fucking nutter. If the girls were available to talk to, that would be a great help. I give you my word, nothing more will come of this. But that girl was tortured and murdered, Terry, she deserves to be treated with respect.'

Terry digested her words for a while, and she knew that

his instinct was telling him to keep as far away from Old Bill as possible. She also knew that he was a fair man, and that he would want to see the man responsible for the girl's death locked up. He sighed heavily, as if he was not sure he was doing the right thing. Helping the police was not something he would ordinarily have done.

'OK, Kate. You can talk to Simone. She runs the place, and she is a nice woman. You'll like her. But I would only do this for you, no one else.'

It was a warning, he was telling her to keep the police at bay. Kate smiled, swallowed down her drink, then held her glass out for another. 'I understand that Lionel was a frequent visitor, is that true?'

Terry grinned once more. 'That old fucker? What have you got against him or, more to the point, what do you *want* over him?'

'He needs taking down a peg or two.'

'Well, I won't argue with that. But this sounds personal, very personal.'

'That's because it is. He has looked down on me for years because of Patrick and our life together. I had him bang to rights on the other girls, but the S&M just sounds so much more sordid.'

Terry laughed. 'That Patrick, he's a fecking eejit. Women like you, Kate, are what my old mother would call a keeper.'

Kate laughed then, really laughed. Then she said with heavy sarcasm, 'Yeah? Well, try telling him that.'

Terrence O'Leary was heart-sorry for her. He liked her a lot and he respected her, regardless of her chosen vocation. 'I have, Kate, on numerous occasions. He knows he's fucked up, big time. *Everyone* knows he's fucked up, big time. Even you being a *Filth* hasn't stopped people liking you. They know you're one of the good guys, you look for the *real* killers, the real murderers. That's something to be proud of. It's not like you ever stuck your beak into any of our businesses. And look at you now, you came here personally to save me from any embarrassment, and I will never forget a courtesy like that. But I'll tell you this now, old romantic that I am, he loves you. After his daughter's death, he needed someone, *really* needed someone to turn to. You and him are a great pair, he's a fucking eejit, but then I'm preaching to the converted, aren't I?'

Kate laughed again. 'When can I see Simone?'

Terrence smiled at her, understanding that he had stepped over the unwritten line. 'I'll have her available some time this afternoon, and I'll tell her to be truthful. Remember, Kate, this will never be a statement. She'll talk to you only as a friend. Is that fair enough? That's if she agrees to talk to you, of course. If she don't want to and refuses, that's her prerogative. I can't say fairer than that, can I?'

Kate nodded her acquiescence, there was nothing else she could do. Terrence O'Leary held all the cards and she knew that, unless he gave her the nod, Simone wouldn't talk to her parish priest, let alone the police. Even when the police was Pat Kelly's bird.

'Tell her it's no more than an informal chat, and ask her to be as open as possible. I give you my word that I'll keep her out of it as much as I can. I want a lead, no more and no less. I need someone to give me something useful. It's in all our interests to capture this fucker, not just mine, but yours as well.'

Terrence O'Leary nodded, he knew Kate was speaking the

truth. The sooner the cunt was apprehended, the better for all concerned. It would take the spotlight off them, so to speak. Kate always impressed him with her intelligence and her guts. She managed to straddle two stools, live within two worlds, and she did it all with aplomb. He decided to throw her an added bone. She deserved it, and he knew that she needed all the help she could down the gaff that passed as a police station.

'Going back to Lionel, the piece of shite. Kate, did you know he likes to be beaten with a hairbrush? He's right into the rough and tumble him. Jesus, even I was shocked at his antics. Now that's the truth, Katie love, as God is me witness. He's a fucking strange cove, if you get me meaning.'

They laughed together at the image of Lionel getting beaten with a hairbrush, it was a hilarious thought. The man was a fool, but worse than that, he was a dangerous fool. But Kate knew that Terrence O'Leary was giving her the bullets, and all she needed to do was fire them. It was strange that it took a known criminal to make her life so much easier. But then again, she had known all along that people were never what you thought they were, and that help often came from the strangest of places.

'I hear he likes to emulate strangling the young women as well. Old Lionel is not a man I would ever consider as a suitor for any of my daughters, but he's not capable of a real killing. He hasn't got the fucking balls of a gnat, if you get my drift, Kate.'

Oh, she got his drift all right. Lionel Dart was scum, absolute scum. But then, she had known that for years. He was her boss and, as such, he was supposed to be above all this kind of shit. It seemed to her that, in fact, he was actually using his position to pursue it. Scum rose to the surface, and she was determined to make sure that this piece of scum sank, that it disappeared once and for all. Lionel Dart was a predator, a man who used everyone around him to further his own agenda. He saw himself as above the people he was supposed to be hunting down and yet he took bribes and used those poor girls. All the while doing it without the slightest care for the people he might hurt or crush.

'I think the sooner I get that fucker aborted the better, don't you, Terrence?'

He smiled at Kate's anger. She wasn't a girl any more, but he could see what had attracted Pat Kelly. She had class, and that was something you were born with, no amount of money could fake it. He should know, he had tried hard enough over the years to emulate it.

Terrence picked up the phone on his desk and said quietly, 'Stay, Kate. I'll get Simone here within the hour.'

Margaret was still researching the dead girls' lives, and it made for fascinating reading. She was astonished at how they had been pushed from one care home to another. Did no one think that these girls needed stability, needed love and care?

As she read the girls' private files Margaret felt the sense of futility that she knew had to have become a part of their daily lives. They must have felt worthless. None of them would have known that they were entitled to so much more, were entitled to be treated as human beings.

She saw the same thing over and over again. They were written off at a young age and programmed to believe that *they* were the problem, not the people who were supposed to be taking care of them.

More than a few of the girls had run away on more than one occasion, had tried to make a better life for themselves. They had all been looking after themselves, basically since they could walk. They had been removed from their mothers' care, from their homes, at a very young age and had then been forced through the care system. At sixteen, they were turfed out on to the streets with a few quid and no real hope of a happy ending.

Did none of these girls' mothers care that they had children? That these same children would grow up one day, would become women in their own right? Did they feel no responsibility to their offspring? No affection or love?

Coming from a very good family, it occurred to Margaret Dole that she had, in effect, lived a charmed life. She understood now just how lucky she had been with her parents. They loved her. She had grown up surrounded by the love of her mother and father, and later she had fought against that love with all her being. She had felt they were holding her back somehow because they loved her *too* much. Now though, reading these files made her realise just how fortunate she really was. Holidays, good clothes, nice food, people who cared for her, had seemed the norm. She had never understood how other people's lives could be, how that might make them rebel, and rebel in the worst possible way. Abuse and violence had been a way of life for most of the girls, they had come out of the so-called care system and been ripe for the job that had finally killed them.

Margaret only wished she had known how fortunate she was a long time ago. Her parents had been absolute fucking diamonds, and she had not understood that until now. It had taken the deaths of these young women to make her understand just how lucky she had been. How lucky she still was. She had a saviour at the end of a phone line, she had a haven to go to whenever the world got too much for her. She had the opportunity to spread her wings knowing she had the back-up of two wonderful people who adored her, warts and all. Picking up the phone, Margaret dialled her parents' home number. Suddenly she felt a desperate need to make contact with them, to tell them how much she loved and cared for them. She had finally grown up, and it had taken these tragic deaths for her to achieve that. It was a sobering and troubling thought.

Annie had looked everywhere for Kate and she couldn't locate her. Her mobile was turned off, and Annie finally concluded that she obviously didn't want to be found. That was up to her. She guessed, rightly, that Kate was following a lead that was best left in the wind for the time being.

Annie had learned early on from Kate that, sometimes, you needed to talk to people who didn't really want to be interviewed. Consequently, their statements, such as they were, had to be corroborated by someone else. They just gave you the heads-up, it was up to you to make something concrete from it. She knew Kate was revered in the criminal underworld because she never used anyone, or asked anything of anyone that could put them in harm's way. Kate made sure that they knew whatever they said would be in complete confidence, that she would take what they had told her and make a truth from it without their names ever having been even mentioned.

Because Kate dealt with gruesome, senseless murders and child abuse cases, telling a Filth sometimes wasn't wrong in these circumstances. These people were bullies and liars, predators of children and the weak. These were people even the hardest criminals would see dead and buried before they had anything to do with them. They were the equivalent of drug dealers who sold to kids, the men who preyed on little children, and the scum that penetrated the vilest corners of society. Cowards who hid behind the scenes, who didn't have the guts to show themselves for what they really were. Kate knew that when she was looking for scum, even the hardest men were willing to give her a helping hand. They had families and they loved them with a vengeance.

Also, as Kate was the love of Pat Kelly's life, she was regarded as one of their own. Almost, but not quite. She was still a Filth, but a Filth to be not only tolerated, but respected. After all, she had the protection of Patrick Kelly, and that was worth fortunes in her world, and theirs. Kate knew her worth, and she used it to its full advantage. She had always trodden a fine line between the criminals she mixed with and the criminals she took a pride in apprehending. But it worked for everyone. She kept the *real* scum off the streets and they could ply their trades without her feeling the urge to go after them. It was a win-win situation for all concerned. Kate was one of the good guys, she made the streets safer for the average person while, at the same time, overlooking the skulduggery in front of her face.

As Annie waited for Kate to get in touch, she knew how lucky she was to have her on her side. Seeing Margaret's spite and jealousy had been a real learning curve for her. It had shown her how petty and childish she could be. She depended on Kate's experience to help her get on in her chosen profession, but she also accepted that Kate's reputation was distracting. It didn't matter how experienced she was, Kate would always be the one people listened to, respected. After all, she had, during her illustrious career, brought in not one, but *two* serial killers. That was something most people in her world could only dream about. Mainly because serial killers were actually few and far between. Films and books might make them seem commonplace but, in real life, they're rare. So rare as to be almost unheard of in most police stations around the country.

Sitting back in the chair, Annie hoped that Patrick and Kate resolved their differences, once and for all. Kate was always happier when Patrick Kelly was in the equation. Annie envied her the trust and the love she had had for so many years. She envied Kate's happiness. Kate had once said that the best thing that had ever happened to her was Patrick Kelly.

Lionel Dart was almost hyperventilating. Kate sitting there like an avenging angel was not something he felt comfortable with.

'We've been here before, haven't we, Lionel? Many times.' Kate's voice was pure venom, her dislike for him spewing from her like a fountain of hatred.

'It seems that you were a regular visitor of a young woman called Candy Cane. What a great name. But she was also known as, or aka as we say in the force, Valerie Kent. Now I know about your other peccadilloes, the hairbrush and the play-strangling. You like brasses but, unfortunately, they don't like you. They all say the same thing. They talk about your sexual dysfunction, your need to be used by them. Now, you got away with all this for a long time. I couldn't prove anything conclusively against you and, believe me, I tried.

But Candy's house is owned by Terrence O'Leary. This puts a completely different complexion on everything, as I am sure you understand. While Patrick is not what you would call entirely straight, he's straight enough. The O'Learys on the other hand . . .' Kate left the rest of the sentence unfinished.

Lionel was terrified. He knew that Kate would not be there without a good reason, without some kind of proof. He knew she hated him, and he also knew that she had good reason to. He had thought of himself as untouchable, but now he knew he was fucked, as he would put it.

Candy was his Achilles heel. He had recognised that from the moment she had taught him the meaning of sexual satisfaction. He had always known that if it came out, he was finished. But that it was Kate who had outed him was more than he could bear. He had accepted money and bribes over the years, and he would hold his hands up to that much, but he had also done a lot of good as well. He might have a weakness for young women, but what man *didn't*? Who didn't feel the urge for the fullness of a youthful breast and the firmness of a younger girl's body? What man was really happy with a wife who was scarred physically and mentally by the act of childbearing and who was uninterested in trying to explore the sexuality they were born with?

Was it any wonder men turned to strangers for their succour? Was it any wonder they didn't come home any more unless they absolutely had to? Why did people like Kate Burrows, a gangster's fucking moll, put themselves above the likes of him? Who gave her the right to fucking stand in judgement of him? He was a man, a man with needs, needs that were not going to be assuaged by his wife of thirty years.

He hated that he had been lumbered with a wife who was not only sexless, but who was also an imbecile. He had married a pretty, slimmish girl with a nice smile and a pleasing look about her and ended up with an overweight idiot who avoided him like the plague. But he was a man with a man's appetite. He had wanted to be loved, and he had wanted to feel the warmth of another human being close beside him. Personally, he couldn't see the harm in that.

'Are you listening to me, Lionel?'

He wasn't, but they were both aware of that fact. Kate saw the fear in his face and was glad. She knew she had to make this fucker walk. He was dangerous, he was a bully and, worst of all, he was a tyrant who preyed on the vulnerable and the weak. He bullied people who couldn't argue back because they depended on him for their livelihood, their jobs.

'I want you to take early retirement or whatever else rings your fucking bells. But your days of running this place while lining your own pockets are over. I can prove it. You have no interest in the girls who have died except to get your face in the paper or give a statement on *Sky News*. You're a fucking parasite, and I am determined to see you outed and gone from here sooner rather than later. You've got a week before I expose you for what you are.'

'You can't do this to me, Kate.'

Kate grinned. 'Can't I? You just watch me.'

Chapter Nineteen

Strangely, Kate hadn't felt any euphoria at Lionel's downfall, she just still felt the disgust that police like him engendered inside her. She *loathed* him, she always had. But still, she knew a scandal would not do anyone any favours, least of all the person who would be taking over his position. You always had to think ahead in her profession and try and protect your colleagues. Not because you agreed with what they had done, but because anything that tainted them eventually tainted everyone around them. It was like a disease that spread and infected everyone it came into contact with.

If Lionel's association with Candy Cane ever became common knowledge, the whole case would go down the toilet. Anyone she apprehended would have their lawyer arguing that it was a police fit-up, that they were protecting the real culprit.

Simone was in her early thirties and all lip gloss and well-cut hair. She came across as being open and friendly, but she was as hard as nails. She had to be, but she didn't look it yet, she was still young enough and new enough to the game, to keep the impression of youthful naivety.

'Thank you for seeing us.'

Annie's voice sounded friendly and approachable. Kate was pleased, she was really getting the persona right now. She used to talk to people like someone from *The Sweeney* and Kate knew from experience that that kind of behaviour only worked on a certain type of person. Generally, it was easier to chat and gain the trust of whoever you were interviewing, that way they tended to open up more. Kate had learned, early on, the power of respect, of treating people as an equal. With a suspect you could make them see that you had their number straight off. They were, in essence, fair game. But witnesses were a different ballgame. Even if you believed they could be the perpetrator, you couldn't treat them like dirt. So many young policemen and women didn't understand the game until it was too late. The law stated that a person was innocent until proven guilty and for Kate, that meant just that: until you could prove their guilt, you treated them like visiting royalty. Once you had the proof, of course, you were then within your rights to fucking slaughter them, left, right and centre. Kate had explained the process to Annie on more than one occasion and her nagging was finally paying off.

Simone was someone who could unwittingly give them the push they needed, but she had to be coaxed. She might not even realise that she had information that could be of relevance to them. If the person interviewing them was aggressive and intimidating, if that person came across as an avenging angel, anything of value was often lost. It was the minutiae, the little things that really mattered.

Unlike Annie, Kate could see through Simone's friendly demeanour. Annie, God love her, missed the hardness of her eyes and her natural distrust for the police. Kate knew that O'Leary would have primed her about what she could, and could not say. Kate understood that, and would work within those parameters. Simone would only tell them what was relevant, she would never tell them anything she thought could be used against her or, more importantly, the people she worked for.

Kate deliberately took over the conversation, doing it with a flourish that left no one in any doubt about who was in charge. 'Look, Simone, I've spoken to Terry, and I know he has already talked to you about this meeting. Well, I just want you to be clear that I have no interest in your daily grind, OK? I simply want to ask you a few questions about your clientele. I swear to you that we are not questioning you about your daily life. Your job is private and personal and I guaranteed Terry that. But you have to be honest with us. We're not making a statement of this, we are just interested in your take on the people who use your establishment.'

Simone didn't answer for long moments, and both Kate and Annie knew that she was wondering how to answer their queries without putting herself or her workforce in danger.

Annie Carr had enough sense to keep quiet at this point, she realised that it was in her interest to let Kate orchestrate the interview. She saw Simone weighing up her options, and she knew that if she sat back and kept out of it all, they would be rewarded.

Kate smiled. 'Just tell me if there were any punters you were chary of, anyone that you felt wasn't right. I know that you girls have a built-in shit detector, it's what keeps you from being hurt, and that's what I'm interested in now. We know about James Delacroix but over the last twelve months, has there been anyone else who gave you food for thought? Who you felt was dangerous? Was there anyone you had problems with, no matter how small or insignificant they might have been? We need to know.'

Simone started to relax, she felt more comfortable now. This wasn't a real interview by the Filth, all they wanted was an opinion and she was more than willing to give them that much at least. She wanted this fucker caught as much as they did. Probably more, if the truth were known. She had seen the fear that had spread through the working girls, saw the unease and distrust that had become even more a part of their daily lives. She knew that their fear was interfering with not just their work, but with their real lives, with the lives they lived with their families. It had taken its toll on them, they were all terrified that they might become the next victim.

Simone knew Kate Burrows by reputation and she knew the girls were pleased she was involved in the investigation because that meant they were being looked after by one of their own. She had tamed Patrick Kelly, and that in itself was kudos enough. She was still wary though, still felt the need for reticence. It was what had kept her safe all these years, it came naturally to her.

Kate said quietly, 'Is there anyone who came to the house that made you feel uneasy? Was there anyone who you felt was capable of hurting someone, and not in a kinky way. Really harming them? Someone you felt was wrong somehow? You'd be surprised how often a woman's intuition is proved correct.'

Simone sighed heavily. She was racking her brains for anyone she could think of who fitted their bill. But there wasn't anyone. She shook her head sadly. 'I'm sorry, but there is no one who springs to mind. I really want to tell you what you want to hear, but I can't. None of the girls have said anything along those lines about the men who currently frequent our establishment. And, believe me, they would be very vocal about something like that. They know the value of honesty when it's about safety. They aren't fools, they wouldn't compromise their safety for money. And in reality, we are at the *safest* end of the market. The men who come to us are actually completely honest about what floats their boat.'

Kate listened intently to Simone's words and she saw she was being truthful. She really was trying to be helpful. 'I understand that, but if that's the case, then what the fuck do you think happened to Candy Cane? Why her? Who killed her?'

Simone wasn't rattled, and Kate knew that wasn't because she didn't care, it was because she didn't want to show her feelings.

Simone shook her head in denial. 'I don't know. I don't even know who half her customers were. She entertained out of office hours, if you get my drift. She had her private customers and I don't know who they were. Why would I? She looked after the house, she lived there, rent-free. All I do know is that she should have been alone the night she died. No one was in the book. Whoever she let in, she let in without a second's thought. It was either a private regular or a newbie. Take your pick. But I can tell you now, categorically, that whoever killed her only got into the house because she trusted them.'

Kate looked at Simone. 'So what you're saying is that she knew the man who killed her?'

Simone nodded. 'Yeah. Maybe not as a customer at that house specifically, but they were someone she had seen before.'

Kate was disappointed, but she persevered. 'So you haven't seen anything that you would class as untoward with any of the other girls in the house? None of them getting a hard time from somebody, or being given preferential treatment? Let's face it, lunatics come in all shapes and sizes. He may even be someone the girls like, someone they would never guess could be so violent.'

Simone again thought long and hard about what she was being asked, but finally she shook her head. 'Nothing springs to mind, but I'll ask the girls, and if they can think of anything I'll let you know.'

Annie said evenly, 'Is there anyone who helps maintain the houses? Can you think of anyone the girls might have in common?' It was a long shot, but she thought it was worth a try.

Simone shrugged. 'Valerie was like a lot of the girls, she came out of the care system. A few of my Brookway House girls were even away together. Myself, I came from a home in Wales. My mother was a nut-bag, my brothers were out of control, and my father was a bully who didn't care who he punched as long as he could punch someone. We've all done the halfway houses and the social worker route. Is it any wonder we end up as outcasts? We've all felt like outcasts all our lives.'

Kate didn't know what to say. This was such an honest depiction of so many young people's lives. Was it any wonder that the papers were full of children murdering children? If they were brought up like animals, was it any wonder that they acted like them?

'Thanks for coming in, Simone. We'd appreciate it if you asked the girls to try and think of anyone they think might stand out from the crowd.'

Simone shrugged. 'With our clientele that might be asking a bit too much. They ain't exactly the norm.' She laughed quietly. 'Let's face it, if they were, they wouldn't be coming to the likes of us, would they?'

Kate smiled. As Simone left the room she looked at Annie and they both shook their heads in bafflement. They were no further in their quest to find the man responsible for the murder of so many young girls. It was as if he was a fucking ghost. He left nothing behind, not even a fractured memory.

Margaret Dole was looking at all the information she had found on the dead girls. All their lives were there, in black and white. She was staring at it all, willing it to give her some kind of a clue, desperate to be able to see something that might give the merest hint about the person responsible.

She'd placed all the girls' lives into numbered files. It seemed fitting somehow because that was exactly how they had been treated. They had always been at the mercy of the social services system. None of them had ever had the luxury of a caring family. None of them had been wanted. They were just a number in a file on a social worker's desk.

Margaret glanced at the clock on the wall opposite her desk. It was nearly midnight, and she stifled a yawn with the back of her hand. She had finally learned that these girls were not robbers or violent thugs, they were a product of their environment. Without their early lives, and without their childhood dependence on the welfare system, these girls would never have turned out this way, their lives would have taken a very different path.

She now understood Kate's attitude to these women. She now knew Kate was actually far more savvy than all the people around her, and that included herself. Kate had experience and, alongside that, she also had something she knew could only ever be earned. She had genuine respect, not just from her peers, but from the outside world. Margaret felt ashamed as she remembered that she had tried to mock her, had seen her as an old fool, when she should have been grateful to be taken on board in the first place. That she had forced Kate to make her a part of the team now rankled. She wished that Kate had *invited* her to be a part of it because she wanted her. That would have meant more to her than anything else in the world. But she had to live with the choices she had made, and she realised that now she had to make not only Kate, but also Annie, glad she was part of their team.

Margaret's psychology degree told her that this killer was dominant in their private life, but passive in their daily life. This was a person who people were easy with, a person who people felt they were safe with. He accessed people through this veneer of niceness. He was someone these girls would have believed was on their side. They would have never once suspected him of anything even remotely dangerous. It was this persona that had gained him easy access time and time again, even after the first murders. He came across as unthreatening, the people around him saw him as someone they could trust. As someone they thought was on their side.

As Margaret yawned once more, she heard the door open and saw Kate standing there with a slight smile on her face. Margaret knew Kate had not expected to see her there so late at night, and this hurt her. She wanted Kate to think she was willing to put in as many hours as she did. She'd learned that it was by working as part of a team that would eventually get them that arrest. It was now important to her to be classed as one of the gang, as someone worth listening to. For the first time in her life, Margaret Dole wanted to be a part of something, part of a team.

'You still here?'

She smiled and said softly, 'This is everything I could access on the dead girls, I've been able to hack into more sites than I originally thought possible. What I've done, Kate, is given them all a timeline. It charts the girls' lives through the information I've gathered on them from the databases. I was amazed by how easy it was to hack into their private records. It's as if they don't warrant any kind of real protection. Most of the files were not even encrypted. A child could have accessed them, it's laughable.'

Kate knew Margaret was trying to play down her role in the gathering of so much information, she already saw by the thickness of the files that this girl had left no stone unturned. She also sensed that something had happened to Margaret and it had caused her to see Kate in a completely new light. Kate had a feeling that this wasn't a bad thing. In fact, listening to the new, humble timbre to the girl's voice, it could only be a good thing.

Kate picked up the files and said with genuine amazement, 'It looks like you've really been working hard on this. Well done, Margaret.'

It was a genuine compliment, and it made Margaret feel that she really was being included.

'How did you get on with Simone?'

Kate shrugged nonchalantly. 'How do you think? She didn't have anything of any real use. She was as honest as she could be, given the circumstances. Like all those girls, she had to think twice before responding to the simplest of questions. It's strange, really, Margaret. As the years go on, you find yourself pre-empting them. You know the answers before you even ask the bloody questions. But she tried, she really wanted to tell us what we needed to hear. But I feel as if I've heard it all a hundred times.'

Kate went to a chair and opening her Burberry bag, she took out a half of Grant's whisky. She then emptied a Styrofoam coffee cup into the bin, and poured herself a generous measure.

Margaret had heard about Kate's legendary all-nighters with only a bottle of hard and all the evidence laid out in front of her. She was known for her absolute dedication to the job in hand. As she watched her scanning the papers and placing them in orderly piles on the empty desk by the window, she understood she was watching an expert at work. Kate instinctively knew what was important and what was worthless. Margaret watched her, enthralled. It was as if, after her speech, she had forgotten she was not alone.

Margaret sat back in her chair and wondered when this kind of innate knowledge would be hers. She knew that experience was the key word, Kate had honed her instincts through each and every different case.

Margaret had looked up all the newspaper coverage of Kate's career, had become engrossed in George Markham's story and the vicious murders he committed.

Margaret now wanted to be like Kate Burrows more than anything else in the world. She knew that it was the Kates of this world who, in their inimitable way, made the most difference. And she wanted to make a difference. She wanted to know that she was making the world safer for the average person.

Kate looked up from the desk and seemed surprised to see Margaret still there. Smiling widely, she said, 'Can I interest you in a drink?'

Margaret nodded happily, her heart filled with pride that she was finally being invited into Kate's world. She finally felt the warmth of Kate's attention to her and what she had achieved.

'Get yourself a cup, and then I want you to look up some things for me. Do you think you can get back into those databases?'

Margaret grinned. 'I can access anything. You just tell me what you want, and I'll get us in.'

Kate laughed. 'Oh to be a young woman again! Don't waste it, before you know it, girl, you'll be just like me.'

Margaret looked her straight in the eye, she had taken the words as a compliment. 'I can think of worse things to be.'

Kate poured herself another stiff drink and said sadly, 'No, you can't. You think you can, but take it from me, you really can't. I have a daughter on the other side of the world, and an empty bed. This is all I ever wanted, and now it's all I'll ever have. Life has a way of kicking you in the teeth, and it hurts, it really hurts. Remember that for the future when you find yourself sitting here day after day, night after night. When you suddenly realise that your whole life is peopled with the dead, the poor, or the missing. When you wake up one day and wonder why the fuck you even care, but for some bloody reason you do and, somehow, that seems to be enough.'

Margaret didn't answer her, she didn't know what to say.

Chapter Twenty

Annie listened to Margaret extolling Kate's virtues and hid her cynical smile. She understood the girl's excitement at seeing Kate at work, up close and personal. She knew that, like Margaret, she herself had only really understood the pull of detective work after seeing Kate's dedication. The men in the force made every step forward into a major event, they celebrated every little thing with a piss-up. Kate just got on with it, and it was her determination to get to the truth that made people sit up and take notice. Even in this enlightened day and age, the men still reacted like their counterparts from the sixties. It was like watching a rerun of *The Sweeney*, they just wore nicer clothes, and knew how to turn on a lap-top. But they basically had the same attitude.

Kate got her kudos from Kelly and his reputation. Like all Filth, the men here appreciated him as a genuine Face. They respected him for that, and they respected Kate because she had the sense to see what they saw. Margaret was still green enough to think that Kate had earned her reputation by herself – well, she wasn't about to disabuse her of that notion.

Instead she said, in as friendly a voice as she could muster, 'Kate knows what she's doing. I heard her arrive home in the early hours. She won't surface until lunchtime, and then she'll expect us to be as wide awake as she is.'

Margaret heard a note of reprimand in Annie's voice, it was as if she had somehow criticised her in some way. But she was still determined to make herself liked, make herself wanted, so she swallowed down her annoyance and said loudly, 'Have you heard about Lionel? He's taking early retirement.'

Annie nodded. She whispered, 'About fucking time and all, he's as bent as a fucking corkscrew. You do realise it was Kate who put the hard word on him, don't you?'

Margaret was stunned, not at the words and what they conveyed, but more by Annie's saying them to her in the first place. Annie was enjoying what she saw as the girl's first real sojourn into police force politics.

'He was a frequent flier by all accounts; he was Candy Cane's best customer.'

Annie saw Margaret's eyes open to their utmost, saw the shock and the disbelief on her lovely face. She assumed it was because Margaret had not heard the gossip. Annie couldn't resist the urge to taunt her and said nastily, 'Fucking hell, Margaret. Everyone knows about Lionel and his little peccadilloes, it's the joke of the station. He used to be first in line for the new WPCs at one point. He's never had a real fucking case, got a real collar, never arrested anyone of importance. He's a career Filth, he's climbed the ladder through arse-licking, combined with his association with the people he was *supposed* to be arresting. And yet he's only going now because Kate put the hard word on him.'

Even though she had known all about Lionel and indeed had secretly given Kate the information, Margaret was surprised at Annie's candour, and it showed. But she felt honoured that Annie felt she was important enough to say all this to, even though she knew about it all anyway. Police stations were like any other large establishment, they thrived on gossip and innuendo.

'Did Kate seem interested in your research?'

Margaret nodded. She was back on her own turf now. When it came to computers and such like she knew there was no one to beat her. No one here anyway. She had a real knack for searching in cyberspace. She had been computer literate from a girl, and she enjoyed the challenge. She was a natural-born hacker and she loved the feeling she got when she found out what she wanted to know. She had understood a long time ago that policing was now more about paperwork, than actually going out and finding the people necessary. She had unobtrusively taken over Kate and Annie's. Paperwork irritated them, but she liked to put it in order and enjoyed collating it all. Margaret was determined to become indispensable to them, and by doing that she knew she could truly earn her place in their team.

She decided to come clean. 'I couldn't resist it. I hacked into Lionel's bank accounts, he earns fuck all in comparison to his lifestyle. He is definitely getting a second income from somewhere.'

Annie grinned. This was more like it. The girl was learning, slowly but surely.

'Not exactly front page news, everyone guessed that years ago.'

Margaret didn't answer her.

'But by the same token, it's gratifying to have it all proved true. I hope whoever takes over from him is someone we can at least respect, if not like.'

Margaret had hoped that would be the case too, but she knew it wasn't to be. She had also hacked into the police database, she had been hacking into it for months. She knew that, sadly, the man who was to take over was as bad as Lionel Dart, if not worse. But she decided to keep that gem of wisdom to herself.

'Did you make any copies of the files you gave Kate?'

Margaret shook her head 'Most of the information was *hacked*. I hardly want that circulating around the station, do I? Kate can photocopy what she deems important. I'm sure she'll bring us both up to date on her thoughts when she judges it necessary.'

'Did you see anything of value?'

Margaret said truthfully, 'No, it was all basically the same thing. They were all in care and, at sixteen, they were dumped into a halfway house. Then they ended up dead through their involvement with brassing. It's as if they were enrolled in the school for the unwanted, the unneeded and the uncared for. I never realised how many kids are out there on their own, no one to claim them, no one for them to turn to. It puts Miriam and her old man into perspective, I mean, at least they cared. Which is more than I ever did. But I tell you something now, I'll take more interest in the future.'

Margaret looked sad and Annie knew exactly how she was feeling. She also knew that, once this case was over, she would forget all her good intentions, and do what they all did. Forget all about the girls and why she cared about them in the first place. It was the only way to survive in their job.

You had to concentrate on the task in hand, and emotion couldn't come into it. Otherwise you couldn't make any rational decisions. They made you vulnerable, and that was something you daren't feel in their game. You had to put your emotions away, and start afresh with each new case.

But Margaret would learn all that in her own time. Until then, she would leave her in blissful ignorance. Margaret had not yet encountered the young men and women who were so damaged they were capable of the most heinous crimes. She hadn't yet been threatened or attacked by someone who had no kind of real feelings. Who saw everyone around them as a mark, as somebody to either rob, blackmail or harm. She had only got herself put on this case because she was a computer whiz-kid.

Annie wondered how Margaret would fare on her own with the scum and the detritus they encountered on almost a daily basis. The wife-beaters, the child-molesters, all of them liars, all of them trying to justify their own failings. These were predators who saw a chance to make a few quid, and pounced on it without a second's thought. She had seen pensioners battered and children slaughtered, and she had seen the people responsible walk away because they had manufactured themselves a good sob story.

But she kept her own counsel. After all, she had once been like Margaret, and she had learned the hard way that life was not all it was cracked up to be. She was over thirty years old, and she was alone. She could see herself in Margaret. A younger, more eager self and now, with all that was going on, she was wondering where that girl had gone, and if she could ever get her back again.

Margaret didn't realise that Annie Carr was crying for

long moments but, when she finally noticed, she got up from her chair and placed a gentle arm across her shoulders. 'Hey, Annie. What's wrong?'

Margaret was frightened by Annie's tears and she didn't know what she was supposed to do. She didn't yet know that this was part and parcel of the job. Feeling completely useless, and wondering why you couldn't find the perpetrator of such a vicious crime eventually took its toll on you. Margaret didn't yet understand just how hard it was to try and come to terms with other people's hate, other people's viciousness. She hadn't experienced the sheer disgust that many of the people they had to get involved with would engender within her.

Annie was really sobbing now, and she turned her face into Margaret's outstretched arms and finally let her emotions get the better of her. Margaret held her tightly, wondering how this situation had come about. Of all the things she had expected from Annie Carr, this wasn't one of them.

Patrick was aware that Kate was doing what he would usually refer to as *stronging it*. She had not answered any of his calls, nor replied to any of the numerous messages he had left for her at the station house. He was getting pissed off.

As he opened the door to Terry O'Leary he was not his usual jovial self, and Terry noticed it straightaway. 'Patrick Kelly, you look like you lost a sawn-off and found a fucking cap gun. I take it Kate's still not talking to you.'

Patrick scowled, and that just made Terry laugh even more. 'Jaysus, Pat, have you seen yourself?'

Even Patrick had to laugh at his friend's incredulity.

'She's missing you, I saw it in her eyes. You two are like Bogart and Bacall; great together, shite on your own.'

Patrick opened the fridge and took out a bottle of white wine. As he poured out two glasses he said snidely, 'Fucking white wine, you're a right tart, do you know that?'

Terrence laughed good-naturedly. 'Less calories than beer, and I still get as drunk. It's a different world now. I don't do a full Irish breakfast every day, just on a Sunday after Mass, and I eat sensibly and drink in moderation. Short of getting shot by someone with a grudge, I reckon I'll live longer than most.'

Patrick handed him the glass of wine and, sipping his own, he swallowed the golden liquid appreciatively. 'Even I have developed a taste for this stuff. Now, what brings you here on a bright and frosty morning?'

O'Leary was suddenly all business. 'I have a proposition for you. Bates wants in, and that's fine by me. But what I want from you is an investment in my *new* business venture. I have the opportunity to purchase a rather large scrapyard in North London. Now, as I am rather well known these days, and therefore have to keep a low profile, I thought you might like first offer as partner. It's a guaranteed earner, and it's owned by two brothers who are, for some strange reason, *not* of the criminal persuasion. A friend of mine has convinced them that it would be in their best interests to unload said scrapyard at the going price to my good self. Now, this yard is ideal for us in that it's not on anyone's radar, not the Filth's, nor any rival families'. It has a lot of land with it that could be utilised by us in a variety of different ways and, best of all, it's a seriously legitimate business. In fact, I had a forensic accountant give the books a quick shufti, and he was hard-pressed to find a penny out of place.' Terry gulped at his wine before saying sagely, 'I mean, come on, Patrick, what kind of eejit runs a straight scrapyard? It's fucking outrageous. Why wouldn't you try and get an earn on the side?' He shook his red-haired head in consternation. 'Anyway. I think it's the real deal.'

Patrick grinned. 'Is it the McCartneys' place?'

Terrence was impressed and it showed. 'You fucker, how did you find out?'

'Danny Boy told me a few weeks back. He's a real ferret him, finds out everything. Not that I'm complaining, and you're right, there's a lot of potential there. Me and you are just the fellas to tap into it. What's the initial outlay?'

'A million each. The equipment alone is worth over a mill and, as the two brothers are happy to take a twofer, we can get the sale over within a month. I thought we could do a nice sideline in crushing motors. Obviously we would not really be crushing them, only the ones that are shite. I think it could be a front for misplaced prestige cars, Mercs, Porsches, and the like, that we can sling into containers and send overseas. It's a booming business, especially with all the cunts who have bought into the Dubai dream. Personally, I hate the place, it doesn't do anything for me. I think it's like Vegas but without the atmosphere.'

Patrick laughed loudly. 'Kate hated it there when we went out for Jimmy Doyle's sixtieth. It was too hot and completely charmless. You know like Italy, say, or even fucking *Glasgow*, there's a bit of culture, some nice buildings, decent architecture. There was nothing to actually go and *see* there. It was all too staged. All right for a few days, but I couldn't do more than a week there at a time.'

Terrence smiled. 'My old woman loves it. Shopping is all she does out there. Mind you, that's all she fucking does here. So, can I take it you're on board?'

Patrick nodded. 'Yeah. I'll buy in through one of my offshore companies, that way I won't be on any paperwork that's important. Danny will keep an eye out for me, he's a good kid. Now I'm unloading the flats and houses, I'll need something to keep me busy. Danny can do all the legwork, just ring him and he'll sort it. He understands the business too. He bought Dicky Bolton's place not so long ago.'

'You and him make a good team, Pat, he's a nice kid. Everyone speaks well of him. And he was useful when we had our recent difficulties.' Terrence held his glass out for a refill and, leaning casually against the kitchen sink, he said quietly, 'I hear the sister put your front window in?'

Patrick smiled ruefully. 'She did. And she was well within her rights. I treated her abysmally, and she is quite a feisty character, if you know what I mean.'

'So I hear. Is Kate back on the scene yet?'

Patrick sighed heavily. 'What do you think?'

'I saw her the other day and she more or less said she was making you sweat. She'll be back, Pat. You dropped a hefty old bollock, but we've all done it. You two are like me and my old woman, you fight, you fuck, you make up, and you fight again. It's nature's way of keeping you on your toes.'

Patrick grinned, and Terry could see the lines that were accumulating around his eyes, that he was getting on in years. He still looked in great shape, but he had the looseness of skin that said you were getting past your sell-by date. It was strange seeing Pat like that, he always thought of him as being in his prime. It was something he was noticing a lot recently, the ageing of his friends. He hated that he himself was spreading, that he couldn't run any more. He hated that he was breathless at times, and that he felt tired out halfway through the day. It was funny, you spent all your life making money, but when you finally cracked it, you were too old to enjoy it.

Terry watched as Pat opened another bottle of wine, and he waited for him to refill the glasses. 'Here, Pat, could I ask you a favour?'

Patrick nodded affably. ''Course. What is it?'

'Do you think you could get Kate to talk to that ugly bird from Victim Support? Only she's turning up all over houses and flats in Grantley. The girls like her, but I think she might see a bit too much of what goes on. Giving them Bibles and having a chat is one thing, but not on my clock. Two girls have fucking left over her, said they wanted a different life.'

'Well, you can't blame them for that.'

'I know, but not only is she making a dent in my earn, she's also seeing too much of what goes on. Some of those girls entertain the local dignitaries.'

Patrick laughed again. 'What, like Lionel, the dirty old fucker?'

'And the Mayor, the little fat fuck. He gets his goolies slapped with the Chief Planning Officer from the council, that's how I got planning permission for that block of flats in town. But, that aside, she's a weird old bird and I want her to start conducting her business off my premises.'

Patrick nodded. 'It'll give me an excuse to talk to Kate, she'll know what to do.'

'She'd better, because if she doesn't give her the soft

word, I am going to get Simone to turf her out with a flea in her ear.' Terrence shook his head sagely. 'Fucking Bible bashers, no good ever comes from those kinds of people. I go to Mass, I take me penance every few months, I don't try and ram it down anyone's throat. Once me mum pops off, I'll leave all that to the wife and kids. But it's strange the way the girls act towards her. Simone reckons they like her because she makes them feel good about themselves. Fucking birds, eh? Beyond understanding.'

Patrick laughed loudly. He loved Terrence O'Leary. Not only was he one funny man, he was also as shrewd as a gaggle of barristers. He knew the law to the letter, and he listened closely to everything being said around him without ever giving away his thoughts. Patrick wondered briefly what was actually going on in the houses and flats that worried Terry so much but pushed the thought from his mind. Terry had his reasons and concerns and that was his affair. He clearly lived by the old code: people only know what you tell them.

Kate was still perusing the files that had been provided by Margaret. She was impressed at the girl's acumen. She hated computers herself, but she understood that they were a part of daily life now. Even Patrick played online poker when he couldn't sleep.

As she read about the girls' early lives, and about the problems they had encountered, she felt a deep sorrow. These girls had once been newly born babies. They had been brought into the world, and then basically left to fend for themselves. Some women had a lot to answer for where their children were concerned. Kate saw it so much more now, a generation that had grown up wanting everything, but not wanting to work for it. Celebrity was the new religion, and it caused just as much trouble as the old ones.

Kate had now looked over the files for so long that her eyes hurt, and she knew she needed a caffeine hit. There was something there, she just had to find it. To make the connection. Getting up, she heard her mobile ring, and she answered it quickly assuming it was Annie telling her to get home and get some sleep. It was after eleven thirty, and she was beat.

'Kate?'

It was Patrick's voice and, like a young girl on her first date, she felt the flutter of butterflies in her stomach. All her anger was gone now, she just felt raw emotion. He had always affected her like that. From their first meeting she had wanted him, and that had never diminished.

'What do you want?' Her voice was low and she heard the catch in it. She knew he would be waiting for her to speak first. She stayed quiet. This was his chance to make amends and she only hoped he didn't muck it up.

'Can I see you?'

He seemed nervous, and she smiled into the phone.

'What about?' She sounded hard now, as if she didn't care whether she saw him or not. The thought of him and Eve together suddenly crowded her mind. A vivid imagination worked for some people; novelists and artists, but, for the average person, all it brought was heartache. Kate pictured him with that young woman and jealousy threatened to subsume her. It was a destructive emotion, she knew that better than most. She had cleaned up enough murders that were the result of jealousy and bitterness. Bitterness grew from jealousy, bitterness was what festered inside a heart and made a person capable of overwhelming hatred that was without logic or reason. A hate so real, so tangible, that it could cause an international incident at the drop of a hat. Bitterness was the stuff of legends, it was the reason people became fools, and it wasn't until the bitterness had literally caused murder that those people suddenly realised just how far off the scale their emotions were.

For Kate, hearing his voice after all this time was like ambrosia to the gods. She also knew that, if she could, she would smack the fucker's face until he squealed in pain. He had hurt her, really hurt her, and she knew it would take a long time for her to even consider forgiving him.

'Are you still there, Kate?'

She sighed, her earlier euphoria gone now. 'I'm still here.'

She was determined that she would not talk to him, he had to talk to her.

'Please come and see me, Kate. I need to talk to you.'

Suddenly she hung up. He had thrown her and made her feel too vulnerable. She also felt furious, who the fuck did he think he was? That he loved her, she had no doubt. That he still craved a bit of strange, was something she had forced herself to overlook. But it was the simple fact that it had been *Eve* he had turned to, his protégé's sister. It was so fucking crass and so shaming, not just for her but for him as well. She knew that everyone in their world would know about his liaison, would know that he had replaced her within moments by a younger model. That was what really hurt. She hated him for that, not so much that he had found someone else, and found them so bloody quickly, but that he had then paraded the young woman in front of all their friends. She had been left a virtual outsider, dumped like a hankie full of snot. It had galled her beyond belief that Pat had not once thought about how that would make her feel. He had removed her belongings from the home they shared, had not even had the guts to say anything to her face; he had left Desmond to do his dirty work.

The Desmond who was now what was commonly referred to as MIA. Not to be confused with the military term, missing in action, of course. Desmond, the stupid idiot, was assumed to be murdered in action. Desmond's widow had tried to claim on the insurance already, so the mortgage would be paid off. She would be well off. The fact that she had tried to scam the missing money herself had not been held against her. She had coughed up eventually, and finally seen the error of her ways.

Kate didn't bother herself with this kind of crime, she accepted that, from the moment Desmond had resorted to skulduggery for his own ends, he had been living on borrowed time. He *knew* that the people he mixed with were *not* the kind of people to overlook that kind of a piss-take and so murder was an occupational hazard for someone like him.

Kate always felt that the one thing in her favour was the fact that she was more interested in what she deemed the real crimes. She liked defending people who couldn't defend themselves. She knew it was wrong to overlook blatant criminal activity, while pursuing other crimes, but she also knew that pursuing some so-called crimes were a waste of her time and effort. There were certain crimes, especially those that were part of the criminal network, that would not, and could not, ever be solved. Not until it was too late anyway.

Kate deliberately distanced herself from everything that

pertained to gang-related crime. She didn't feel the urge to investigate those crimes. She had learned, over the years, that the real criminals, the real rogues, were actually not that important in the grand scheme of things. It was the burglars, the car thieves and the nonces that people wanted off the pavements. It was the bullies who terrorised old ladies for a couple of quid for a few pints. Rob a bank, and the criminal world would protect you to the hilt. After all, you were only earning a crust, murder an enemy *before* he murdered you, and that would also be ignored. It was no one's business but *yours*. But to try and scam your own was a different matter entirely. Try to force an earn that you had no right to only guaranteed that you were shunned by the local populace, that you were seen as the parasite you really were. If you tried to make a penny from any of your peers, you were deemed as scum because you had stepped over the unwritten line. You were loathed by everyone concerned, family and neighbours included and, worst of all, you would forever be classed as grade-A scum. A *marler*, a *thief* of other people's hard work, you'd be seen as an outcast, forever remembered as an idle ponce. Too lazy to work for yourself.

Kate understood and accepted that. She knew, better than anyone, that it was a necessary evil because the same loyalty and the same ethics were expected in *her* job, were needed in the police force. Like the criminals they tried to apprehend, the police lived by a similar hierarchy, it was another profession that relied on not just loyalty, but trust.

Kate overlooked Patrick's lifestyle and she had fitted into his world, but he had never really fitted into hers. The worst part being that she felt more comfortable in his world than she ever had in her own.

Her phone rang again and this time she looked at who was calling her. It was Annie. She answered the call, gutted that Patrick had not bothered to call her back.

Chapter Twenty-One

Kate was annoyed with herself. She knew she shouldn't have aborted Pat's call, but she was still hurting. She believed he was sorry now, but it wasn't enough for her, it still didn't make things right. Although she had forced the issue, had been angry at his involvement in the flats and houses the girls worked out of, she could have overcome that. Deep inside, she had always known he was not directly involved. After all, he had been running women when she first met him. She had accepted him for who he was.

As angry as she was, though, she was very aware of how hard it would have been for him to make the first contact, and she had been batting off his calls for days. Patrick had completely wiped her from his life, had ejected her once and for all from their home. He had to have known she would have come back sooner rather than later. Even though she loved that man, much more than he deserved, she still couldn't get over the way he had completely blanked her. She had lived in that house for years, she had felt that it was *her* home as much as it was his. And he had pushed her out, like she counted for nothing.

But that he expected her to welcome him back with open arms, knowing he had slept with a girl who was, in effect, younger than his dead daughter had she lived, having treated her so badly, made her feel hot with shame and anger.

She didn't want coffee now, she needed a drink. She opened up her desk drawer and took out her half bottle of whisky. Pouring a generous measure into her cup, she gulped it down. She felt the warmth of the burn as it slid down into her chest, then the second burn as it arrived in her belly. She swallowed down another shot of whisky and opened the files once again. She knew them practically off by heart now, she had read them so many times. But she went back to the beginning.

Her phone made a quiet beeping sound. As she opened the text message, she smiled widely. *Please come home, Kate. I need you.*

She knew how much it would have taken proud Patrick Kelly to send her that message and, even though he had broken her heart, and even though he had taken young Eve into his bed, she wanted him. She still felt the pull of him even after all these years. She picked up the files and left the building.

As she approached the gates, she saw that they were already open, and she drove in. She saw his outline as he stood in the light of the front door. Getting out of the car she felt the sting of tears in her eyes.

Pat walked out of the house towards her, arms outstretched and, pulling her into a tight embrace, he said raggedly, 'I didn't think you'd come. I didn't think you'd ever forgive me.'

She relaxed into his body and he breathed in the familiar

scents that were his Kate. Harmony hairspray, Boots moisturiser and Chanel No. 5. Pat felt as if he had died and gone to heaven. She was there, she was in his arms, and he knew that, no matter what he might try to tell himself, no matter how much he tried to convince himself that he didn't need her, he couldn't exist without her.

'I missed you so much, Kate. I missed you so fucking much.'

As they walked into the house together, Pat felt all the tension leave his body. Shutting the huge double doors behind them, he locked them both.

Kate caught her reflection in the large Venetian mirror that was opposite the front door. She knew she looked awful, that she looked every day of her age, and she saw she was crumpled up and grubby from being in the same clothes for over fifteen hours. But it was pointless to start worrying about that now, she could never compete physically with a young woman like Eve Foster, she wouldn't even try to. What she focused on was that she was here, and Eve wasn't. She knew that if she thought about it all too much, she would only make herself unhappy.

Kate looked around her. It was all so familiar, and yet it all felt so strange. After all, Eve had been here, she had slept in their bed, she had showered here, and she had eaten here. It was hard for Kate to accept that truth, but she knew she had to get over that obstacle if she wanted to get her life back. Their old life back. Percy Sledge was on the CD player, and as they walked into the kitchen together, Pat looked at her and said happily, 'Fuck me, Kate, you don't half look rough, girl.'

*

Annie was fast asleep when the phone rang and she picked it up groggily saying, 'What?'

She was tired out, she had also had a few drinks and the combination of the alcohol and the tiredness had sent her into a deep and satisfying sleep. She was not happy about being woken out of it.

'Who is this?' The voice was garrulous and high-pitched. Annie was annoyed, it was obviously a nuisance call.

'Is Kate there?'

Annie yawned, and the noise was loud in the darkness. 'Who is this?'

'It's Miriam.'

Annie was so tired she couldn't place her for a few moments. 'What do you want, Miriam? It's late.'

Miriam didn't answer for a few seconds, then she said softly, 'Is Kate there? Only I have a woman here who has been attacked. She won't go to the police station. But I still think that somebody should talk to her. I think she should report it, or at least have the conversation on record.'

'Who is it?'

'I would rather not say. If Kate's not around, you'll have to come.'

Annie sighed heavily. She knew she would have to go. Still, she was intrigued, and she wanted to see what had happened. 'Where are you?'

'St Saviour's Hospital. Can I take it you'll be coming instead of Kate?'

'Yeah. Give me twenty minutes.'

Annie replaced the receiver and jumped out of bed. As she pulled on her street clothes; scruffy denims, and a dark-green fisherman's jumper, she wondered where Kate was.

A few minutes later, as she dragged a brush through her hair, she popped her head around Kate's bedroom door. The room was empty and, assuming that she was probably still at the station, she dialled the number quickly. No answer. She tried her mobile and it was switched off.

Annie pulled on a raincoat and left the house. She was freezing cold and wondering what the fuck she was doing driving around Grantley in the middle of the night.

As she pulled into the hospital, Annie wondered whether Kate was on her way home. Perhaps she'd just missed her at the station. She turned her attention to the job in hand. Miriam was waiting in the light of the ambulance bay. She was hard to miss, she looked like a demented social worker, all flowing clothes and wiry hair. Her fat feet were encased, as always, in her open-toed sandals.

Annie smiled briefly as she walked towards her. 'Is it a domestic or a working girl?'

Miriam sighed sadly. 'It's a domestic, but she's been beaten very badly, Annie.'

'Why all the hush-hush? Is she well enough to make a statement?'

Miriam rolled her eyes in annoyance. 'Why don't you just come with me, and if you can manage to keep your mouth shut long enough, I'll explain the situation.'

Annie was shocked by Miriam's manner. She bustled through the overly bright hospital corridors and into a small ward where she turned around and, putting her finger to her lip, she said quietly, 'You can't say anything to anyone about this poor woman or her plight unless she says that you can. Do you understand that?'

Annie was annoyed. She knew the law, after all, she was in the police force. 'Of course I do.'

As they walked down the ward, Annie saw that there were only four beds. Three were empty and the fourth was by the window. As she approached it, she saw a woman of a heavy build with one arm in a plaster cast.

'It's all right, Hayley. It's only me, Miriam. I've brought a friend to see you, Annie Carr.'

As the woman turned her head to look at her, Annie saw that she had her jaw wired up, that the fingers on her good arm were badly broken and missing a couple of nails, and that her face and neck were covered in small cuts. It looked as if she'd gone through the windscreen of a car.

She looked at Miriam for some kind of explanation, of course she wanted to know what had happened. This was clearly not a car accident, it was a beating. But she also knew that battered wives often needed time and space before they were ready to leave the abuser.

'This is Hayley Dart, Lionel's wife. I thought that someone should see what he is capable of.'

Annie looked at the woman in the bed, and tried to hide her shock and surprise.

'This isn't the first time he's done something like this, he's always been a violent man. But the attacks are escalating in their severity. I just wanted someone else to see her, someone else to bear witness to her injuries. I want her to know that when she is ready, there will be a whole network of people she can rely on. I want her to see that she is not alone.'

Annie was open-mouthed with astonishment.

'He's going to take early retirement. I hear Kate put the

idea into his head. I think it must have prompted this latest attack.'

Annie nodded her head slowly, trying to take it all in. The woman in the bed was once more looking out of the window, and Annie knew that she was ashamed and embarrassed by her predicament. Battered women often believed that they brought the violence on themselves, it was a classic symptom. The bruises made them feel self-conscious and often they ended up colluding with their attacker simply because they were too ashamed to admit what was happening to them.

'How long has this been going on?'

Miriam shrugged heavily. 'Years, but this time I felt I needed to bring in an independent witness. He's shattered her jaw and broken her arm. He bent her fingers back until they snapped and he ripped her nails off. Her ribs are also broken, and she has internal injuries. It was a neighbour who called the ambulance. She won't press charges, she never does. But he needs to know that other people are aware of what he is doing. He is a bully, and bullies need to be confronted. Bullies need to know they won't be tolerated.'

Annie nodded in agreement. The door to the room opened and Lionel Dart scurried in. He saw Annie standing by the bed and he stopped. Then he turned around and walked from the room without even uttering a sound. Hayley Dart looked at Annie and there was fear and pain in her eyes.

Annie watched as Miriam grasped the woman's hand gently, saying softly, 'I'm sorry, Hayley, but sometimes this is the only thing that works. He will be chary of Annie and Kate knowing his secret. He will be frightened that they will spread it around, and it will make him think twice before he does this again.'

Hayley was crying quietly, with hardly any sound at all, and Annie knew that this woman had cried in silence all her married life. She looked at Miriam as if for the first time, and she wondered at a woman who was so unlovable and yet spent her whole life trying to make other people's lives that little bit better.

'How did you know about this, Miriam?'

Miriam shrugged. A nonchalant and expressive shrug. 'The nurses call me if they have a victim of domestic violence. I come straight here and I advise them of their rights, or I just hold their hands, depending on what they want. I don't judge them, and I don't tell them what to do. I just keep them company, try to show them a little kindness. Often, after a violent attack, all the victim needs is a friendly face.

'Lionel Dart has been getting away with this for years. Well, hopefully, now that he knows you are in on his secret, he might rein himself in a bit. He has been given an easy pass for far too long.'

Annie didn't answer her, she didn't know what to say. She couldn't help wondering whether, if Lionel Dart liked hurting women so much, he was capable of killing them.

Patrick was thrilled to have Kate back. He watched her as she slept beside him and marvelled at her being back in the home they had shared for so long. She was the only woman he really cared about. She was the only woman he could ever trust.

As Kate snored gently beside him he slipped his arm underneath her body and pulled her into his embrace. She felt different after the softness of Eve, and she was like a rail. She was thinner than ever, and he knew she needed feeding up. He felt so content as he lay beside her that he knew, no matter what happened in the future, he would never take her for granted again.

When he closed his eyes to sleep, the landline started ringing. He had to lean over Kate to get to the receiver and as he heard Annie's strident voice he stifled a small smile before saying loudly, 'Wake up, Kate, it's for you.'

'Never in a million years. He's a wife-beater, not a serial killer.' Kate's voice was dismissive, and Annie was aware that she was not pleased at being dragged out of Patrick's bed in the middle of the night for a wild goose chase.

Annie still wasn't convinced.

'Look, Annie, as soon as I knew he was on the nest at the house where Candy Cane died, I checked him out. He was at dinners with local dignitaries or showing off at masonic dos when the majority of the girls were murdered. But I must admit, I am shocked at what you've told me.'

Kate could see that Annie was outraged at Lionel Dart's behaviour. 'He's broken her jaw, her arm. I was really shocked. I mean, he's a fucking wife-beater, and none of us knew.'

'Well, Miriam knew. She is deeper than an ocean, Annie, don't you think?'

Annie nodded. 'Well, Kate, he's up for early retirement, but where will that leave his poor wife?'

'We'll keep an eye on her and Miriam will monitor the situation, I am sure. If she doesn't want to press charges, then there's nothing we can do.'

'Did you talk to Margaret today?'

Kate shook her head. 'She's hacked into another government site, she says it has the records of some of the dead girls' sojourns in the care system. She is a funny one, she really loves hacking into computers and snooping into other people's lives. I think she's fucking brilliant though, don't you?'

Kate grinned. 'I mean, I am a computer illiterate, and proud of it. I can do just enough to get me by but, other than that, I'm with Shirley Conran. Life *is* too short to stuff a mushroom and it's certainly far too short to spend so much of it hunched over a fucking computer. Still, in this day and age it's essential to have someone good with computers on the team and I'm glad we've got Margaret.'

Annie rolled her eyes at the ceiling and said with puzzlement, 'Who's Shirley Conran?'

Kate was too disgusted to answer her. Instead, she said, 'Where are the files Margaret accessed today? Did she leave them for me?'

Annie walked over to the desk Margaret used for her research. Picking up a bunch of pale buff envelopes she brought them over to where Kate was sitting. Kate was sipping a cup of black coffee and as Annie dropped the files before her, she said on a wide-mouthed yawn, 'I don't know whether to go home or stay here. It's nearly six, so I might as well start on these now, I suppose.'

She opened up each of the envelopes and carefully placed the papers from each of them into neat piles. She scanned them quickly before saying quietly, 'Jesus wept, she has accessed all the victims' medical records. Fucking hell, I don't like the thought of anyone being able to do something like that. Do you? I mean, this really is an infringement of people's privacy. Well done, Margaret. There might be something in this lot that could help.'

Annie nodded in agreement. 'She's bloody good, Kate. I mean, she has accessed every part of their lives and, even though we know it's wrong, to be honest I can't help feeling that, given the circumstances, we need everything that we can get on them all.'

Kate was determined to collate and cross-index these poor girls until something somehow gave her a pattern of sorts. Something that she could use to tie them all to a person or a place. Something that gave the girls a common denominator. She was desperate to link the dead girls up in some way, and that was why she was suddenly wide awake and trawling through the files as quickly as she could. It was another angle for her to look at, and it gave her a renewed vigour because she might just find something, however small, that could trigger a breakthrough. Often it wasn't huge big clues that set you on the right course, it was something simple that, on its own, would have no real significance whatsoever. But when you placed it alongside *another* little clue it would sometimes take on a completely different significance.

Looking up at Annie she said gaily, 'By the way, how did you know I was at Patrick's?'

Annie laughed, her slim shoulders shaking with mirth. 'Fuck me, Kate, you obviously don't have much respect for my skills as a policewoman! It was easy. You weren't here, you weren't in your own bed, so you had to be with Patrick.'

Kate wasn't amused any more. She didn't like the thought that she was so transparent, she wondered when she had become so easy to read. It was as if she was seeing her life from someone else's perspective, and she didn't like what she was seeing. Did Annie really believe that she only had three places to go? Then she thought about it and she had to admit that there *were* actually only three places she could, or would, go. Was this what getting older meant? Did you suddenly stop having options because one day you decided that it was easier all round to choose the least demanding one? She knew why she was thinking like this. Ten years ago, she and Patrick would have argued and then they would have made a point of making up with long, slow, deliberate sex. Last night they had both been too tired to have make-up sex and, if the truth be told, the thought had not even crossed their minds. The knowledge rattled her, plus she didn't like the fact she was so predictable.

'Am I really that easy to work out?'

Annie raised her perfectly arched eyebrows.

Chapter Twenty-Two

Kate was still smarting from Annie's comments about her so-called predictability. She was back in her own house, she was not going back permanently to Patrick's until she felt they were both ready for it. She couldn't get past the fact that he had basically ordered her out, and she knew that her pride was not only wounded, it still needed a very large bandage. But she consoled herself with the fact that they were at least back on speaking terms. The lines of communication were once again open, as American talk show hosts say.

But she still felt that there was something missing. She guessed it was because for the first time ever, they had not had make-up sex. She wondered if Patrick was thinking the same thing. Was he also secretly questioning their failure to consummate their new-found togetherness? He had not even caressed her in a sexual way and, although she had not thought about it at the time, now, as she remembered it, she felt slightly snubbed by him all over again. She assumed he had been shagging for England with Eve and the fact that he didn't seem to want her was now taking hold in her mind. The two-faced bastard had not even tried to kiss her properly, he'd just lain there, holding her in his arms, until she had dropped off.

She quickly went to the bathroom and looked at herself in the mirror. She was still slim, still attractive and although she wasn't a spring chicken, she wasn't that much different to the woman he had met all those years ago. She put on some lip gloss and brushed her hair, immediately feeling much better just for doing it.

Back in her front room, she sat on the floor and spread everything she had on the dead girls out in individual piles. She accepted that there could be a man out there somewhere who was just choosing the girls at random, who had no real reason other than that he wanted to kill somebody. But the viciousness of the girls' deaths told her that this was personal. It was someone with an axe to grind. Why they wanted to grind the axe in the first place, she still couldn't work out. She felt though that, if she *could* work that much out, she would be a step closer to finding the man responsible.

They had interviewed so many people, had investigated so many men, and yet they were still no nearer fingering a suspect than they had been at the start of the investigation. Kate had spent hours poring over the details of the crimes, re-reading the witness statements, and trying to look at it all from a fresh perspective.

She picked up Janie Moore's files, then she picked up Sandy Compton's paperwork and placed it on the floor beside Janie's. She stared at them for long moments then, sitting back against the sofa, she placed Candy Cane's papers in the middle of the other two. She picked up the first piece of paper from each pile and read them. She did the exact same thing with each piece of paper that came to hand. She read them all again, as if she had never read any of them before. She picked up the other girls' files and read them again too, placing them in different orders, straining her eyes as she tried to see something, anything, that would make her feel she was in with a chance of winning.

The phone rang and she answered it quickly, annoyed at the intrusion. It was Patrick, and he was trying to be as affable and friendly as possible. She gave him a few Brownie points for that much anyway.

'Why don't you come over for dinner, Kate?'

Kate shook her head, forgetting he couldn't see her. 'No, Pat. Thanks for the offer but I really need to work. I can't concentrate at your house and I have all my paperwork here.'

Pat couldn't be sure, but he felt that there was a note of censure in her voice. But he knew better than to remark on it. He knew she was still smarting from his fling, and he didn't blame her for that, he would have felt the same if the boot had been on the other foot.

He sighed. 'OK. I just thought you might like a bit of dinner, that was all, love. How is it going, like? Any nearer to a collar?' He laughed then. 'That's not a sentence I ever thought I would say.'

Kate laughed with him, and she realised she missed this, the chatting, the closeness. 'It's hard, Patrick, we have nothing, literally nothing.'

He sighed. He racked his brains for something interesting to say to her to take her mind off it for a few minutes. 'Oh, Kate, I just remembered. Terry O'Leary came round the other day, and asked me if I could do him a favour. He wants you to tell that woman from Victim Support to stop coming round the houses. The girls love her, by all accounts, but I think he's worried she might put off the customers. Or see too much of what's going on. Either way, he wants her to meet the girls off the premises. Would you mind having a word with her for me? Apparently she's talked a few of the younger ones into leaving the life but, as I said to Terrence, you can't blame the girls for that. But he don't like her there interfering and, reading between the lines, if she doesn't take the hint, he'll have her out by the scruff of her neck.'

There was a long silence and Patrick broke it by saying, 'Are you still there, Kate?'

'Do you know the names of the girls who left?'

Patrick was annoyed now, assuming she was being sarcastic. 'Now, how the fuck would I know something like that, Kate? It's not like I frequent them places, is it?'

Kate laughed good-naturedly. 'I didn't mean it like that, I just wondered if he had mentioned the girls' names, that's all.'

'Well, he didn't and, not to put too fine a point on it, why the fuck would Terry O'Leary know the names of two Toms in his employ?'

Kate heard the incredulity in Pat's voice and decided that, as much as she loved him, he had a lot to learn about, not just basic manners, but also the safety of the people who earned you a good wedge. 'Get off your high horse, Patrick. I like Terry, but it doesn't change the fact that he is a fucking pimp and, just because he doesn't mix with his girls, doesn't spend time on the premises they all work out of, it doesn't make him any less of a pimp in my eyes. He is a ponce, as the old Faces would put it and now, if you don't mind, I need to go somewhere. I'll talk to you tomorrow.'

Kate had already put the phone down before Pat had even had the chance to say goodbye.

*

Terrence O'Leary was not impressed to see Kate standing, larger than life, on what was generally referred to as his *official* doorstep. His wife, on the other hand, was thrilled. 'How are ya, Katie love? Come away in, you look frozen to the bone.'

Kathleen O'Leary was a beauty, and even after giving birth to six children, five of them boys, she still managed to turn more than a few heads. She had the thick black hair and violet-blue eyes of the real Irish along with the tiny bone structure of a fairy and good deportment and, all these things put together made for a winning combination. She was truly lovely, inside and out, and Kate had always had a soft spot for her. 'Has that eejit seen the error of his ways yet?'

Kate laughed as she followed Kathleen into the large and expensive kitchen. It was like something from *Doctor Who*, all brushed stainless steel and expensive gadgets. Kate knew that it would have been what Terry wanted, not what Kathleen would have desired. Kate knew Terry well enough to know that he saw everything around him as something to either be admired or coveted. He felt that even his home wasn't somewhere to relax in, it was somewhere to prove how well he had done for himself.

It was a shame really, but Kate understood Terry's need to show off his wealth and his need to prove that he had expensive but elegant good taste. Unfortunately, he looked uncomfortable in these surroundings, and that was the shame of it all. Instead of enjoying his home, he spent all his time wondering how the fuck to fit himself into it.

'Do you want a coffee?'

Kate nodded. 'I came to talk to Terry about Patrick.'

Kathleen scowled. When she had put Kate's cup of coffee in front of her, she said angrily to Terry, 'Now you tell her what she wants to know.'

Kate knew Kathleen assumed that she was round there asking about Eve, and she was sorry that Pat's fling was such common knowledge to all and sundry.

'He's as fecking bad. I've caught him out more than once, Kate.'

Terrence O'Leary was terrified of his little wife because, for all his bombast and his machismo persona, without her he would crumble. She was his life, but he never let on to anyone about that. He saw his enormous love for her as a weakness, whereas she saw his love of her as a bonus. Their boys were handsome and strong, and their only daughter was a beauty, a beauty who it seemed had inherited all the brains of the family.

Kathleen smiled at Kate, and left the kitchen quickly. Like any woman, she understood the need to find out everything you could about your rival and, from what she had seen, this Eve was a rival in more ways than one.

Terry looked both shame-faced and less than impressed.

'I want to ask you about the girls who left your employ because of Miriam Salter.'

Kate saw him visibly relax, and she knew he had not expected her to ask him something so mundane. Like his wife, he'd obviously thought she would be quizzing him on Patrick's affair with Eve.

'Is that all? Why are you interested in them?' Then Terry was suddenly concerned, and he looked worried as he said, 'They aren't dead, are they?'

Kate shook her head. 'I don't know, but if you give me their names I can track them down.'

He frowned. 'Ring Jennifer or Simone, they'll know more than I do, Kate. For feck's sake, I've told you before, I rarely step foot on the premises.' He was almost whispering now, worried that his wife might be earwigging from outside the door.

'To be honest, Terry, I would rather you spoke to them. All I want is their names, but I don't want anyone to know that I am looking into their lives. Believe me, Terry, I wouldn't be here if this wasn't important.'

Terry felt the urgency in her voice and, looking into her eyes, he said softly, 'Are you sure they aren't dead?'

'Not that I know of, but I just want to find them and ask them if they left the house because someone had frightened them. I need to ask them if they've ever been hurt by a punter or threatened.'

'Why not ask the loony woman, she's the one who talked them into leaving. Why not ask her where they went?'

'I tried her, but she's not answering. Anyway, first off, I just want to get the girls' names, and I want to research them. Their lives, where they come from et cetera. This is a hunch, no more, and it's probably nothing. But if you could get me the names, and not let on it's me who is asking after them, I'll owe you a favour until the day I die.'

Kate had appealed to the criminal side of Terry's charac ter, and he knew that. He liked the idea of her dragging him into her conspiracy theory, or whatever it was. He liked that she didn't want to involve anyone, not even her fellow plods.

'Let me make a call. Drink your coffee. I'll be back in five.'

*

Hayley Dart was frightened. She knew that Miriam bringing in that young DC to see her in all her battered glory would only make her husband ten times worse. He had beaten her from the day they had got married and, over the last few weeks, his anger and his frustration had caused the violence to escalate, until he was now almost out of control. Miriam was keeping a vigil by her bedside but, as much as Hayley appreciated her concern, she wished she would just go away and leave her alone. She knew that at any minute, she would be back beside her bed, Bible in one hand and a cross in the other.

Lionel would be on his best behaviour soon. He would lapse into his sorrowful mode and would be like a little child asking her to forgive him and assuring her it would never happen again. He would appear to be mortified at what he was capable of, and he would be terrified of someone he knew finding out about it. It was when he stamped on her face that she had realised he was now totally out of control. In the past, he had always taken great pains to beat her where the bruises wouldn't show. He had only broken her fingers once before, and that had been explained away by him telling everyone she had shut her hand in the car door. This time, however, he had not been able to control himself, and she had been seriously beaten. She knew that the hospital staff had guessed long ago that she wasn't really that clumsy. But he was the Chief Super of Grantley nick and he had power. This ensured that they didn't probe too much into the circumstances of her accidents.

Hayley knew that her jaw would take a long time to heal and that she would be kept in for as long as the nurses could swing it. She appreciated their kindness, but she knew that her husband always held all the cards. He stood there and joked with everyone, brought the nurses chocolates, filled her bedside with expensive flower arrangements and spoke to her as if they were love's young dream. She had seen the way women on the ward looked at him, the way they watched as he fussed over her and she knew that they wished their husbands were as attentive. She knew they looked at her and wondered what she had that made her husband still treat her like a new bride all these years later.

He was a bully and a coward, incapable of fighting a man, but more than capable of threatening and intimidating a woman or a child. He spewed filth at her, and she knew that he enjoyed doing it, knew that he was so weak and emotionally feeble that all he could do to make himself feel powerful was to vent his hate on those he knew couldn't fight back. He had bullied the girls too but, unlike her, they had got away as soon as they could. She was ashamed that she had not stuck up for them, ashamed that she had been too terrified and too weak to defend them from his tyranny. He had a way of making her feel it was all her fault, he made her think that the girls were not good enough because she didn't know how to raise them properly. He had even bullied his own *mother*. Like her, she had been weak, weak and frightened of the son she had spawned and had eventually come to loathe.

Hayley now knew she had to do something. She knew inside herself that if she stayed with him for much longer, he really would kill her. She was so glad her jaw was broken. It meant she didn't have to talk to him, didn't have to play the game, didn't have to pretend she wasn't hurting all over. She didn't have to act like she loved her husband so that people, even strangers, would believe that they were the perfect couple.

Hayley heard the door open and saw Miriam walk to the chair beside the bed. She sat down, her heavy body appearing to collapse in on itself. Miriam always sat with her shoulders hunched up, body hanging forward, she looked as if she would fall off the chair on to the floor at any minute. But she meant well, and Hayley was grateful to her because, all the time Miriam was sitting beside her, Lionel couldn't get away quick enough. He knew that Miriam was more than aware of what was going on and he also knew that she was a busybody. That scared him because he depended on people thinking well of him, he needed people to think he was a nice man, a good person.

As she saw Miriam smiling at her, she tried her hardest to smile back, but with her jaw wired up it was an uphill struggle.

Kate looked at the computer screen as if it would give her the information she wanted through sheer willpower alone.

Margaret Dole was laughing at her. 'Go and get a coffee, Kate, I'll be a while getting the girls' details.'

'I am amazed that their names didn't bring up anything at all.'

Margaret shrugged. 'Maybe they have never been nicked, did that occur to you? Oh, hang on, I've got something. They've all been residents in the same home.'

Kate felt a stirring of excitement inside her chest.

'Nicky Marr, seventeen years old.'

'Brookway House.'

'How did you know that?'

Kate grinned. 'Something Simone said. Now see if Donna Turner turns up there and all.'

'Wow, I'm impressed, Kate. They were both in Brookway, but not at the same time. But, have a guess who else was there with Nicky Marr?'

Kate looked at Margaret for long moments before she said, 'Terri Garston?'

'Give the lady a cigar. Do you think this is the connection between them all? Brookway House?'

Kate shrugged. 'I don't know. Nicky and Donna have both left the life, Miriam saw to that. I wonder if Miriam got involved with the girls at the halfway house her husband ran. Margaret, can you check which one it was, she may be able to help us. Also what we need to establish is whether any of the girls who were killed ever resided at Brookway. It seems to me that a lot of them rolled up there after leaving the care system or, in some cases, after getting out of prison. Now the girls all help each other out, and I think they were steered towards Grantley with the promise of a nice house to live in and easy money. Whoever killed these girls knew them well enough to ensure that they opened the door to him without a second's thought. So, after we establish that the girls were all in Brookway at some time or another, we need to look at the people who worked there.

'You started me off with this because the files you hacked into had some of the girls living there. Now both you and I know that the care system is sometimes lax and we know that these homes are a breeding ground for girls who are ripe for the life.'

'Are you really saying that you think someone who worked there was cherry-picking girls and giving them the contact details for the houses and flats here? In Grantley? That this person was grooming them for the life?'

Kate nodded. 'I think there was someone they trusted, and I think that person was the one who pointed them in the right direction. I have to say, however, that I don't think they were being paid for each girl they provided. I think they just wanted the girls here, so they had access to them.'

Margaret looked up from the computer. She was stunned. 'You're not going to believe this, Kate, but they all had a sojourn there at one time or another.'

'I knew it! That's the trouble with the halfway houses, their records are always scant. But they always make sure that they put the residents' full names down. Right, start searching the work records and see what comes up. Get names, addresses and phone numbers and track them through their social security numbers. Then let's see what or, more to the point, *who*, pops up in Grantley.'

'Fucking hell, Kate. This is freaky. I mean, if we hadn't hacked into all those files, we wouldn't have had any idea about this, would we?'

Kate laughed. 'Keep your voice down! Not only have we committed a serious crime, as you well know, we, or more precisely, *you*, have not only invaded these people's privacy, we have also cyber-stalked them, and that's without the fact that we have also broken into government databases. That's just for starters. And we've done it all without a second's thought.'

Margaret laughed with her and Kate knew that the girl was experiencing the rush of adrenaline that a breakthrough always brought with it. There was nothing on earth to beat it.

'But remember, Margaret, if anyone finds out what you've done, we're up shit creek. Not so much me, my love, I'm only here as a part-timer these days. You and Annie, on the other hand, have your careers ahead of you. So make sure no one can follow your trail. Or prove that we got all our information on the knock.'

Margaret nodded solemnly, she understood the importance of Kate's words better than anyone. 'Listen, Kate, I could hack into the fucking Pentagon and they wouldn't be able to trace it back to me.'

Lionel was scared. He knew he had gone too far this time, and he also knew that now he had requested his early retirement he was, to all intents and purposes, finished. He had dedicated his life to the police force, had seen it as a platform to bigger and better things. He had learned, very early on, that it could be a lucrative profession if you played your cards right. And he had played his cards well, they had provided him with a lucrative little earner. He had always been willing to bend the law for a good cause, and money was as good a cause as any.

Lionel had never really walked the beat, had never really nabbed a criminal. He had come into the force from Hull University with a second-class degree, and the desire to make something of himself. A natural-born paper pusher, he had always preferred sitting behind a desk. He had moved through the force with lightning speed and although he knew he was not a go-getter as such, he knew his limits; he also knew that men like him had their uses. Desk jockeys as the uniforms called them. Arrogant pricks if you listened to the CID. But, for all that, he was their boss. He was the man in charge. But he had never even read anyone a Miranda; he had never once been on a shout. He had done what he did best; he had sat on his arse and filled out the paperwork. He had seen that the brass above him had been free of everything from drink-driving charges, speeding tickets and, once, he had even made sure a senior officer had not had to answer a charge of gross indecency in a public toilet with a minor. The boy had been all of fourteen, and the gentleman concerned had promptly invited Lionel to his daughter's twenty-first birthday party. He had been promoted three months later as a thank-you. When a shit job needed doing, he was the man to call on, and Lionel prided himself on his ability to sort out any crisis, no matter how complicated it might seem.

Then one day in walks Kate Burrows and, in a few minutes, she forces him to not only leave his job, but to also do it so quickly that he knew everyone would think it was to avoid a scandal of some kind. After all, he had enjoyed the services of those young girls with not only his senior colleagues, but also most of the local dignitaries.

Now he felt cornered and because of his anger at the unfairness of his situation, he had made another mistake. He had inadvertently given his wife Hayley a serious hammering this time, and Miriam knew the truth of it. Like that fucking skuzzball of a husband of hers, she felt it was her *duty* to stick her fucking ugly mug into everyone's lives. Alec had been the same and when he died, it had taken Lionel's considerable willpower not to laugh his bloody head off. If only Miriam had known the truth about *her* lovely Alec. Well, there was still time.

Miriam thought that by sitting by his wife's bed day and

night, she was protecting her from him and his anger. Well, if Miriam used that ugly fucking head of hers, she might suss out that he wasn't fool enough to batter the fucking imbecile he had married while in a public building. He would just bide his time, and beat the crap out of her in the comfort and privacy of his own home. But for all that, Miriam was still sitting there, watching over Hayley like a retarded Rottweiler, and he knew he had to be nice to her until the time when he could take his wife home.

As Miriam stood up, Lionel smiled at her. She didn't react, she just stood there, her dead eyes looking at him and her heavy body, as always, emitting the odour of her sweat. It was sharp and cloying, and if you stood close enough to her, it seemed to permeate through your skin, you could almost taste it. She was what his father would have referred to as soapy. She was a soap dodger all right, and she clearly didn't understand the value of a decent deodorant. Even her hair was a greasy mess. Yet she still managed to make herself busy. She still managed to find people to look after. He moved away from her, the smell of her body odour was making him want to gag.

Hayley stared at him balefully from her swollen eyes, and he decided to give up for today, he had had enough of these two to last him a lifetime. Blowing Hayley a kiss, he left the room as fast as possible. As he walked out into the cool night air, he decided to pay Simone a visit. He wouldn't be able to do it for much longer, not for free anyway, so he might as well make the most of it while he had the chance.

Chapter Twenty-Three

Kate saw Miriam first when she walked into Hayley Dart's hospital room.

'Hello, Kate, what a lovely surprise. How are you? Can I get you anything, a coffee, a tea?'

Kate shook her head and said gently, 'Can I have a quick word with you, Miriam? Only I need your advice about something.'

It seemed almost as if Miriam was about to burst with pride at Kate's words. 'You'd like my advice? *My* advice?'

Kate nodded. She was aware that Hayley Dart was observing everything with wary eyes. Lionel had really done a number on the woman, she looked like she had been in an RTA. Her poor hand, minus some nails, looked so painful and raw that it made Kate shudder. The bastard had broken one arm and then he had destroyed her other arm by breaking the fingers and snapping off her nails. She felt a moment's queasiness as the sheer horror of the woman's pain and degradation washed over her. It grieved Kate that this man could bully his wife and, unless she found the nerve to speak up, or fight back, he would get away with it, time and time again.

Lionel had known exactly what he was doing, and she knew he had probably taken great pleasure in it. Kate leaned over the bed and said quietly, 'Listen, Hayley, you can't go on like this any more. Let us take a few photos of your injuries and I promise that I'll personally make sure you are safe. But you have to find the strength to walk away from him once and for all.'

'Thanks, Kate. I think Hayley needs people to let her know she is not alone. She can't talk because of her poor jaw and both her arms are destroyed so she can't even communicate with a pen and paper. I swore to her that I would stay here night and day until she was on the mend, and to make sure he doesn't use the time alone to torment her.'

Kate narrowed her eyes as she said, 'How long have you known about all this?'

Miriam shrugged as if she didn't really know.

'Have you known this for a while, Miriam?'

Miriam nodded slightly.

'Why didn't you tell anyone? We could have helped.'

Miriam sighed then and she said gently, 'Now, you know better than that, Kate. If she doesn't want to report him, then that's her business. We aren't here to force people into doing what *we* want, or what we think is right. We're here to stand by them, even if we don't think they are making the right choices. I met Hayley a few years ago when she had to drive herself to A&E, dripping blood. Lionel had stabbed her with a kitchen knife, had ripped her arm open. She said she had had an accident and I knew she was lying. I've counselled enough battered women in my time to know the truth of a situation like that. So me and her became friends, and Lionel knew that I knew what was going on. But if it's any consolation, I think she'll leave him this time. Now he's taken early retirement, she knows deep down that it will mean it's open season for him.'

Miriam looked at Hayley then and said loudly, 'You are going to leave him this time, aren't you?'

Hayley nodded her head, and Kate saw the scope of the damage that Lionel had inflicted on his wife, and the enormity of it hit her. For all of Miriam's faults, she was here for the woman, standing over her and making sure that Lionel didn't get the chance to finish off what he had started. Hayley's jaw had been completely unhinged, and she would never again be able to chew her food properly or pronounce certain words. She would for ever look odd, her face had lost its natural shape and she would be reminded of her husband's anger every time she looked in a mirror.

'Hayley, I hope you do leave him. And I hope you will feel better soon, love.'

The words were so trite, so banal, but what else were you supposed to say? The truth? Wow, Hayley, he really did the business on you this time, eh?

Miriam smiled at the woman sadly and led Kate from the room. Outside in the corridor Kate sighed with relief. 'I need your help badly, Miriam.'

Miriam was thrilled to bits. 'Anything you need, Kate. I'll do my best to provide you with it.'

Since Kate had visited her in the hospital, she knew that Miriam now classed her as her number one friend. 'Come to the canteen, and we'll get a couple of teas and I'll explain in more detail what I need from you. Is that OK?'

Kate was aware that Miriam was suddenly looking

decidedly nervous and grabbing her by the arm she said mischievously, 'Cheer up, Miriam, you always look so sad.'

Miriam attempted to smile and Kate saw that she was really trying hard to do what she thought was wanted of her. It was sad to see her like this, and Kate wished for a brief moment that the usual Miriam, the heavy-jawed and defensive Miriam, would resurface once more. She actually preferred her, this coquettish lump of a woman seemed so outlandish and she really didn't know how to deal with her.

Patrick was looking through the safe in his office. He was looking for some papers that Danny Boy needed to sign, and he also needed to make sure that Kate's jewellery was all ship-shape and sparkling. He wondered why she had not asked for it, after all, he had bought it for her, it was legally hers. But she had not even mentioned it.

He felt a wave of shame once more as he recalled his pettiness towards Kate. He knew he had a lot to make up for, and he also knew that Kate was not a person who would throw his actions in his face at every available opportunity. Whereas he would do exactly that in a heartbeat; he would happily sling anything, however dirty, he could at the person he was arguing with. It was his nature.

As he opened the leather jewellery box he smiled happily. Inside the box was the proof of his love for her. The diamond earrings he had once given her for her birthday, the gold Rolex she was too frightened to wear in case she lost it. The rings and the bracelets that marked their time together, and Pat realised that these presents, all this proof of his love for her, would still be around when he and Kate were long gone.

He had never thought about that before, never wondered what would happen to the diamonds, the emeralds and the sapphires.

He picked up an antique ring that had set him back the national debt, it was a seven-carat diamond surrounded by emeralds. It was over two hundred years old. Some other woman had once worn it with pride, some other woman who was now dead and buried, and yet the ring was still here. He decided he liked the thought of some things being constant, and he swore that if Kate let him back into her life for good he would be as constant as the ring he had bought her all that time ago.

Danny came into the room and Patrick turned to him and said happily, 'All right, son?'

Danny grimaced. 'Yes and no, Patrick. We have a problem.'

Patrick was immediately all serious faced and prepared for the worst eventuality. 'What's up?'

Danny shook his head in absolute consternation. 'Terry is in Ireland, as you know. He gets back tomorrow.'

'What is this, Danny Boy? A fucking news update or have you got something serious to say to me?'

Patrick never ceased to amaze Danny. He had gone from being the jovial, happy patriarch to a morose and dangerous villain in less than three minutes. Danny sighed, he was slightly irritated by Patrick's quick temper. 'Simone's been on the blower. It seems our local friendly chief of plods has gone off his trolley. He's attacked one of the girls and she's been taken to hospital. He is refusing to get dressed and leave the premises.'

Patrick shook his head in annoyance. 'That fucking idiot Lionel is a real pain in the arse. Bring the car round, we'll have to go and sort it.'

Patrick proceeded to put everything back in the safe and, five minutes later, they were on their way. Patrick was fuming now. Lionel Dart was a has-been, an also-ran, he was on his last knockings as a Filth with any kind of clout. To all intents and purposes, it was now open season as far as Pat was concerned. He had been looking forward to this day for a very long time.

'What I need from you, Miriam, is anything you can remember about the staff from your days at Brookway House. I understand it was your Alec's first posting as a social worker, at least that's what Annie says.'

Miriam nodded, her dead eyes suddenly animated. 'Oh my, that's a blast from the past as they say. I was very happy there, we both were. But what has this got to do with anything?'

'I think there's a link between the dead girls. They were all, at one time or another, at Brookway House. It seems odd to me that they all came to work in Grantley, and that every one of them ended up being tortured and murdered.'

Miriam was sitting opposite Kate, and her jaw was hanging open with the shock. 'No, that has to be a coincidence, surely? I mean, you know what these girls are like.'

Kate knew exactly what the girls were like, but this wasn't about how they acted, it was about how they had all started out at Brookway House, and ended up in Grantley as dead as doornails.

'You worked there with Alec. Who do you remember?'

Miriam thought for a few minutes before saying seriously, 'There was an older man there, he was called David Floyd. He was very, very overfamiliar with the girls, I mentioned it to Alec on more than one occasion. He was the team leader as they were called in those days. He was there all the time that we worked there. In fact, he was still there when we left.'

Kate wrote the name down in her notebook. 'Can you recall anyone who might have been in a position to give the girls information on working the flats in Grantley? Was there anyone you can remember who might have been around the girls who could have met up with them at a later date? I mean, they must have attracted boyfriends. I know it was a place for females only, but I'm sure they would have attracted plenty of interest from the young lads around and about, all those girls together. Surely you must have noticed something, Miriam?'

Miriam just sat there, staring at Kate as if she was unable to comprehend what she was saying to her. It occurred to Kate that Miriam had probably not looked much different then to how she looked now. She was one of those ageless people who seemed to stay exactly the same from eighteen years old onwards. She probably looked old then, and she looked old now. She was not interested in fashion or clothes, she wasn't bothered about getting a decent cut so her hair looked nice. She didn't attempt to control her intake of food, she was always eating something, and she was not a person who valued hygiene. Her teeth were her best feature and she obviously looked after them although her breath could be overpowering at close quarters because of her love of garlic. Yet she still managed to do what she could for people she saw in need of help and somehow the people she helped liked her and depended on her. It would never cease to amaze Kate how the world seemed to work.

'Were *you* working there when some of the girls were there?'

Miriam smiled. 'Yes.'

'Why didn't you tell us that?'

'I felt that the girls were entitled to their privacy. I wasn't to know that they had *all* spent time there, though it doesn't surprise me.'

Kate heard the hardness creeping into Miriam's voice and she was staring once more. She could do that, she could just sit motionless and stare, it could be quite unnerving.

'Drink your tea, Miriam, you haven't touched it.'

Miriam shook her head then and smiled. She was suddenly almost her old self again. 'I don't really like the tea here. It's like the tea at the station house, overly strong and bitter.'

'So who were the girls in residence when you were at Brookway House?'

Miriam thought for a few seconds before saying dismissively, 'It's all closed down now. What does it matter?'

Kate was getting slightly irritated now. She leaned across the table to answer Miriam's question and it was obvious that she was losing patience fast.

'It *matters* a great deal, Miriam. We are in the process of getting all the relevant information about Brookway House, but these things can take time, as I am sure you know. Social Services are always worried they'll be stuffed with a criminal accusation and the way things are with the care system at the moment, who can blame them? But as you were there for some time, I thought you *might* be able to help us get a heads-up.'

Miriam shrugged again. Kate could tell she was getting rattled about it for some reason. In fact she was getting the feeling that Miriam knew a lot more than she was letting on about Brookway House.

'Which girls were there at the same time as you?'

Miriam was staring again. Eventually she said dismissively, 'To the best of my recollection they were Janie Moore and Danielle Crosby. You must understand, Kate, these girls must be allowed their privacy. They were there because they were not long out of the care system or, in some cases, they had just left prison. You also need to remember that they were all basically transients. No one wanted them, you see, and if you read the files on some of them, you can see why.'

Kate was puzzled. Miriam was normally the champion of these poor girls, why would she say something like that now?

'What was in their files, Miriam?'

Miriam shrugged again, a slight smirk on her face. 'What do you think would be in there?'

Kate was unsure where this was going, and she said quietly, 'I don't know, that's why I am asking you. After all, you read them. I didn't.'

Miriam sighed heavily, 'Listen to me, Kate. These girls are all damaged somehow, they were all the product of unwanted pregnancies or were born to people who quite frankly should not have been allowed a dog, let alone a child. It's always amazed me that, at one time, you had to have a licence before you could purchase a puppy, but anyone could have a child. Still can. These girls are all capable of anything if they think it will get them what they want. Now, if you'll excuse me, I need to get back to Hayley. She really *is* an innocent victim.'

As she bustled away, Kate watched her warily. They had most of the files from Brookway House, Margaret had accessed almost all of them. They were now awaiting the personnel files on the people who had worked there. She now felt that there was something more to Miriam's time at Brookway House. Alec Salter had been a social worker there and she wondered if his files might be worth looking at. She looked down at her notebook and saw David Floyd's name. She wondered just what he was doing now. Well, she would soon find out.

'Lionel is naked and drunk out of his head, Kate. He's locked in a room at a local house and with him is a terrified young girl. So could you please call me when you get this message?'

Simone was fuming, she was also very frightened. Lionel was unhinged, he was really out of control. She knew that he had snapped for some reason. He had always been a very uptight man, she knew all the signs. He was a verbal bully, but a coward at heart. But the ruckus he was causing would soon bring the police and if the neighbours heard any of his raging they would wonder what the fuck was happening. They would call the police, as any good citizen would do. This was publicity they could well do without, especially with Terrence O'Leary in Ireland and Patrick Kelly on the premises.

As she poured them all a coffee she saw Peter Bates come in through the back entrance and, rolling her eyes to the ceiling, she thought that this was all they needed. Another bloody man to add to the mix.

'Come out, Lionel, or we'll kick the door in.' Patrick banged on the door.

'Fuck off to hell, Kelly, and take that fucking whore Burrows with you.'

The words were followed by another crash and the terrified screaming of the young girl locked in the room with him.

Danny shook his head in consternation. 'The door's solid wood, we'll need a battering ram to get through it. How about the window? We can get up there with a ladder.'

Patrick nodded. 'Let me try and calm him down first. All we need is that mad bastard throwing a table at us, or the poor girl, come to that.'

Lionel was bashing at the door again, demanding their attention. 'She was always out to get me, your fucking Kate, she was a fucking leech. I wanted her out but *they* overruled me. They let her stay on as a fucking *consultant*. Her, a consultant, *her*. Living with the biggest villain since Al Capone!'

Patrick sighed in annoyance, his face was screwed up with anger and hatred for what Dart was saying about him and his Kate.

Danny put his hands on Patrick's shoulders and said in a whisper, 'Don't retaliate, Pat, that's what he wants. Listen to him. He is unhinged. He's also drunk as a skunk.

'Look, Lionel, this is Danny Foster. Remember me from the casino? I used to deliver your envelope of money every week, remember? I'm asking you nicely, *let the girl go*. Just let her leave the room. Let's face it, you are in enough trouble as it is. And if you don't stop all this now, we'll have no option but to call the police, and none of us want that, do we? Least of all you.'

Lionel was laughing now, a loud, deep laugh. 'I am the fucking police, remember? I am the Chief Superintendent of Grantley Police Station. Until next week, of course, and then

I am fucking no one. And why is that? Because of that cunt, Kate Burrows. How the fuck is she still around? She was supposed to have fucking retired. After all this fucking time, she is still here and I am out. *Out, finished,* my career is over. She even had the gall to come to the hospital. My wife had an accident, a simple accident, and she even turned up there. Is nowhere safe from her? Is she going to go to fucking Iraq next and stick her beak in there as well?'

They heard another crashing noise and the whimpering of the girl trapped in the room with him. Simone had come upstairs once more and she looked at Patrick and Danny helplessly.

'Look, we need to get into that room. If he hurts that girl, I'll swing for him.'

'I'll go up a ladder and try and bust in that way,' Danny said.

Simone nodded. 'There's a small en suite. The window is not that big, but you could probably get through it at a push.'

Patrick laughed. 'You're right, we need to get in there and knock this ponce out.' He pointed at Simone. 'You get a ladder from somewhere and I have a baseball bat in me boot.'

Danny walked down the stairs saying happily, 'No need for that, Pat. I have a cosh in the car, it's small and it's lead, lethal in the wrong hands.'

Simone shook her head in a gesture of angry bafflement. 'There's a ladder in the garage. I'll sort it out. Fuck me, Pat, this is mental, he has to know that we won't be able to keep this quiet. It's like he's out of control.'

Pat laughed then and, rolling his eyes to the ceiling, he said seriously, 'Well, I don't know if you've noticed, Simone, but personally I think the banging, crashing and the shouting, along with holding that girl hostage, are all strong hints, so I think we can *safely* assume that he is *out* of control, Simone.'

She was hurt at his words, and he felt bad immediately, but he was worried about the girl's safety; Lionel was capable of hurting her, he had no doubt about that. He knew Simone was also worried about the girl, and he should have taken her feelings into consideration.

'Look, love, he's always been a strange cove, old Lionel, he's always blamed other people if things didn't go his way, or he fucked up. He only got as far as he did in the force because of people like me and Terry. We *bought* him, and now he's been sussed out, he's been exposed for what he really is. Without his job he is nothing. Unfortunately, he was nothing to most people, even when he had the job, and that must have finally occurred to him as well. So go and organise the ladders, and tell Peter that he can come up now.'

Simone didn't answer him, she just walked slowly down the stairs. Patrick scratched his head in bafflement, how the fuck were they supposed to sort this all out?

Peter Bates came up the stairs and, opening his coat, he said quietly, 'I've brought a sawn-off with me, Pat. I thought maybe we could blow the fucking door open?'

Patrick looked at the gun, placed neatly in a specially designed long pocket inside Peter's overcoat, and he knew then, without a shadow of a doubt, that it was finally time for him to retire.

Annie and Kate were both looking over the files that Margaret Dole had managed to access. Margaret was busy looking for David Floyd and anything pertaining to him.

411

'Is there any way we can get the relevant files about Brookway House, Kate? It's critical we do, as all the girls were there at some point.'

Kate shook her head and lit a cigarette. The no-smoking ban was, as usual, ignored. They had locked themselves into the office and had all the windows wide open, consequently they had to wear their coats and Margaret had to wear gloves. The room was freezing, but they didn't care. Kate had taken up smoking for England and Annie was following suit.

Kate opened her handbag and took out her phone. 'Oh shit. Do me a favour, Annie, plug that in for me. The charger is in the bottom drawer of the filing cabinet. I must have forgotten to put it on last night.'

Annie took the phone from her and did as she was asked. It was this kind of little thing that irked her. She felt she shouldn't have to do menial tasks, Kate could do these things herself. She swallowed down the annoyance. Kate was used to being in the driving seat, she knew that. But it still rankled.

'David Floyd is no longer in the employ of the social services. He's working as an adviser for, of all things, the Youth Workers' Association.'

'Have you found anything pertaining to him and Brookway House, or anything that says he was ever accused of being a bit too friendly to the girls?'

Margaret shook her head. 'Nothing like that at all. In fact, he was only ever given glowing references. He seems all right, Kate. There is nothing I can find about him ever being nicked or questioned. Nothing.' She held up her hand then as if to stop Kate answering her. 'But you are not going to believe this, girls.'

Annie and Kate were now both staring at Margaret expectantly.

'Well, come on, Mags. Out with it.'

Margaret looked at Kate in utter amazement. 'I should not even be looking at this, right, so remember we can't use it in any way. I don't even know if it's relevant.'

Kate was losing her patience. 'Go on. For fuck's sake, Margaret, what is it?'

'David Floyd made more than one complaint about Alec Salter. It seems he accused *Alec* of being overfamiliar with the girls.'

Kate sat back in her chair, trying to understand.

'So Miriam saying Floyd was the nonce is a lie? Is Miriam protecting her dead husband? Tell me, Mags, was Alec ever pulled up over any of this? Was he accused of anything by anyone else, not just by this Floyd, but by any of the girls for instance? By anyone at all?'

Margaret smiled. 'Not that I can find. David Floyd seems squeaky clean and there is nothing else about Alec, nothing that I can find anyway. But by the same token, Kate, me and you know that where government agencies are concerned, it wouldn't be the first time stuff was erased, would it?'

Kate nodded slightly in agreement. 'You got a current address for this David Floyd?'

'You won't believe this, Kate, he lives in the *next* road to Miriam Salter.'

'You're joking?'

'Not a bit of it. I flagged up all the girls, along with all the people concerned, just to see if there was a connection, and he came up in Maple Terrace. Number twelve, to be exact.'

She was very pleased with herself and it showed. Annie

watched Margaret as she practically preened at her own cleverness.

'Do me a favour, Margaret. See how long he has lived there, and find out where he was living and working before. Also, see if you can find anything more at all about Alec Salter.' She stood up then and motioned to Annie. 'Looks like me and you are on our way to Maple Terrace.'

Annie had just turned on Kate's phone and the sound of her text message alert was loud and constant. 'Seems like you have lots of messages.'

Kate took the phone from her and dialled her voicemail. Five minutes later, she said in absolute disbelief, 'It's Dart. According to Patrick, the arsehole's gone off his rocker at Simone's house. We'd better get there and sooner rather than later, by the sounds of it. Pat's been trying to get me for ages.'

'Why not just ring here?'

Kate looked at her as if she couldn't believe what she was hearing which, of course, she couldn't. 'Use your loaf, Annie. He wouldn't say anything like that over a landline, let alone one in a police station.'

Margaret laughed then. 'Jesus, this is better than the fucking telly.'

Annie looked at her and said primly, 'Yeah, that's as maybe but, unlike the telly, our victims really are dead.'

Kate smiled grimly as she said, 'We'll sort Dart out first, see what the score is, then we'll go and check out this Floyd. Now, can you two stop with your petty digs for the foreseeable future, only it's starting to get on my tits.' She looked at Margaret then and said harshly, 'Keep digging and see what else you can find out. If my phone rings, take a message and then just ring it through to Annie's phone. And remember, keep the door locked until all the smoke has dispersed. The last thing we need now is a fucking sergeant on our backs about the smoking rules. Like we haven't got enough on our plates.'

'If anyone asks where you are, what shall I tell them?'

Kate unlocked the door and said heavily, 'Tell them we've gone out for a fag.'

She could hear Margaret's booming laugh all the way to the car park.

Chapter Twenty-Four

'Oh, Patrick, if what you say is true, how am I going to be of help? He loathes me, always has.'

Patrick was getting more and more aggravated by the second, and he knew he had to keep a lid on his anger. 'All I want is your opinion, Kate. You know the best way to deal with nutters. All we need is advice.'

Kate felt his annoyance and, looking into his eyes, she said angrily, 'My advice would be to phone the police.'

'You are the police, Kate, that's *why* I phoned you.'

'Is the girl all right? Do you think she is in any danger?'

As she spoke, Lionel started ranting and raving again, and Kate looked up at the ceiling as if that would tell her something she didn't already know.

'It's like the exorcist, he screams, we listen. Danny went up a ladder, but Lionel was standing there, holding a chair above his head ready to sling it at him. As you can understand, Danny retreated as quickly as he could. But he saw enough to see that the girl is unhurt. Frightened, but unhurt. I think Dart is a weak and stupid man who won't open the door, so

I have arranged for Georgie Twofer to come and open it for him.'

Kate nodded in agreement as Annie wondered who the hell Georgie Twofer was.

'Good idea, Pat. But make sure he doesn't go too far, you know what he can be like if he thinks it's the Filth.'

'All sorted. I'm paying him, and I've given him the hard word. He just gets us in, we sort out the rest.'

As he spoke, a car pulled up in the drive and Simone answered the front door to reveal the biggest man Annie had ever laid eyes on. He was huge, over six foot seven, and he had a body that made Arnold Schwarzenegger look like a wimp. He was totally bald, and his face was not what could ever be called handsome, but his expression was one of affable kindness. That was until he spoke. 'Where is the prick? I have to be in South London by ten.'

He walked up the stairs with surprising speed for a man of his build, and everyone followed him. He was shown the bedroom where Dart was holding the girl hostage and he said quietly to Kate, 'OK. Lovely strong wood, mortice lock, piece of piss. I've knocked down fucking metal doors in both Durham and Highpoint. Love a fucking locked door, me. Move back, darling, and let the dog see the rabbit.'

He then took a few steps back and with a resounding shout kicked the door in with one heavy foot. The door was falling now, even the hinges were no match for this man's physical strength. It was George's incredible strength coupled with his expertise in breaking through any door he felt was offending his sense of freedom that was his talent. He had taken off a few cell doors in his time, and once he had even managed to break through a door on the punishment block in Parkhurst. Hence the name, Georgie Twofer. It took two doors to keep him locked away for any reasonable length of time, one for him to kick down and the second door so the officers concerned got a chance to run away from him and get the medic on call to inject him with the strongest drug they could legally find.

'Fucking hell. That was excellent.' Danny's voice was filled with awe and admiration.

Georgie gave a mock bow. 'All in a day's work, my son.'

Lionel was standing in the room half naked, he looked demented. Kate saw that he was in no fit state for anything. He looked for all the world like a cornered animal which, in some ways, was exactly what he was. A wife-beating, bullying animal who had finally been found out. The room was completely trashed, and the young girl he had trapped was already running towards Simone, her face covered in mascara from her tears and her body wrapped in a sheet. Patrick went in and, drawing back his arm, punched Lionel Dart with all his might. He went down like the proverbial sack of spuds.

'What shall we do now, Kate?'

Kate glanced at Simone and said archly, 'Personally, I would remove the locks from any doors that the girls use for entertainment purposes, that will ensure this never happens again. As far as that little shit is concerned, you can do what you fucking like. I'll ring the commissioner and fill him in on the latest developments. He'll call you, Pat, and tell you what's to be done. He knows the score so far and he'll make sure this is kept as quiet as possible.'

Kate looked at Annie and saw the amazement and shock on her face and said gently, 'Come on, let's get going.'

'Thanks, Kate. I didn't know who else to phone.' Pat spoke quietly.

Kate looked at Patrick as if she was seeing him for the first time. She saw his greying hair and his battered face and, walking to him, she kissed him gently on the lips. ''Course you didn't, Pat. I'm the only Bill you have on speed dial.'

He grinned then. 'Well, you took your time getting here if that's the case.'

They looked at each other for a few seconds until Patrick said softly, 'I'll see you later then, Kate, at home.'

She nodded at him and, for the first time in what seemed like for ever, she felt as if things might actually be OK. 'I can't give you a time.'

'So what's changed?'

It was what he had always said to her when she was embroiled in a case. It was his way of saying that they were back on an even keel as far as he was concerned.

Georgie Twofer walked into the bedroom and, picking Lionel Dart up by the scruff of his neck, he said loudly, 'He's coming round, where do you want him?'

David Floyd was a tall man, thin to the point of emaciation, with kindly brown eyes. He had opened his front door wide, something Kate knew from experience was often the act of an innocent man, that, or the bravado of a guilty one. She always waited until she had spoken to the person directly before making up her mind. 'Mr Floyd?'

He smiled easily, looking at them both expectantly, 'Yes, can I help you?'

'We were wondering if we could have a word with you about Brookway House?'

They both saw his face cloud over, he was immediately put on his guard. 'And you are?'

Annie stepped forward and flashed her ID. 'We are the police.'

He sighed then, a heavy protracted sigh. 'Then you had better come in.'

They followed him into his hallway then, opening a door to his left, he waved them into his lounge with a flourish, like an old-time courtier. When they were seated, he said easily, 'So, how can I help you?'

Kate looked him in the eye as she said, 'This is not an official visit, we just need some information from you about Brookway House and, in particular, Alec Salter. Your name came up during our inquiries, and we would appreciate it if you could help us.'

'Alec is dead, surely you know that?'

Kate and Annie both nodded. 'We know that. You are aware, I take it, of the recent spate of murders here in Grantley?'

David Floyd looked at them both with well-disguised distaste before answering, 'As they are the only thing about which the press will write at the moment, I think we can all safely assume I have heard of them. What I don't understand is, how are they in any way connected to me?'

'All the girls who were murdered had, at some point, been residents of Brookway House.'

David snorted then, and taking out a handkerchief he coughed violently into it before saying archly, 'Some were. I recognised the names, but I didn't know they were all there at some point. The others must have been there after I left.'

'Have you ever seen any of the girls from Brookway in

Grantley? Did you ever have any kind of contact with them?'

'Oh God, no. If I had seen them I would have walked the other way. I mean, those poor girls really don't want to be reminded of their early lives. If they had spoken to me, then that would be different, but I would never have approached them.'

Kate looked over at Annie. Annie raised her eyebrows as if to say, *What do we do now?* Sometimes she got on her nerves.

'I was given to understand that you were there at the same time as Alec Salter, did I get that wrong? Was I misinformed?'

David nodded, and Kate realised that he was not a well man, his wrist was all bone, and as he brought the handkerchief up to his mouth again, she saw his hands were shaking. Not the trembling of fear, but the shake of heavy medication or illness. 'You did get that wrong, dear. Alec took over from me.'

Kate sensed he was hiding something from them. 'I don't want to bring up any unpleasantness from your past, but I have to tell you that we have been told there were certain accusations against you pertaining to Brookway House and the girls who lived there. Is that why you left?'

David Floyd turned white with anger. He was also having difficulty controlling his breathing. Eventually he said in a whisper, 'Would you be so kind as to pass me that bottle of brandy on the dresser? I need a little nip before I carry on.'

Annie went to the dresser and poured him a generous measure, then she took the glass to him and waited as he swallowed it down in one gulp.

'Thank you. Please help yourselves.'

He coughed again, only less hard. He was clearing his

throat now, ready to speak. 'Alec didn't accuse me of anything, it was his girlfriend Miriam. She was not what you would call an easy person to get on with. They had both come through the care system together and they were so close it was sometimes uncomfortable to observe. She was very damaged and she was jealous of Alec. I got on well with him, then she came there on a volunteer basis. As I am sure you know, they were very religious, and she had a good relationship with the girls which, in some ways, was amazing. She was so different to them in every way but she seemed to have a knack of getting them to trust her.'

He looked at Kate and Annie then and motioned for another drink. Annie got up and was pouring it for him when he said, 'I don't really know what happened with her and me. She just seemed to take against me one day. I never understood why.'

'I understand she said you were too friendly with the girls at Brookway House?'

He accepted another drink from Annie, but he sipped at it this time. 'Oh yes. In fact, she actually accused me of a lot more than that. But no one ever took the allegations seriously, they knew she was wrong.'

Annie said quietly, 'And how would they know that?'

Kate laughed gently. 'Because I think, Annie, you will find that Mr Floyd is gay.'

David nodded and laughed with her. 'Well spotted. What gave me away, the photos of me and my partner all around you, or the fact that I am in the final stages of Aids?'

'Is that why you left Brookway House?'

'Partly. My partner at the time, who contracted it first, was very ill, and I went part-time so that I could nurse him.

Which I did. Alec took over from me, I recommended him. My partner and I bought this house years ago and we rented it out as an investment property. I moved here after I retired. It was smaller and without memories. I still do some stuff for the youth organisation. I help raise money et cetera. Nothing too strenuous, I just like to keep my hand in.'

'Have you ever come across Miriam since?'

David laughed, and Annie saw the difficulty he had in even speaking for any length of time. He was so weak, so fragile. 'Once. She saw me a while ago at the doctor's surgery. As you can imagine, I spend a lot of time there. I tried to say how sorry I was about Alec, but she cut me dead. She didn't acknowledge me at all.'

He frowned then, and Kate knew he wanted to say more.

'Mr Floyd, if you can tell us anything, no matter how small it might seem to you, we really would be grateful.'

He raised his hand to his mouth, cupping his lips as if the action might stop him saying a word. 'I sometimes thought that Alec was not as good as everyone believed. Not that I ever saw anything that was untoward, of course. But he watched those girls, I mean, *really* watched them. It made me uneasy at times. But it was only a feeling, I had nothing to substantiate it. And as I say, he was never even *suspected* of anything, and none of the girls ever made a complaint as far as I know. He *always* went the extra mile for them, I can't take that away from him.'

'How do you mean, the extra mile?'

David smiled then, and it made him look younger, it wiped away the lines of pain. She could now see the man he had once been. The handsome, smiling man in all the photographs around the room. 'He was very good. He had this contact he would use, she worked at the job centre I believe, and she was very good to the girls. She found them jobs and that was not easy I can tell you, not with their backgrounds. She was wonderful. I never met her personally, you understand, I only spoke to her over the phone. Her surname was James. I think Alec called her Jenny.'

Patrick smiled easily, he was relieved that everything was over at last. The Chief of Police had been a diamond. After a call from Kate, he had phoned Patrick and having been given the whole sorry saga, he had arranged for Lionel to be sectioned into a private facility. It was amazing what you could do with money and power.

As the ambulance left the drive, Patrick and Danny had looked at each other and they both started to laugh. It was nerves, they knew that. Laughter was nature's way of relieving tension. They walked back into the house, and Simone handed them both a drink. 'Thank God that's over! Who would have thought he was such a nut-bag?'

Danny sniggered as he said half-jokingly, 'The fact he fucking comes here. Let's face it, this isn't exactly a health farm, is it?'

Simone was not impressed by his words or his tone. 'Listen here, you. We're a top-class establishment and it ain't the girls' fault that some men are a bit touched. We provide a service, that's all.' She looked at Pat then as she said, 'You tell him, will you? He needs a lesson in the real world.'

Patrick didn't answer her, he was looking around him at the sumptuous décor and he knew that getting rid of his involvement in the houses and flats was the best thing he had ever done. 'Oh, don't worry, Simone. I think he'll learn all he needs to know soon enough.'

'Hello, Kate. I wasn't expecting you.' Jennifer sounded nervous.

Kate pushed her way past her without saying a word. Jennifer shut the front door gently and waited patiently for Kate to say something. Anything.

'How could you, Jenny? How could you not tell us who was providing you with young girls? Did you think we wouldn't find out?'

Jennifer nodded, her face tight with anger. 'Yeah, that is exactly why. Alec is dead. So what's the fucking difference? He provided me with loads of girls over the years, and a lot of them are still alive and kicking.'

'Did Miriam ever know about it? Was she involved?'

Jennifer laughed. ''Course not. For every girl he put forward I gave him a couple of hundred quid.'

'How did you meet him? How the hell did *you* and *him* ever come to meet?'

Jennifer walked into her lounge and Kate followed her.

'It's a long story, but as you're here now, can I get you a drink? I'm having Scotch, can I pour you one?'

Kate nodded. 'I fucking need one.'

Jennifer put two glasses and a bottle of Grant's on the coffee table. She poured out two generous measures and then lit a cigarette. Settling herself down in her white leather chair, she said nonchalantly, 'I met him when he came to a flat I had years ago. Ugly fucker he was and all. He was a regular, he liked this particular girl. Turns out she had been at that Brookway House. She had got in touch with him for some fucking reason or another, and that was what brought him to the flat. Anyway, we got talking, and I said as a joke, any more like her at home? And he said yes. The rest, as they say, is history.'

Kate was scandalised and disgusted at what she was hearing. 'And that was it? That easy?'

Jennifer shrugged and, opening her arms wide in a gesture of puzzlement, said, 'Yes, it was that easy, as it happens. He had a fucking constant stream of girls willing to work for the right person. He sounded them out, and if they were agreeable, then he led them to me. They were all over the age of consent, and they did it willingly.'

'And you honestly didn't think that this information was relevant? You *knew* the dead girls, you *knew* how they had died. *You* recruited them and yet you are honestly telling me that you didn't think that any of this was worth mentioning? They died in absolute terror, they were paralysed, but they still knew what was happening to them. Doesn't that mean anything to you?'

Jennifer laughed again, but it was a false laugh; she was ashamed, embarrassed now. She knew she had been caught out by someone she genuinely liked. Someone who had always treated her with respect. She knew any friendship they had, however tenuous, was now finished. She was also worried about Patrick's reaction when he heard all about it. She knew he would not find her reticence too clever. Like Kate, he would want to know why she didn't tell everything she knew. She attempted to justify her actions. 'Alec is *dead*, Kate. Why would I think he was involved and, for that matter, why would you? He is dead and gone, mate. He was still feeding me girls right up until he died. They were the girls he counselled through his church. He knew the type. He was a fucking scavenger, he could see a troubled teen from thirty paces. But as he was *dead*, I didn't think he would be a suspect, know what I mean? The *dead* part being the giveaway.'

'You stupid, stupid woman. Do you realise what you've done? How you could have stopped all this if you had told me?'

Kate stood in the dark, chilly night air, and wondered how long it would take for Annie to get to her. She felt sick with apprehension as she waited for the warrant to arrive. She knew she had to make sure everything was legal and above board. There could be no room for a clever barrister to tear their case apart.

As Annie pulled up in a small squad car, Kate nodded to the uniforms around her. They all stood out of range of the front door so it would look like they were there alone. Kate rang the doorbell, and they waited patiently for the door to be answered.

Miriam opened the door and, looking at Kate's serious face, she said quietly, 'Is it Hayley? Is she all right?'

'She's fine, really. I was wondering if I might come in? Only I need to have a little talk with you.'

'What about? What do you want to talk to me about?' Miriam's voice was querulous now, frightened. 'Why can't this wait until the morning?'

She stepped out of her hallway and peered through the darkness around her. She saw the panda cars parked nearby, saw the uniforms waiting quietly for the word to move in. She saw Annie walking towards her with a warrant.

'It's over, Miriam, it's all over.'

Stepping back into her house, Miriam walked heavily into her lounge, Kate and Annie following her. They motioned to the uniforms to wait until they were needed.

Danny and Patrick were sitting in Pat's kitchen drinking expensive brandy and smoking expensive cigars. 'I want all this, Pat. I want a nice drum and a nice life.'

Patrick nodded. ''Course you do, son. Who wouldn't? But this – ' he waved his arm round to encompass his whole life – 'doesn't guarantee you happiness. It's family, good friends, someone to share your nights with. That is what gives you the real happiness in your life. I would gladly give everything I possess to have my Mandy back. Even for just one day, for one hour. So I could hold her in my arms, tell her how much I miss her, how much I love her. You can replace *things*, son, but you can't replace people.'

'I know that, Pat. I ain't ever lost anyone that close though, have I? Me and Eve, we always had each other, looked out for each other. We had to, we were all we had.'

Patrick nodded in understanding. 'I have Kate. I have my Kate back. She is an awkward mare at times, and she is argumentative as well. But she is also clever, funny, and she is the only person in this world who can make me forget my losses. She can make me forget, for a while, my heartache.'

Danny heard the raw sadness in Patrick's voice and knew that his loss was so vicious, so destructive, that it would never truly heal. A child murdered would always leave the question, why *my* baby. Why *my* child? A question that, of course, could never really be answered.

Danny held his glass up for a toast. 'To Mandy, always in your heart.'

Patrick clinked glasses. Then he smiled, remembering her lovely face. 'To my girl.'

Miriam sat at the small kitchen table and she was calm, too calm. Kate sat opposite her, and Annie stood by the back door. The house was filthy and the smell overpowering.

'You know why we're here, don't you, Miriam?'

She nodded slightly, her face resigned as if she had known that this would happen eventually. 'You want to ask me about the girls.'

'What about the girls, Miriam? What can you tell us about them?'

Miriam stood up quickly and her chair made a loud scraping noise as it was pushed away from her cumbersome body. Annie and Kate both waited to see what she would do next. She went to the kettle and filled it with water, then she turned to put it on the gas.

As she sat down, Annie said softly, 'I'll make the tea, shall I?'

Miriam smiled. 'Thank you. That would be lovely. A nice cup of cheer, that was what Alec used to call it. A cup of cheer. He was like me, he loved a cuppa. We might have had to scrimp for some things, like everyone has to at some time, but not on our tea. Lipton's, that was our favourite. Not that it was that expensive, mind. But we never bought the cheap supermarket own brands. It was our favourite, you see. Now he's gone, it seems to bring us together again. Our cup of cheer.'

Kate nodded and smiled. 'I can see that. But, Miriam, what can you tell me about the girls? The girls that Alec used to help.'

Miriam sat up straight in the chair and she shook her head angrily. 'Fucking whores, all of them. He was a good man, he was a good man, Kate.'

She was wiping her hands across her face now as if she was trying to wipe away a stain of some kind.

'I know he was, Miriam. How did he know the girls?'

'Do you know, all the years we were together, all those years, we never once did anything we shouldn't do. We had decided that we would stay pure, all our lives. Like the Bible, the people in the Bible. We were above the sins of the flesh. Because it's a sin, you see, even if you're married. It's a sin. But he was tempted, like many a good man before him, he was tempted. I saw the result of his sin, you see. I saw it all.'

The kettle boiled and Annie began to make the tea. Miriam was quiet for a few moments, she was very upset and Kate let her collect herself once more. Annie placed a cup of tea before her, and Miriam smiled her thanks.

'How did you see his sins, Miriam? I can't understand how you could have seen anything.'

Miriam sipped her tea. 'I found the books a while after he died. He kept them hidden away upstairs. He had a small fortune in a savings account, did you know that? And he had pictures of the girls, of the girls and him. Their heads in his lap looking up at him. Filth. But then they *were* filth. Complete and utter filth. Hard as nails, all hard cases, all those bloody girls.' She smiled again sadly. 'I knew I had to do something, and so I did.' She gulped at her hot tea then, swallowing it down quickly. 'I remember when I was small that, if I swore, I would have my mouth washed out with soap. So that is what I did. I found them, and I cleaned them up. I explained to them that they were wrong, very wrong to

431

do what they had with *my* husband. *My* Alec. You see, he was mine. He loved *me*. He never wanted to do those things with me, do you see what I am getting at, Kate? He didn't do anything like that to me because he *loved* me.'

Kate nodded as if she perfectly understand what Miriam was saying, as if what she was saying was perfectly normal.

'Come upstairs, I want to show you something.' She giggled then. 'And you lot didn't know it was me. I was clever. I knew what you'd look for, so I hid things and I tidied up.'

Kate and Annie followed her up the stairs and the smell was now even more overpowering. On the landing she pointed to a door saying happily, 'They are in there. The others.'

Kate felt physically sick now. The stench was everywhere. She knew what the smell was, and she held her hand over her mouth as she said, 'What are you talking about, Miriam, what others?'

Annie opened the door slowly and, as she turned on the light, Kate heard her friend dry-heaving. It was a few moments before she heard her whisper, 'Jesus Christ, Kate. Jesus Christ.'

Kate walked towards the doorway as Miriam said gaily, 'See, Nicky Marr and Donna Turner.'

Kate looked at the two decomposing bodies, their faces still recognisable as human beings. She turned to where Annie was almost bent double and, taking her firmly by the arm, she led her down to the front door. Once they were outside, drinking in huge gulps of the fresh, cool night air, she said sadly, 'It's over, Annie.'

Epilogue

Kate looked around her at the happy faces of her friends and the people she had worked with over the years. It was a lovely party but she knew that, for her, it was nearly over. Seal was blaring out of the CD player, the drink was flowing copiously, and most of the people there were almost legless. She looked at the gold watch on her wrist, it was inscribed with the words, *From all at Grantley, with love.* She would treasure it, it meant more to her than anyone here realised. She had finally admitted defeat, she was too old for this now. It was the time for Annie and Margaret and all the other young officers, her time was long gone.

She sipped at her glass of whisky. It felt good as it warmed her throat. She was a drinker now and she wondered if that was something else that came with age. Her mother had loved a quick nip. She loved a drop of Scotch in her tea or her hot milk. Kate missed her, she still felt her loss acutely. She offered her up a silent toast and she knew her mother would appreciate it.

She looked around her again. The canteen was packed with people, and she was pleased that so many of them had come to wish her well, to see her off. The top brass had been and gone, had given her a few words of praise, and remembered her finest moments, then left at the earliest opportunity. She knew she frightened them, always had. Firstly because she had been a better detective than all her male counterparts put together, and secondly because she had been the lead detective on not one but two serial killer cases. Both of which she had solved. She had also been a consultant on the biggest case Grantley had seen in years. She had a lot to think about where Miriam Salter was concerned. She knew that that was not for *now*, though, that was for another time, another place.

But what really bothered the brass, she knew, was her relationship with Patrick Kelly. It was because of him that she had got to know everything there was to know about her superiors and their close relationship with the people they were supposed to be trying to put behind bars. It had been a real eye-opener for her, right from the start. She had been so naive back then. She was embarrassed just thinking about it. How could she have been so blind not to see what was going on right under her nose? Now she knew the real deal, inside and out, and she had learned to live with it. Well, she had not really had much choice.

She smiled at Annie as she danced with a dark-haired young uniform with kind eyes and a killer smile. She had taken over Annie's case, she knew she had acted as if she was the lead on it. Annie had not only had to put up with her at work, she had also had to put up with her in her home. In reality it was a wonder they were still talking, were still friends.

But what else could she have done? She had been, to all intents and purposes, homeless. Pat had been livid, but then so had she. After all, they were both of a temperamental nature. It had gone too far, too fast. Patrick had nearly broken her heart, but she had forgiven him. At least on the surface she had. Inside her, she knew it would take longer. Eve was still there, like a ghost between them. Both of them were too frightened to say her name out loud in case it made her real again, reminded them that they were nearly destroyed.

She shook herself mentally, telling herself not to get maudlin, depressed. This was her going-away party, her leaving *do*, as Annie put it. This was the last time she would ever come into this station, this canteen. She knew that as if it was already a proven fact. This phase of her life was finally over, and she knew it was not before time.

Annie was half pissed and she held up her glass of wine to Kate as she shouted across the room. 'A toast! Come on, everyone, I've got a final toast.'

Everybody stood still, and the music was turned down. Kate smiled widely as Annie shouted at the top of her voice, 'To the end of an era!'

'To the end of an era!' The sound was deafening as all the voices rose up to toast her one last time. Kate was happy and sad at the same time, it *was* the end of an era, her era. She belonged to another time, she belonged to the past. She was never going to come back here again, she knew it was time to let go.

As Kylie started singing 'Can't Get You Out Of My Head', Kate decided it was also time for her to leave her party. She picked up her handbag and quietly slipped out of the door. She walked slowly through the station house, lingering over her last moments there.

Her head was crowded with images, people she knew past and present. She saw her life as a policewoman as if it was a film, as if it was about someone else. She knew it was time for her to leave, knew deep inside that she should have looked into Miriam sooner. Her shit-detector had always felt there was something not quite right about her, and she should have listened to it. Miriam Salter was never going to see the inside of a courtroom and that was as it should be. She was, as Patrick had so succinctly put it, out of her fucking tree.

As Kate walked through the back door of the station for the last time, she was pleased to see Patrick waiting for her in his Bentley. She got in the car, savouring the warmth of the leather seat. It was freezing outside.

'How was it?'

She smiled at him. 'Lovely, it was really lovely. I wish you had come though.'

He started the engine up and laughed. 'Now come on, Kate, you know how I feel about police stations.'

She laughed with him and, as they pulled out on to the road, he said seriously, 'Are you sure this is what you want, Kate?'

She sighed heavily. '*Yes*. I'm sure, Patrick, for the hundredth time.'

'All right, keep your hair on. I just can't see you sitting around all day doing nothing, that's all.'

She lit a cigarette and blowing the smoke into his face she said quietly, 'I won't be sitting around all day doing nothing, I will be sitting around all day doing nothing with you, there's a difference.'

'I wish you would give up smoking again, I hate to see you puffing away.'

She grinned. 'We'll see.'

'Anyway, I will still be playing golf twice a week so you'd better find something to do with yourself. Let's face it, if we're together twenty-four-seven we'll drive each other up the wall.'

Kate opened the window and threw out the cigarette butt. 'Do you really believe that, Pat? Do you think we will get on each other's nerves?'

She was serious, and he felt the question in her voice. He grasped her hand and pulled it into his lap, squeezing it gently as he said, 'I love you, Kate, always have, always will. We are getting older, girl, and whatever time we have left together, I want it to be happy and fulfilling. So no, if I was with you all day, every day, you wouldn't drive me mad, I would love every second of it.'

She knew he meant every word, and she felt a sudden urge to cry. It had been an exhausting few weeks and a very emotional evening.

Patrick squeezed her hand again, and she looked at his handsome profile as he said, 'Have you heard about Lionel?'

She laughed. 'What about him?'

'He gets out next week and, by all accounts, his old woman has packed up, sold up, and gone to live in Spain with the eldest daughter.'

Kate laughed. He always could make her smile, it was what she loved most about him.

'Good on her, eh, Kate? Measly little ponce that he is.'

She nodded. 'Is the bar in Spain anywhere near Eve's new club?'

Patrick was silent now, and she felt the tension as it gathered between them.

'Look, Kate, that was her choice. Nothing to do with me.'

'I know that, Pat. I just need to know that you don't have any regrets, that's all.'

He shook his head slowly. 'Not one, and I'll swear to that on my Mandy's grave.'

She believed him. They drove in silence for a few minutes, neither of them knowing what to say.

Eventually Patrick said light-heartedly, 'I nearly forgot. I have some more good news, Kate.'

'What's that then, Pat? No, don't tell me, let me guess. Terry O'Leary is going straight, and Georgie Twofer is really a woman.'

Patrick was chuckling at her words. 'Georgie is a case, he used to work for me years ago when he was a lad. Strong as an ox even then. His old man was a hard bastard and all. He was good pals with Charlie Bronson. 'Course, he was called Micky in them days. But, like him, Georgie hated being banged up, and he took it out on every door that was ever shut in his face.'

Kate watched Pat as he spoke. In the darkness he looked young again, she couldn't see the grey that had crept into his hair, or the lines that were suddenly so prominent around his eyes. He looked good, he looked just like he had when she had first known him.

'So come on then, what's this good news?'

He grinned at her for a few seconds, winking at her saucily before looking back at the road. 'As of today, I have retired. Really retired this time. I've sold up, got shot, and I am free of anything even remotely criminal.'

Kate sat back in her seat and, lighting up another

cigarette, she took a few drags before she started to laugh. Really laugh.

'What are you laughing about? What's so funny?'

She took another puff on her Benson & Hedges, savouring the taste of the tobacco, knowing it was doing her no good whatsoever, and not caring about that.

'*You*, Patrick. You make me laugh. Have you got rid of the scrapyard you bought not so long ago? Have you got rid of the casino or the other clubs? Have you got rid of any of the betting offices or the cab ranks? Shall I go on?'

He didn't answer her.

She laughed again, louder this time. '*Well?*'

He pulled the car into a lay-by, and turning to face her properly he looked deep into her eyes. Then he shook his head in mock anger, saying quietly, 'Once a Filth, always a Filth.'

He kissed her gently on the lips before pulling out on to the road again. Then he was quiet until they approached the gates of the house. As he slowed the Bentley down, he said jovially, 'Anyway, how the fuck did *you* know about the scrapyard?'

Kate laughed at the genuine astonishment in his voice. It was so good to be with him again, it felt right when they were together. He was all she really wanted. All she really needed. She punched his shoulder gently and, laughing once more, she said happily, 'I know *everything* there is to know about you, Patrick Kelly, and don't you ever forget that.'

He smiled at her words and, as they drove through the electric gates, she knew they would be all right.